TIC

LIES

TIGHT
LIES

TED DENTON

Urbane
PUBLICATIONS

urbanepublications.com

First published in Great Britain in 2019
by Urbane Publications Ltd
Unit E3 The Premier Centre Abbey Park Romsey SO51 9DG
Copyright © Ted Denton, 2019

DISCLAIMER

This is a work of fiction. Names, characters, places and incidents are either products
of the author's imagination or are used fictitiously. Any resemblance to actual events
or locales or persons, living or dead, is entirely coincidental. The author takes no
responsibility for the validity of factual research conducted during the writing of this
book. Please note that there is no insinuation that the British Government and its
officers nor the PGA European Golf Tour, its employees, players, caddies, sponsors
or agents are in any way or have ever been corrupt. There is no deliberate intention to
relate Russian criminality to the oil and gas industry, to sport or to politics except for
solely creative purposes. References to the companies Rio Tinto and British Petroleum
are only used to add corporate authenticity within the book around the subject of
the oil and gas and mining industries and there is no insinuation that they are or ever
have been involved in any political or commercial corruption. Rublex Corporation is an
entirely fictional entity with no reference to any existing or previous organisation.

A CIP catalogue record for this book is available
from the British Library.
ISBN 978-1-912666-48-5
MOBI 978-1-911583-77-6

Design and Typeset by Michelle Morgan
Cover by The Invisible Man

Printed and bound by 4edge UK

URBANE

urbanepublications.com

The author acknowledges and is grateful for the copyright usage of and references to the lyrics of Bob Dylan (Copyright © 1974 by Ram's Horn Music; renewed 2002 by Ram's Horn Music).

For 'the wild unknown country where I could not go wrong'.

For MJP. Always.

For the brave members of the British Armed Forces who deliberately put themselves in harm's way to try and help make our world a safer place.

...and for a once in a lifetime dog...

Definitions:

In the sport of golf, a *'tight lie'* is deemed to be the position (or lie) in which one's ball has come to rest either upon bare dirt, very short grass, or where there is very little grass beneath the ball. This often makes the connection between the club head and golf ball harder to strike cleanly and therefore the outcome of the intended shot is harder to execute with accuracy.

Tight – (adjective): difficult to deal with or get out of; experiencing a feeling of constriction.

Lie – (noun): a resting position; a false statement made with deliberate intent to deceive; a falsehood.

Chapter 1

Occupying the back corner of some piece of shit dive of a bar and nursing a chipped half-tumbler of bourbon. I sat alone chewing on the end of a splintered match. The place was a dark rancid hole. To tell the truth I looked just about bad enough to fit right in. Hell, the regulars hadn't even looked twice at me with my three day old stubble, dirty oil-stained checked shirt. None of the usual lingering stares at the thick angry white scar that scores its way up from my neck, petering out across my left cheek.

I scanned the bar at leisure. An old scab-ridden whore, skin wrinkled and ravaged from too much sun and cigarette smoke, was staggering on skinny legs encased in tattered, torn pantyhose. She wobbled between two time-worn tough looking men, labourers or mechanics with nothing waiting for them at home most likely, sitting on solitary barstools, connected only by discarded shot glasses and a near-empty tequila bottle. She was bothering them for drinks, hoping to turn a quick trick in the filthy alleyway behind the building.

The whole desperate scene was played out in front of an ox of a man who was lazily tending the bar. Heavily set with broad rounded shoulders, his long greasy black hair hung down to a massive protruding stomach. He wore an ironically cheerful short-sleeved Hawaiian shirt, fashion which appeared starkly out of sync with both the dismal surroundings and his pockmarked, humourless face. The shirt stretched over his massive arms, unbuttoned to the navel, displaying a mat of tangled hair covering his bulky torso.

The side of his neck and chest was covered in intricate green and blue patterned tattoos and to cap it all off he was missing most of his front teeth. He wouldn't be making front page of the local tourist board's promotional brochure anytime soon.

I took a swallow of bourbon. Chased it with a couple of painkillers. Savoured the burn as the scene played out in front of me. The whore cackling with laughter. Two spindly, decrepit drunks squabbling at a table to the side of the bar. They began to scrabble at each other, knocking down chairs as they tore at their shirts and faces with grubby fingernails, spilling glasses and drinks as they went. A pretty pitiful sight. But nobody seemed to notice. Ox nonchalantly surveyed the saloon bar with not so much as a raised eyebrow, polishing a grimy looking glass with a dirty rag. Above him hung what looked like an oversized pickaxe handle mounted upon two nails. The scrawl of a thick black marker pen beneath simply read 'The Peacemaker'. I smiled to myself. My time spent within the murkier elements of the British armed forces had instilled in me a twisted appreciation of a man who took pride in his work.

●

The heavy door banged open. A stream of light flooded the bar room as a couple entered. My focus heightened. A rat-faced man with sinewy arms led the way, his blonde ponytail trailing down a leather waistcoat threaded with silver chains. He dragged a young Mexican girl by her upper arm. She was petite and, in tight denim Daisy Duke cut-offs, ankle cowboy boots, and midriff revealing tank top, certainly cute to look at.

She squirmed in his rough grasp. He threw her down at a nearby table and gestured to the barkeep for service. Ox duly appeared with two bottles of beer, still soaked from the cool of the fridge. He set them on the table. Retreated. The blond man took a long swig of beer and, in one motion before swallowing, sparked a Marlboro Red from a battered Zippo lighter and inhaled. This was plainly not an establishment which concerned itself with pandering to the ubiquitous American anti-smoking laws. He reached across the table and grabbed a fistful of the young girl's hair. She was sixteen at the most but with a whole lot of living in those pretty brown eyes. He pulled her forward across the table and kissed her roughly on the mouth. His bony hand thrust itself down the front of her tank top. He laughed and pushed her back into her chair, a tiny crumpled and frightened mess trying to play the grown up woman.

I watched, grinding my teeth in anger. Through force of habit, I traced my thumbnail down the deep scar on my face. Etching slowly. Scoring it deeper. Partly seeking reassurance from the familiar contours, partly working it to ensure its permanence as my defining mark. I drained my glass, sat back, breathing deeply to retain control. I studied the bar. No one else had seemed to take a blind bit of notice. Another biker mistreating some lowly slut— just part of the fabric of the place. I closed my eyes in resignation. The fickle lens of my mind's eye transported me so vividly to my service within the Regiment. A time where respect was earned through action and deed. A life governed by a much-needed structure which had, at that time, brought order to my worthless life. There was a time, way back, when the name Captain Tom Hunter, youngest commander of A Troop based out of Hereford and indeed of any of the four squadrons of 22nd Special Air Service Regiment of the Regular Army, had been spoken with pride, even held up as an example of excellence for fellow soldiers to emulate.

How things had changed.

A fist slamming into a table and the sound of a shattering glass brought me round. I looked up and the blond biker had the little Latina girl by the arm again and was forcing her to her knees under the table. She was sobbing. He leant back chuckling, one hand on his beer and the other on the top of her head as she reluctantly busied herself with attempting to pleasure him. After a fashion, he moved to hold his drink over the girl's bobbing head and proceeded to pour splashes of beer pattering down over her. The sound jarred me. A painful memory, not buried deep enough, came bubbling over. That was enough.

I rose slowly and surveyed the bar, scanning for threats. The rest of the punters continued about their business. Ox was leaning forward, meaty forearms resting on the bar, smirking and enjoying the show.

I staggered across the bar in feigned inebriation, as if solely intending on ordering yet another drink. Approaching the Target, I took two quick steps forward and kicked the edge of the table hard and purposefully into the chest of the unsuspecting biker. The force smashed him backwards off his chair, onto the floor. I flew after him and, pushing the girl aside, stamped on the knee joint of his flailing leg. I pulled the table off, held it up and over him. Shouted at the girl to stand up. He screamed out in pain, hands groping hopelessly at the shattered kneecap. Going nowhere fast. Without pause I slammed the table's sharp edge downward into his windpipe.

I looked up to see the huge bartender, moving faster than his corpulent body belied, wielding The Peacemaker in both hands and smashing it down towards my head. I dived sideways as the bat collided with the table, cracking the top in two. Momentum slid me into a table of three older guys with long greasy grey hair wearing tasselled leather jackets.

One of the men pulled me off the floor by my hair and hit me in the temple hard, scrambling my senses. The Ox was coming for more, swinging The Peacemaker with gusto like he was batting out the ninth inning for the Dodgers. I stooped and, reaching into my boot, pulled out the eight-inch hunting knife strapped inside. I thrust out wildly into the armpit of my mature assailant and twisted. It was enough to free me from his grip and I lurched forward again pulling out my Beretta.

'Stay the fuck where you are!' I shouted in general at the bar, spinning and pointing the gun towards the motley crew assembled at ringside. 'Nobody fucking move and we are out of here. If so much as a fucking finger reaches for a gun I swear I will shoot it the fuck off.'

Ox stood still. Breathing heavily, sweat pouring off his fat acne-scarred face. His expression contorted with rage. The Peacemaker rested still in his double-handed grip, making him look like an oversized tennis player. All he needed was a headband. 'You've fucking killed him, man,' he howled, glancing at the biker sprawled on the floor of the bar. 'He's not moving. You're dead, you son of a bitch. I'll lose my licence. I promise you are fucking finished, punk.'

I backed up slowly, covering the bar evenly with the barrel of the Beretta as I moved. I reached the young girl who was crying and shaking. 'You cool?' I said, briefly glancing into her mascara streaked face. She nodded. Taking her wrist I continued to edge backward together until we reached the door. We piled through into the sunlight; behind us a cacophony of cursing and shouting.

'Who are you? Where are we going? What the hell is going on? You killed my boyfriend asshole,' she cried, tears streaming down her pretty face.

'Listen, I don't know how the fuck a nice girl like you got caught up in this shit but from where I was sitting it didn't look like you were having much fun. Your parents hired me to get you away from that bastard. It's a done deal. My car's down the next street. You're coming with me and we've gotta run. NOW!'

We turned the corner on the block as a throng of people rushed out onto the street behind us, followed by the throaty punch of gunned motorbike engines. I was practically dragging the girl off her feet and, by the time we reached the car, she was missing a boot. The beaten-up rusting red jalopy was specifically picked for this job so as not to stand out in this low rent gang-infested neighbourhood in Bell, the predominantly Hispanic suburb of Los Angeles. Right then I wished I'd gone for speed over style.

I ripped open the unlocked car door and pushed the skinny brown girl onto the seat. Jumped into the driver seat and turned the ignition. On the second time of asking it spluttered into life. As it backfired I shouted across, 'Consuela—there's a blonde wig in the bag at your feet. Put in on now.'

'What? Like no way. This is all just so fucked man.' Her tiny fists were balled up tight in her lap. I could swear she was pouting.

'Connie, put the fucking wig on now.' I urgently swivelled my neck around me checking the streets. 'We've got to get out of here. We're dead if they catch up with us. Do it now!'

Scowling, she pulled on the wig. It was thick and heavy with platinum blonde curls. I threw on a baseball cap and sunglasses kept ready in the dash box. Rolling down the window halfway, I stuck my elbow out and casually slid the vehicle into the road. We weren't going to outrun anyone in this thing— we'd have to bluff our way clear. We approached the intersection. A screech of tyres and two leather clad bikers pulled out sharply, skidding into the path of a fast moving blue Ford pickup truck running in the opposite direction. One of the hogs bailed onto its side in the effort to stop and slid under the wheels of the truck, the rider's leg trapped underneath. Its driver, fully moustached and mulletted and wearing the obligatory checked flannel shirt, threw open his door shouting and gesticulating wildly at the pair. The fallen biker rose to his feet and wiped his bloodied mouth on the back of his hand. As if watching some carefully rehearsed synchronised dance move, he pulled out his handgun at the identical moment his wing man and mirror image did so too. They started to pump holes in the side panelling of the sky blue Ford, tearing the metal apart.

This was the perfect opportunity for us to slip away unnoticed, so I threw the jalopy in reverse and backed up down the street. Spun the vehicle in a neat skid, flipped into a side street, and put my foot down, leaving nothing but dust behind us.

We drove for twenty clear minutes on the freeway out of town, most of which saw Connie sitting with the blonde wig on her lap and a sorry pout across that cherubic face. I punched some numbers into my cell phone. 'Mr Rodriguez, I've got your daughter. She's safe and well,' I said, grinning over at Connie. The girl's instant response was to wrinkle up her nose and dart her little pink tongue out at me. 'We're ready to make the drop as arranged, Mr Rodriguez. See you in an hour.'

Chapter 2

Daniel splashed cold water on his face and exhaled. He ran wet fingers back through his floppy blond hair. Looking in the mirror, he straightened his collar and forced a smile. This was it. He was finally taking control of things for himself. The door was opening to a new world of infinite possibility.

He took in the opulence of the cavernous washroom nestled inside the lobby of the Bayfield Mandarin Hotel. What he saw was a classic example in traditional Spanish finery and the unmitigated deployment of wealth: gold plated mirrors, marble tops adorned with carefully folded pristine woollen washcloths, glass bottles of exotic looking oils and thick white creams. The setting only served to exaggerate the long distance he already felt from Sheffield and the life he'd grown up in. The home town from which he had left early that very same morning, amidst a depressing swirl of cold, gloomy drizzle.

The meeting had taken place only five weeks ago now. It was hard to believe he was actually here. Daniel had been working as an intern in a small publishing house in Sheffield—a business still clinging to the fading success of the single celebrated author they had ever been lucky enough to represent. The Ego, as he was referred to somewhat churlishly, had delivered them a bestseller, a clever and well-regarded spy thriller. The book was a well-researched, technical and refreshing view on modern espionage. For its time. That The Ego hadn't yet managed to deliver the much vaunted and over-promised sequel meant that things had moved on with the subject matter. There were doubts, from those that knew him, whether he would be able to keep up. It was the cause of serious consternation and turmoil amongst the partners in the business. The significant advance he had already been paid was having a deleterious effect on company cash flow and the whole situation snagged intemperately on an increasingly fractious and frayed working atmosphere. If Daniel had been asked to sum up his working environment in just one word he may well have selected *toxic* as the descriptor.

He'd studied computer science at Sheffield University before taking forensic accountancy as a vocational option to satisfy his father, coupled with modules in sports science and investigative journalism to sate his own wider interests. He lived at home to save money in line with parental advice, rather than studying further afield, stifling any possible claim to genuine independence. Only two of his classmates who came through comprehensive school with him had secured a coveted place in higher education. It wasn't hard to envy their shared flat, succession of drunken escapades and tales of daring-do documented through an endless stream of Facebook boasts and Instagram updates. Still, surviving his parents and keeping sane for twenty-one years was, he considered, an epic achievement in itself, albeit one that might not generate as much attention from girls on social media. Daniel had been blessed with an overprotective mother who was beset with an unending stream of premonitions and predictions which appeared to be gathering urgency and momentum daily, whose genesis no one could quite identify; and a down-to-earth, no-nonsense father whose life mission was to preserve as much money as possible for some future, but as yet unspecified, purpose. This was coupled with a near-paralysing fear of the repercussions of any form of law breaking, however moderate they may be. On one occasion, the curtains had been kept drawn and the milk left on the doorstep for a week to maintain the pretence that the family were abroad, having returned to the car some six minutes after their parking ticket had expired, albeit unnoticed. Despite his cruel caricatures, Daniel knew they were good people. Good ordinary people who wanted the best for their only child. Irrespective, it was suffocating and depressing to have his entire life bleakly sketched out far in front of him. Being forced to share his parents' lives was a slow and torturous death. In his mind he knew he was destined for more.

He had met Silvio working at the publishing business. A portly, permanently tanned, silver haired gentleman of Italian heritage with a predilection for snugly fitting waistcoats, brown buckled brogues, and long, indulgent lunches. He didn't work for the company, happening instead to rent a desk there in order to conduct his own business, the mainstay of which was to sell sports content for media consumption across books, magazines, television, and online. He came and went as he pleased with an easy smile and never concerned himself, it seemed, with the bitter undercurrent of resentment emanating from the morose publishing staff whose building he shared. He'd noticed Daniel busying himself around the office and, when the boy had shown a keen interest in some of the sports content across his desk, he had decided to indulge him. When the deal came together, it all happened so fast. Silvio had contacts in golf, an opportunity on the European Tour, and a tie-up with an American sports agency to cement. They had some talented up-and-coming southern hemisphere players currently living in London. There was no one to manage them in Europe as they weren't yet ready to progress to the US PGA Tour, typically considered the hardest to win playing privileges upon. In order to secure the gig, the plan was that Silvio would create the illusion of having a ready-made team. Daniel could be moulded quickly to fit that remit and no one at the American sports agency would be any the wiser. They had already worked with Silvio and he had the solution they needed. Daniel got an exciting opportunity he would grab with both hands. Everyone wins.

Five short weeks and a crash course in the beautiful intricacies of professional golf later, here he was. Like most boys, he supposed, Daniel had enjoyed games at school above academic lessons. He was a naturally gifted sportsman, tall, rangy and athletic with good hand-eye co-ordination. In preparation of the new career, he'd hacked a golf ball round the local pitch and putt track to half decent affect, heralding his father's advice and foregoing the unnecessary expense of a single lesson.

Now he stood in the washroom of the Bayfield Mandarin Hotel in the Valencia region of southeastern Spain at the start of a prestigious European Tour event. He needed to front up and blend in to take this opportunity. Play it cool and make it happen. Would anyone spot that he just didn't belong, he wondered. Daniel Ratchet, Player Manager to some of the hottest young guns competing to win this week's European Tour event, who feels like everyone is looking at him as if he stands out a blinking mile. Who got lucky by meeting an old man in the right place at the right time. Daniel Ratchet, with just one chance to make it work. No turning back.

The door to the washroom swung open. Two swarthy middle-aged guys filed in wearing well-filled matching white polo shirts, navy shorts and long white socks pulled up to the knees. They chatted animatedly in Spanish. Daniel, no longer alone with his thoughts, nodded a greeting, dried his hands, and exited back out into the hotel. The place was a hive of activity, buzzing with glamorous, well-dressed, sun-kissed people. Players, denoted by their heavily logoed caps, crowded around a free-standing noticeboard. An olive-skinned girl in a crisply pressed uniform stood next to it answering questions. A large antique desk stood dominating the space behind which an unsmiling leather-skinned matron in her mid-fifties sat brusquely addressing the impatient queue of players. Notes were being entered into a large binder. A streaky blonde ponytail was scraped tightly back from her forehead exposing deeply etched lines worn into the strong, features of a handsome Germanic face which would not be bowed by age. The scene depicted the epitome of no-nonsense, diligent efficiency.

Daniel joined the back of the throng and studied the noticeboard. The pairings for first round of the event were listed sequentially by tee-off time. These were strict minute-by-minute timings that could not be missed, on pain of disqualification, by even a few seconds. Daniel's role as Player Manager was specifically to look after two young promising guys from the Crown Sports stable, Aaron and François. Australian and South African respectively. Noting the piercing stare now directed towards him from the older of the two women, presumably for loitering and obstructing the view of the board, he double checked relevant times and names, made a mental note, and retreated hastily.

Growing up as an only child, Daniel was quite used to time spent alone. He would break free of the house at any given opportunity, seeking to escape the predictable monotony of family routine by running painfully long distances. Out through the town and into the undulating countryside beyond he would go, leaving the quiet terrace and its cul-de-sac behind. What he felt now though was a different type of isolation. Surrounded by people teaming through the club house, he felt awkward, like something might stand out about the way he was dressed or that he was somehow perpetually in the way.

Silvio had warned him of course, 'Don't be put off when you get out on Tour. There's a lot of what they call 'etiquette' in golf. It's a game for the rich made up of endless rules. So what do you expect, eh? You can either feel part of it or not. A smart boy like you will learn soon enough and until then just keep your head down, your mouth shut, and try to look the part,' he'd told him patting him on the shoulder. 'People will typically assume you are what you say you are until you prove otherwise. Life on Tour is a bubble. Just a week will feel like months have passed. It's intense and addictive and you'll wonder at times if you can even survive it, although you'll soon realise, my friend, that you can't live without it.' He'd finished the pep talk with a beaming benevolent smile.

Daniel flashed the cherished metallic Tour badge at security and entered the vast restaurant reserved for those involved in that week's tournament. There were small clusters of players and officials gathered at the various tables. Eating. Chatting. Studying charts of the course. A few he recognised from their picture profiles in the Tour handbook, but most he did not. To the left, a gleaming wall-to-floor window looked out onto a luscious green course and imposing mountains beyond which traced the curvature of the building. The entire right hand wall of the room was pinned by long tables adorned in crisp white table cloths. They shouldered a regal spread of buffet-style platters and servers. Every style of hot and cold food Daniel could think of had been laid out in deep trays, accompanied by stacks of sparkling crockery. Two moustached waiters ladled generous portions from the silver slavers. Daniel selected a small helping of rice and chicken with a bread roll. Having missed breakfast in his rush to catch the flight, and not having the stomach for a plastic-wrapped aeroplane sandwich, he could certainly have eaten more. Not an untypical situation given that growing up he was often teased for a prodigious appetite and for having hollow legs. Somehow the current situation didn't become an overladen plate.

Daniel found an empty table in a corner and sat there, watching intently, taking everything in. People came and went. There were some obvious cliques, players of the same nationality or age grouped together. He could hear raucous laughter from a group of three South African players. A cluster of serious looking blond Nordic types, perhaps Swedes or Danes, played with their food and spoke in deep tones about their practice rounds and the current challenges in their game. In an attempt to look pre-occupied, Daniel took out a card of the course and toyed with memorising the layout of the holes and their yardages. It made little sense. Swirls, icons, and tiny numbers peppered the pocket-sized chart. He tried to glean what he could. Although more pertinent material for the players than their agents and particularly more so for the caddies, he needed something convincing he could regurgitate at the appropriate moment in conversation which would otherwise expose him as a total golf-fraud. There was so much to all this. He was way out of his depth and drowning fast.

●

'Mind if we sit here?'

Daniel looked up into the friendly brown eyes of a heavily muscled, sandy-haired German man in a tight-fitting polo shirt which looked as if it had been painted on.

'No, please. Be my guest. Er... I'm Daniel,' he said, adding quickly, 'from Crown Sports.' Part introduction, part explanation.

'Hi Daniel,' came a cheerful voice from behind the broad shoulders of the German. 'This is Michael and I'm Matilda.' A slender, smiling vision in white T-shirt and tailored blue shorts.

She placed a bowl of salad onto the table in front of her, followed by two-toned, bronzed legs slipped under it. They looked like the perfect couple. A vibrant advertisement for the human race itself, or least an endorsement for some high-end luxury Swiss spa. He pictured them eating muesli together at sunrise whilst practicing complex yoga moves.

Glad of the enforced company and conscious that he stood out being the only person eating alone, Daniel pushed his course chart aside and began to engage the pair.

'Busy week, isn't it?'

'Mmm, yes,' Michael replied between mouthfuls of a thick slab of bloodied steak that Daniel eyed with pangs of envy. 'For us always busy. Lots of the guys need fixing up in the truck.'

'The truck?' Daniel replied carefully, not wanting to show himself up so soon.

'Yes the physio truck— we're the treatment team— don't tell me you're the only one who hasn't used us yet?' giggled Matilda in a gentle Swedish accent.

'Ah right, I'm new out here actually,' blustered Daniel by way of apology, 'but I'm sure my guys have worked with you before. Do you happen to know Aaron Crower and François Steine?'

'Of course!' Matilda shot a glance at Michael and leaned in conspiratorially. 'Aaron is a perfectionist who likes to be pampered. He uses his maximum quota of stretching and massages before and after every round. I guess François sees using the truck as a sign of weakness or something. He could slip a disc out there and would still rather soldier on than get any help.'

Michael flashed a knowing smile, looked down at the table and shook his head.

'We work together to get to know all the guys' exact training routines, areas of the body prone to weakness, and everything required to get them ticking like clockwork. Each player is very different,' said the German.

'You must have great memories. That's a lot to keep on top of,' keened Daniel, set on making a positive impression.

Michael pulled out a slim white USB memory stick from his pocket and tapped it against the side of his head. 'Yeah. Great memory, us Germans,' he grinned. 'I keep everything on this. All the bio-stats on every player you could want. I keep it with me everywhere, it just plugs straight into any device, even a smartphone, and you are good to go. So, I don't need to be so smart myself you see.'

Daniel felt foolish again but then Michael was smiling at him good naturedly and, before he had time to change the subject, a French player with heavy stubble and a slightly disgusted look on his face tapped the German physio on the shoulder. Explaining that he had an early tee time in the morning he insisted that he be slotted in for urgent treatment to fix a tightening in his calf muscle. Michael looked first at Matilda and then at Daniel with raised eyebrows before pushing his plate of half-eaten steak out in front of him, easing his massive frame up out of the chair. Holding an arm out in front magnanimously, he invited the Frenchman to lead the way from the restaurant, longingly staring over his shoulder at the uneaten food with a comic look of exasperation.

'Is that always how it is?' Daniel asked. Matilda smiled. An open and easy smile. Daniel was suddenly aware of how beautiful she was. 'It's how it always is with Michael. He can't do enough for the players and they take advantage, you know?'

'And what about you?' Daniel retorted, a smile playing around his lips.

'No one takes advantage of me, I can quite assure you,' she

replied, her perfectly manicured blonde eyebrows arched above a challenging blue-eyed stare.

'Oh that's not actually what I meant at all. Sorry, it's just that, well, are you as dedicated to the job as Michael is? You must work together closely as a team I suppose. I bet it's hard work with so many guys on Tour and a new event every week?'

'I can assure you that there's no choice but having to work closely when you spend all day together in a sixty foot truck crammed with all our equipment. We even have to share the same email address, so no escape—even in cyber space! But, hey, you get used to it. The Tour is my life and Michael is a sweetheart. Guess what? I finally realised my ambition to travel to Russia and spend six years studying business at the famous Stockholm School of Economics in St. Petersburg only to end up with no job and heavy bills to pay thanks to the global recession. I was lucky to get the job here and now I don't know anything else I suppose.' She paused before checking herself. She turned a piece of crispy salad over with her fork and continued playfully. 'And you? You must be one of these hot shot player agents then, Daniel.'

Another challenge. She speared a crouton and crunched it between pearly white teeth. It clearly amused her to see how easy it was to put her new acquaintance on the back foot.

He felt himself flush, first with embarrassment, perhaps with a little pride, at the reference to his new job. He looked awkwardly at his plate of uneaten and rapidly cooling chicken and rice. 'I'd hardly say that. I don't even feel like I know what I'm doing most of the time.'

And then their eyes met. Matilda snorted in surprise. 'Well now that makes a change! Usually you know-it-all agents out here are all the same: full of testosterone, confidence and swagger. It's quite sweet to hear you asking for help.'

'Thanks, I think,' said Daniel. 'I'm not sure I was asking for help though, was I?'

'It's quite okay, Mr Hotshot,' she replied, reaching forward from across the table and displaying an elegantly presented diamond on the ring finger of her left hand as she gently squeezed his. 'I'm sure we can make sure that you don't get too lost out here.' Again, that sweet infectious giggle.

And with that, her salad barely touched and the conversation apparently over, she eased out of her chair. Daniel watched the gentle roll of her hips as she glided smoothly through the maze of tables out of the restaurant. It was several moments after she had left that he finally felt himself exhale.

Chapter 3

ENGLAND. LONDON. WHITEHALL.

'Your meeting with Boris Golich is scheduled for 4 p.m, sir,' a stiff young man announced in an impeccable rendition of the Queen's English. The grey haired civil servant, encased in perfectly creased dark pinstripe, sat deep in thought. The small, yet smartly presented, office sat just off the corner of Whitehall. He barely acknowledged the aide as he was presented with a bulky folder. 'Everything you require to know about the co-funded gas exploration deal is within, sir. Please do not hesitate to enquire if there is anything further I can assist with.'

The phone on his desk rang and, after watching it rattle in its cradle for a little longer than was polite, Derek Hemmings, who had been staring wistfully out of his rain-streaked window, moved hesitantly toward it, took a deep breath and answered. It was the call that he had been dreading since arriving that morning at the refined environs of the Foreign Office. Andy Bartholomew was on the line. Derek's senior counterpart at the Department of Trade and Industry was a short, balding, pugnacious Scot whose name was pronounced in the manner in which one might clear unwanted phlegm from the back of one's throat.

'Right, the pressure's really on this time, Hemmings,' he snorted. 'We can't afford another fuck up on the seismic scale of the Rio Tinto deal. There are seven thousand British jobs on the hook for this gas operation in the Falklands. Boris Golich's Rublex Corporation is co-funding the operation and will be piping gas into Europe with a big fat BP badge on it. And in case you missed that, old man, the B in BP stands for British.'

'Thank you for the insightful synopsis as ever Andy,' Derek responded coldly. 'Forgive me that I don't share in your unfounded ebullience but my consternation is simply thus. I'm due to meet Boris Golich at sixteen hundred hours today. However rich and powerful he may be and with whomever he may now be friends, the man is purported to have a rather unsavoury past. I'm not really sure that the British Government should be working with him at all. Job creation or not I'm afraid.'

'Not your concern, pal. BP has agreed terms. We're shutting out the Americans on this one. The Prime Minister has ratified it. It is as they say…' he paused for dramatic effect, inhaled, then exhaling as he spoke his punch line, '…a done deal.' The 'A' was pronounced 'hay'. Derek shuddered.

'Then what do you need me for, pray tell? Surely I don't need to be dragged into this viper's nest at all if everybody is seemingly so keen to work with this gangster?'

'Do as you're told, Hemmings. Your department is there to dot the I's and cross the T's. Can you manage that, son? Don't fuck it up this time and do not come back without a signed agreement. I hope that's clear.'

'All I'm saying is that it would be illegal and in contravention of our manifold international trade and energy undertakings, to say the least, for Great Britain to enter into a long term and far reaching commercial partnership with a criminal organisation. This relationship requires pipelines to be laid across several international borders. The geopolitical implications will be huge and could place global trade relations at significant risk.'

'Criminal organisation?' spat Andy. 'Show me some proof of that then pal. There is nothing criminal about Rublex and you know it. They might be an aggressive high-growth corporation but that's no crime. And they have capital to invest with the UK. That's been a fucking rarity in recent times. You do remember the fucking recession, don't you? Do you remember the sodding Brexit farce? Besides, the Americans had their chance to partner in the exploration on the Falklands with us and they wouldn't put their money where their mouth is. Without developing that territory for all its rich natural fossil energy, Maggie's war would have been in vain. Tumbledown would never have happened, Hemmings. We should have left it to the bloody Argentinians if we followed your view of the world. Is that what you would have wanted?' A rhetorical question. He continued unabated. 'You're pathetic. Rublex Corporation is our only option to make this deal happen and deliver economic growth to Britain. If we don't take this opportunity, the Chinese will step in to finance the deal with Rublex, who have now acquired the exploration rights in the international waters. That will leave Britain out in the cold.' Derek squirmed in his seat, shifting from buttock to buttock. 'They will build an offshore infrastructure platform to house thousands of Argentinian workers, instead of Brits, and enjoy the proceeds of what is rightfully ours. I'm sure you find all that just fine and dandy, don't you Hemmings?'

'It's a fine argument in the grand scheme of things' he conceded 'but I'm still uncomfortable, Andy.'

The abrasive Scot sensed the older man's resolve weakening. He decided to change tack, display some contrition. 'Listen Derek, we both know what these things are like, don't we? Both of our departments need to work together on this one. For Christ's sake, we all need a big win, you know that. Some good news to put out in the media for once is much called for. You play golf don't you pal? What's your handicap playing off these days?' He swished a pen through the air for his own amusement, pleased with himself for his new line of approach on the phone. 'Well, Rublex sponsors the European Tour now. Those guys are squeaky clean. They are a trusted corporate brand right across Europe and all over the world. Boris Golich has invested millions in the game personally. What gangster have you ever come across now that plays golf? It's a gentleman's game, Derek. I should bloody know, it was us Scots who invented it. When you meet, just talk to him about birdies or ostriches or eagles or whatever you lot are into.'

Derek hung up and looked gloomily out of the window. He watched a child in brightly coloured Wellington boots stamping gleefully in the rain puddles below. He'd seemingly risen as far as he could in the Department, with the appointment of Senior Executive Officer his last just over five years ago. His retirement was planned for seven months-time at the end of the year. His forty-third year in service of Queen and Country, an honour he had taken most seriously for the main part of his adult life. Of course, for some time now, he'd noticed the rise of a younger, more aggressive breed of political animal superseding him. Career politicians and slick, ambitious civil servants drunk on power and hungry for success. Less concerned it seemed with the responsibility of long term judicious governance but led moreover by avarice for political headlines and personal glory. He lacked the energy and bite anymore to stand up to the Andy Batholomews of this job. Quite simply, Derek was weary of the posturing, the personal positioning and one-upmanship that came with the brief.

Chapter 4

Two days and a hangover from hell later, I sat in a sports bar at LAX waiting for my flight back to Europe. Hunched over a frothy glass of beer and a roast beef sandwich cursing my aching joints. My phone buzzed. I opened the text to find an encrypted message flashing for urgent attention. I grimaced. Complexity was the Hand of God's chosen method of communication. Frowning, I jotted the letters and numbers of the code down on a beer mat in front of me and duly added the sum of my birth date to the total numbers, then multiplying it to the letters of the code which were assigned a numerical value by their position in the alphabet. There was a reason I never played Sudoku and this was it. I found using code an unnecessary and frustrating process. There had been times when I'd been simply too wasted to calculate the code out and respond in good time. I once got a girl lying next to me in bed to do the sums. I think it freaked her out a little for a one night stand. But Charles insisted on security at all times and if I wanted the number to the current secure phone this time then there was only one way of figuring it out.

I headed to the back of the bar and punched the long number into the neglected payphone. Another of Hand's frustrating rules: Never make contact on your mobile unless you absolutely have to. Charles answered on the second ring, his voice bright and polished. Imposing. Commanding.

'Thomas, dear boy, I gather everything was a success.' It wasn't a question.

'Yeah, all sorted and full payment on its way from Mr Rodriguez. Although I gotta say, in my opinion, I think Daddy is going to struggle keeping that little minx under control.'

'Enough with the family psychoanalysis Hunter, that's not your concern.' And then after a beat he said gravely, 'Now listen up Tom. We've got a problem I'm afraid.'

'What is it?'

'A comrade, a gentleman I served alongside in the forces by the name of Bob Wallace, has been in touch. He believes there's been a kidnapping or something worse in Spain. He's got no proof but a sports agent has vanished, gone for two days and nights unaccounted for.'

'Come on Charles, the bloke's probably stopped out with some saucy senorita for the night and is getting the fuck of his young life. This is not our area. Besides you know after a job I like to kick back a little, take some time out. Get a little crazy.'

'We need to act. The clock is ticking. Bob Wallace would not bother me unless this was critical. He mentioned that this chap had uncovered information regarding alleged fixing on the professional golf tour stored on a tablet. Sounds volatile. He will pay the Unit's fees and your bonus for bringing the Target back alive himself, out of his share of a recent win bonus he earned from one of the golfers he coaches. I have of course agreed to discount our costs on account of our history in the Forces together.' I pumped another few coins into the phone and picked at the peeling paint on the wall with my thumbnail.

'Tom right now we're in the golden period.' Hand continued, 'You know as well as I that if we don't get onto his trail within eighty hours of the snatch, then our chances of finding him again will be diminished by over a hundred and fifty per cent.' I sighed, nodding resignedly to myself.

'I want you on this now. Ella will send you the relevant mission information and full briefing notes to your phone in encrypted files. When you land, please liaise with Mickey to pick up fresh unmarked weaponry and ammunition on the ground, again Ella will send you the co-ordinates.' I wrapped my knuckles against the metal box, seeing my next few weeks of planned partying evaporating before me.

'Take this seriously Tom and make sure you bring this lad back. His life is now in our hands.'

I hung up and scratched the stubble on my chin. The Rodriguez girl was the seventh job that we'd completed together as this discreet self-contained Unit available for private hire. We'd been put together by the Hand of God after his official retirement from the mob. He'd tracked me down in a Guatemalan squat two years before using crystal meth and too much dirty cocaine, between earning money from bare-knuckle fights and shaking down dealers for their ill-gotten gains. He found me in a world of pain, rock bottom, and once again he had to save me from myself. Now the system was strong. Charles found the jobs and negotiated the payments. Mickey, a tenacious, life-hardened cockney, worked ahead of us on the ground and set up vehicles, weaponry, communications— anything we needed to make a job run smooth. He was a tough little bastard, the best I'd ever worked with. If he said it would be there and your life depended on it, you would always bet on Mick.

Another on the team was Phil Manning, a big affable guy, with a ready laugh and as reliable as they come. He was a dedicated family man, married for what seemed like forever to his childhood sweetheart Leanne and doting father to three little girls. He'd trained in the Marines. When he'd been injured in combat in Iraq, Leanne had insisted that he pack in the job. The Army was all Phil had known and he'd struggled to hold down a normal civilian job.

Cash-strapped and needing to put food on the table, a mate had put him on the radar of Charles Hand. Kidnap rescue seemed like a compromise to Leanne. Phil could keep his sanity and she hoped it meant he wouldn't be shot at day in day out, or so she thought. He was a solid man to have beside you in a firefight. We'd been teamed on a few jobs and our styles seemed to complement each other. I could kick in doors and crack some skulls whilst Phil had our backs.

There were a few other guys, all ex-military and usually prior acquainted with the Hand of God's maverick leadership style, who came in and out of the crew. Sadly, we'd lost some good men during the seven jobs that we'd taken on so far. It never worked out that easy.

Then there was Ella, a bright and pretty brunette, whom Charles had enlisted as researcher and operations hub manager back at our London base. Rumours abounded that she had been completing a PhD in Military History when they met. Charles had been delivering a guest lecture on the effective strategies of guerrilla warfare. She was fascinated by him and by his battlefield and covert operations experience spanning every continent of the world. When he finally confided in her about the new private Unit and our ambitions, she was intrigued and determined to participate in any way which was welcome. Yes, Ella of the big brown eyes, those large heavy breasts, and a wickedly flirtatious smile. Regardless of how she had ended up with the team, she had certainly added a different dimension to the HQ.

Of course, then there was me. Tom Hunter. The nothing to live for, the no job too dirty, self-abuse junkie, Tom Hunter. Who, it had been said, leaves a wanton trail of destruction wherever he goes. And a man for whom heavy violence and the darkness of killing come with unnerving delight.

I stood over the phone and traced a lazy thumb down the tract of my scar; a subliminal habit to check it was still there, I guess. Perhaps to prevent it from ever properly healing. I reflected on the conversation. Charles Hand had brought me back from the dead at least three times. So far. I owed him everything and now he had made it clear that he needed me on this one. The call had been unequivocal. Forget about taking time off, a young man's life was in the balance. *Hunter was back in play*.

Chapter 5

An unrelenting sun beat down, burning though a canvas of azure sky. A solitary wisp of cloud flirted with the apex of the rugged sprawl of red mountains, providing a dramatic backdrop to the golf range. The only sound to be heard was the swish of metronomic golf swings and the pop of golf balls drilled across the range. Daniel exchanged a flash of his Tour access pass for a courteous nod from a smartly dressed, Spanish attendant who unclipped the white rope which divided the players and coaches on the range from spectators. It was perhaps the first time he'd been on the receiving end of this type of deference and Daniel greedily admitted that he could get used it. As he stepped onto the range his heart beat faster. He didn't recognise anyone. Panic rose in his throat. He felt as if a massive searchlight was now trained directly on him, highlighting his every sound and movement. His mind drifted to the story recounted by Silvio of a spectator's phone going off on the backswing of one of the more successful and famously bad tempered stalwarts during a competitive round. Said player had thrown his club to the ground, crossing the ropes to scream in the face of the unwitting spectator now fumbling frantically in his pocket trying to silence the hues of an absurdly inappropriate comedic ringtone. Needless to say, the guy didn't take the call. Daniel checked his mobile was off for the fourth time.

A line of immaculately dressed golfers each stood in their own space next to a stacked pyramid of clean new white balls. Huge golf bags emblazoned with their names in heavy stitching were set slightly behind. Some were striking balls alone in their own focused rhythm. Others worked with a coach who stood behind them, holding the shaft of the club at the top of their back swing, tweaking angles to reset by tiny margins. Some golfers were chatting away to their caddies, who industriously polished club heads or fished about inside the manifold deep pockets of their golf bags. Others refreshed themselves with cool drinks from one of a number of small well-stocked fridges that adorned the range. Daniel noted a couple of slick, well-groomed guys in reflective sunglasses pacing up and down behind the line of players. Sometimes squatting down and watching the swing, sometimes moving forward and having a quiet word in the ear of a player, sharing a joke, a touch of the arm. These guys were the real deal. Long-standing player agents and managers. Confident and natural with an overt hint of arrogance.

'Jeppe's swinging beautifully today, don't ya think?' came a broad Scottish brogue from behind him; delivered as a statement of fact. Daniel swung around to face a short stocky man in his late sixties, wearing a tatty navy blue flat cap and holding a thick hand-rolled cigarette between his teeth. 'Ay, the kid's in the groove for sure. I think he could be tough to beat this week, that one.'

'Yeah, I think you might be right there actually,' smiled Daniel. He had no idea which golfer was Jeppe and, following twenty minutes of deliberately intense and studied observation of the players on the range, he had noticed no discernible differences between the lot of them.

'Mark my words, sonny. Jeppe's the one to watch this week. My boy Stephen's coming along too, got him releasing the club head nicely now after a fashion.' He nodded down the line to the end of the range where a tall languid figure in yellow carefully set his knees and fixed a perfect acute angle between his spine and the back of his long legs.

'You're Stephen's coach then?' Daniel enquired deciding he needed to take risks in exposing his ignorance if he was ever going to learn anything. 'Ay and I've worked with a bunch of the boys out here over the years. This is my twenty fourth year on the Tour and you could say I've seen most things come and go.'

'That's incredible,' gushed Daniel. 'You must have seen some changes over the years I bet.'

'For sure, sonny. Just more assholes than ever,' came the deadpan retort. Daniel laughed a short, nervous rasp, uncertain if the old coach was even joking. 'Really? Why's that then?'

'More money and distractions getting in the way of the game. Golf used to be the last bastion of fair play, I'm just not so sure anymore.' And with that he threw the brownish yellow stub of his beleaguered cigarette onto the ground between them and shuffled slowly off towards the end of the range. Daniel considered that the stooping gait could be a deliberate coping mechanism against years of chronic back pain.

●

Now his forearms were starting to burn from the unforgiving sun. He'd forgotten to wear sunscreen. He couldn't find Aaron or François on the range and desperately wanted to meet with them before they began the first day of the event the next morning. Grabbing an ice cold bottle of water from the fridge at the back of the roped-off range area, he walked quickly and purposefully back through the ropes and headed for the clubhouse. At least he could try to look as if he knew where he was headed.

It didn't surprise Daniel when he found that the changing

rooms of the clubhouse affixed to the hotel were nothing short of sumptuous. He didn't really have a frame of reference to make a comparison but they were more luxurious than, say, any fancy bar he'd ever stepped foot in during his time at university. And they were a different scale altogether to the musty office of Mr Pembridge, managing director of the small insurance firm in Sheffield where his father had worked for thirty-six years. His eye traced the blue and gold motifs patterning the elegant marble floors, up to thick piles of freshly laundered fluffy white towels which lay folded upon polished wooden benches. The immense lockers themselves had doors made up of single pieces of heavy mahogany, each carved with an intricate coat of arms. Two very dark-skinned black men in starched white tunics, pressed trousers, and white deck shoes busied themselves carrying armfuls of towels, wiping vast glistening mirrors and polishing golden coloured taps.

A shirtless fat man was picking lazily at the dried mud on the bottom of a pair of expensive-looking golf shoes. The mud was flaking all over the marble floor and scattering disregarded under lockers and benches alike. One of the attendants looked on nervously. The man chewed absently on the end of a wooden golf tee humming jauntily to himself. A massive hairy belly flopped over the brim of his shorts, completely obscuring any belt. He was in his late forties with closely cropped black hair speckled with patches of salt and pepper. His fat, creased face sported a rasp of greying stubble.

'What the fuck are you looking at, sunbeam?' he said out of nowhere in an unexpectedly high pitched Liverpudlian accent, now looking up at Daniel with beady eyes.

'Sorry, excuse me. I'm, er, looking for a couple of players actually,' said Daniel.

'And you are, mate?' came the response, scathing and immediate.

'Oh, I'm Daniel Ratchet, an agent with Crown Sports. Have you seen Aaron Crower or François Steine by any chance?'

'No Danny, I haven't, okay? I'm Jeppe Ossgren's bagman here and he's the only bloody player I need to worry about.'

'All right then. Thanks. Nice meeting you,' Daniel murmured as he turned on his heel, somewhat chastened by the whole experience.

'No problem, sunbeam,' was the singsong call behind him.

Daniel stopped and checked himself. *Fuck it*, he thought. 'So, er, Jeppe's swinging beautifully today isn't he? He's in the groove for sure. I think he could be tough to beat this week.'

Silence. Then after a few moments. 'Yeah you're dead right actually there mate. You've seen something there you know. He's got the bit between his teeth. We're due for a big cheque this week.'

'Well, good luck,' said Daniel pleased for having successfully positioned himself as an expert.

'Hey sunbeam,' came the voice behind him. 'You know what? You'll probably find Aaron in the physio truck getting stretched into shape before his early round tomorrow. And François just came off the course from a practice round so he will probably be grabbing a shower before he heads out to eat with the other Saffas.'

'Great. Thanks very much,' Daniel replied but the burly caddy was back to scraping golf shoes again, humming away to himself and paying no attention.

Feeling a bit more in control of things, Daniel strolled back out towards the sunshine. He drained his bottle of water, depositing the empty packaging in a bin before threading his way along the paved walkway up to the massive free standing trailer truck that served as the Tour's mobile physiotherapy service. The door was open and he hauled himself up the little metal steps, poking his head around the gap. The internal space was much bigger than expected. To the right, a self-contained office with soft seating, a coffee table, white board and drinks dispenser. The main central space contained a weights machine with all manner of levers and pulleys dangling above plastic seats. To his left, two massage tables were bolted to a hard plastic floor. Beyond the tables were compact medical cabinets containing a stainless steel wash basin and flanked by wall-to-ceiling cupboards. Matilda was leaning over the half-naked torso of a man lying face down on a towel and pulling his arm out ahead of him as if simulating a swimming stroke.

'Excuse me,' Daniel said in a low voice, conscious of startling anyone.

'Oh hello, hotshot.' Matilda smiled back at him, looking up from her exertions of kneading the tired knotted muscles of the golfer below her.

'I was hoping to find Aaron Crower here.'

'You found him mate,' came a voice emanating from the hole at the head of the massage table.

'Hey Aaron. It's Daniel Ratchet, from Crown Sports. We met briefly in London a few weeks back after you had secured your Tour card.'

'Ah yes, my fellow new boy out here,' Aaron replied thoughtfully now sitting up and rubbing the suntanned shoulder which Matilda had been stretching out. 'How are you finding life on Tour then?' he continued. 'Not a bad way to make a living is it?'

'Not at all,' Daniel replied truthfully. 'Just wanted to make sure you had everything you needed before play tomorrow?'

'Good on yer. Well I'm out freaking early unfortunately but it should give me a fair crack before the wind picks up in the afternoon.' He slowly rotated his wrist one way and then the other studying the movement carefully. 'I've been having a tinker and could do with a new thicker grip on the wand and a wedge adjustment to fifty-two degrees. That's one and a half wraps of grip tape by the way, not two, in case you were thinking about getting carried away.' He looked directly at Daniel, unsmiling. 'Go and see the boys in the Callaway van to get it fixed up for me, will yer mate? Andy, my caddy, has got the sticks. Oh and a new box of Pro V1s will work a treat too.'

'No problem Aaron— I'm on it— I'll pick that up with Andy for tomorrow,' said Daniel, frantically repeating over in his head what he had just been told.

'On yer mate,' came a relaxed and muffled response as Aaron pushed his face back into the massage table and Matilda again began working the knots in his back.

Daniel backed his way out of the truck slowly, hoping to catch Matilda's eye as he left. He was rewarded. She glanced up from her charge, smiled coyly at him and made a little wave.

Kicking his way along the neatly paved walkway behind the hotel complex Daniel felt a surge of energy well up inside him. He thought about Matilda. This was coming together nicely. Was it possible a girl like that could actually be into him? Wasn't she engaged? He'd always done all right with girls. A diffident charm and boyish good looks made him sought-after boyfriend material at a comprehensive school filed with boorish, testosterone pumped football and PlayStation obsessives who saw girls as a necessary inconvenience. Still considering this point, grinning inanely to himself, he was sharply awoken from his daydreams by a massive German hand slapping him on the back.

'Can't keep away from Matilda I see,' boomed Michael, shaking his head. 'Just like all the rest.'

Daniel smiled uncomfortably. *This is pretty awkward,* he thought. *It may be claustrophobic them working together but it's not cool to get caught paying too much attention to another man's fiancée. Still she seems to know what she wants and the ball is very much in her court. I guess I'll go along for the ride and let her make the running.*

He playfully punched Michael on the arm in response before quickly sloping away to find Aaron's caddy.

⬤

Andy Sharples was clearly a stylish man. He'd come into caddying fairly late by conventional standards but by all accounts was highly regarded amongst his peers. He was meticulous in his preparation and thorough in his care of whichever golfer, on whichever Tour, he was working.

Randy Hughes, the renowned larger than life founder and Chief Executive Officer of Crown Sports could be considered, amongst several more unpleasant things, a man of guile. His dealings were deliberately centred on North America for financial reasons alone. He dabbled in big-time boxing, UFC, NASCAR, and in managing US PGA Tour golfers. Crown Sports did very well out of it too. They put together some of the very highest value and most creative sponsorship deals for those individuals, assets and events which they had come to represent. Randy's contact book was legendary. It included Hollywood celebrities, leading sportspeople, and leaders from their fields in the worlds of finance, business, and crime. His prodigious energies were focused where the big money was and, where golf was concerned, he viewed the European Tour as merely a stopgap for young players to learn their trade before they progressed up to the 'major leagues' in America to play for the big bucks. Aaron Crower and François Steine fell into this bracket. The opportunity for Silvio and Daniel was one of mutual convenience. It meant Randy could keep control of his young international rising stars and earn out of them without the hassle and expense of having to set up a European satellite office. Experience told him that talent needed a measure of nurturing and a good deal of control. He had wanted to match the precociously talented Aaron Crower with a steady experienced hand who could filter the right kind of messages as he plotted his first full season in the sport. Andy Sharples knew the nuances of the game at the professional level. He was the perfect choice to help a new boy on Tour to make good game management decisions and keep his head in pressure situations. With very little persuasion except of the dollar bill variety, he had ditched his last employer's mid-tournament preparation to make himself available for the rising star.

Daniel approached the cluster of caddies sitting together on cheap plastic chairs and nestled behind the enclave of massive golf equipment trucks which were parked at the back of the main hotel complex. Something struck him instantly. Andy was dressed, and seemed to hold himself, differently to the rest of them. More like a player than a bagman he noted. He was lean, with a neat black quiff and perfectly crafted goatee. His clothing was comparatively expensive and impeccably turned out. The others in the group played a hand of cards, Andy smoked a long, thin cigarette and pondered a small black pocket book. As he approached, Daniel noted pages filled with endless lists of unintelligible numbers and letters. But by this stage, weary and already bewildered enough, he had given up expecting things to make natural sense. Recognising Andy from the description he'd been given he addressed him directly.

'Andy, hi. Daniel Ratchet from Crown Sports. How you doing?' offered in the soft northern lilt he had worked so hard to dilute.

The group stopped talking amongst themselves almost as one. Backs straightened. Sets of surly expressions fixed back at him.

'A pleasure…' replied the caddy slowly, putting on a slim pair of square sunglasses to avoid squinting into sun setting over Daniel's shoulder. He presented his hand limply with a half-hearted nonchalance.

'I wondered if you could help me out. Aaron's got some requests for tomorrow regarding his clubs and he told me you were looking after them.'

'Looking after his sticks is my domain. It's not a problem.' He was economical with his words. Efficient with the unnecessary use of language. It seemed to suit him.

'Right. So the wand needs a new grip and he wants his wedge tweaked to fifty-two degrees and a new box of Pro V1s.' Daniel repeated the list verbatim, hurriedly unburdening himself of the detail which sounded more like a foreign language as he spoke it aloud. Somehow the perception washed over him that he was now standing with the cool kids smoking behind the bike sheds in school, desperately wanting to be accepted by the gang. 'Is that something you can help with Andy?'

'I've already taken care of that,' Andy sighed, flicking his eyes back at the group who seemed to be still staring at Daniel with some measure of passive aggression. 'We discussed it on the range and the guys in the van have worked their magic.'

Daniel visibly relaxed, glad the conversation didn't warrant an interrogation. 'You're a star. Thanks so much,' he smiled.

'You the new Jerry McGuire round here then?' Andy followed with a staged throaty chuckle causing the whole group to laugh openly.

'Not sure if you'd say that, but I'm managing the Crown Sports stable out here now. I've heard you're a steady influence, Andy, helping Aaron to get some good consistency out of his rounds and scores. Helping him to keep his head in check when under pressure,' replied Daniel, ignoring the jibe and wondering if and how he should exert himself at the right moment. He'd been apprised of the apparent pecking order on the Tour by Silvio, and managers thought of themselves up near the top of the food chain with the players and the caddies more like the hired help. Caddies, of course, felt the reverse was true.

'Sure, it's working well. You can back that scoring consistency with your wallet if you fancy, Danny,' said Andy, waggling the pocket book at him. 'Billy Boy tells me you think you know a thing or two about who's got game. Something of an expert are we then? Stick your money where your mouth is and I'll give you odds against who you reckon is going to place this week.'

'I'll get back to you on that mate. I'm running about a bit at the moment right now so can't stay and chat I'm afraid.' *Don't get into a discussion on player form*, Daniel chided himself. He turned to leave. The moment passed.

'Listen Dan,' soothed Andy after him in a velvety, accent-less voice. 'Some of the caddies and Tour staff are heading out tonight for a few drinks and you're more than welcome to join us,' he suggested. Paused. 'Unless you've got something better planned that is?' he cast a quick look over at the card players, who were definitely more hostile audience than contented gamblers, and was rewarded with a smirk or two in response.

Daniel considered his options quickly. A night alone in his room in front of whatever boring movie repeat or soft porn that might be found on late night Spanish television, following an uncomfortable dinner for one in the posh hotel restaurant? Or the chance to grab a few beers and ingratiate himself with the people who seemed to really know how this place worked, even if they seemed a tough bunch to crack. He needed to begin getting to know people and this was as good a start as any. He was in.

'Sounds good actually. Where and when?'

'Excellent,' replied Andy in a disinterested drawl, already returning his attention back to the pages of his notebook. 'Meet us in Muldoon's Irish bar in the centre of town about eight-ish.'

He didn't look up as Daniel hurriedly left.

●

'I think I really like him, Michael,' said Matilda as she cupped her hands around a mug of green tea.

Michael smiled a toothy grin as he stacked bandages and bottles inside one of the storage units in the truck. 'Nothing I haven't heard before my sweet Matilda. We both know you seem to have a thing for the agents out here'.

'Stop it!' She giggled. 'He's different. One of the good guys.'

'He does seem a little more innocent, that's for sure.'

'I feel like he needs protecting, Michael. I want to give him a chance. I want to help him find his feet out here. What do you think?' She swivelled in her chair to face him directly.

'Well, if you want my opinion, I agree he seems to be one you could trust and he is certainly interested in you. You must follow your heart if you really like him. But treat him gently, if he is serious about you. He may not get over you quickly.'

'I'm glad you like him too, Michael. That's important to me. You're the closest thing to family I have out here.' She beamed up at the giant German.

He stepped towards her and gave his response. A simple, gentle kiss placed upon her angled blonde head. Both his blessing and a signal that their conversation was at an end.

Chapter 6

I refuelled and grabbed a few hours of well-earned sleep on the fourteen-hour flight to Spain from LAX. Ella had been highly efficient in changing my schedule without undue delay. The muscles in my shoulders and arms ached from a few nights of sleeping rough. I'd crashed in the back of the old jalopy as I had staked out the movements of the Target and her captor prior to the take down in the bar. The luxury aeroplane seat slid back and reclined. Ella always booked business class for overnight flights. In the scheme of things it was probably when I managed to rest the most. I slipped the sleeping mask down over my eyes. Not only was I dressed differently to the other passengers in this section of the cabin but after my exertions of the previous few hours I was also aware that I stank. I could already hear the disaffected murmurings around me as I started to drift away. Memories of how far I had come to be sitting here now, travelling the world, amongst these well-to-do folks danced into my dreamlike thoughts.

I'd enlisted in the mob at sixteen and despite being, to quote my Sergeant Major, 'an angry, feral, under educated toe-rag', managed to work my way up quickly inside two years. There, I tasted motivation I hadn't dreamed existed following an unceremonious expulsion from the school I'd barely attended in the preceding few years. School was a waste of time for a kid like me. Authority was a line to be crossed. The way I saw it, I wasn't interested in learning and the teaching staff were simply too jaded or too exhausted to make me. Mine was once described by an army psychologist, intent on ticking a box on a neatly compiled form, as an 'unsettled childhood'. I got caught up in some bad situations. Some I got away with. Some, much to the chagrin and futile disdain of my caseworker and the police, I did not. Trouble always had a knack of being able to find me and I bowled through my teenage years with a cavalier confidence born of early physical development allied to raw natural strength. It led to a lot of confrontation and more than my fair share of notorious and bloody fights with the older gangs which haunted our neighbourhood. When the time came for me to get out, the army had been recommended as the only viable chance I stood to start afresh. To see a bit of the world. The truth is, back then, I had no idea that the one thing in life I would display any given talent at was also the one thing I would end up battling a compelling and seductive compulsion towards: killing people.

That was how it began. I was too young and arrogant when I signed up as a private in the Royal Fusiliers infantry regiment. I was treated like shit. Beasted regularly to break my spirit. One cold grey afternoon, spitting with icy rain on Exmoor, it had got too much. I'd flipped out. Broken the jaw of the cruel, supercilious, privately educated, didn't-know-his-fucking-arse-from-his-elbow senior officer in charge. It had felt good at the time. The two weeks in solitary, not so much. In the aftermath of the enquiry, I was offered a deal. Face a dishonourable discharge or be assigned to a new platoon in the regiment, run as a separate unit under its own auspices. The small group was put together under the supervision of the apparently soon-to-be retiring Major Charles Hand. A man who came to be known by those who served with him simply as 'The Hand of God'. I was still only a boy.

We were trained like athletes and disciplined like prisoners. Put through hours of intense physical endurance and multi-form combat training every day. Hand took us to the very edge of anatomical limitation. My mate Steve, a tough kid from a council estate in Bolton, also hand-picked to be in our elite team, was running next to me on an ultra-marathon across the moors one night when his ankle just snapped. Nothing touched him. He didn't trip. The bone had simply been put under so much pressure that it had nothing left. Steve was stretchered away and we never heard of him again. He was presumably kicked out of the mob on the basis of previous misdemeanours. I don't get the psychology behind it but somehow I responded to Hand. I thrived in that challenging environment.

Over time, I grew up. Learned respect and I learned discipline. I learned how to fight. And I learned that killing came naturally to me. Unnervingly so.

And I was promoted. I was trusted and given my own tactical team to lead. I saw so much torture and death. Tasted betrayal. And it was only the start.

I felt replenished from the long sleep, waking only when the plane bumped to its final halt on the hot Spanish tarmac. I always travelled as light as I could. Usually just the clothes on my back, cash, and a phone. Weapons would be collected from Mickey once we got into theatre and the job was primed. Fresh clothing could be picked up if needed as we rolled. I headed out into the terminal, flashing a cheeky grin at a couple of simpering stewardesses on my way past. *I'd have to remind myself to bang one of those if I ever came back this way.*

The task at hand now was simple: familiarise myself with the mission brief and background. Set up the rendezvous with Mickey who had no doubt already arrived from London a few hours before me and had begun to put things in motion. From there it was going to be a long drive to the golf course and I was impatient to get going. With time to kill, I ordered a double espresso from a quaint independent coffee shop inside the terminal building. It was good to see the little guy holding their position against the mighty Starbucks and rebuffing their indefatigable quest for global domination. Better coffee too. And that was something I knew a bit about. I'd have myself hooked up to an intravenous drip of the stuff if I could.

I pulled out my phone, opened the application, and punched in an access code to download the case files. As analytical and micro-detailed as she was, Ella Philips, our administrative manager and expert researcher, was also a fun, quirky individual. It was no secret that I would have liked to get to know her a little better, in more senses than just one. The pressure of the jobs and a few different time zones hadn't seemed to allow for that. Yet. It felt like she was the human glue that held the guys together in the Unit. She was always fussing over us, especially me. But I suppose someone had to. It really wouldn't have surprised me to find a packed lunch or some little note or other in my assault kit after it was assembled at base—although so far it hadn't got that bad. The Hand of God had found a real gem with Ella, that's for sure. A valuable resource, she had gotten me out of some tight scrapes in theatre through providing live intel on a Target or serving up some GPS co-ordinates to deliver an innovative escape route right on time. I smiled at the computer screen as I was reminded of another of her traits. The woman had a PhD in military history. That, coupled with an irreverent sense of humour and spookily poignant timing, inspired her to surprise us with resonant historical quotations throughout a job. As the data file loaded before me, a quote in italics swirled across my screen:

There are four columns marching on Madrid and yet a fifth within.

I recognised the quote as one from the fascist General Franco. It was both a reference to the origin of this job in Spain and a warning of the insidious nature of war, often enemies or allies may not be as easily identifiable as they would first appear. The demarcations of allegiance can sometimes be blurred. *Duly noted Ella*, I thought and then busied myself with digesting her report and the background to the job which included a detailed set of mug shots and personal profiles highlighting the individuals I may need to recognise and interrogate on the European Golf Tour. I also committed to memory the coordinates of where I'd meet Mickey in a couple of hours, a little outside the city.

I sucked the final dark coffee grounds into my mouth, running the grit between my teeth. Ordered a second double espresso with a nod of the head. My mind drifted back to previous visits to Spain. Vacations. A typical story of a bunch of twenty-something year old British lads letting their hair down. In our case we were probably worse than anything the tabloids might have conjured.

Try imagining a gang of highly revved up squaddies who had deliberately been kept away from women and alcohol for months at a time while training intensely. Those few breaks we got to decompress were pretty messy affairs as you may imagine: lots of drinking, lots of fighting, lots of fucking, and a few instances that seemed to involve the lot together. On one of those rare occasions when we'd hired a car instead of motorbikes, we decided to save money and opt for the cheapest box with four wheels that we could fit our gear into. I remember the tiny Ford Fiesta with an engine so small it could barely make it up the hills in second gear. I can still hear the sound of my crew, squeezed into the back, howling and crying with laughter like braying donkeys as I bounced on my arse behind the steering wheel as if bucking a set of reins. It was a comic sight, the jolting and overloaded motor struggling to make it up the incline as local families stared and pointed in disbelief from the sidewalk.

I wouldn't be hampered for speed like that this time round. With the clock ticking, I approached the car rental desk, deciding on a top of the line Range Rover, with all mod-cons.

Cost no issue this time, I thought as I handed over the Unit's credit card. The transport is a gift straight from the Hand of God.

Chapter 7

Admiring himself in the full length mirror of his fifth floor hotel room, Daniel nodded. He'd showered and shaved carefully. He wore a black short-sleeved shirt with blood red trim, dark blue jeans set off with a stylish black leather belt. Boots which sported a slight Cuban heel added further to his natural height of just over six foot. He'd caught some colour in his face from today's sun and could see his wavy blond hair even picking up some lighter streaks already. He smiled. Back in Sheffield with his mates, he'd definitely be heading out on the pull tonight.

The room that Crown Sports had arranged for him was beautiful. The bed was vast with a solid wooden frame and carved head board. Everything seemed to be operated by a chunky remote control that opened and closed the window blinds and patio doors, operated the massive wall-mounted plasma TV screen and changed the lighting and air conditioning with so many permutations that it would be a challenge to set it the same way twice. The bathroom was done out in marble with a large corner bath punctured with Jacuzzi jet holes and a walk-in shower so big it even had lighting controls, music speakers, and a seat. The balcony was decked out with a simple white wooden table and chairs. It overlooked one of the hotel's pristine swimming pools. Inviting blue water surrounded with greenery and palm trees. Daniel sat out on the balcony dripping wet after his shower, drinking a cold beer from the mini bar, an act in itself that would have induced a minor aneurism in his father. *Just think of the mark-up they put on those drinks boy, it's criminal in itself.* He cast his mind over the day, the amazing hotel, the new way of life, the vibrant characters and nationalities he had met already and yes, of course, Matilda. He closed his eyes and hoped that she might be there tonight.

When he arrived at the bar just after eight o'clock the party was in full swing. The place was heaving. Squeezing his way through the throng of bodies, Daniel scanned the bar for recognisable faces. He waited an eternity as a succession of animated and attractive girls got served before him. With beer duly secured at last he pushed back through the chaos into an outdoor area at the back. It was cooler outside but poorly lit.

A pretty girl in a red T-shirt and sarong that barely covered her ample bottom was dancing on a table, waving a bottle of tequila. People were standing around talking and laughing and some were jumping up and down in unison to the raucous beat of the music. Daniel caught sight of Andy waving from a table at the back and threaded through a group of lobster pink sunburnt tourists clinking beer bottles and passing around a jug of sangria. There were twelve guys sitting together. Aside from Andy, Daniel recognised four others from the earlier card game behind the equipment trucks and the belligerent fat Liverpudlian from the locker room. It was he who greeted Daniel first, clearly the worse for wear.

'Hey sunbeam, come over here and give Billy Boy a kiss,' he cooed, crashing his massive elbow into the ribs of the guy sitting next to him and laughing.

'Settle down, Billy,' said Andy whilst deftly pulling an empty chair from under the table of the couple behind him without asking and swinging it in one motion beside him. Daniel sat and Andy, nattily dressed in white linen, complemented him on his clothing, watch, and choice of beer in turn, before the introductions. They were all caddies except for one who represented the bottled water company, responsible for keeping the fridges on the range and the tournament tee-off areas replenished. Daniel forgot the names almost as soon as they had been spoken.

The night wore on and the table heaved under the increasing weight of empty glasses and discarded bottles. The jokes and banter seemed to grow in proportional volume. Daniel got into the swing of things. He held his own both in rapid consumption of alcohol and the quick-fire conversation, ensuring of course he was careful to avoid any strong opinions on the game of golf itself. Sean, a twenty-three year old ginger skin-head from Glasgow, was lining up a long row of grubby looking shot glasses and loosely pouring a stream of some indeterminable liquid into them from a bottle held unsteadily a foot or so above. And he was making a total mess of it too. Daniel was relaxed. He was coming to equate these guys more with the earthy Sheffield blue collar workers he'd known so well, as opposed to the polished perma-tanned multi-millionaire golf professionals you watched being interviewed on TV. Despite his new found pretentions of grandeur, the reality was that this was probably more his speed.

Despite regular replenishment of his glass from a personal bottle of expensive looking vodka, fetched discreetly from an inside jacket pocket, the only person keeping any semblance of sobriety and control around the table was Andy Sharples. As Billy Boy returned to the subject of his 'miserable bitch-of-an-ex-wife', pounding the table repeatedly with a meaty fist, spilling drinks asunder while bemoaning the fact she keeps screwing him over for more alimony, Andy pulled Daniel to one side and enquired, with a single arched eyebrow, if there was anything the new boy needed to know about life on Tour.

'You guys do this all the time?' Daniel questioned.

'What's that bullshit expression?' Andy pondered, lighting one of his long slender cigarettes. 'Ah yes. Work hard, play hard! Well as you can see, Danny, you could say out here that life's a ball—a golf ball!'

'But don't you have to get up early to be on the course and play in the morning?' Daniel asked earnestly.

'Don't be soft. It's Aaron and the rest of the pros who have to be sharp tomorrow. The guys you see here have all done the hard work earlier in the week.' He waved his hand around him towards the table. 'We've walked the course, we've studied the yardages. Our hard work's done. If your man makes the weekend it's quids-in and we're laughing. If he misses the cut, then we don't get a bonus but we still get our wages so who cares? We usually hit a strip-club or tap up some whores depending on the city and where we have to be next week.' One of the group howled and began to simulate sex with the table.

'Don't some of the guys bring their wives on the Tour though?' asked Daniel, intrigued. He noticed that, like the others, he too was becoming increasingly intoxicated as time wore on.

'Schoolboy error if you ask me Danny. Besides, it's easy to spot the players who got married before they made it on Tour from those who got hitched afterwards. Right lads?' Sniggers from the table.

'Yeah,' chimed in the cheeky mixed-race cockney, referred to by everyone simply as Razor presumably because he was not the sharpest, 'their missus is about three shades blonder and a double-D cup,' followed by a hyena-like cackle at his own joke.

Flushed with the apparent success of his wise-crack and now seriously slurring his words he continued, 'Tell him Andy. He'll find out soon enough. It's the caddies who pull the strings out here. We're the ones who really run the show. Right boys?'

From out of nowhere, Andy suddenly lurched to his left, grabbed Razor by his throat and flung him backwards off his chair and onto the ground behind him. 'When are you going to learn, you dumb fucking mongrel? You keep your mouth shut until I tell you otherwise. Do you fucking understand?' Andy leered down at his prey as he pinned Razor to the floor by his neck. The rapid sudden violence of movement stunned Daniel and by the time he had recovered and considered whether he should perhaps intervene or move somewhere safer himself, Sean was helping Razor to his feet, Andy was back in his chair smoking, looking completely unruffled and the party had picked back up again. And then Billy Boy was standing on his chair clapping and conducting a choir of drunken Danish guys in football shirts and Sean was leading Daniel over to take his turn on the row of shots and the whole incident blurred into the long tapestry of the evening.

Chapter 8

At ten to four in the afternoon, the gleaming black Mercedes pulled smoothly to a stop in front of the alabaster pillars of a St. James's Square Gentleman's Club. Rain splattered the windscreen of the car, drumming an erratic, hypnotic rhythm. Derek sighed and stuffed the manila folder deep into his suit jacket to protect it from the wet. A portly, heavily-jowled man in the standard Club uniform of long black overcoat, replete with black felt bowler hat, stepped forward and opened the passenger side door, offering the protection of a vast umbrella as he did. Hemmings trotted up the steps and sidled inside into the warm and familiar surroundings of The East India Devonshire Sports and Public Schools Club. He nodded at the wiry Italian butler, thinning hair scraped back over his forehead. The greeting in response was warm. 'It's a pleasure to see you again, Mr Hemmings. If you please, sir, your guest is waiting for you in the Ladies' Drawing Room.'

Derek grimaced. The irony of holding a meeting with this dirty Russian gangster within the refined, elegant surroundings of the Ladies' Drawing Room was not lost on him. Being a privately owned, members-only club the establishment retained strict rules on the entry of and usage by ladies. It may be unfashionable and antiquated in this day and age but Derek respected the traditions and felt they represented a sanctuary of order in this hectic, all-access, politically-correct world. Ladies weren't permitted in the bars, the Library, Smoking Room (the lighting of cigars in the club was now sadly no longer permitted but the name of the room endured in glorious defiance) or even the Dining Room at lunchtime. To enjoy lunch at the club a lady must be accompanied as guest of a gentleman member in the Luncheon Room only. The Ladies' Drawing Room represented a refined environment in which to entertain female guests away from the main rooms, so as not to impinge on the relaxation or important matters of discussion and debate among the other members. It was the very room where, on 21 June 1815, The Prince Regent (later George IV) first heard the news of the English army's victory at Waterloo. Major Henry Percy, aide-de-camp to the triumphant Duke of Wellington, interrupted the dinner party to present four captured French eagles and the Duke's victory dispatch. Today it lay empty, reserved exclusively for Derek's important meeting.

Hemmings trudged up the stairs with heavy feet, stopping outside a set of tall delicately hand painted wooden doors. He knocked hesitantly, at once annoyed with himself for already ceding the psychological advantage of the meeting. This was his Club: he the member, Golich the guest. He had no need to knock. If there was knocking to be done it should be Golich who should be doing the bloody knocking. 'Useless, Hemmings. Simply useless,' he murmured beneath his breath.

Entering the room in a fluster, folder clasped deep within sweaty palm, Derek was halted as he stepped over the threshold by a huge hand attached to a huge man, muscles straining inside a shiny, jet black suit. Further ignominy was suffered through the intimate patting down of his bony, sixty-four year old body in the thorough search for a weapon. The very notion of which was, of course, quite preposterous. Derek stood there limply with his arms outstretched, blushing and assiduously trying to avoid any eye contact whatsoever.

The large room was empty, save for one small round tea table at which sat a stocky man whose age Derek could only place somewhere between his mid forties and early fifties. His face was round. Cold grey unblinking eyes were framed with thick black eyebrows. *The eyes of a hardened criminal*, Derek mused to himself disdainfully. He studied the man at the table as he sipped mint tea from a delicate china teacup, fat fingers struggling to hold it with any sense of refinement. Derek wondered if the cup might fall as it wobbled its way to fleshy lips. It struck him, on examination, that Boris Golich had a perfectly wrinkle-free and lineless face. A baby face. It was bizarre. His smooth features were accented by a short cropped black beard flecked with grey. Hair was of exactly equal length and colour. An oversized diamond earring twinkled from his left ear. Derek was heartened at least that the man had made an effort to respect the opulent surroundings and rules of the club. He wore a light grey suit, stitched of the finest cloth, with neat, precise creases. It was set off by a black shirt and surprisingly tasteful tie of deep purple interwoven with fine gold thread. Much to his annoyance, the whole outfit came together rather well, emanating an impression of wealth and elegance. Well what had he really expected? Trainers and a denim jacket? Perhaps Disney characters on the socks and tie?

'May I offer you some tea?' came the offer.

'Oh yes, very kind. English breakfast if you please.' Unfailingly courteous to the last. *Actually*, thought Hemmings, *isn't he supposed to be my guest?*

Seizing the initiative Derek began. 'So Mr Golich, I understand that you wish to do a little business with Great Britain?'

'Well only if Great Britain wants me. And of course the little business of my money.'

He laboured the word, clumsily attempting to draw every last grain of irony from his point. They locked eyes. And then the oligarch began to laugh. Loudly. Heartily. After a short period his mirth spread to the muscle in the unforgiveable suit who joined him with an obsequious snigger. He stopped laughing and straightened the knot in his tie. He cleared his throat.

'This little business, as you call it, is billions of pounds invested by MY Rublex Corporation into gas exploration in the international waters off YOUR British Falkland Islands, and the infrastructure for YOUR British workers living on them.' The emphasis of his words was used to make the crude point. Derek reciprocated.

'Yes indeed. OUR Falkland Islands. YOUR money in exchange for Britain's co-operation in transporting this gas for sale across the world under our protection and licence in the good name of British Petroleum. Joint enterprise, sharing in the proceeds, potentially one hundred billion pounds over the next ten years.' A stiff retort.

'Correct. I'm pleased you have an understanding of the arrangements, Mr Hemmings.' He tapped his fingernail crisply against the edge of the teacup. 'It seems your Prime Minister wishes to move ahead as soon as possible. He told me so himself when we played golf at Queenwood, other day. I love you British because of your famous justice, the sense of honour. Not like the bitch traitors in US. You say you make the deal. You make the deal.'

Golich spat out the word 'bitch' with genuine venom causing Derek to glance around him to see if they had been overheard. *Well, the old stager thought, the rumours are true, they are golfing buddies after all.* Followed quickly by a second thought: *I wouldn't mind an invitation to play Queenwood with the Prime Minister myself.*

'British Prime Minister gives me his word. He tells me this is stronger than the mighty British oak tree. Deal happens, okay.' Again the hard stare. Unblinking eyes. No invitation to respond.

'With all due respect Mr Golich, whilst I am indeed here to discuss and ratify the deal with yourself and Rublex Corporation, we do have due process and procedures to follow. And I intend to satisfy myself with the full probity of this deal before we make a commitment to you or anyone else. Now, I have some questions regarding the origins of your investment stake for the gas development station. We need to be satisfied with regard to international money laundering rules and regulations.'

Boris Golich stood up from his seat raising a hand to silence the civil servant in mid flow.

'The talking is over now Mr Hemmings. The offer stands for one week only and then is off the table forever.' He waved his hand dismissively, curling his upper lip. 'We know plenty of governments who will make such a deal with Rublex during this period of, how do you say, "global economic uncertainty"? So you have no business asking questions of my wealth. It will simply do no good for you.'

The word *you* was definitely emphasised. These not so subtle messages were certainly being telegraphed. He stalked from the room followed closely by the gigantic minder, a disproportionate shadow. Derek was left feeling distinctly uneasy. He peered from the huge bay window out onto the square, partially hidden behind a long, elegantly embroidered drape. Watched as the Russian climbed into the back seat of a waiting Silver Fox Rolls-Royce which purred away in the direction of Park Lane. *Well that went better than expected Derek old boy*, he chided himself ruefully. Scuffed his foot deliberately against the leg of an antique table in self-disgust.

Chapter 9

Daniel awoke fully clothed on top of his still made bed. The morning sun streamed through the window, stinging his eyes. He rubbed his face and coughed. The rancid taste in his mouth made him gag and, looking down gingerly, saw he had been sick over his once pristine black shirt. He clambered off the bed and into the bathroom and splashed cold water over his grimy face. He looked sheepishly in the mirror, then away just as quickly, unable to face the pathetic image reflected back at him. He pulled off his shirt and winced. Two deep parallel scratch marks ran the length of his torso diagonally across his chest, alarmingly sore to the touch. In the shower his scratches throbbed and burned under the water.

After, he stepped out into the room in just a towel and worriedly scoured the room for his wallet and watch. They hadn't been in his trousers and weren't lying anywhere he could see them. He checked the wardrobe and under the bed. 'Stupid bastard,' he groaned. 'Mum's going to kill me if I've gone and lost Granddad's gold watch.'

After five minutes he gave up, the exertions making his head thump in raw, uneven pulses. There was little doubt about it, he was in bad shape, probably still drunk. Doubts and questions flooded over him. *If he was this bad now how had he got back to the room last night? If he didn't have his wallet how could he even get back in the room without his key card? How was he going to pay his hotel bill this week without any credit cards?* He couldn't face the idea of explaining this mess to Silvio. Closing his eyes, Daniel tried to redact the intense throbbing in his head.

●

An eternity later, the digital clock wobbled back into vision. A red 09.28 blinked back at him, boring into his skull. It was the first day of the tournament and Aaron and Andy would be half way through their round by now. *Fuck. Hadn't Andy been with him up till the end last night?* He struggled to remember as he dragged himself back over the preceding evening, fighting to recall any real detail from incoherent snatches of memory and a whirling carousel of blurred images and faces. There's just no way that Andy could have been with him in this state if he had to be up before the birds to prepare the gear the way Aaron wanted it for tee off at 06.45am. The man wouldn't have been to bed at all and he seemed to be drinking as hard as everyone else. As the fragmented pattern of thoughts coursing through Daniel's head smoothed into a cohesive stream of consciousness he was hit by a deep sense of foreboding once again as the realisation landed that he would be late out onto the golf course having promised that he would be there to walk the ropes and show support on the first day of the tournament. The very least he could do. And this was the very first professional tournament of his new career as a golf agent. A cold sweat beaded across his face and neck. *Fuck.*

He dressed hurriedly, pulling on a powder blue polo shirt and neatly creased grey trousers from the hanger. What had Silvio said about looking the part? The imperative now was to move as quickly as he could without throwing up. The fresh air would clear his head and if Daniel still couldn't find his belongings when he got back to the room then he'd simply have to front up to the mess he'd got himself into, cancel the credit cards and file a report with the local police for insurance purposes. Frustration and anger bubbled up within him. He cursed himself: What a bloody fool for getting into a drunken mess on the first night. For jeopardising the one big chance he had at a new career. At that moment Daniel wasn't exactly repaying the faith that Silvio had shown in him.

●

Out through the hotel and still in one piece, Daniel stalked his way past the practice range. His sole objective was to avoid eye contact that might draw him into an unwanted conversation about this game that he really knew so bloody little about. Daniel skirted the line of enormous black television trailers connected by an umbilical cord of endless thick black cable. He strode over to the imperious white scoreboard standing in splendid isolation. Squinting into the morning sun Daniel scoured down the names on it alphabetically until he came to CROWER, A. With not half the players out on the course yet he could see that Aaron had begun the day well. In fact four under par after nine holes was a blistering start and the stylish Australian was tied in second place at the turn. Daniel calculated that they must already be playing the tenth hole. He quickly consulted his crumpled score card for its crude map of the golf course and headed directly to the eleventh hole to intercept the group.

The eleventh was a beautiful par four hole. It snaked around a rugged head of sublime Andalucían coastline. The tee consisted of a postage stamp of well-watered grass positioned on the edge of an exposed headland, surrounded on three sides by sheer rocky cliffs and the shimmering blue and green Mediterranean Sea. The coastline cut in dramatically to the cliff top leaving the tee precariously positioned and set apart from the rest of the course. Whilst lush fairway stretched up to the green on the right hand side, the greatest reward and a seductive temptation for a glorious birdie or eagle chance was to aim your sights directly across the natural rocky cove carved over centuries of attrition from the lapping of the unrelenting waves. To attempt to 'drive the green', those players who needed to score aggressively would fire their ball across the aqua swell aiming at the flag beyond. Watching intently, praying it wouldn't get caught in a capricious swirling wind and drop down into a watery grave. The green itself was surrounded by deeply hollowed, perfectly raked bunkers of pure white sand. It was an epic hole, designed for risk and reward golf. Like a siren's beauty calling a ship's captain towards the rocks, the hole's allure was set to tempt even those players whose 'course management' mindset was of the most puritanical.

A small crowd had gathered behind the ropes surrounding the green and were facing back up to the players on the tee. Daniel headed there directly, noting Aaron's group trooping up from the recently completed tenth hole. The group ahead were putting out on the green and a caddy moodily raked one of the bunkers which had just proved so costly to his boss. He claimed a place between an elderly couple and two women, ripe to the point of plumpness, in their late teens, both wearing rather short shorts and jostling each other whenever the handsome players walked near. Sweat dripped from his brow. It was starting to get hot and Daniel was still feeling decidedly ill.

'Mind if I join you?' came a voice behind him. Daniel turned to face a tall, good looking man dressed in black slacks and an immaculately embroidered white collarless shirt, buttoned up to the neck. His ashen blonde hair was perfectly parted to the side, not a strand out of place. He enquired again, 'May I join you Daniel?'

'Of course,' replied Daniel, wondering anxiously how this man happened to know his name and if they had already met. 'I'm Aaron's manager,' he said as if in some justification for him being there and pointing to the silhouetted figure now crouching to insert a tee peg into the turf some distance away.

'Yes Daniel, this much I already know. Good morning to you, I'm Sergei Krostanov, Head of Golf Sponsorship for the Rublex Oil and Gas Corporation.' He extended his hand in greeting and Daniel caught sight of a small crudely drawn star in blue ink tattooed on the flesh between thumb and forefinger. It reminded him of something a bored student might have doodled during an oppressive maths lesson. It seemed incongruous given the way the man was dressed. 'We support the Tour very much you know?' he said and continued without waiting for an answer, 'I also do much business with Randy Hughes who owns the Crown Sports.' Daniel thought of the huge sponsorship billboards he had seen around the course promoting Rublex Corporation, the Russian Oil & Gas conglomerate, in addition to the title sponsorship they held for the race of champion golfer of the year.

'It's a pleasure to meet you,' Daniel replied quietly, offering his hand and half turning to look Sergei in the eye just in time to miss Aaron's tee shot from across the cove.

'We all like to help each other out on the circuit, as they say, Daniel. We look after our own out here so any problems, anything at all, you must please let me help. Do you understand?' Sergei purred. He moved to stand next to Daniel behind the roped off green, not once lifting his lifeless pale blue eyes from his face. Daniel shifted one foot to the other. Although his English was excellent there was still a noticeable undercutting Russian bite to Sergei's speech, an unmistakeable hard edge to the consonants in his diction. Not sure why he was feeling under interrogation, he decided that the omnipresent beads of sweat bubbling up on his forehead were determined to visibly betray the hidden throbbing inside his skull. He wanted to crawl away and vomit. But there it was, once extended, incapable of being ignored. Just left hanging out there. A platitude. A kind but empty promise of future help. That was all surely. The last thing he wanted to do was further humiliate himself by admitting to this important cog in the machinery of the Tour that he had lost his watch and wallet, or had them stolen, after getting drunk on his first night on the job. But this was a big deal to Daniel. Nothing like this had ever happened to him before. Sergei seemed friendly and might know whom to speak with about it. And so inevitably the awkward silence did its work and Daniel found himself drifting inexorably towards the point of confessing his predicament. After a long uncomfortable period of time had elapsed between them Daniel practically blurted out loud:

'Sergei, my wallet and watch were lost or stolen last night. It was my grandad's watch and the wallet had my company credit cards in it and I thought you might know the best way to register this with the local police or with the Tour, if there was a lost property department or something?' He inhaled sharply.

Sergei chuckled. 'Lost property? This isn't school anymore, Daniel.' The young man's face turned a fierce shade of burning crimson in response. 'It's serious if you have lost those things. Okay, I will ask some questions and try to help you. I too know what it is like to treasure a gift handed down through the family. The family is the only thing in life with any true meaning.' His voice seemed serious, hard edged. But then he continued chirpily, 'And golf as well of course. Few things have more value than the golf.'

'Thank you so much. I feel like such an idiot.'

'Not as much of an idiot as when my friend Randy Hughes finds out that you lost his company credit card. Your boss, the owner of Crown Sports is not, shall we say, a patient man where money is involved.'

'I'm not looking forward to telling him to be honest. I haven't had the chance yet.' Daniel looked crestfallen.

'I tell you what. Let's not make a drama out of all this.' Sergei reached inside his trouser pocket and pulled out a neat shiny black leather wallet. 'Take this credit card. It belongs to Rublex. Use it for expenses while you find your wallet. If you don't find it then you should cancel the card and you may hold onto this one for the week of the tournament in Spain. Give it back to me at the next event. Okay?'

'I don't know what to say. That's incredibly generous. Thank you.'

'Please Daniel. Rublex does what it can to support golf in every way. We have a strong working relationship with Crown Sports and I'm sure you will find a way to make it up to me. Besides I can't let you get on the wrong side of our Mr Hughes just yet, not when you have just started out in your career on the Tour.'

Then the discussion was over and Sergei pointed with his jaw beyond the ropes. 'Yes, he's got the fierce talent indeed, that one,' as Aaron skilfully skimmed the ball out of the bunker, plopped it onto the green, and watched it roll past the hole to within two feet. 'I've been speaking to Andy Sharples, the caddy, about Aaron's aptitude and he thought you might like to enrol him in the Rublex Corporation sponsorship programme?'

●

Daniel brightened up at once. Sponsorship was one of the key facets of his job and a measureable element of how well agents are looking after their players. Silvio had warned him that it was also a lever that rival player managers used to pry star golfers away from management stables. In golf, money spoke and it spoke loudly.

'That sounds most interesting Mr Krostanov. I really would be delighted to discuss terms,' answered Daniel, trying to sound as professional as he could under the spectre of his debilitating hangover.

'It's Sergei, please, if we are to be working together. Everybody just knows me as Sergei.' He ran his fingers through his hair, continuing, 'I'll have my secretary draw up the papers specifying the terms and send them to your hotel room.'

'Yes, thank you. I really appreciate it,' answered Daniel. This man was turning out to be quite the savour of his disastrous morning.

Aaron drilled his two foot putt and followed up with the obligatory fist pump. Applause rippled through the gallery. Sergei slapped Daniel once on the back, hard and firm before turning to head back through the trees towards the hotel.

Stepping under the ropes, eleventh hole now complete, Aaron approached Daniel who stood smiling gently to himself. 'Good to see you made it out here mate,' he drawled pointedly as he made his way down a short dirt path that led to the twelfth hole tee box. 'Andy didn't seem to think you'd be getting out of bed today for some reason. Sloppy stuff on your first day I reckon, we've been up since the crack of dawn.' Andy smirked in the background.

Daniel trotted to keep up and immediately wished he hadn't. His skull rattled. 'Actually I've been busy working on a new sponsorship deal for you with the Rublex Corporation this morning,' he countered with as much false enthusiasm as he could muster. 'It's all looking good.'

'On yer mate,' came the lazy unenthused response and a fist offered in congratulation for Daniel to bump with his own.

'The greens are like putting on a glass table this morning, mate. Lightening quick.' And with that Aaron Crower was back in the zone, standing to the side on the twelfth tee, swishing his driver back and forth like a fly fishing rod. His stocky Italian playing partner stared doggedly down the fairway focusing assiduously on executing his pre-shot routine.

Pleased with the way the morning was shaping up after its disastrous start, Daniel watched the golfers stride off down the tree lined fairway following a pair of precise booming drives. If I'm going to survive today without fainting I'd better try and get some breakfast down he thought, and began the long loop back towards the hotel.

Chapter 10

At the appointed time and place, or near enough, I found Mickey leaning on the bonnet of his Jeep, tinkering with a tiny screwdriver in the back of a two-way transistor radio. He was a wiry man of about five foot seven, always clean shaven, with a thick brush of spiky black hair. His angular inquisitive face, protruding nose and furtive dark eyes generated the perpetual impression of a badger in the wild poking his snout out from the inside of a hedgerow. I don't think anyone really knew Mickey's surname. Perhaps it was long forgotten, perhaps never been shared. He'd been working with Charles Hand for many years prior to the set up of the Unit. A talented engineer and communications expert, he was also just the guy you wanted to have your back in a firefight. Calibrated to be unquestionably dependable and I liked it that way. You can't afford to be left wondering if you've got a bullseye on your back during a job.

He glanced up at me and grinned

'What fuckin' time d'ya call this then Hunter?' he called out in mock exasperation, making a dramatic show of checking his watch.

'Tommy Time, baby,' came my response. 'Been here long then, have you Mickey?' I laughed.

'You'll be late for your own funeral Hunter,' he flashed back. 'I've got something to show you Tommy-boy. And I think you're gonna like it too.' The words sang out over his shoulder in that rasping cockney lilt. I scooted round to the back of the Jeep and he slid back a green tarpaulin under which sat an array of equipment that we would require for the job. I scanned the neatly compiled arsenal, noting everything in its place. The gear was strapped onto a square cut piece of thick green material. This would fold up tightly, wrapping the weaponry to be stowed into one or other of the two grey and sandy brown camouflaged rucksacks sitting to the side. The equipment was set up with the precision that a heart surgeon might lay out their life saving equipment with prior to a major operation. Tools of the trade. There were two Berettas, both with attachable silencers. Mickey knew it was my favourite handgun because the model came without a safety-catch to hamper a quick draw, the double squeeze trigger preventing accidental fire. Next, there were two stub-nosed Mack 10 machine guns, a sickening bull of a weapon which could extinguish the occupants of a room in mere moments at close range, its roaring clatter of thirty bullets a second pronouncing death on arrival whenever it was called into play. There were boxes of ammunition clips and both stun and flash grenades. Handier and less volatile than their destructive TNT-based cousins, these grenades can be used to cause a distraction or temporarily blind assailants without the risk of collateral damage. In addition, Mickey had stocked a water bottle, energy bars, a field medical kit, a magnetised GPS tracker button and three razor-sharp knives.

Long ago, Mickey had told me a tall tale of how back in the mob, a Sergeant Major in the Marines had requisitioned one of these same trackers from Mickey's munitions store. He'd affixed it on the underside of his buxom wife's car, as he suspected she was having an affair. Given his fearsome reputation and violent temper, the attractive blonde had always been extremely careful that she wasn't being followed when she left the base, doubling back on herself and constantly checking in the rear view mirror.

The tracker had located her. The Sergeant Major waited until she entered the cheap motel and was deep in the throes of passion with a strapping chef from the military base when he stormed inside. The story went that he'd made the chef watch as he forced his wife to swallow both her engagement and wedding rings. As she sat sobbing on the floor he pulled out an array of knives that he'd taken from the young chef's kitchen. He sharpened them right there in front of the petrified couple and then proceeded to slowly remove the skin from the lovers' arms and legs before slitting their throats. Rough justice indeed.

Completing the kit were two-way radios, binoculars, and a slim box of industrial cable ties. I had always found these plastic ties the most efficient method of securing necessary captives on a job with the least hassle. I wasn't surprised that he'd been so thorough but it was good to know we were well prepared.

'You don't do things by halves do you Mick?' I laughed, punching him on the shoulder. 'Do you know something about this job that I don't get, mate? You've pushed the boat out. How come we're so tooled up on this one?'

'The Hand of God says that fella Bob Wallace is on the level and he's a man to be trusted. They served together and Hand doesn't forget a man he's shed blood with. Now he needs help. We talked this job over whilst you were in the air catching up on your beauty sleep. It's not straight forward. Wallace can't go to the police and he blames himself for the boy's disappearance.'

'The weapons are untraceable I take it?'

'I tapped up a contact who deals hardware to some of the more unpleasant elements of Spanish criminality. He's very good. This lot has never even existed my friend,' Mickey waved his hand regally over the weapon haul before him, beaming like a proud father.

'Nice. Thanks for sorting things, Mick. I appreciate it.'

'The pleasure was all yours,' he retorted smugly, accompanied with an overplayed sardonic look.

'I'm heading to the golf course where Daniel Ratchet was last seen so I can find out what I can about this situation. With a bit of luck Daniel will turn up nursing a hangover and a sore cock before we're even required. In the meantime, if there are leads on the ground, we'll turn them up. If he doesn't make an appearance sharpish, we'll have to figure out what went down and if he's still alive, who's got him, where the hell he's been taken, and make the intervention.'

'Good luck, Hunter. The clock's ticking hard on this one.'

I loaded the new gear onto the back seat of the Range Rover, stamped down on the gas, wheels squealing, dust cloud swirling in the air behind me. The motor pulled sharply out onto the smooth tarmac and I watched as the arrow on the speedometer forced its way doggedly round the stylish metallic dial, eating numbers as it went. Heavy downward pressure to the accelerator urged the metallic beast onwards, seeking out the angular horizon. Red rugged mountains filling the bottom inch of the windscreen. Sharp, clean lines jutting harshly against the soft aqua sky. Sun rising lazily to preside over a beautiful morning.

Keeping one eye on the empty road ahead, I rapidly scanned through the mobile phone for any new alerts from base. I'd barely averted my attention for more than a brief moment when, from out of nowhere, a battered articulated lorry swerving wildly on the wrong side of the road came careering right at me. Bloody typical that practically the first other traffic I'd encountered on the quiet Spanish roads early that morning and the driver must be asleep at the wheel. I slammed my fist into the horn blasting it loudly and swerved defensively to avoid a smash. Pulled the wheel sharply down, skidding over to the other side of the road where the lorry should be driving. Closing in on a tight corner just ahead. A heavily laden family hatchback turned into view on the road, heading straight towards me, oblivious of the carnage that had just ensued. Instinctively I heaved at the wheel and pulled the Range Rover back across the face of the road and slammed nose first into a sandy verge beyond. The truck, avoided by mere inches, skidded on two wheels as it struggled and fought to grip the tarmac. I'd swerved a clean side-on figure of eight and just missed smashing into the oncoming traffic to avoid a certain collision. The startled face of the driver in the truck cab was gripped in a mask of fear as he grappled with the unwieldy heavy machine. He finally managed to pull it back across the dotted white lines, the lorry rocking capriciously from side to side until it settled squarely back upon its rows of huge spinning wheels, slowing to a crawl.

Cursing under my breath, I watched stationary as the meat wagon, its side panelling emblazoned with a vibrant livery detailing a cargo of happy and succulent looking pigs, continued on its journey past me. The image of the truck driver's horrified face close up through the windshield held firm in my mind.

●

A green, open-top army Jeep flies out from nowhere, bouncing off a dirt mound and taking a clean two meters of air. The machine gun affixed to the back rattles a menacing timbre. Our car swerves sharply on the dirt road leading into the village, hits a pothole, flips onto its side. Screams fill my ear from behind me. Stu, injured in the crash, is speared through the torso by a twisted metal shard from the damaged vehicle. Blood spewing everywhere, thick and sticky. I struggle with the impacted passenger door and crawl forward furiously wriggling on my front. Dirt and grit in my eyes and filling my mouth. Now Jeeps, armoured vehicles, surround us from every angle. Guns fired into the sky indiscriminately, shouts and howls of excitement reverberating in the thin air. An ambush. An angry brown face thrust down at me, huge yellow blood shot eyes, inches above me, shouting loud, flecks of snow white spittle spraying from his mouth. 'Where is Mahood? Where is Mahood? You come to the village for a munitions cache but instead you will die a hostage. This is our trap. We trade soldiers for Islamic prisoners. And for you now this is very dangerous.'

The butt of a rifle descending hard toward my face. Shooting pain. Then nothing.

The incessant tapping on the window grew louder, more insistent. Woken from the haunting flashback I turned my head to face the pristine starched uniform of a local Spanish traffic cop standing beside the Range Rover. He peered quizzically inside, speaking loudly at the glass. The response to the descending electric window was a futher torrent of rapid agitated Spanish. I held out my British driving licence and after careful examination he nodded dismissively.

'No sleep here. Very dangerous. Trucks. All come very fast here,' he pointed at the road shaking his head as another truck ploughed past us, smashing a wall of hot compressed air up against the passenger window. I couldn't be bothered to try and explain, instead placating him with a lopsided grin and a goofy thumbs up. He stepped backwards quickly as I fired the engine and after making an exaggerated show of checking the mirrors swung back out onto the dusty road and continued on my way at speed, still shaken by my visions of the past.

Chapter 11

SPAIN. EUROPEAN TOUR. DAY TWO. MID-MORNING.

Daniel sauntered back towards the hotel, weaving his way past the crowded practice putting green, speckled with players and a scattering of gleaming white balls. The old Scottish golf coach he had met the day before hovered hawkishly at the scene. He greeted the affable manager with a nodded salute. Still in his navy blue flat cap, cigarette stub gripped firmly in mouth, the old boy leaned on a seven iron watchfully directing his lanky charge who stood trapped passively captive inside a neat semicircle of balls. Bob Wallace, whose name had been discussed in disparaging terms last night, was by all accounts quite a character. Sean, the ginger haired Glaswegian caddy and self-anointed Master of Ceremonies for the previous night's debacle, had recounted various nefarious tales about his fellow Scot regarding clashes with the establishment, flared tempers and one legend back from the 1980s on falling into disagreement with an over-celebrated Hollywood actor concerning his tuition style. He had chased the Hollywood star brandishing a nine iron straight off the golf range and into a nearby pond. These stories always got distorted and built up over time but Daniel chuckled to himself, picturing the scene as he tracked the pathway back towards the side entrance of the hotel.

'Hey hotshot,' called out a voice from behind him. He turned to see Matilda, sitting in the sun on the steps of the physio truck, clutching a well-thumbed paperback. Daniel waved in response. 'Got time for a coffee?' she cooed.

'Absolutely,' he replied, instantly regretting sounding so keen. By the time he reached the truck, Matilda was inside filling a cheap plastic kettle with bottled water. He bounded up the succession of tightly spaced metal steps like an energetic puppy, reaching the top only to trip on the frame of the truck as he entered, stumbling over his feet. Feet followed torso as he lurched forward clumsily, chest first into the sharp corner of the glassed-off office space that dominated one side of the truck.

'Hey, steady there, hotshot,' Matilda laughed as Daniel, looking sheepish, rubbed the painful point of impact. 'You okay?' she asked concerned, a cute furrow appearing on her brow just at the top of her button nose. 'Yeah, no, actually I'm fine, really,' he said. 'Just caught myself there. It's cool,' he said before offering, 'Sorry,' as an afterthought and wondering why.

'Really, are you sure, Daniel?' Matilda replied. 'Because that looks pretty sore,' motioning to the dots of blood soaking through his powder blue polo shirt.

'Ah, shit. I got scratched somehow last night and I must have knocked it again when I fell back there.'

'Here, show me,' she said, patting the massage table next to her, encouraging Daniel to sit.

'Matilda, it's really fine, honestly. Nothing to worry about.'

'Listen to me,' she retorted, her accent more pronounced, vowels drawn longer, 'I may not have studied medicine but I know that if you got scratched it needs to be sterilised properly.'

Daniel carefully peeled off his shirt, wincing a little as he did so.

Matilda soaked a ball of cotton wool in iodine dabbing in confident darts at his chest. 'So, how did this happen to you then, hotshot? You have to tell me. It was a woman wasn't it?' she teased and tutted, shaking her head. 'I knew all you sports agents were the same!' she followed, exclaiming in mock horror.

'I don't think so, unfortunately. Not one I'd want to meet again at any rate,' Daniel replied, scrunching up his face as the iodine stung into him.

'Oh well! I guess she can't have been that memorable then,' Matilda answered playfully as if she were philosophising.

'Rough night I'm afraid,' offered Daniel by way of explanation. 'I went out with some of the caddies on the lash. Lost my wallet. My watch. Everything. Pretty sure they were stolen. It's a major bloody disaster.'

'You poor thing. You don't deserve such bad luck just when you start a new job.'

'Well not all bad, fortunately,' he responded brightly. 'An important Russian guy out here on the Tour who works for one of the big sponsors came and found me this morning and has offered to sponsor one of my players. Could be great news and set me up well in the eyes of the new boss.'

'Sergei Krostanov by any chance?'

'Yes, how did you know?'

'Because he's involved in everything round here. I'm not surprised that he spotted the chance of a deal to be done. He always ingratiates himself with the new player managers the second they arrive. Especially if their guys have game.'

Daniel pulled a face.

That infectious giggle again. 'Okay. Sorry. I guess you deserve some credit and for something good to happen after all those issues. But let's say I'm not surprised. Somehow Sergei even gets to set the budget of the physio-truck each season and decides that it's a prerequisite that he needs to discuss it personally with me over dinner. People talk and say we must close but business is business.'

'What does Michael say about that?'

'Michael? Nothing, Michael does what he's told.'

'But I thought you guys were together?' Daniel tried to make it appear like a natural casual enquiry as he fished for information. He needn't have fretted.

'No, no. I'm a very independent woman, Daniel. Michael takes it on himself to protect me from some of the slime-balls out here on Tour perhaps, but we aren't together. I prefer a man with a bit more of an edge to him. Besides, he's got a family: a wife and a baby daughter back in Hanover. He works every hour he possibly can to send money back home to them, but they always want for more. And I'm more than capable of looking after myself, I can assure you. I have done so for a very long time indeed and that isn't about to change.'

'I have no doubt about that. I'm sure you are very capable,' Daniel said, grinning in admiration at her, then suddenly aware that this may not have been an appropriate response to verbalise. After a little while he asked thoughtfully, 'If you aren't with Michael, what about the engagement ring?'

'Oh, the ring,' Matilda replied coolly, avoiding eye contact. 'It's my mother's. I feel that it keeps me safe.' A pained and distant look held in those enchanting pale blue eyes and Daniel awkwardly decided that this avenue of conversation was better now closed.

'Just leave that to breathe,' Matilda instructed, regaining control. She turned to pack away the iodine and threw the damp ball of used cotton wool into a small metallic wastepaper basket under the sink. Daniel pulled on his shirt and fished out his phone. He switched on the company-owned phone and INSERT SIM flashed up on the screen. *Bollocks* he thought, flipping it over and removing the hard outer casing. *Where's the SIM card gone?* he wondered, worrying now because of all the details that were on it, all of Crown Sports' business contacts. It was useless without a SIM.

He discarded it with contempt, letting it spin over to one side of the massage table as his mind turned to his missing wallet and cash card. He considered ruefully how any more than only very modest spending on his cash card at this point would obliterate his overdraft and that he might be left liable for any theft on the company account.

'Matilda, listen, thanks for the patch up,' Daniel called as he bounced off the soft, padded therapy table, starting to feel an urgent need to get control of things. 'I've got to get back to my room and sort a few things out.'

'Okay,' she replied, hugging the corner of the medicinal storage cabinet and in the process exposing a long, sun kissed and perfectly toned leg. 'Will I see you later?'

He gambled.

'Well if you aren't busy we could maybe meet for dinner tonight? If you're free that is?'

Matilda hesitated, smiling. 'Sure, why not?'

'Great. Come to my room in the hotel, 503, for about seven-thirty?'

And with that Daniel was gone, spirit restored, grinning from ear to ear and trotting back down the steps of the truck towards the hotel, firmly resolved to sort the grief he was in and get his new life back on track.

Chapter 12

Derek Hemmings sat alone in the secluded gardens of St. James's Square in the gathering gloom. Across all corners of the Square, people were heading home from their day jobs, rushing to get back to their families. These days, Derek had only his wife Alice to go home to, his two children, Robin and Samantha, both having flown the nest many years ago now. Their visits were becoming less and less frequent and he felt he barely recognised them as the bright inquisitive little people he had helped bring into the world, raised with his own impeccable values and manners. No, these days as they navigated themselves through the onset of middle age, their own bustling social lives, demanding partners, and burgeoning careers took unrivalled precedence above their aging and unfashionable parents.

Derek cast his mind back to when he himself had been a vigorous young man. He might be weary of all the political games now but when he'd first joined the Foreign and Commonwealth Office as a sharp, intelligent and dedicated twenty-one year old Cambridge graduate, he'd been intent on changing the world. Selected by MI6 as potential Intelligence Unit material and fast-tracked through the training set up, Derek had thought of himself as very much in the mould of Ian Fleming's James Bond in the secret service. Equipped with sharp suits, boundless confidence and high aspirations, everything had seemed possible. So he put himself about, volunteered for assignments and cut a dash with army commanders and politicians alike. His patriotism and unstinting sense of honour made him determined to make a difference to that which he cherished most, his beloved Great Britain. For Queen and Country: Do the right thing. The mantra by which he had lived all these years.

And as quickly as it had begun, it was over. He'd met Alice, a secretary in the typing pool at Whitehall, introduced by his sister Mary with whom she was friends. They shared cocktails and theatre visits on the Strand and romantic walks through Covent Garden entwined arm in arm. Within two months, Alice was pregnant with Robin and Derek couldn't bring himself to take the posting to Cairo. He'd done the honourable thing, followed his immutable moral compass. With a young family to raise and a burdensome mortgage to pay, his fanciful ambitions of secret spying missions and glamorous foreign travel would simply have to wait. And wait they did, as his work and the family settled into a comfortable routine all together. As the wee baby grew into a toddler, Derek was handed greater responsibility within the department. Alice fell pregnant again with Samantha and Derek's ambitions were pushed further into oblivion, curtailed by the administrative quicksand of a civil service position, albeit with a slow-moving rise toward seniority and respectability. Too slow moving for Alice, perhaps, but by appointment of The Queen no less. The eventual nominal promotion was in reality on paper only but it still caused Alice to weep tears of pride and fetch out the best china for an extended family celebration. Derek was nonplussed. He had known it was dead-man's shoes right from the very beginning.

And here he was, forty-odd years later, sitting outside in a cold St. James's Square, contemplating the course of his life, decisions taken and choices made. And too stubborn to go home yet again and drink tea and finish the crossword and listen to the *pick pick pick* of Alice's knitting needles.

His mobile phone rang. The jaunty whistling theme tune to *The Great Escape*. Robin had changed it for a joke when 'the old man' was out of the room on one occasion, presumably to poke fun at his old fashioned sense of patriotism. Derek had never changed it back. It was a standing joke around the office that Derek was too out of date and inept to understand how these gadgets worked. The truth was that Derek liked the tune and what it stood for. It flared up some of the old bulldog spirit somewhere still inside him. The ring tone remained unchanged.

He answered the phone and listened as Andy Bartholomew oozed his rich, unctuous Celtic tones down the line. This was the particular tone reserved only for when he either needed something very important indeed or on returning from a lavish booze-fuelled lunch spent entertaining an enthusiastic and comely young researcher looking to climb the greasy pole. With junior female researchers of this type it was an open secret that in order to properly progress their careers it would need to be Andy's own greasy pole that they would be climbing first.

'So Derek my fine sir, how did it all go today?'

'How did what go Andy?' Derek sighed.

'That would be your little tête-à-tête with our new friend Mr Golich, Derek,' came the smarmy reply.

Derek Hemmings considered the state of play. Something didn't sit well with him. He was being rushed and he didn't like it. For Queen and Country: Do the right thing. He was tired of being pushed around by Bartholomew... by Golich... by Alice....

'Ah yes, Andy. Everything went very well with our little friend thank you. He just wants to move some cash around before he signs and we need further clarification on one or two things. There's no problem. But he says it should be about a week or so. Leave it all with me and we'll have everything wrapped up pronto.'

'Sounds fine and dandy, Hemmings. Just keep me informed and be sure bring me a signed copy of the agreement personally.'

Andy hung up.

'He's bought it,' said Derek aloud to himself in disbelief, standing to his feet. Then a little louder: 'I've just lied to a senior government official and he's only gone and bloody bought it.'

The Great Escape.

Chapter 13

The soft bed linen billowed as he flopped back onto the mattress, letting the cool of the air-conditioned hotel room wash over him. Not much by way of exertion had taken place, but he still felt drained from his short time under the baking heat of the demanding Spanish sun. He grabbed an ice cold can of lemonade from the mini bar, soaking wet from precipitation as if it could have been perspiring from its own exersions in the heat. He pressed the metal hard against his neck.

Daniel dialled down to reception and asked for the number to International Direct Enquiries. In an efficient sequence of activity, punctuated by slugs of the refreshing drink, he spoke first with his mobile provider, requesting an alternative SIM to be couriered to the hotel, and then to his bank to put a stop on the cash card and check the account balance. Just as he'd feared, the damage had already been done. The fuckers had drained his account to its maximum overdraft limit taking him two thousand pounds into the red. Worse than this he was still missing his grandfather's gold watch. Come home without that after chasing some 'Flash-Harry dream' with a bunch of foreigners and it would not go down well. Not one little bit. He stared listlessly out of the window, despondent. In blissful contrast to his sombre mood, two colourful rotund little birds danced and hopped outside on the terrace.

Sitting up on the edge of the bed, now, trying to breathe steadier, Daniel spied a slim tan file lying upon the coffee table at the side of the room. He didn't recall seeing it before. Couldn't be his. Something from housekeeping perhaps?

He hauled himself off the bed, head spinning, and steadied himself before unenthusiastically dragging himself over to the table to examine it. The outside of the folder was blank. He opened it to find several neatly bound pages of stiff crisp document inside. The first page was adorned solely with the large imposing logo of the Rublex Oil & Gas Corporation. *When did this arrive in my room?* he wondered. He scanned the following twelve pages quickly, unable to absorb too much detail or comprehend the legalese which framed the salient content. Daniel gathered it was a private and confidential proposal outlining some type of financial option scheme. Rublex Corporation was offering to make a series of significant upfront payments to Aaron Crower, care of Crown Sports, in exchange for a percentage of his winnings throughout the year. Accompanying pages outlined a schedule of bonuses, some of which appeared markedly discretionary on meeting 'required expectations' and payable to him on achieving specific positions in a number of listed events. Daniel gawped at the figures, counting out the zeros with his fingers twice to be certain. There were enormous sums of money involved. They dwarfed the sums that the major equipment manufacturers paid the higher profile players on Tour to represent their clubs, shoes, clothing and balls. There was no reference to Aaron overtly representing the brand or wearing logoed apparel. This was usually the heart of any standard player agreement, branding and player appearances at corporate golf days, in the media or at certain specified events. Instead it was written as if Aaron was a company and Rublex would become a silent investor, calling the shots behind the scenes. Secondly, he couldn't make sense of the bonus schedule. The ones that Silvio had emailed him by way of example all grew in denomination as the player achieved a higher position in the tournament, with an emphasis on the Majors. That's why they were called 'win bonuses', the better you did in an event, the more time on TV the sponsors got and the more exposure could be derived in media value and brand awareness from association with that player. The difference with this agreement was that these bonuses seemed to reward failure in certain events above victory itself.

It made no sense, Daniel thought to himself, tossing the folder back onto the table in front of him. It was the first agreement of its kind that he had read and with a combination of his fuzzy head and bleary eyes, he was convinced that the document was littered with mistakes and missing pages. I'll run it past Silvio and see what he thinks, he thought. Perhaps I can make it sound like I've delivered a serious coup in my first week, prove that I'm worth my salt after all. That will overshadow all these teething problems when they hear about the money I've brought in, as long as we can iron out the errors in there regarding the performance bonus. *Silvio will know what to do.*

It didn't stop the uneasy feeling in his stomach that was beginning to pervade.

He flicked on the TV to check the player scores of the tournament which, ironically, was playing out on a golf course only metres away from him. Aaron had finished his round on three under par after a difficult back nine. François, whom he'd also met briefly in London at a Crown Sports summit but hadn't caught up with so far this week, was fairing much worse. A later tee-time had left him combating the worst of a blustery afternoon wind and he was two over par after three holes. Daniel hoped he would be able to keep his head out there and battle round in a decent score to make it to the weekend. He'd been warned that François had a fiery temper and a tendency to get disconsolate if his game wasn't producing the results he felt his talent was capable of delivering. Missing the cut wouldn't help at all. Jeppe Ossgren was leader in the club house at six under par. Daniel smiled to himself. *Well, that's worked out just like I said it would! After all, he was swinging it just lovely on the range.*

He leaned back in his chair, hoping his luck was truly starting to change. Daniel felt his head loll to one side as he willingly succumbed to sleep's seductive summoning.

He awoke at six that evening, refreshed and invigorated. Next he showered and shaved, liberally applied aftershave and cleaned his teeth with newfound zeal. He dressed in a red and white checked short-sleeved shirt and faded blue jeans, going for the casual look. Someone had once told him: where women are concerned don't make it look like you're trying too hard.

But fighting the desire to try and impress was, of course, impossible. He could already feel the butterflies whirling in his stomach. Although these could also be attributable to the remnants of the malingering hangover, manfully navigated thus far. There was no denying he was excited by the prospect of dinner with this sexy worldly woman, a woman who was displaying genuine interest in him. And in this testosterone-rich environment with so much wealth, talent, and the very essence of competition on display, she would certainly have her fair share of suitors. She'd practically alluded to as much herself. The thought lingered and annoyed Daniel, unsettling him more than he quite expected. Yes, he wanted her for himself. There was something else about her that intrigued him too. She was confident, certainly aware of her own self-worth and possibly the devastating mind-numbing affect that she had on men. That was if his own reaction were anything to go by. Yet she remained vulnerable. She was grounded and down to earth and seemed to shield a secret hurt. But she enjoyed teasing him and could establish her superiority with just a look. Above all else, Daniel loved a challenge.

He was, however, getting ahead of himself. He'd overslept and hadn't made dinner reservations. With no access to money, except for the Rublex corporate credit card which Mr Krostanov had so kindly extended to him, impressing Matilda was going to be a tough job. And he could hardly ask her to pay. He toyed with the idea that Sergei would consider that buying dinner for the Tour physiotherapist was a fit and proper use of his generosity when the time came for expense reconciliation. It was, after all, a favoured activity of his own apparently. Thinking on his feet, Daniel figured that at least he might be able to arrange for his hotel bill to be covered by Crown Sports HQ at the end of the week, buying him some time. He grabbed the room phone quickly and dialled to order room service.

As a lad growing up, Daniel had been told that he displayed an easy manner, a relaxed charm. Perhaps it was the natural antidote to being the only child of a neurotic mother and uptight father who calculated and affixed risk to each of life's everyday decisions. To say that they had been shocked and concerned when he'd taken the job with an American company at such short notice, without the usual period of intense and expected due diligence was an understatement. This was compounded when they learned that he would be travelling abroad for his job, a different country week on week, living out of hotels. His father was naturally suspicious of the type of money that a man of twenty-one would be earning in these endeavours. Was Daniel quite sure what would be expected of him by these foreigners? His mother repeatedly warned of impending doom with so many flights to be taken during the year across the busy international golf schedule. Above all, they didn't consider sport to be a serious, sustainable career, nor the best use of a university education. A bunch of show-offs, dressed up like clowns, trying to hit a little white ball into a hole was, to them, a frivolous affair.

Daniel gently persuaded the friendly, female voice on the end of the phone to open up the full restaurant menu to him for room service, rather than the limited listing on offer in the room. He ordered with gusto, the classic trap for anyone who has chosen food whilst gripped in the pangs of hunger. Hoping Matilda would be pleased with his choices, he added a couple of bottles of champagne and hung up the receiver. It was 19.15.

He briefly considered phoning François to touch base and offer some words of encouragement. On balance it was probably safer to let him stew in his own juices on the range, beating out his frustrations on dozens of innocent inanimate objects instead. He opted to leave a simple, upbeat message of support for him to be collected at reception. Boxes ticked, he sprang off the bed and sauntered out onto the balcony, gazing below at bronzed couples in light evening dresses and linen shirts, smoking cigarettes and sharing pre-dinner drinks by the pool. He hadn't really comprehended it when Silvio explained that he would be staying in five star hotels on his trips with the players, all paid for by his new employer. When he had queried it, Silvio had explained that the beautiful golf courses on which the tournaments were played often had hotels affixed to them or situated close by. Staying at these made total access to the players, your own stable or perhaps even those of another agent if you were seeking to build an illicit relationship, much easier. The caddies take care of themselves, sharing in whatever cheap flea pit they can find between them during the week to keep costs down. But it simply wouldn't do for a player manager not to be close at hand for his stars.

Daniel was woken from his thoughts by a rap on the door. He scampered across the room, opening it to allow two smartly dressed waiters to bluster inside wheeling long metal trollies adorned with white table cloths, ice buckets and several large silver salvers stacked up together. They looked with concern first at the room's small coffee table, and then in turn at the writing desk and patio furniture calculating the lack of surface space versus the plethora of dishes steaming patiently on the trollies. The waiters enquired politely in heavily accented English where 'sir' would like dinner to be presented. Daniel considered the balcony for a moment but then pulling one of the folded white table cloths from a trolley, shook it free and laid it on the floor at the foot of the bed. 'I think it's going to have to be picnic time,' he grinned.

At 20.03, the door knocked twice, softly. The minutes had ticked by. He checked himself in the mirror one last time before taking a deep breath. He peeked through the tiny fish-eye security peephole out into the corridor. Matilda was standing before him holding a single flower in both hands, a large drooping yellow and white daisy. He sprang the door open.

'For you,' she said coyly, offering Daniel the flower, kissing him on the cheek and stepping into the room in one single motion. He turned to see a vision standing before him, her shoulders swaying slightly, hands clasped in front across her lap. Matilda's long, straight cut, platinum blonde hair cascaded down her shoulders. Her dress was made of white embroidered lace, cut an inch before the knee to reveal two long shapely, tanned legs in a pair of strappy black heels. Her look was natural with make-up used simply and sparingly, perfectly highlighting strong Nordic cheek bones and those big blue eyes. Full, lightly glossed lips glistened at him, soft and inviting. Daniel hadn't realised quite how hungry he actually was.

Gesturing behind them to the generous picnic spread which adorned the table cloth stretched over the carpet he mumbled aloud, 'I was going to take you to a restaurant but…'

'Daniel, you did all this just for me? It's wonderful. I can't believe it.'

'Oh, it's no problem. Really. I just figured it might be fun. I hope you brought your appetite,' he said, fumbling to open a cold bottle of champagne from the bucket and fill two glasses, spilling half of the spurting bubbles and losing the cork somewhere behind an arm chair in the process.

They toasted each other, 'To new friends,' and stepped out onto the balcony to enjoy the view.

'You are so lucky to be staying here, Daniel' said Matilda looking carefully around. 'You realise I have to share a room with some old dragon in a cheap downtown apartment. Michael prefers to sleep in the truck.' Daniel wondered if the old dragon might be the efficient, line-faced matron he has seen registering players on the first day. He couldn't help but envy her being able to share a room with the sumptuous woman standing in front of him.

'I know. I can't believe it myself. I think I could just about get used to living the life of a golf agent.'

'Don't you fucking change on me though,' said Matilda, fiercely placing her hand on Daniel's shoulder. 'There are enough assholes around here already.' The Swedish accent was coming through stronger again.

'Who do you mean exactly? Although I think I've already met a few to be honest,' replied Daniel, draining his glass and then refilling Matilda's.

'Well, some of the caddies you already know I believe? Your new drinking buddies? They give me the creeps, always hanging around, staring, whispering, making lewd remarks. It can be a bit menacing really sometimes. Most of the agents are just slimeballs, always making innuendoes with me and ordering Michael around.'

'No one ever takes your fancy then?' asked Daniel.

Matilda giggled and playfully punched him on the leg. 'Well a girl's got to have some fun, right? I've been on a few dates, got to know a few of the agents out here. But they are all so boring. I went out with one guy in particular, Ollie. His daddy started the company managing sports stars years ago and now Ollie runs around on Tour sucking up to the players and pretending he's very important to everyone else. I guess you could say we had some fun. He really made it big though when he got his whole stable to be sponsored by Rublex on their player programme. You should think about that too I guess. That's real money.'

Daniel thought back to the slick looking guys he'd seen on the range, gelling with the players and their teams so naturally. *Was Ollie one of those guys?* he wondered. He found himself bristling with jealousy.

'Righto. And I met that Russian guy we talked about. Sergei, right? He's such a nice guy. He's already been so kind to me. What do you know about him?' enquired Daniel earnestly.

'You're just all business, you hot shot agents, aren't you?' answered Matilda smiling at him. Daniel sensed she was also trying to change the subject.

'Sorry. It's just I'm new here and any information is a help. I've got one chance and I'm determined to make my mark.'

'He's the face of the Russian Rublex Corporation on the golf Tour. They did this massive deal with the Tour a while back, supporting tournament infrastructure and building up the big prize funds to attract the best international players. Sergei delivers it all and ensures they get what they want. Not everyone approves though. Some of the more traditionalists like Bob Wallace, you know that tough little Scottish swing coach with the blue hat and always with the cigarette, he's one of the longest serving guys out here. He says the Tour has "sold its soul" to compete with the US Tour.'

'Surely that's a good thing for the game, a bit of competition. Must be good for the players too,' Daniel challenged.

'Rublex has certainly divided opinion but they are the future. Sergei is a clever guy. He always has an eye for a deal and knows the right levers to pull at the right time. He's a good man to be on the right side of. But he understands the importance of family and loyalty, although Bob seems to think he is somehow resentful of the game's exclusivity and traditions. He is actually very committed to golf. His heart is in the right place.'

'Sounds like a bit of an enigma,' scoffed Daniel. 'But he has certainly helped me out this week, that's for sure.' And then, 'Look our food's getting cold. Shall we eat?'

Leading Matilda by the hand back into the bedroom they sat facing each other on corners of the table cloth which served as their make-shift picnic blanket, he cross-legged and Matilda sitting with her knees curled beneath her. He busied himself removing the numerous lids that covered the delicious-smelling food unpacking baskets of warm bread rolls and small jars of exotic looking sauces. Since the aborted restaurant plan, he had decided against choosing a specific meal on behalf of his date, equipped with little prior knowledge of her tastes. Instead he had decided on ordering a vast array of delicate tapas.

'It could get messy,' joked Daniel, 'please just get stuck in. There's no order to it really.' He reached across the spread to ease a ladle full of fearsome looking, paprika-rich chorizo and some folded pieces of thickly-sliced rustic ham onto his plate. Matilda helped herself in turn to a modest portion of thick lamb stew with a side of lush green salad leaves. Daniel replenished their glasses and, after a second helping, he leant back sighing contentedly.

'I really don't know that much about you,' Matilda stated shyly peering over the rim of her glass.

'Not much to tell really,' he replied. He was met with a disappointed look. 'I'm a straight forward bloke I suppose. Guess I'm just running scared from my boring life back in England. I want to do well but I'm not sure I fancy having to cut corners and compete with the supposed sharks out here doing my job.'

'A man with principals. That can be very sexy you know,' Matilda teased. He flushed red up the sides of his neck and cheeks. *Steady on with the champagne* he chided himself, *you're getting a bit loose here.* 'I suppose I'm trying to escape from my background, my parents, my life as it was meant to be, all mapped out for me. I only got this job through luck. You know, right place right time. I feel like a bit of a fraud most of the time. Like I don't fit in.'

'Oh, Daniel, of course you fit in. You fit in because you're real. A real person. You don't find that too often. You're not someone pretending to be something that you're not. I really appreciate your honesty in sharing with me.' She clasped her hands against her heart as if showing the depth of feeling. 'There's not much genuine conversation or guys showing their feelings and making themselves vulnerable out here. Thank you'. She reached out and held his hand in hers, keeping eye contact.

'What about you?' Daniel asked gently softening his voice, his head cocked slightly to the side.

'Me? I'm a bit of a mess too actually. Only in my case I wish I had parents to run from.'

'Seriously? What happened?' said Daniel, not releasing the delicate hand from his grip.

'They were killed in a car crash outside Stockholm when I was nineteen. I lost the plot after that for a while. I didn't know where to turn, Daniel.' She held up her other hand and offered it to him. 'I wear this ring you noticed because it's all that I have left of my mother, she gave it to me on my eighteenth birthday, it had been her mother's too you see and it's always protected me.' She pulled back, retreating a little. 'I should have been on that trip with them that day. I only wish she had been wearing it instead of me, you know?' She looked at her hand and twisted the small stone around on her finger. A moment of silence passed between them and she continued. 'After a while I managed to get it together and I just threw myself back into my studies. My brother Nils, he took it harder, he went off the rails, got in with a bad group, turned to heroin to escape. It's a fucking dirty, horrible drug, Daniel,' she spat. 'He damaged himself permanently. Now he's trapped in a state clinic in Malmö. Lost. Alone.'

She looked up at Daniel and he could see her eyes brimming with tears. He reached behind and tucked a strand of fine blonde hair behind her ear.

'It's okay,' was all he could manage.

Matilda reached forward and traced her finger down his shirt over the scratch on Daniel's chest which she had treated some hours earlier. He let her nearly finish before grabbing her and pulling her towards him. Wiping the tears from her cheeks Daniel found himself suddenly kissing her tentatively on the mouth. He cupped the back of her head and, feeling her yield, he kissed her soft lips again harder.

He pulled back, holding her face in his hands and gazed for an age into those pretty blue eyes. With an impish grin escaping across his face, Daniel Ratchet couldn't contain himself. Still kissing her at delightedly random intervals he asked, 'So why me, Matilda? A girl like you could have anyone she wanted out here.

I'm curious to know because I get the impression you don't do this sort of thing very often?'

'Right place, right time! Didn't you say that yourself, hotshot?' She giggled pushing him away and easing herself up and onto the edge of the bed. 'Okay, you want to know what I like in you? You're sincere. Honest, vulnerable, even. You didn't act all cool and in control like most of the other guys out here when we met and I really liked that. Besides, despite all the people out here performing with this travelling circus, it's actually a pretty lonely way to live and although I'm with Michael in the truck all the time, he's married and treats me like a kid sister. Can you blame a girl for getting excited when some fresh meat arrives on the scene?' Daniel blushed. 'Besides, I need an escape plan to get off this merry-go-round at some point. So play your cards right and make sure you sign your players up to lots of juicy sponsorship deals out here and make it big. I heard you are looking after the hottest young international talent on the Tour right now so as far as escape plans go you might just be it.'

Daniel grinned and, standing directly in front of her, pushed Matilda onto her back. She squealed with laughter, thrashing around playfully as Daniel kneeled on the bed, pinning her by the arms and planting quick playful kisses all over her face as she snorted with laughter.

Chapter 14

ENGLAND. LONDON. WHITEHALL.

By the time Derek strode back into his office, chest thrust out, the blood coursing through his veins, there were only a few lights left on in the building. He marched down the corridor with a spring in his step he'd not felt for many a year. A lone chink of light emanated from under a single door. The small office of his diligent assistant Alexander Gontlemoon. A double first in languages from Oxford, the immaculately groomed young man was tipped as a rising star of the department and, Hemmings had noted to himself at the interview, was cut from the right cloth. That didn't hurt one jot around the corridors of power. Tall, expensive suits, perfectly parted hair, and always prepared to go the extra mile. Not like his own son Robin or the rest of this self-entitled Facebook generation, he mused.

He rapped twice on the door and cleared his throat as he pushed it open. 'Alexander, dear boy. Would you be so kind as to come to my office? I could use your help with looking into something important, something gravely sensitive to the interests of our great nation.' Derek straightened his back and drew out his words as if to labour their significance. 'And I do hope you don't have plans. It may be a long night'.

'I'm at your disposal, sir,' came the reassuring reply. 'It all sounds rather intriguing. Is it by any chance concerning the Russian Gas deal you were looking at today?'

'I need to know I can depend on you Alexander.' Derek Hemmings' response was grave and considered, his voice choked thick with emotion.

'Of course, sir, rest assured you can trust me with anything.' An earnest reply sure enough. 'I will be the very soul of integrity in the matter.'

'Well you should be made aware that there are factions right here within our esteemed governmental departments, Alexander, that would wish for this commercial agreement with a certain Russian businessman to be signed sealed and committed to without the proper and correct due diligence it warrants.' He laboured the word 'businessman', lacing it with heavy irony and looked resolutely into the handsome face of his young aide. 'I can't allow this to happen I'm afraid, Alexander. No, not on Derek Hemmings' watch.'

●

Over the next thirty minutes, Alexander was fully apprised of the situation at hand. They ran through the stringent timelines imposed upon them and the dire implications of getting this decision wrong. The UK could imminently be entering into a legally binding commercial agreement with an international criminal organisation. This would de facto mean that Great Britain became little more than a conduit for money laundering on an epic scale and a reseller of dirty energy. By sanitising it with Britain's good name and transporting it for sale in the western open market, there would be a significant risk of damaging carefully fostered international relations and crucial trading partners. It could take decades to repair the fallout. If such misuse of the Falklands Islands was seized upon by Argentina, with all their usual sabre rattling, the result could possibly prompt another war or having to cede the territory once and for all under pressure from the United Nations on the basis of illegal occupation for financial gain. The desperate alternative meant pulling out of this deal at the last moment and sacrificing seven thousand British jobs. It would mean passing up on a huge industrial infrastructure investment and boost to the ecomny of nearly seven billion pounds, plus the share of a projected hundred billion in sales over the next decade, whilst spending cuts, tax rises, increasing unemployment, refugees, and a contracting European economy ravaged a fragile continent. It also meant potentially handing a prime opportunity with the Russians over to an aggressive Chinese-Argentinian axis intent on exploiting the natural resources for themselves. Derek's hands began to sweat. Get this one wrong and he'd be assured of a legacy in the annals of history all right.

For Queen and Country: Do the right thing. Do the bloody right thing.

●

They worked through the night, fuelled by endless rounds of coffee and packets of custard creams raided from the office tea trolley. Derek worked like a man possessed. His heart soared, energy abounded. A man on a mission once more. Under his close direction, Alexander scoured reams of intelligence data and financial records, seeking to understand the complex financial ownership of Rublex Corporation and its meteoric rise from such humble beginnings. By sunrise, they were both agitated and exhausted in equal measure. Some of the individual elements of what they sought to expose had been identified but they had been unable to pull the pieces together to make any sense. Without that golden thread tying facts together, the information would be as potent as the other unsubstantiated and unpleasant conjecture about Golich. Nothing had stuck. Derek was in despair. He tugged intermittently at his forelock as he worked, brow creased deeply in concentration. Gut instinct told him under no circumstances to trust the Rublex Corporation, despite the fact that he could still prove nothing. *Innocent until proven guilty old boy,* he chided himself. The deal would be on the table only a few more days. And the clock was ticking.

Chapter 15

A shard of warm sunlight streamed across the bed through the open blinds. Daniel stirred and stretched lazily. He rubbed his eyes, blinking at Matilda as she stooped at the foot of the bed pulling on her crumpled white dress.

'Morning,' he smiled, pulling his pillow behind him and scooting up to lean back against the head board.

'Morning sexy,' cooed the womanly silhouette framed by a backdrop of fragmented early morning sunbeams. 'Last night was amazing darling. But I'm so sorry, I've really got to run. I need to shower and change in time for a really early appointment this morning.'

'What's the time?' mumbled Daniel.

'It's five-fifteen, sleepyhead,' Matilda replied, moving to the bed and ruffling his hair. 'Thank you for a beautiful evening,' she murmured, kissing him full on the mouth. 'But I'm so late. Come and find me at the truck later, will you?'

'Sure thing,' Daniel replied, shuffled back down the bed yawning, 'Have fun.'

The door pulled shut and Daniel, with the sunlight causing vibrant colours to bubble and dance across his eye lids, slipped back into a dreamlike state, peppered with snapshots and memories from a night of passion with an intoxicating Swedish siren. Ratchet was in freefall and he was falling hard.

Rising at just past seven, he dragged himself out of bed and forced himself to stand, limply hunched under the powerful jets of the slippery walk-in shower. He dressed hurriedly and left the room, hair still wet. The elevator doors pinged open and he trotted out, whistling down the hotel steps and out through reception.

'Excuse me. Mr Ratchet?' an over-groomed man at the front desk called out as he passed. 'We have a package for you, sir'.

Daniel signed for a neat square box, tightly wrapped in plain brown paper. Ripping it open and lifting the lid of the navy blue cardboard box, Daniel pulled out a gleaming new gold watch coiled around a Perspex cuff adorned with smart lettering that announced a Rolex Datejust Oyster no less. Daniel fished out a stiff black business card stuffed into the side of the box and turned it right way up. The bold logo of the Rublex Corporation filled the centre of the space. Beneath it in gold leaf: Sergei Krostanov / President / Golf, complete with phone number, email, and an office address in Perm, Russia, on the reverse. Daniel felt his jaw go slack. 'You sure this is for me?' he enquired of the receptionist, eyebrows raised.

'Yes sir. It was left by Mr Krostanov's assistant this morning. He was very insistent that you received it personally. We were about to send it up with this letter to your room.'

'Thank you,' said Daniel slowly to the man. He tore open the note. It was handwritten in spidery blue ink. Ink from a traditional fountain pen, Daniel noted. Somehow the old fashioned touch added deeper cadence to the sentiment of the gift. It read:

Dearest Daniel,

I was saddened today to hear of the loss of your treasured watch. A gift from your grandfather, no less. This modest replacement will not recompense for such a thing but I hope will go some way to showing that we all work together as one on the Tour and as the newest member of our family, I feel great responsibility for your wellbeing. Enjoy the Rolex.

I look forward to completing many deals with you in the near future.

Yours,

Sergei.

Daniel shook his head. Exhaled sharply through his teeth as he walked away, cradling the box in both hands. This was a different world.

●

By the time he reached the practice green the new watch was snugly on his wrist and the accompanying guarantee and documentation stuffed into a back pocket, the box deposited into a nearby litter bin. Bob Wallace knelt on one knee holding a stimpmeter in place to record the ball speed of a patch of green. A row of balls were neatly lined up in preparation of the pre-round warm-up session he would be giving to one of the players later that morning. 'You surviving out here, are you laddie? ' he chirped without glancing up from under the tattered flat cap.

'You could say that,' replied Daniel. 'In fact, so far, I think it's coming together quite nicely.' He glanced down again at his new watch.

Wallace struggled to his feet with an overt display of effort. 'That new then is it, m'boy? Mighty fine time piece you got there.'

'Yeah. Thanks. It's great isn't it? I was just given it at the hotel, a gift from the Rublex Corporation. It works out pretty timely though, excuse the pun, as I had my watch stolen the other night. It was my granddad's. It was all I had left of him since he passed and I'm still gutted it's gone, to be fair.'

'I see, laddie. I thought it looked like the sort that some vulgar Ruski might wear to show off their bloody money. As they say, there's always a deal to be done out here,' the old dog sniffed, practically turning away with contempt.

'I'm not quite sure what you're saying?' replied a brooding Daniel, stuffing his left hand deep into his pocket as if wishing to conceal the watch from view. It now felt unnaturally heavy and conspicuous on his wrist.

Wallace looked back towards Daniel. 'There's a lot more going on out here than meets the eye. Some unsavoury characters who don't have the game's best interests at heart to be sure.'

'Who do you mean? I can't really imagine that myself.'

'I've long been of the belief that those celebrated Russian benefactors of ours, with all their boorish money and ostentation, actually resent the British game deep down. I think they hate our history, our rules and exclusive clubs, because they dragged themselves up from the dirt. They could never be part of it and now that some of them have made a fortune by raping their own people, they want to own it. Well it's our bloody game, laddie, and this Scotsman isn't giving it up without a fight.'

Daniel stood quietly, uncertain what he should say in response to this quite unsolicited rant.

Red faced and worked up into something of a sweat, Bob continued, 'Have they approached you about your players shaving shots yet? I know that damn well goes on out there.' He nodded darkly towards the lush green golf course that stretched out behind him.

'What are you talking about?'

'They always start with some sort of a sweetener.'

'What are you saying Bob?'

'Some of the caddies. They like to get the agents onside all right.

They work a system out here, I'm sure of it. There's secret gambling and players' results not matching up to their form and all sorts. I've raised it with the Tour's top brass at the AGM before now but the ramblings of an angry old man have just been laughed off. I've got a bit of history with those fuddy-duddies who run the game, a bit like Will Carling's fifty-seven old farts at the Rugby Football Union back in the day, you see, laddie. No one takes a blind bit of notice of angry ol' Bob anymore. Not one bit.' He took a hard drag on his tatty cigarette end.

'Are you suggesting that they're really fixing tournaments then? That's all a bit too Moon Landings/ Area 51 conspiracy stuff for me. Besides you can't fix golf, the best guys stand to win too much money, don't they?'

Bob ignored the attempt to lighten the mood. Straightening up, like a wizened minister readying a scathing sermon to his chastened congregation, he began.

'It breaks my heart, Danny, it truly does, but it is only about the money now, and there's too much of it out here for sure. You can forget about the love of the game. The honour and tradition. Proud and honourable gentlemen founded this fine Tour and grew it from nothing but an impoverished sideshow into a genuine rival for the US Tour. They made it so that there was no longer one show on the world stage and the cream of European golfing talent had bigger and better tournaments and purses to compete for right on their doorstep.'

Daniel nodded sagely.

'Ay, that indeed built some confidence,' Bob muttered to himself. 'We started beating them in the Ryder Cup, filling the top spots in the world rankings, and winning more and more Majors. That attracted the best international players to our events and in turn the commitment of the sponsors and TV.' He picked absently at the dirt under his thumbnail with a metal pitching fork.

'Europe doesn't mean Europe any more. We play in any country that is willing to foot the bill. The cycle self-perpetuates. You see, laddie, money attracts talent. But time moves on as they say and I think the new guard at the Tour got greedy with the success and wanted even more.' Bob shook his head.

'It wasn't good enough to simply compete anymore, they wanted to out-gun the US PGA altogether and stick it up them after all the showboating about the huge money available in the FedEx Cup. So in came Rublex with all their dirty energy money, and how things have changed!'

'You're pretty passionate about this.'

'I still know a thing or two about this ancient game of ours. But it's always been fair. The best golfer won out. It doesn't feel like that anymore,' said Bob, pawing at the turf with his foot. 'Maybe some of them are just happy to take a cheque and do what they're told and forget about the winner's circle.'

Daniel nodded. 'I want to keep away from all that if it is going on. I wouldn't want to lead any of our guys down the wrong path or get Crown Sports into any bother either.'

'You might want to catch up with that big lump Michael Hausen from the physio truck for his take on all this then. He told me that last month a player leading an event came to him in tears on the Saturday night asking for a medical exemption to withdraw from the tournament. Daniel, there was nothing wrong with him. Michael didn't want to sign anything but apparently he had a little visit afterwards from the player's bag man which helped him to change his mind. He was left with little option.'

'I don't get it,' said Daniel shaking his head again. 'Golf's always been beyond reproach. It's so skilful that drugs can't really enhance performance and the huge prize funds available mean it will always be a meritocracy with the best talent winning out on the course.'

'Like I've said, it just seems to me that a certain element doesn't want the best guys to win out here at all.'

'Right. Thank you, I suppose,' Daniel said sullenly. It felt like he'd been punched hard in the stomach and he was keen to leave.

The old man nodded once solemnly, casually swung the trusty seven iron in his hand, swishing it across the top surface of the grass in front of him. He turned back silently to the arrangement of balls and practice drills on the green. Daniel sloped away. He had some figuring out to do.

The rest of the morning was spent following a brooding François as he moped his way around the golf course. Each hole appeared to deepen the darkness of his mood as a succession of errant drives and lipped-out putts forced the South African farther and farther from the cut mark and the chance of making it into the weekend money. Daniel welcomed the silence and his anonymity amongst the galleries as an opportunity to clear his head. It had been a hectic few days. He needed space to reflect on the enormity of what he'd learned about the dark workings of the golf Tour. And it was distinctly uncomfortable, leaving him feeling vulnerable and frighteningly exposed. There was no way he could act on any of the information until he knew more and was sure of the facts. He couldn't do anything simply on the hearsay of one angry old man. He would be risking his job too. A job he was beginning to love. He figured he'd already been on the receiving end of how some of the caddies, to whom Bob had referred, operated out here. *What if he got drawn in deeper? How would it play out if his own players were asked to co-operate in any kind of results fixing?* he fretted. Suppose there was actual proof showing guys in the field misshaping the Order of Merit through deceit? By ignoring and avoiding this, he would be tacitly assisting a dishonourable practice to thrive, cheating the sponsors, and the paying public who adored the sport and supported the players. And perhaps this wasn't even Daniel's choice anymore. Even if he wanted to keep his head down, hold a low profile, and stay away from trouble; it seemed apparent that some of the people on the Tour were determined to get him involved one way or another.

Daniel made up his mind. He needed to know the actual state of play, to understand how far this went for himself. Making eye contact with François for a final time after he had splashed his beleaguered ball out of a bunker and straight into a patch of thick penal rough, Daniel pumped his fist in solidarity, willing the erratic streak to rescind. He splintered away from the throng of fans scurrying between hole and tee, vying with each other for premium vantage points along the fairway. He headed back towards the hotel complex, deciding to pay a quick visit to Matilda before getting to grips with Aaron's Rublex agreement and trying to learn more about the depth of influence that this cartel of malevolent caddies really leveraged in affecting tournament scores and finishing positions.

He stole a shortcut through a grassy parking area, closed to the public this week and used for housing the wealth of trailers and trucks required to service the infrastructure of the event. Daniel's eye was drawn to two figures in heated discussion, partially hidden behind a massive generator. He decided not to approach but, intrigued to get a better view, sidled up between two black articulated lorries and edged closer until he was within ear shot.

He recognised the men in the throes of a vociferous argument. Sean, the ginger Glaswegian caddy, whom on the balance of probabilities Daniel blamed as at least one of the authors of his first night drunken ignominy, was grabbing the hulking frame of Michael Hausen, Matilda's co-worker, by the scruff of his T-shirt and was shouting at point blank range up at him. Sean's face was screwed up into a hateful snarl, a grotesque spray of saliva emanating from his mouth as he berated and admonished the German. From the shadow between the trucks, Daniel tried to make some meaning out of the ranting. He had trouble understanding Sean in casual conversation, let alone when he was screaming and swearing uncontrollably. Michael owed some money. He had gambling debts that needed to be repaid and it sounded serious. The sight was somewhat farcical. The muscular German dwarfed the pugnacious Scot in both height and bulk yet he was being totally dominated in the exchange. He seemed genuinely scared. Daniel was transported back to school where, one hot afternoon, his geography teacher had yet again decided that actually teaching something would be too much bother and instead switched on a video about cattle ranching in Australia. The enduring comic image was of a small, yet acutely aggressive and determined cattle-dog perched on the back of a huge dumb cow nipping and yapping away until the beast bent to its will and returned to the ranching station.

But this was heavy. Michael was pleading for more time to pay and it was falling on deaf ears. What happened next shocked Daniel to his core. Uncontested, the Glaswegian grabbed a fistful of Michael's hair, dragged him forward and slammed his face into the hot metal grate of the generator, twisting and grinding it against the scalding hot grill. Daniel's instinct was to intervene. To take on the bully. To get the victim away from his torturer and the dreadful situation. Gripping the side of the Callaway equipment trailer that was shielding him from sight he suddenly paused, checking himself. Something was wrong about this situation. Michael could easily overpower the little thug tormenting him. He wasn't even resisting, instead he was allowing it to happen. When finally Sean pulled Michael free from the grill he was moaning in pain. The entire side of his face red with raw welts and burns. Next, Sean opened a can of Red Bull, casually took a swig admiring his handy work, before emptying the rest over the pitiful German's head. 'Fockin' pay up this time sausage meat or you're a dead man. You know all about our connections, Sauer Kraut. The Russians have always despised you Germans. Things could start to get very nasty for you indeed pal,' he hissed. Turned and strolled away.

Daniel felt cold sweat streaming down the back of his neck. He didn't stop running until he reached the hotel.

Chapter 16

Sergei Krostanov shook the hand of the tanned young Australian and handed across the oversized trophy. Applause resounded in the winner's circle on the 18th green. Aaron Crower raised the cup aloft and beamed his pearly whites towards the bank of flashing camera bulbs. His maiden victory was evidence that his much vaunted attributes as a strong front runner during a glittering amateur career could translate into the big money Pro Tournaments. It was one thing being able to shoot the lights out and get on a hot streak to execute a run of birdies. It was quite another having to sleep on a lead in the first professional golf event you were in contention for, with a hungry chasing pack snapping at your heels ready to prey on any sign of weakness. Only the purest of swings and those players endowed with genuine self-belief and mental toughness would make a habit of it. He was now an official winner on Tour, recipient of a fat winner's cheque, a one-year playing card exemption and, most significantly, he had become 'the one to watch'.

Aaron scanned the crowd gathered behind the ropes as they showed their appreciation with polite applause and searched for Daniel. It annoyed him that the new manager Rudy assigned to him hadn't bothered to show up on the biggest day of his career to date. He turned to Sergei standing beside him and asked if he had seen anyone from Crown Sports.

'I hear a rumour that Daniel Ratchet has returned to England I'm afraid. I don't think he was quite up to the job. Didn't seem to have what it takes to make it out here. I take it he didn't discuss your new contract from the Rublex Corporation with you either Aaron? It's a sixteen million dollar contract so to me it seems a little remiss of him to not have raised this with you. After such a fine display on the course today, now seems like the perfect time to have that conversation, don't you agree?'

He ushered the lean athletic golfer through a roped off pathway, dismissing requests for interviews with a wave of his hand. They weaved through the temporary cabins serving as Tour offices, which were assembled at every scheduled event, and entered one of the private meeting rooms together. Aaron sat at the table. Sergei laid paper and pen before him and stood hovering behind like a hungry buzzard studying a mouse. 'Let's get down to business,' he began dryly.

Andy Sharples was counting money. It was his favourite thing to do and he liked to take his time doing it. Stacks of crumpled notes sat piled beside his little black notebook as he tapped away on his tablet, doing sums and accessing accounts. The other caddies sat around him in a semicircle drinking bottles of beer, rolling dice, and animatedly discussing the golf round that day. A dark-skinned Spaniard named Salvatore was lazily tipping ash on the back of an Asian girl as she moved between him and Sean on all fours, ready for his turn to receive the soft attentions of her mouth. They had 'borrowed' her from behind the counter of a Chinese takeaway in the town which hadn't been able to contribute adequately to their protection fund. It was clearly in their own best interests. A kind of business protection insurance they had explained. And, pleasingly, the group had found this 'payment in kind' to be more than compliant. Sometimes it just worked out like that.

'Great numbers lads! We've earned our trip to The Pussy Palace this time and no mistake,' exclaimed Andy, slapping his thigh.

'With the wire transfers from Macau and Gibraltar we are nudging two and a half million euros in takings this week. Such a shame for the punters that the house will never lose big and then each week we just ship on out of town to the next event.'

Razor, who had been holding a lighter flame to the charred bowl of a ceramic hashish pipe, spluttered out a lungful of silver smoke by way of agreement.

Sharples smirked in satisfaction. In one swift motion he used his foot to deftly flip the Asian girl from her crouched position to flat onto her back. Then he slowly poured the remainder of his beer bottle over her small pointed breasts, drawing howls of laughter and derision from the room.

They had earned the celebration.

Chapter 17

Daniel Ratchet bolted the chain across the hotel door before slumping onto the bed, head in hands. He was sweating hard, his mind racing over and over what he'd just witnessed. He took a Coke from the mini bar, hoping to rapidly increase his blood sugar levels and help to regain some control. He reconsidered. Removed a miniature bottle of Jack Daniels from the door-rack of the fridge, emptying it into his glass in one motion. Took a deep swallow.

After a few minutes had passed, settling himself somewhat, Daniel reached for the room telephone. He punched in the international dialling code followed by the familiar digits of the family home number in England. He yearned for the reassuring voices of his parents, hoping for solace and comfort. Something to cling to, far from the storm of the escalating and dangerous situation that he was inexorably gravitating towards.

'Seven two four double nine eight, Ratchet residence,' came his mother's shrill voice down the line.

He smiled, answering enthusiastically, 'Mum, it's Daniel.'

'Oh Danny, how are you love? Are you well? Wait, hold on I must just get your father.' In the background frenetic squawking, 'Malcolm, Malcolm, it's your son on the telephone. Malcolm, come quick, it's our Danny.'

Daniel waited. Heavy, measured footsteps grew louder through the hallway.

'Hello, Daniel. We'd thought you'd forgotten us back in Sheffield.

How are you, son? Are you enjoying the big swanky job? You are being careful, aren't you Danny?'

'Yes, Dad. The job's great. Better than expected even,' he lied. 'How's Scruff? I hope that rascal pup is keeping out of mischief without me?'

He was trying his best to sound cheery. And by the time his mother had joined them on the other line and they had discussed the rain, an unmarried neighbour from number sixty-three who was starting to show as pregnant, and his dad had warned him twice about rising foreign exchange rates, Daniel simply couldn't bring himself to ask for the help and advice he needed. He couldn't disappoint and worry his parents further by confirming their worst fears about the job. He played out the call with a raft of insipid platitudes and hung up.

A renewed sense of purpose surged through him. Yes, Danny Ratchet was ready to understand things better for himself and take some firm decisions now. He flicked on the tablet. He searched through his old university files, finally settling on a localized version of a unique statistical analysis programme he'd created with three of his fellow students for their dissertation. It uncovered patterns in data flows. They had hoped it would become an acceptable application for the medical industry, spotting patterns in drug trials. Now Daniel wondered if it would make some sense of the mass of information which accompanied the performance of every player currently participating on the European Tour, both before and after Rublex's involvement. He set out the parameters of his analysis, cross-referencing the ranking of top performers in every separate element of the game: driving distance and accuracy, greens in regulation, sand saves, putting, lowest rounds in sequence. Next he matched these statistics against the players who won out at the end of the events.

The findings were astonishing. Final round scoring increased significantly for a specific set of otherwise high performing players going against the run of form from their preceding three rounds in any given event. It seemed to show that these particular players, with a track record of shooting very low scores and a history of winning tournaments, would seemingly always do worse than would have been expected of them going into the final crucial round of key events, albeit never at the same time. It might perhaps have been barely perceptible to the galleries and Tour officials, but when charted out using a timeline of in-depth performance data, the trends were clear. There was no doubt that this was the tournament fixing that Bob Wallace had known was happening intuitively. A sickness at the heart of the game.

Next Daniel carefully re-read Aaron's sponsorship proposal from Rublex. The Russian conglomerate was paying a premium for the best up and coming international stars of the game yet were happy, even encouraging of them, to underperform. The question was why?

Message alerts for new emails flashed up on the corner of the screen. Daniel dragged a new window open and watched four new messages drop into his inbox in orderly fashion. A Tour memo advising of travel arrangements for the tournament the following week, an update on the Order of Merit standings now that last week's Money List had been updated, next an email from a very earnest sounding African lawyer bequeathing him the lost fortune of one of his newly deceased clients if only Daniel would part with his bank account details—how the hell his new work email had already fallen into the hands of the internet scamerati he had no idea. And, lastly, an email from Sergei Krostanov with an attachment copy of the contract, politely yet insistently enquiring if Daniel had managed to progress the matter with Aaron yet and that with keen interest from other managers and their players on the table, he sincerely hoped he could expect a signature very soon.

Daniel got up and paced around the room, exhaling hard. This was all getting a bit heavy. He didn't know how he'd been drawn into all this so fast and he couldn't yet fathom the implications. But it now all appeared unequivocal. You might get some anomalies through the beautiful quirks of sport, the psychology of pressure, luck, or through human error; but time after time for the top players to throw away events on the final day against the run of form was untenable. They were taking it in turns to hide the true extent of the malaise. It may have been buried deep, but once unravelled the data painted a clear picture. And it didn't lie. Given what he'd already seen of how the caddies rolled out here with the gambling, drinking, the petty crime, extortion and intimidation, actual tournament fixing didn't seem so far out of the question. There must be a connection with the gambling ring he had stumbled upon. He hadn't warmed to Andy from the beginning, with his little book of numbers, the dominant display of aggression he had shown towards Razor on the night out, and for mocking him the next day for being late out onto the course when he clearly had something to do with getting him into that mess. Now with the pieces appearing to fit into place, the implications were unnerving.

With the SIM card of the company mobile still missing, obviously taken by the same bastards who had his grandfather's watch, Daniel grabbed the room phone again and dialled the mobile number that Matilda had scrawled upon the back of a napkin at their romantic dinner. It bounced straight to voice mail and Daniel left a long rambling message, which he started to regret even as he was garbling his way through it. He hoped it didn't come across as if he was blowing her off. He vaguely drawled on about wanting to meet up but needing to do further research on some data tonight. Now was not the moment to expose insecurity and paranoia to this sexy new woman that he was really starting to like. It would probably make her run a mile. Besides, he'd share all with her later once things were somewhat clearer. And when he'd worked out what the hell he was going to do next.

●

Outside the window, a thick black storm cloud emanated across the darkening sky. Daniel picked at the fearsome scratch that was now starting to scab across his chest, his brow furrowed in deep thought. Having been steered by the old Scottish golf coach to make connections between the key protagonists in this sordid tableau, there were some hard choices to be made. Aaron was in contention to win the event at tomorrow's final round. Was his caddy, Andy Sharples, a threat to possible victory given this new information? He might influence the outcome of the tournament. It was impossible to know whether presenting the massive Rublex contract to Aaron was the right thing to do now given that he better understood the implications. He had a duty of care to the player, both in looking after his commercial interests and in protecting his career. He also had a duty to Crown Sports who were expecting him to drive sponsorship value for his stable and yield some juicy commissions. Either way he felt uneasy about being pressured into getting the agreement signed. Perhaps this was just the way that business got done around here, he wondered, before taking a deep breath and punching in the digits to Silvio's mobile back in England.

'This is Silvio,' the silky voice purred down the line.

'Hello Silvio, it's Daniel Ratchet out in Spain.'

'How's the big time my friend? Have you settled into the life of a high flying sports agent yet with all its, how shall we say, attractive benefits?' He chuckled earthily before Daniel had the chance to speak.

'It's okay Silvio. But to be honest I'm not too sure what's really going on out here. I'm a bit confused to be fair and wanted some advice. Have you heard of the Rublex Corporation?'

'Rublex? Don't be naïve. Obviously, Rublex are one of the biggest sponsors in golf. They headline the Order of Merit. That's the equivalent of asking me if I've heard of an equipment manufacturer like say a Callaway or a TaylorMade, isn't it Daniel? They are huge in golf. Please. What's the point of all this?'

'I wanted your opinion really. I've found some information which seems to show that players out here are cheating on the Tour. Sergei Krostanov, the Rublex Director of Golf, has offered a sixteen million dollar sponsorship contract for Aaron. It's great but it's drafted like they would prefer him not to win all the time. Why would they sponsor someone and incentivise them to underperform? He's really pushing me to get Aaron to sign it quickly. And to cap it all off I'm feeling pretty uneasy about the fact he gave me a Rolex to keep as well. It feels very strange.'

'That's a great deal Daniel. Fantastico! Well done. Don't concern yourself with these trivial details. It's just the way the Russians do business you understand. Are you in possession of the paperwork?'

'Er, yeah. I've got a contract. But it doesn't make any sense?'

'What the fuck are you talking about boy? We've just made twenty percent on sixteen American large. Has Aaron seen the contract yet?'

'Um, no. Not yet. Have you heard of Bob Wallace? He's a coach out here for some of the players, seems to have been around for years?'

'Sure, I know of the man. Wallace is a trouble maker, a firebrand, he got drunk at the PGA dinner last year and made a big scene. He publically accused the Tour of being in conspiracy to bring down the game of golf from within. What a ridiculous man, spoilt a good dinner. Sergei was the most indignant. Bear in mind that this is the civilised world of golf, Daniel, not some dangerous shadowy cult from a Dan Brown novel.'

'Silvio, the data shows a group of top players getting into contention to win tournaments and then dropping away on the final day. They don't finish the way their statistics and tee-to-green form suggest they would. I think it's got something to do with gambling as well. A group of caddies out here seem to be running a book and shaking people down for money.'

Silvio raised his voice with unbridled, caustic anger. 'For Christ's sake, will you listen to yourself, Daniel? These things are none of your concern. You've been in this job for five minutes only. If Randy knew you were sitting on an agreement of this size he would skin your knackers, cut them off and feed them to you himself. Daniel, please, what's wrong with you? You disappoint me, boy. You were nothing when I scraped you off the floor at that dead-end job. Are you telling me that this is the way you repay me for setting you up in a new life? Your job is to do what you are told. Crown Sports have worked with Rublex for years. They helped broker the original deal with the European Tour in the first place. The way it works? You have to give them what they want. Keep your nose clean and don't fucking call me back until you get that contract signed.' Without another word uttered, he cut the call.

Daniel cursed and cracked the back of the receiver against the bedside cabinet. His neck flushed red in uneven blotchy patches. He paced around the room for some minutes, throat dry and palms sweating. His head was swimming. He stepped onto the balcony, breathed slowly and cooled down. Relaxing a little, he allowed himself to be temporarily distracted by an energetic female water-aerobics instructor leading a lacklustre gabble of flabby hotel guests splashing through their late afternoon activity.

Daniel was starting to get a sense of himself again. Here he was in a luxury foreign hotel, the like of which he had never set foot in before, doing his dream job, dating a super-hot Swedish chick he'd just met, and holding in his hands a multi-million dollar sponsorship agreement for one of the talented golfers he managed. And all in the first week. *So who cares what was happening out here on the Tour? Like Silvio had said, it was none of his concern.* Besides, by all accounts, this Bob Wallace character was a bit of a nutter, and certainly an outcast from the close inner sanctum on Tour, which is where Daniel felt he needed to be if he wanted to make a real success out of this career.

With his dinner fixed for eight o'clock, he took his tablet out onto the balcony to refresh himself with the finer details of the agreement. The sun melted away over the red mountains, dissolving through an unsettled sky. Daniel soon lost himself in the nuances of the contract, memorising terms and clauses so he could create an erudite impression and deliver an illusion of control to the young Australian. It was important to reassure the rising star that his manager was on top of his game, a safe pair of hands to represent him in these complex commercial matters so he could just continue to focus on delivering results on the course.

It might just serve as the boost he needed to go on to win the tournament in his final round tomorrow.

Order somewhat restored, Daniel decided that he would head out for a stroll to clear his head, study the agreement terms and build on this new sense of perspective. He would swing via reception where he would leave a message for Aaron to meet him for dinner when they could discuss the contract before the final round in the morning. If Silvio wanted a contract, then Daniel would make sure he bloody delivered one and hang the consequences. It wasn't up to him if they wanted to cheat on this stupid Tour. He would go along for the ride.

He followed the pathway away from the hotel. His eyes studied the tablet screen as he ambled, reading and re-reading the clauses and terms of Aaron's agreement, whispering some of the more complex ones aloud to himself, as if studying for an exam. Daniel was determined to get this finally right after all these early teething problems in the new job. He wandered past the practice putting green, a scattering of players still grinding out their drills before tomorrow's round. The neatly kept pathway eventually led round to a cluster of porta-cabins where equipment was stored, officials were briefed prior to the day's play and scores were collated and signed off following it. Daniel squatted down on the steps of one of the cabins and scrolled down the document. He needed to appear confident in front of Aaron so the contract signing would go smoothly. Silvio was counting on him.

The sound of voices cut through the peace of the evening. Two men were walking together on the other side of the cabins, talking animatedly. They moved within earshot of Daniel, unaware that he was sitting out of view mere metres away.

'Aaron hasn't signed the contract yet. He won't be onboard before tomorrow's final round.'

'That fucking useless new agent Ratchet hasn't delivered then?'

'I tried playing nice. I don't know if the boy is simply stupid, doesn't understand how these things work or if he knows more than he lets on. He has after all been spending quite a lot of time with that annoying Bob Wallace.'

The hairs rose on the back of Daniel's neck. He recognised the voices at once. Sergei Krostanov and Andy Sharples. And they were discussing him in very disparaging tones. He rose on impulse with the intention of interrupting them. He would bloody put them straight if they were going to talk about him behind his back indeed. But he checked himself. Instead Daniel avoided the confrontation and decided to let them talk. Hear what else they might say about him and reveal. He dropped to the ground. Crawled forward into the space under the raised cabin and edged across the corner to where the men were standing. He manoeuvred himself a little way down and on instinct flicked the tablet onto video record mode. Angled the screen upward and held it breathlessly as it filmed the two men as they continued their private discussion.

'This is a problem Sergei. Aaron is looking strong. He is leading the event and I don't think there is anyone playing nearly as well in the field this week. There is a weight of money on him and this is one we could do with having him throw so we could clean up.'

'I understand Andy but there is nothing I can do at this time. He hasn't signed the contract. He doesn't understand that the Rublex incentive scheme will demand that he loses certain events on the last day rather than win them so that we can rig the book and take our high rolling Asian sports betting clients to the cleaners. We will have to find a way to make up the shortfall somehow. How have the local shakedowns gone?'

'Not the best in terms of producing cash Sergei. But me and the boys secured ourselves a tasty little Chinse takeway in part exchange if you catch my drift?'

'Ha! Not another girl Andy?'

'This one is very compliant. There won't be any trouble like before.'

'I should hope not. Keep Billy Boy away from her then.'

'You want a turn Sergei?'

'No Andy. Thank you. I have business to attend to.'

Daniel froze. Pulled the tablet back fully under the cabin unnoticed and watched as the legs of the men strode away from where he lay.

Breathing raggedly he returned quickly to the room, somewhat shaken. Things were getting very heavy. There was clearly some kind of serious conspiracy taking place right under the oblivious noses of the European Tour officials. Had he really overheard what he thought he had between Sergei and Andy just now? He might have been mistaken. Taken it out of context and be jumping to a wild assumption. He double checked the video recording saved on his tablet to be sure; to listen to it again.

The video clip ended for the second time. Daniel dropped his head into his hands. It was crystal clear. The angle had captured both Andy and Sergei's faces. There was no doubt about it. This was incriminating evidence. He swiped back onto the spreadsheets to re-examine them. There it was, as plain as day, a statistically provable positive correlation in the data that indicated cheating on a grand scale. Now backed up with a videoed admission of guilt straight from the Head of Sponsorship of Rublex Corporation, the Tour's title sponsor. Daniel swore under his breath.

A new email alert blinked onto the screen catching his eye. He opened it. Sent from **physio-truck@europeantour.com**. A single line read:

DANIEL, PLEASE BE VERY CAREFUL

Why would Matilda be emailing him this? Attached to the email was a scanned newspaper obituary of a veteran Russian investigative journalist. She had published a series of articles in the mid-nineteen nineties about a vast corporation named Rublucon and its links to both serious organised crime and the upper reaches of the post-Soviet Russian government. The huge energy deals brokered had apparently provided a convenient cover and conduit for money laundering for the notoriously violent Russian crime families who had originated in the gulags of the oppressive Stalin regime decades before. They had been formed as a secret society living an alternative, strongly structured and codified way of life. Known as the Vory, they lived by the thieves' code, rejecting all work or acknowledgement of the state or religion. They had thrived over the years and, as capitalism had spread, many of the more charismatic leaders had seized considerable power and wealth. The journalist had dedicated her life and career to uncovering corruption and the obituary was posted defiantly on the front page of the newspaper she had represented. She had apparently taken her own life, jumping from a bridge in St. Petersburg. She had no record of depression and the authenticity of her suicide had been questioned with calls for an investigation into her death. No action had ever been taken.

Sweat dripped off his forehead, a droplet splashing onto the screen of his device. Daniel punched in a hurried text message to the number he had dialled a little while earlier when he had left his voicemail for Matilda.

Thanks for the warning. Russians do seem dangerous! You have to see the video I just took of Sergei admitting cheating out here on Tour! It proves me and Bob right!! Let's meet up. XXX

●

His intense concentration was broken by the sound of a card clicking in the door. The maid had been in hours before. He swivelled in the chair and peered through the glass door of the balcony to see two men step inside the room looking around furtively. He recognised Razor immediately, flashing back to Andy Sharples throwing 'the mongrel', as he'd called him, off his chair at the bar. He didn't recognise the other guy but the man was huge, probably standing around six foot five. Massive muscular thighs bulging through tight jeans, supported a towering frame. He sported a thick leather belt complete with a large metal buckle in the shape of a hissing cobra's head. Two evil looking fangs protruded menacingly from the serpent's open mouth. Instinctively, his hand touched tentatively at the tender scratches on his torso. *Could that belt have caused the cuts on my chest?* The beast stooped naturally to avoid the frame as he came through the door behind Razor who by now was quickly tugging at drawers and opening cupboards, rifling through Daniel's bags and clothing.

Frozen outside on the balcony, his natural instinct would have been to challenge the men who were clearly breaking into his room. Given the recent grotesque violence he had witnessed, coupled with the menacing presence of this mono-browed giant accompanying Razor, Daniel held himself back. He edged to the side of the balcony further out of sight and peeked through a chink in the blind back into the room. By now, Razor was frenziedly rifling through Daniel's briefcase, strewing papers over the floor. He was hell bent on finding something specific it seemed. The 'mono-brow' twisted his neck to the side, cracking his bones with a sickening, audible crunch. He bent down to lift the bed with a single paw, peering underneath. They'd be coming out on the balcony soon, no doubt about it. Daniel was sweating again. He scurried back to the table and hurriedly grabbed the tablet. Sticking it under his arm he looked around for a way of escape knowing he'd never make it out through the room and past the uninvited guests. It was too far to jump onto the concrete below and besides he seriously hated heights—just the act of looking straight down over the railings made him reel back with his head spinning. There was a four foot gap between his and the next balcony, which was deserted except for an array of brightly coloured swimming shorts, frilly black bikini bottoms and enormous beach towels drying over the back of chairs. No time to waste. Steadying himself against the wall and hoisting his foot onto the balcony rail Daniel strained to pull himself up so that he was standing balanced on the top edge. Puffing his cheeks and blowing out sharply, he bent his knees and sprang frog-like as far as he could towards the adjacent balcony just as the glass doors clicked and slid open behind him.

●

It was an impressive leap and Daniel cleared the metal railings of the adjacent balcony with inches to spare, landing on his toes in a squat. The force of the jump banged his knees up into his chin hard. He grunted as his mouth filled with the bitter iron taste of blood, as teeth bit into tongue. The tablet remained tightly clenched into his chest.

'The fucking computer's not here, is it Razor?' came a deep Russian accent above him, spitting out like a machine gun. Staccato. Cold. Stone on stone.

Daniel held his breath and, twisting his neck uncomfortably for a better view, peered upwards through the crack in the railing. Razor stood on the balcony just a few feet away, wiping sweat from his forehead in the heat. On his wrist glistened a slim gold watch with an old cracked black leather strap. Daniel swallowed hard. His granddad's watch. No doubt about it. The bastard must have stolen it on the night out at the Irish bar. The night when he'd passed out. Had he been drugged? He'd certainly been robbed. And sliced up, he now presumed, with the snake's teeth on that monster's belt buckle as he was probably dragged back and dumped in his room. He wanted to scream, to fight, to exact some form of retribution. He checked himself. Closing his eyes tightly instead, Daniel waited. Frozen still with fear, sweat dripping off his nose and onto his shirt, desperately trying not to breathe, to make no sound whatsoever.

The door slid closed above him and after another few minutes of no further movement or sound Daniel figured he could finally dare to move. Crawling across the concrete floor of his neighbours' balcony he tugged on the door handle. His only chance of escape. It opened first time, the heavy door smoothly gliding across the well-oiled gear mechanism. Stolen glances inside the room revealed it was empty and he slithered inside. Steam swirled, billowing around the floor. The sound of the shower and a woman humming a lazy, sweet melodic tune emanated from the bathroom. Without waiting to be announced Daniel covered the floor of the bedroom in just a few short strides and entered out into the hotel corridor, peering nervously around him. His heart pulsed urgently inside his chest.

He had no idea where the room invaders were but he needed to get out of the corridor. Fast. Rather than take the elevator down into the main lobby Daniel took a strategic decision to head quickly in the opposite direction and darted down a maze of eerily deserted corridors past endless rows of identical rooms until a heavy door marked with the green sign for an emergency exit came into view. He ripped it open and lunged into the back stairway panting hard. In stark contrast to the opulence of the hotel rooms and finely wallpapered corridors, the stairs were left cold and bare; an unloved functional afterthought. But they were empty and Daniel needed to escape the hotel without being seen. His footsteps clattered a noisy echo, reverberating around the concrete stairwell and filling him with fear, unable to separate his own noise from the sound of any pursuers. He knew he was now embroiled in something dangerous and no matter what Silvio had ordered him to do, this was now about survival. Daniel had to look after himself.

He cleared the stairs in just over two minutes, keeping a consistent rhythm trotting down through the floors, twisting and turning down towards the ground. On arriving at the ground floor Daniel dropped his shoulder and slammed into the metal bar of the fire escape at the end of the stairwell, not stopping nor caring if it triggered an alarm. He burst out into evening dusk. Night was closing in.

He scoured the immediate surroundings for Razor and the mono-browed giant. Nothing. Gripping the tablet in his hand he walked briskly away from the hotel as naturally as he could in the direction of the only person he felt he could trust out here. Matilda. A pair of well-nourished middle-aged women in brightly-coloured shorts chatted animatedly as he passed by in silence, head down. He assiduously avoided eye contact with them as he trod the winding cobbled path towards the service truck park.

Daniel rapped his knuckles on the door of the physio-truck. The door was unlocked but no one was inside. He tested the locker with Matilda's name stencilled on it, but it was locked shut. Looking around at the empty space, he considered for a moment the best course of action. It was clear that he needed to find a safe, discreet place to hide the tablet which was the focus of so much apparent unwanted attention. At least until this was all sorted out. Remembering how he had watched Michael store some equipment in the space beneath the bench-seats at the side of the truck, Daniel flipped the cushions up and eased the quarry inside, covering it with some discarded towels. He'd let Matilda know later.

He headed directly to the practice green where he hoped to find Bob Wallace. There, the old gnarly coach was sat in crumpled fashion on an upturned bucket of balls, cleaning a sand wedge with a damp rag, puffing at a tatty, yellow-stained, hand-rolled cigarette.

He cleared his throat to announce his arrival and the old man looked up into Daniel eyes and nodded. It all poured out after that. In a single continuous and emotional diatribe Daniel recounted the nefarious happenings of that afternoon. The break-in. His granddad's stolen watch on Razor's wrist. The data pointing to the truth about Bob's own theory on the tournament fixing. Underpinning it all was the video that Daniel had taken that very day, recorded on his tablet from under the portacabin, of Sergei and Andy themselves discussing their illegal gambling ring and the conspiracy to fix tournaments by the undue influence on players to drop shots. It was cathartic and, by the time he'd finished, Daniel felt emotionally drained. He waited, expecting some profound response.

Instead Wallace coughed up a dose of mucous from deep within the recesses of his beleaguered lungs and spat it quivering onto the grass at his feet. Finally he spoke.

'Those fucking dirty bastards. I knew it,' he snorted, taking a final drag of his dying tab before stubbing it out on the side of his golf shoe. 'I've got some thinking to do, son. If we're gonna get these guys out of the game for good, we've got to make sure we do it the right way. I've been laughed at and dismissed as a crazy old fool for bringing this to the PGA's attention before. We need to take your proof and nail them once and for all and that's for damn sure. Meet me in Muldoon's Irish bar in town at ten tonight, laddie, and we'll make a battle plan.'

Tired, conflicted and aching as the adrenaline depleted from his bloodstream, Daniel mooched slowly back towards the hotel complex in the fading light. Dusk was falling and the fireflies danced together in chaotic spirals. As he passed the immense and eerily silent Tour equipment trucks, well-secured for the night, Daniel's eye was drawn to an attractive woman with bright red lipstick and heels, pink tailored shorts and a snugly filled white T-shirt. She stood alone in the shadows of the trucks fiddling deliberately with a large, wide-lens camera.

'Excuse me there,' she called to him as he passed by. 'Excuse me sir, you don't by any chance know how to get this to work do you? My husband will be so cross.' She was smiling now and holding out the camera towards Daniel, imploring him to take it with big, sad, heavily made-up eyes.

'Technology's not my thing I'm afraid,' he replied somewhat untruthfully, holding his hand aloft apologetically and continuing by.

'Oh, please take a look, I'm sure you're much better at it than me,' she continued, batting those long eyelids and stepping towards him.

Daniel softened. He had always been one to assist a damsel in distress even if he just wasn't in the mood at all. He wondered where she was from. What was that undercurrent of an accent? European? Slavic? Not Russian?

Suddenly a sharp blow to the back of his head sent him sagging down onto his knees. A second clinical strike followed. And Daniel Ratchet became enveloped inside a sickening, velvety darkness. Floundering. Helpless. He was falling in slow motion. Towards silence. And then...

...nothing.

Chapter 18

I had managed to buy a fresh set of clothes and underwear en route from the airport. Looking and feeling now a lot less like an extra from a 'Die Hard' movie and somewhere closer to a semi-respectable member of society, I sauntered amongst the dispersing golf fans at the conclusion to the presentation ceremony. Avoiding any eye contact, keeping my head down, studying my phone. People tend to remember a big man with a long nasty scar across his face staring at them. Besides, I was reading updated intelligence from Ella that had beeped through on my device. Even serious messages and highly detailed encrypted data packets were signed off with kisses or some emoji or other depending on her mood. Bemused at first, after a fashion it had begun to really tickle me. Showing that someone cared. In this instance the intel was a steer from HQ outlining a second interview with Bob Wallace taken over the phone. And a detail previously missed: he had recalled that Daniel was upset with regard to the behaviour of some of the golf caddies. His grandfather's watch had gone missing, presumed stolen by the same. It wasn't much to go on but it was the start that I needed. Hunter was in the game.

I neared the 18th green and caught sight of a gangly Spanish teenager polishing the blades on a set of irons, meticulously replacing them into an empty golf bag. I sidled up to him, casually explaining I was the brother of a caddy involved in the tournament and asked where they might typically be found.

Steered in the right direction, I soon reached a sprawling amorphous cluster of oversized trailers and trucks parked to the rear of the hotel, casting oblique angular shadows in the late afternoon sun. Voices rumbled from behind one of the trucks. I flipped onto my stomach and commando-crawled under the supports of the massive trailer. I manoeuvred to a vantage point where I could see and hear the scene playing out perfectly in front of me whilst remaining completely out of sight. A fat man in long blue shorts and white socks was sitting on a red plastic chair which looked as if it might collapse at any point under the strain. He was leafing lazily through a ledger with freshly-licked fingers whilst a slighter man with a head of cropped ginger hair peered over his shoulder. A third man with olive skin and a thick glossy mane sat disinterested on an upturned crate. He smoked a cigarette.

'I see Michael paid up this week then?' the fat man chirped in an unexpectedly high pitched Liverpudlian accent, an incongruous fit with the vast bulk of his body.

'Aye, paid up in full. The big German sausage won't make that mistake again in a hurry. Account closed shall we say,' sniggered the ginger rat in a guttural Scottish patter.

'Good to see we're on track, Sean. Sharples will be pleased to see we've made up the lost ground on shakedowns from the town this week too.'

'Aye. No bother at all big man,' came the casual response.

The two men left together. Their remaining companion silently removed a handgun from a clip on his belt, stripped it slowly down to its constituent parts on his lap and began to delicately oil the mechanism with slick droplets from a miniature pipette. He remained seated on his crate and I surmised that he was actually guarding the door to the truck behind him. It would be good to take a look inside and find out more about these 'payments' and the 'shakedowns' that the caddies were making.

Daniel's instincts had been correct all along. Right now I didn't have the time though. I needed to contact a number of key individuals on site whom Ella had identified might hold vital information on the background to the agent's disappearance. First and foremost I needed to locate Matilda Axgren, Ratchet's girlfriend, and Bob Wallace himself, the coach who had initially contacted the Hand of God about this escalating situation.

I wriggled back out of my hiding place and pushed myself up to my feet, wiping the palms of my hands across my trousers. As I turned to leave, I noticed two blonde women walking through the car park together, one older than the other. The first wore a tight pony tail scraped back to reveal a sour scowl of discontentment on her heavily tanned, deeply lined face. Her taller companion glided beside her. The face of an angel, beautiful piercing blue eyes framed with long platinum blonde hair, falling in loose curls around her shoulders. I recognised her instantly from the photograph downloaded from the research file. This was Matilda Axgren. And in real life she was some hot piece.

I let the women pass by a short way and followed at a discreet distance. The older of the two turned and headed towards a green sign which pointed in the direction of the hotel spa complex. Matilda continued further into the car park and finally stopped to unlock the boot to a black Nissan Micra, fishing about for something inside. I came up beside her silently and she spun round startled, incapable of disguising the cocktail of surprise and anger splashed across her face. 'Who the fuck are you? Get away from me,' she snapped, recoiling as I outstretched my hand to reassure her.

'Relax Matilda, I'm a friend of Daniel Ratchet. I'm trying to find him'.

'Get away from me. Daniel's got nothing to do with me anymore. Leave me alone'.

'Please. I just need to ask you some questions Matilda. I need to find Daniel.'

Matilda slid round the side of the car and fumbled with the keys in the lock. She was obviously not in a talkative mood. I followed round the vehicle reaching her as she opened the car door, clambering hurriedly inside. I forced my knee into the gap to prevent her from locking herself in and driving away. She slammed the door angrily against my thigh in petulance.

'Stay the fuck still, you crazy bitch,' I ordered, one hand gripping the door frame, the other drawing my gun.

Matilda froze, her pale blue eyes widening as she looked up at me. She flicked her hair, jutting her chin forward in defiance. She composed herself, paused a thick five seconds and then spat back at me.

'What the hell do you want? I suppose you're going to try and rape me now like a big tough man? Right here in the car park?'

The words hit me like a sucker punch to the gut. Bad thoughts. Too many haunting memories. The brutal weapon of war. I steadied myself against the car window, head reeling. *Maria... please... don't hurt her... it's me you want to punish....*

I breathed in hard. Exhaled.

'Calm down. That is not going to happen. Give me the keys. Put your seat belt on and the gun goes away. Now please. Just do it.' I struggled to bring control and measure to my voice. Matilda reluctantly buckled up. I put the gun away and walked around to the empty passenger seat, climbing into the car beside her. Locked the car doors and looked at her in silence. She was now crying softly to herself. Whimpering, shaking.

'Matilda, listen to me. I'm not going to hurt you. I just need some information about Daniel Ratchet. We believe that he's been kidnapped and I'm here to bring him back.'

She looked through me with haunting tear stained eyes.

'Who has taken him Matilda and where? Do you know? If you know you must tell me and now. We haven't much time.'

'I don't know much about it. He left me a voicemail saying there was a problem with a contract. He was studying some strange data patterns or something. I think his room in the hotel had been burgled. He needed my help and now he's gone. They're saying things didn't work out for him on Tour and he went home. I thought we had something special.'

'Okay. Do you have any idea where he's gone or why? I need to get the facts here and fast.'

'Try asking a golf coach called Bob Wallace. He's been peddling some theory about how the winners on Tour are all fixed. It seems totally far-fetched. Everyone knows Bob has an axe to grind but Daniel was the new boy out here. Bob got him sucked into these crazy ideas and now he's gone. Perhaps he got disillusioned with it all. Couldn't hack it. I know that feeling too sometimes.'

She looked so sad.

'Do you know any more about this tournament fixing theory? If it is for real and Daniel was poking about where his nose didn't belong, it could it be a reason for someone to want him out of the picture, don't you think?'

Matilda turned and looked at me dispassionately. A coolness revealing itself behind those watery blue eyes, cutting her off from the pain. 'I already told you I don't know anything about it. We all have to survive and make our living out here. Now just leave me the fuck alone will you'.

It wasn't going the way I had hoped.

'Thank you,' I replied with as much sincerity as I could muster.

'You've been helpful. I know it's difficult. I only want to bring Daniel back to you and his family.'

I left Matilda in the car, defiant. People react in a variety of ways following the kidnapping of a loved one and defensiveness was a common characteristic. She was hurting right now but something told me she would pull through. I figured that she was tougher than that pretty feminine exterior suggested. I'd learn more from Bob Wallace, when I located him. Perhaps he would be better apprised of the complex relationship between Daniel Ratchet and the group of caddies that I had overheard before. One thing was for sure. I needed a trail to locate the Target before I could act.

And there was no time to waste or, when we did get to him, there might be nothing more than a stiff cold corpse waiting.

Chapter 19

Throbbing. A dull, deafening pulse. A relentless beat drumming menacingly inside his brain. He opened his eyes to darkness and struggled onto his side. Hands and feet tightly bound. A coarse, thick, prickly rope bit into his skin. He groaned against the rancid gag. The taste of stale blood pervaded his mouth. Ribs felt like they had been smashed in on his left side. The ear drum shattering sound continued unabated. He worked hard to get a better sense of his surroundings. A vast, cavernous, pitch black space. The room felt empty—cold and malevolent. His thoughts stifled by the imposing clatter of old clunky machinery. He wondered if he was in some sort of factory. He wondered what the hell had happened. Last thing he could recall he was talking to an attractive woman outside the hotel at the golf course. Something about a camera? A stabbing jolt jarred through his back as Daniel was bumped up into the air like a rag doll and smashed back down hard onto his throbbing ribs. Pitiful groaning. This was no old fashioned factory. He was inside a moving vehicle.

The articulated lorry junketed, bumped and swerved wildly across the white lines of the road on two side wheels. Tyres screeched as it clumsily avoided a collision with a white Range Rover travelling fast in the opposite direction. Up front in the hot cramped cab, the agitated driver behind the wheel slapped his face hard to clear his head from its dreamlike trance. He had driven hard all night, barely passing another vehicle, lost within the seductive trails of his own thoughts, the mesmeric sound of turning wheels and the bare tarmac stretching endlessly ahead. He'd woken from his daze to find his lorry driving on the wrong side of the road. It had been everything he could do to prevent a head on collision with the other vehicle. Too close. He shook his head in disbelief. Face and neck slick with a sheen of cold sweat.

And after what seemed like endless hours of blackened hell to Daniel's aching limbs and battered ribs, feeling every imperfection in the road beneath as his helpless carcass banged and buffeted against the unforgiving wooden trailer bed, the sun began to rise. Shards of fractured sunbeams prised themselves into the lorry through the cracks and chinks in the side panelling.

As the heat rose steadily with the sun, so did the unmistakable stench of rotting meat, ascending to an unbearable peak. Daniel retched as his body reacted to the enforced environment. The sunlight stung his eyes. He couldn't remember when he'd last had something to drink and his mouth and throat were so dry that he couldn't swallow. It hurt to try.

Huge sharp metal hooks, like menacing inverted question marks, creaked in the gloom above him. Some of the hooks held enormous carcasses with what could only really have been skinned or untreated pigs fixed upon them, presumably those not fit for refrigeration or human consumption. The stench of death, of flesh and smoke was everywhere. Daniel Ratchet was imprisoned in some kind of moving abattoir.

'I'm telling ya. He was supposed to meet me at the Irish bar, lassie. Daniel had figured it out. He'd made the connections between the stats and the decline in specific players' form at specific times. He was on to those miserable cheating bastards and I think they knew. We were going to draw up the battle plan on how to get the Tour cleaned up and rid of this scourge of corruption.' They were sitting closely together in the busy and brightly lit atrium of the hotel. Safe. Drawing comfort from each other.

'I can't understand it. He wouldn't just up and leave the Tour. Not without saying goodbye. This was his dream job. And we'd only just met, Bob. He told me he loved me. I know it sounds strange but until I met Daniel I have always felt so alone out here. He was the only one to ever really understand me. Not just wanting to get me into bed. He really wanted to get to know the real me.' She pulled earnestly on the old man's shirt sleeve as if to emphasise the point.

'I figured he was sweet on you, princess. Suppose there's not a man out here that ain't. I wasn't buying that little ring you wear. It never kept Krostanov away from you neither, what with all those fancy dinners and the like.' Bob always played the straight bat, whatever the wicket.

'That was business, Bob. I didn't have a choice. And I never said I was with Michael or anyone else, I let people make their own assumptions. They can think what they want. I just want the creeps to stay away. I was so happy I had found Daniel.' She twisted the lace of the table cloth between tense fingers.

'And I'm telling you sweetheart,' Bob reiterated grimly, 'he's not left. He didn't bottle it. Danny wasn't like that. That's just some official nonsense that the pubic relations people have put out so no one will make a fuss, so he wouldn't be missed. Nobody will care one jot out here if some upstart agent decides he can't hack the pace and ups and leaves the Tour to head home, tail between his legs. People are always coming and going. And as you well know there are always plenty of young bucks ready to grab their chance with both hands when they get it. He'll be replaced without missing a beat.' He banged his fist on the table top as he spoke the word.

'What those bastards couldn't sanction would be some salacious crime or story about missing persons. Oh no, that would be picked up by the media and besmirch the precious name of the Tour. Reflect directly on their golden goose sponsors and the like. This is a fix up Matilda.' They leant together, faces only a few inches from one another. He spoke in a low voice cracking with emotion. 'They've taken Danny because he knew something about the dark forces at work out here and he told me he finally had the proof to make it stick.'

'What's going to happen? Who do you think is responsible, Bob? Do you have any real evidence that you can take to the police?'

'I've long held the belief that a certain criminal element amongst the caddies out here run a black market gambling ring. I know they have bullied certain players to miss puts during rounds and manipulate the scoring to meet their own ends.'

Bob peered about the hotel searchingly, as if expecting to be overheard.

'They even go so far as to get some of the coaches and managers in on the act when it serves them to score a big pay day. I don't know how high up this goes but I wouldn't be surprised if the bloody sponsors and officials were in on it too for all I know.'

'But you don't have any proof of this?' Matilda asked. Again touching Bob's arm.

'Danny was going to show me the stats he had uncovered which showed the best players throwing tournaments away at the last minute against the run of form. Very convenient as a bookie if you have a lot of money piled on the favourite I'd say. I was going to ask him to use his position dealing with sponsors to see how they felt about it.'

'The sponsors?'

'I know you have to work with Krostanov, sweetheart, seeing as the company he works for sponsors the physio-truck along with everything else around here. Lord knows I've seen him sniffing around you enough like a dog on heat, but I have a bad feeling about that mob from Rublex too. Why would a man of his position spend time with those lowly bag men? Especially cretins like Razor and Sean? My guess is that they are up to their necks in this too somehow.' Face stony and resolute, meeting the girl's eyes.

'Bob that's crazy! Sergei talks to the caddies because Rublex sponsor the players they work with. And they would only want their players to do the very best when they play. That's surely the point of sponsorship after all. You have no evidence of impropriety whatsoever, Bob.' Matilda shifted a little distance between them. Bob's conspiracy theories had been known to become contagious over the years.

'Listen. I've called in a favour,' the old coach growled in his gravelly Scottish drawl, eyes narrowing to hardened slits. 'I've brought in some help from the best I know, back from my time in the Services. They'll get the evidence if it's there. We're going to have to fight to get Danny back and figure out this mess. These are the fellas you want on your side and no mistake.' He looked down at the floor and spoke in a softer voice, the passion drained.

'Matilda, it's my fault the wee lad got dragged into this. I'm so sorry for that. I need to make it right.'

The old man sat back in his seat, a single tear snaking its way down his wrinkled cheek. He buried his head in his hands. Matilda gazed back at him numb, again lost to a familiar world of hurt. After a minute she straightened from the table and wordlessly walked away.

Chapter 20

The meat truck pulled up to the side of the road and finally came to a slow grinding stop. Daniel waited. Held his breath, listening intently for the faintest sound, anything to provide a clue as to what was happening. Everything was still now, even the creaking of the metal hooks straining under the weight of heavy carcasses had stopped. He pulled against the ropes, burning his wrists as he twisted and writhed. But struggling was hopeless. He was expertly hogtied and tightly gagged in the foetal position so that he could barely move. The idea briefly taunted him that he was no better off than one of the stinking slabs of meat above. The cab door slammed shut and Daniel could hear the sound of a man's heavy footsteps rounding the side of the lorry, moving away from the occasional traffic of the road. Whomever they belonged to, they must have been standing not more than a couple of yards away from him now, as he lay helpless inside the lorry. The driver cleared his throat and spat on the ground before scratching impatiently at a lighter flint. The waft of bitter cigarette smoke, rich with tar, pronounced reward for his industry. Daniel could faintly hear bird song. *Where the hell am I and why is this happening to me?*

And then the crunch of gravel told of a car approaching slowly. The double clunk of its slamming doors indicated to Daniel that his driver had now been joined by two new people. He heard footsteps walking away from the lorry and then gruff voices conversing at a short distance. *Fuck my head hurts. Can't think. This is it. I'm going to die. I'm going to die. God help me. Please. Please.*

The men were arguing. Voices raised and angry. Daniel couldn't make out any specific words nor the gist of what was being said, but one thing was for sure, they were not happy people. Footsteps moved briskly towards the lorry now. Daniel shut his eyes tight and prayed. A button was pushed and Daniel could hear the incessant high-pitched whirring of electric gearing at the rear of the vehicle. He could hear the grating of metal steps being set into place. Suddenly aware he was super alert. Bristling with fear, his nerves on edge. The door was flung open and blistering sunlight flooded the inside. Daniel winced, peering through sore and crusty eyelids towards the end of the tunnel at the black silhouetted outlines of two bulky men framed in the square of light at the entrance to the lorry. *They're going to kill me. They're going to kill me. They're going to kill me.*

One of the men clambered up into the back of the truck. He coughed and cursed under his breath as the stench hit him. Daniel gagged again as the man peeled his way through the hanging carcasses which were now wreaking a fearsomely thick and putrid stench in the heat. He paused, slamming his heavy fist against one of the dead pigs in his way forcing it to lash wildly from side to side, metal hook creaking angrily. Punishing the carcass for the unpleasant odour. Daniel heard chuckling. He watched helpless as the shadow stepped closer, hunkering down onto its haunches to assess its bound captive. Suddenly his head was jerked upward by a fistful of his hair. The man stared directly into his fearful bloodshot eyes. In return he saw no hint of compassion. Nothing human to relate to or communicate with. He could taste the repugnant odious breath which warmly bathed his face.

And then, upon satisfying himself with the sorry looking mess within his grip, he issued a cold smirk, and spat directly into Daniel's swollen face. The grip on his hair was suddenly released, his body discarded like an unloved child's toy clattering rigidly to the floor. The shadow turned, gingerly stepped back through the lorry out of the thick funk and into fresh air.

Daniel lay there motionless, heart beating furiously out of his chest. He could feel the thick globule of saliva slowly slithering its way down his cheek and over his cracked bloodied lips. He was grateful of the moisture. It was pitiful. He breathed deeply. The paralysing fear he'd been so overcome with earlier was slowly passing.

If they wanted to kill me then I'd already be dead. Somehow that bastard had seemed pleased. They must need me alive.

Chapter 21

ENGLAND. LONDON. RIVER THAMES.
NORTH BANK. 07.48 HRS.

A rusted tug boat blasted its horn in pugnacious warning at nearby vessels as it jostled for position on the river approaching Westminster Bridge. The sound caused Derek Hemmings to look up from his newspaper and check along the towpath for the twelfth time that morning. He relished crisp, bright, spring mornings such as these and invariably looked forward to his brisk walk to work alongside the shimmering river Thames. Observing the bustle of the boats; marvelling at the industry of a city at work. But today was different. Derek was ill at ease and agitated. He was waiting for a clandestine appointment at the secluded riverside bench which he occupied. And his meeting was late. He glanced furtively at his watch, tutting quietly to himself and shaking his head.

'Still impatient I see, Derek,' Simon Prentice's velvety smooth voice admonished gently behind him.

'I'm so glad you're here, Simon. I'm afraid I don't know who else to turn to, who else may possibly be able to assist.'

'It must be serious old boy. It's been forty odd years since you turned your back on us spooks in MI6. Defected to the Foreign Office. Embraced the Dark Side.' He smiled the same slow calculated smile that had hung long in the memory.

'Come now. It was never like that, Simon and you know it. I loved the job, truly. But when Robin came along so unexpectedly, well, there was just no choice. Alice needed me at home. She insisted that I had to put family first, and rightly so I suppose.' Derek stood and shuffled from foot to foot, somewhat animated.

'We always understood that you are a good egg, Hemmings. And it is formally acknowledged and appreciated that you've kept our chaps informed on what's really going on from inside 'the bubble' over the years. Insight into the Foreign Office's agenda has certainly been useful, particularly given some of the peculiar sensitivities of interdepartmental rivalry. In many ways, you've really been spying for us internally to help the machine work better. I suppose one could say, Hemmings, that you've become the spy you never were.' Chortling to himself, he continued, 'Good title for a Bond film that, don't you say?'

'Oh very droll, Simon. Very droll,' fired back, acerbic, laced with heavy sarcasm. 'Well now it's me that needs you. And I don't just mean a good lunch and a clandestine tour of the field armoury. I'm a desperate man.'

'Go ahead old boy. I'm all ears.' He raised his eyebrows quizzically.

'Ever come across a Russian businessman and erstwhile gangster named Boris Golich?' It was a rhetorical question. 'Well I need to find out everything I can about him and his money and the dealings of his privately owned energy company, Rublex Corporation. I have two days to ratify a massive commercial deal for the government to the tune of a seven billion pound investment in the Falkland Islands and the creation of over seven thousand British jobs to support the exploration, extraction, and deployment of natural gas around the world.'

Simon whistled.

'Personally, I think the whole thing could be a ploy to launder vast sums of mafia money and that Great Britain should stay well clear of it. But the bloody PM himself seems hell bent on driving it through and has now got his pet Scottish pit bull, Andy Bartholomew, on my case; ensuring it all goes ahead for signature on time with no proper due diligence being conducted whatsoever. They're pushing for the positive headlines it will generate in the short term before the election and I'm afraid my conscience is taking a bloody battering.'

He cast his eyes to the sky. Paused for dramatic effect.

'Imagine the gross contamination of the UK's trade portfolio and our international relations if this deal is proved a sham and the selling of Golich's energy nothing but a front for organised crime. The deal goes live at the end of the week and I've looked into it as far as I can. Something is deeply wrong about this agreement. Every instinct and fibre of my very being is screaming out that we have to protect British interests. I have to do the right thing. Help me to do the right thing here, Simon.' Derek looked down and noticed for the first time that whilst he had been talking he had been unpicking a thread from a button on his suit jacket, worrying it loose. Alice would certainly not be pleased at having to stitch it back on. He turned to face the river, shoulders drooped. 'We can't find anything substantial enough to halt this deal and I'm actually beginning to think perhaps we never will.' His words hung in the air, desperation palpable until his companion cut through the silence.

'Alright. I can confirm that we do know Golich indeed, Derek. Have done since the little thug first popped up, illegally seizing oil wells in Uzbekistan with his own private army. Set about displacing ordinary folk from their homes to make way for infrastructure development. Corrupt politicians looking the other way in exchange for his hired muscle conjuring up the right number of votes in their local elections. Fast forward twenty-five years and he's still doing the same thing—only on a far grander global scale. He's a billionaire now who dines and plays golf with world leaders including, I may add, our very own PM. He entertains and influences the great and the good. Has even ploughed millions into the European Golf Tour in order to broaden his reach and legitimise his brand.'

'What else is he into other than oil and gas?'

'Our chaps on the ground in Moscow inform us that he has strong ties to the historic network of Russian Mafia gangs. We'll do some proper digging on his activities now he has become a person of significant interest. I tend to agree with you. This is indeed a critical situation.'

'Thank you, Simon. I'm sure I don't need to tell you that this matter is under the strictest departmental security classification. Very few people know about it. The government wants to steal a march on the opposition and on our foreign rivals. We have apparently lifted this investment from the table of a state run Chinese energy company and the PM is delighted with the coup. The good news announcement in Parliament will be the first sign that this government has cemented the progression into sustained positive fiscal growth with austerity and the mess of Brexit far far behind us. And it couldn't come at a better time to influence the voters.'

'You have my word on behaving with the utmost of discretion old boy. I'll be in touch shortly.'

Derek blinked back the emotion. The two old stagers stood together in the quiet for a short while on the bank of the river Thames, bathing in the morning sun. Letting the moment resonate. A final hand-shake. Turned then left in opposite directions, each in their own ways resolute to claim the morning.

Chapter 22

The breeze dropped the temperature by five degrees at least. It sucked into the back of the open lorry, gently brushing Daniel's face, stirring him awake again as he oscillated in and out of consciousness. It also served to accentuate the sticky, pungent stench in which he lay baking. Daniel wretched as he came round. He worked his blistered lips over the tight gag and listened hard for sounds outside the truck. It felt like they had been stationary for hours but the truth was that any sense of time had become completely distorted.

A single voice spoke now. Talking in rapid bursts, punctuated by equal periods of silence. The seemingly urgent and rising inflection at the end of his sentences indicated he was asking a rapid series of questions. Then nothing, a period of protracted silence. A sudden scuffle. A muffled shout. And in quick succession the snap of a single gunshot shattering the air, the sound of a body crumpling to the ground. Daniel winced and held his eyes tight shut.

Moments later, two men in black leather jackets, one of them the vicious man with bad breath who'd spat into his face, sprang into the back of the lorry. They grabbed his feet roughly and without warning. Dragged him fast over the wooden truck floor, ripping his shirt and tearing the skin on his back over jagged splinters. Above his head the bloodied pig carcasses twirled from the roof like a gruesome oversized baby-cot mobile within some macabre nursery.

Hoisted to the ground and slung limply over a broad shoulder, the hostage was now transferred to the open boot of a gleaming black Mercedes. Lying dumped on his back. Still bound and sucking in what air he could, Daniel stared helplessly up at the colossal expanse of azure blue sky strewn with wispy strips of cotton-wool cloud suspended high above. The view was destroyed when a body was levered unceremoniously into the boot and dropped directly on top of him. His face splattered with globules of blood, sharp particles of sand stung his eyes. The boot slammed shut descending them at once into pitch darkness. The forehead of the dead man nestled against Daniel's cheek causing him to twist furiously to free himself of the touch. *This*, he thought, *must be Hell itself.*

How long the car drove for or in which direction he had no idea. Daniel was completely disorientated with no anchor to fix him in neither in time nor space. He was squashed tightly by the stout and heavy body on top of him. Running low on oxygen in the cramped boot, an unpleasant, syrupy pool of blood now formed on the nape of his neck, dripping intermittently yet relentlessly. By the time the car pulled to a final halt and its human cargo— both dead and barely living—were unloaded, it was cooler and dark outside. Both bodies were dragged inside up broad tiled steps, upon which the back of Daniel's head bounced roughly in near-comedic rhythmic succession. They were laid out onto the stark marble floor of an opulent entrance hall. Only here were the two travelling companions finally separated from their enforced period of haunting entwinement. A period during which Daniel had felt the slow tightening of the dead body pressing upon him until it had finally turned hard and rigidly inflexible.

●

A full bottle of cold water was poured over the hostage's head. He opened his eyes and soon began to take in the splendour of his surroundings. The palatial Hacienda-style entrance hall was encased entirely in white marble. Heavy gold-framed mirrors lined the walls and tall potted palm trees flanked a yawning white spiral staircase stretching up to the solid wooden minstrel gallery and beyond.

'You awake, lazy boy? Yes, lazy boy, you wake up now,' taunted one of the black-leather-jacket-men in heavily accented English as he slapped his bloodied victim callously around the face. Daniel was pulled upright, his feet and thighs at last freed from the bite of their tight bonds. As the blood flooded back into his legs he collapsed to the floor. A hand, now gripping his throat, pulled him to a standing position again. 'Get up little bitch. You stay here with us now, Daniel.'

And then he was shoved hard in the back from behind and Bad Breath Man dragged him away by the upper arm through a blurred series of doors and rooms and finally into a cold back passageway at the rear of the villa. A thick metal-studded door, a small bare windowless cell, paint peeling from the interior walls. The grind of key turning inside heavy lock.

Chapter 23

SPAIN. EUROPEAN TOUR. BAYFIELD MANDARIN
GOLF RESORT. DAY FIVE. 17.00 HRS.

I'd noted practice areas earlier, stamped at intervals around the golf course: putting greens, chipping areas, practice bunkers, driving ranges. I walked briskly towards a cluster of them from the parking lot following the basic logic that I'd likely find Bob Wallace, a golf coach after all, probably located in the areas where golf was taught. At the very least it would be a good place to start. I dialled into HQ as I moved and Ella picked up on the first ring. 'Hunter, how's it going? What's happening on the ground? Everything okay? You haven't had any more flashbacks, have you? I get worried about you.' She spoke as if delivering a single stream of consciousness.

'All good, Babydoll. You missing me then, are you? I think I promised you dinner back in London when we got through the last job. Sorry it had to be postponed. I'll try to make it up to you.'

'Dinner? Mmm. Okay. Sounds nice. You do appreciate that I'm not some cheap date though, don't you, Hunter? It takes quite a lot to impress a girl like me.' It was a sassy reply. 'Anyway, what can I do you for, soldier?'

'Patch me through to Bob Wallace, can you? You guys have his mobile on record right? I want to ask him a few questions about the Target and some of the rats out here that I've already encountered. A few of the pieces are starting to make some sense. I need to assess the level of threat and perhaps squeeze some information out of a few people to help me figure out what's happened to Ratchet.'

'Patching through now Hunter. Be careful, okay?'

The long international dial tone played out repetitively down the line. Although I was probably within less than a kilometre of Bob Wallace in person, the untraceable call was routed via our Unit's headquarters out of a little Victorian cottage in Barnes, South West London, England. Its size and quaint old fashioned frontage, replete with little red bricks and creeping ivy façade, belied the high spec interior. Charles Hand had decked the base out with the very latest computer equipment and military technology. To our knowledge they didn't even possess some of this kit yet at the Pentagon. There was little doubt that being able to access feeds from a massive range of varied global satellite communications enabled us to keep one step ahead and contributed to our efficiency on the ground. Hand always maintained it fuelled our ferocious success rate on jobs and was an investment worth making.

The call hitting Bob Wallace's British mobile phone was now being bounced across various different international exchanges and European time zones. The tone rang out and finally an answerphone message tripped into play. A gruff Scottish voice said, 'Leave your message for Bob after the tone. And remember: always keep your head still and eyes down when you strike a putt. If you haven't heard your ball drop in thirty minutes, then I'm afraid you've missed.' *Beep.*

I hung up. Leaving a message wasn't a good idea. Who's to say that Bob would want to speak to me right now anyway? And besides, if his phone fell into the wrong hands it would just alert them to my presence and compromise any advantage of surprise. I was contemplating my next move when a text message from Ella buzzed through:

Honour is what no man can give you and none can take away.
Honour is a man's gift to himself.
(Robert the Bruce)

I shrugged. *You can't argue with that.*

I needed to move quickly, avoiding contact with other people as far as was practicable. An Indian man in his mid-thirties was working on a series of putting drills on the practice green. He was wiggling his putter back and forth like a pendulum between square set shoulders. I approached from behind. 'Know where I can find Bob Wallace round here, mate?' I called across to him from outside the ropes.

'Yes, certainly. We finished our session together here not one hour ago. Mr Wallace can usually be found in the Halfway House hut off the ninth green about this time. He likes to be alone, save only for his whiskey and his thoughts.'

'Much obliged, friend,' I replied but by the time I had finished thanking him, the head was bowed once more in fixed concentration, golf balls firing off the blade in snappy order, sinking into a cup over six feet away. I continued my way down the paved pathway, following signs towards the ninth green.

The Halfway House was a smallish, boxy hut beautifully carved out of wood from local cedar trees. It was staffed during the main part of the day by a team from the hotel, serving refreshments to golfers as they plotted their way around the course, offering welcome replenishment after their hours under the hot sun. Bob had presumably claimed it as his own when the golf course emptied. It was easy to see why a man who wanted to be alone with his thoughts would select it as a hideaway. Out here in the middle of the deserted golf course, eerily silent and set back amongst a small copse of gnarled olive trees, the hut sat squat in defiant isolation. The low-cut and thick wooden door was ajar, but I rapped on it anyway out of courtesy. No response. Eased it open, slow, cautious. Stepped inside.

What I encountered hit me like a smack in the face—it was

savage. Total juxtaposition to the tranquillity of its setting. A man, only partially recognisable as Bob Wallace from his photograph in the briefing file, was slumped in the corner tied to a chair. His bloodied face had been smashed in entirely on one side revealing the hollow remains of his cheek and jaw. Discarded on the floor next to him lay a pitching wedge, the blade stuck with pieces of grizzled flesh and splinters of bone. His throat had been cut. The deep gaping wound told of a single swift and well-practiced motion. His head lolled to the side lazily, exposing the inside of his neck from ear to ear. Flies buzzed over the body, dizzy already from feasting on the sweet and sticky blood. I studied the room. A small square table in front of him, age-worn with the chips and marks and the scars of a purposeful existence, was littered with playing cards. It was dominated by an overflowing ashtray crammed with a mixture of tatty rolled-up butt ends and blackened cigarette filters. A half empty bottle of Johnnie Walker Black Label was accompanied by a single stained glass. Next to it lay a small square of coarse sandpaper and a wet rag. I grimaced. Searched for the telltale patches of torn skin and exposed bone on the underside of elbows, knees, knuckles and finger tips and was bitterly rewarded. Whoever had done this knew what they were doing. Had taken their time to sand away the skin on particularly sensitive portions of the anatomy, using the alcohol to increase the suffering. I wondered at what stage of the ordeal they had broken him. What the old soldier had finally told them. I hoped, for his sake, that he'd been able to retain his personal sense of honour and integrity before his demise. I would never forget the haunted look of realisation in the eyes of the men I'd watched betray their friends.

I held the grubby glass aloft and swallowed the last inch of amber liquor from the bottom. A risk of contaminating the crime scene perhaps, but the dead man, one of the Hand of God's fallen comrades, deserved a final toast. With the glass wiped free of my prints, I carefully backed out of the hut. This was someone else's mess to clean up now. I wasn't certain that whoever was responsible wasn't still lingering and preparing to ambush me in situ. Plus I figured that if anyone else happened upon the scene then a big, heavily armed and uninvited trespasser stumbling upon a bloody murder on this refined and exclusive golf course would not be easy to explain.

I needed time to think. There was no further information available and the figure central in explaining Daniel Ratchet's disappearance was dead. The who and why didn't matter as much as the where in our job. But time was essential if the Target was still alive and often the most efficient method to get a lock on the hostage location is to assess the context of their disappearance. Get an understanding of the background to the take. Perpetrators routinely leave trails of information. Packets of data to be assessed so we can interpret the situation we are dealing with on a job. As such, the technology deployed back at HQ can tap into real-time transactions from the use of any specified bank and credit cards, vehicle GPS systems, toll booths, and has even been known to lock onto IP addresses and therefore identify the whereabouts of computerised devices and smartphones utilising public Wi-Fi for internet connection. We can quickly build up the profile of a suspect and assess their movements so as to get an idea of their intentions and capability. Whatever the underlying reason for the crime, the planning and actions taken leading up to the execution of a kidnap will also provide an evidence trail that inextricably leads us to where our Target can ultimately be found. Alive or dead.

But that's for the gumshoes. The smart way to do it. And if you have the time, of course. My job is to find the Target. Recapture them if they're still alive. Document the body if they are dead. We get paid either way for reaching the Target but there is a sweet financial incentive for getting them back still breathing. I don't ask questions about who they are or why they are in whatever predicament they're in and I don't need to bother myself with the fallout. Solving crimes is for cops and if there is collateral damage from my work, then so be it. The Unit operates off-radar and I take my orders straight from the Hand of God. Nothing else matters.

The other method of getting information, when taunted by the impatient demands of an officious ticking clock, is a little gentle persuasion fresh out of the 'Tom Hunter School of Charm'. And of those two accepted methodologies, there is no doubt which route I'm more comfortable with.

Experience has taught me many unsavoury lessons. The need to pause for a little strategic thinking before a tear up was one of them. According to an evaluation report made by the Hand of God to the top brass in the mob 'Hunter possesses a positive predilection for preproperation'. Whatever that actually meant. But I do know that if I were to just go straight off wading in to try and extract information on the Target's whereabouts from the key suspects on Ella's list of caddies, such as Razor, Sharples, Sean, or Billy Boy there would simply be no guarantee of gaining reliable information. Even through interrogation at gunpoint or by waterboarding one of the bastards. We've learnt that the perpetrators of a kidnapping or crime of person-disappearance rarely talk quickly when initially confronted. Interrogation can take hours, sometimes days. Being a caddy was also a recognised position within the fabric of the European Golf Tour, which might serve as insulation against any suggestion of impropriety. The on-course security team would handle the fall-out from any immediate disturbances and if the local police were on the payroll, they would look the other way should matters escalate. Given these circumstances, I was well aware that if the authorities got involved, there was no doubt that I was the one who would end up in the clink. With the paucity of information we currently held surrounding the circumstances of Ratchet's disappearance and with time at a major premium, a suspect being forced to talk might decide to deploy a strategy of misdirection. This would cost us crucial time. There's no doubt that if you put the squeeze on someone for information and do it tight enough, they will eventually talk. I don't care how tough you are the world over, it's a rare man who won't sing to me given enough time and the right tool kit. It's the veracity and timeliness of the information provided, that you need to be careful with. And right now I still had other options to explore.

Chapter 24

ENGLAND. LONDON. CROWN SPORTS OFFICE.

'Mr Flavini? It's Daniel Ratchet's father here.' The broad Sheffield accent, firm and true down the telephone.

'Yes, good morning, Mr Ratchet. And please do call me Silvio,' oozed the warm response given between sips of rich Italian coffee.

'Right oh. Er, Silvio then. Yes well, sorry to telephone you at the office, we did promise that we wouldn't use the number except in emergencies, but I'm ringing because, well, to be frank, the boy's mother is agitating. She's concerned that we haven't heard from him for a few days and we were expecting to hear all about the tournament and the ceremony of last week. We read in the paper of the golfer that he's working with winning that big tournament and with that being such a big deal to the lad and the like, it just seems a little odd that we can't reach him. The mobile number he gave us doesn't work and we called the hotel who says that he's up and checked out.'

A pause for breath.

'Mr Ratchet, I'm sure that there's nothing to be concerned about.' A smooth, unctuous response. 'Daniel is working hard for us to put a contract in place and I expect that's what he is focusing on at the moment. I haven't heard from him myself but I'm sure it's all perfectly normal. We all know that mothers like to fuss, Mr Ratchet. And I can myself testify to that, being a good Italian boy myself.'

'Yes, well, that is true indeed. You'll let us know when you hear from him won't you?'

'Of course, Mr Ratchet, of course,' was the silken platitude.

'Now please do try not to worry. Daniel's a big boy. Working on the road as we do, there are the many days when we lose the communication. It's really no problem.' He replaced the receiver in its cradle and smoothed the soft silver hairs of his beard around the creases of his mouth as he considered matters. His next call was transatlantic, placed to the direct line of Randy Hughes, founder and autocratic owner of the Crown Sports Empire.

'Randy, we have a problem. Our new agent, Daniel Ratchet, has gone missing—a few days now. There is the outstanding Aaron Crower agreement to be finalised with Rublex Corporation, part of the incentive programme. I think we may need someone else on the ground out in Europe.'

'You fucked up, Silvio,' came the booming American baritone, 'You hired the wrong guy. A guy who couldn't get the job done and you didn't even fucking tell me that the agreement wasn't signed. What's wrong with you people? Can't you manage to do what you're told?'

'Randy, please. The boy had some concerns about the terms of the agreement and I put him straight. It was due to be signed imminently.'

'That's sixteen fucking million fucking dollars, Silvio,' he shouted. 'Crown Sports doesn't tolerate playing fast and loose with that kind of green'

'I know Randy. I'm sorry, I truly am.'

'It's a good thing one of us is on the ball, you greasy Italian waste of space. I've been speaking with Sergei and Rublex directly. I've been through the agreement and it's the usual format, same as all the others. I've authorised him to deal with Aaron and sign the paperwork in Spain. We can't afford to leave the door open for some other agent to present him with a better offer and snatch him away from right under our beak. Crower is a hot property after that win and those slippery bastards will be all over him.'

'Okay, great news Randy. Thank you. What about Daniel, any word on where he might be?'

'The fuck do I care about that little limey bastard? He was sticking his nose in where it wasn't wanted, Silvio, and from what I hear he was starting to piss off our wealthy Ruski friends. I'm just pleased he's out the way and not obstructing the course of good business being done no more.' The phone went dead. The conversation was very over.

Daniel lay on his side. He'd been staring for hours at a single patch of flaking paint on the cell wall. His body ached. The throbbing in his head had abated but it was still tender and sore to the touch. If he turned his neck suddenly, he was overcome by a sickening dizziness. The cell was empty except for a split and stained pink child's mattress partially spewing its dirty-ish yellow foam innards. A cracked green plastic bucket, presumably for use as a toilet, stood unloved in the corner.

Each day he'd been there so far, a small plastic bottle of lukewarm water for him to drink had been lobbed into the cell. Nothing to eat for the first two days. On the third day, with his strength all but faded, a squashed service station sandwich of limp lettuce, rancid tomato and processed cheese was thrown inside. Daniel gagged as he crammed the food gratefully into his mouth. The stench of the dark heavy urine to which he had grown so accustomed was brought vividly alive to his senses again. The meagre sustenance he was attempting to swallow had a sudden vile impact on his olfactory system, reacting in a painful explosion of dormant taste buds awakened after the long period of neglect. He had been left untied in the cell, presumably considered no threat in being so weak. He was thoroughly secured under lock and key.

Daniel had neither spoken to nor seen any of his captors since first arriving there. *What do they want with me*, he'd often wondered. *It must have something to do with what I'd found out about the cheating on Tour. If they wanted to kill me, I'd already be dead, so there must be hope. There has to be some reason that I'm still alive. For now.*

●

He was awoken from a fitful slumber by the crunch of the key rattling in metal grate. Bad Breath Man stooped and entered the tiny room, watching closely as Daniel sat up and rubbed his eyes. He loped to the corner and then, in one sudden and aggressive motion, scooped up the plastic bucket, hurling both it and its foul contents at Daniel's head. There was no time to roll to his side. The bucket caught him on the corner of the temple, cutting him sharply above the eyebrow and covering him, the bed and the wall, with an ugly slop of rancid shit and piss. Daniel reeled backwards in shock as the assailant stepped forward and screamed furiously into his face, 'Where is computer tablet? Where is tablet you stupid fuck?'

The door banged open on its hinges. A second man whom Daniel also recognised from his capture, roughly grabbed Bad Breath Man and forced him against the wall, jabbing a thick finger towards his face. 'No fucking questions until, Avtorityet arrives. These are rules. Fucking understand?' He pointed towards the door and the two filed out silently, leaving Daniel sitting on the mattress in soiled disbelief, choking on a torrent of frightened tears. Sorrowful, bleeding and dripping in piss.

Chapter 25

ENGLAND. SURREY. RIVER THAMES.
SHEPPERTON LOCK.

Two men approached each other guardedly. Their backdrop, a narrow stretch of the wizened river Thames. Grey choppy waters swirled.

'Simon, it's been a very long time'.

'Good of you to come, dear boy'.

'I don't recall having much choice in the matter,' came the stiff reply.

'From what I remember of you, Charles, there was apparently always a choice,' punctuated with a deliberate and humourless chuckle.

'Not when the safety of my people is involved, Simon, or perhaps you have forgotten that?'

The two men stared into each other's eyes. Hand's steely glare unbreakable, unflinching. The aura still surrounded him. The man who had transcended into army folklore. Some men didn't just command respect, it was a natural and implicit reaction induced on entering their orbit. Simon Prentice finally cast his eyes downward and carefully scratched at a dull mark on the sleeve of his smart, navy overcoat.

'Please, there is no need to dredge up the past. No one will ever forget what happened, Charles. I was compelled to think of the greater good. There was more at stake than just the lives of three British soldiers left back in Pakistan.'

'My greater good was saving those boys. It was my command. I sent them into that village to reconnoitre. MI6 deliberately withheld vital information regarding insurgent activity in the vicinity.'

'Charles, please, you were operating under the radar. Officially deniable. We couldn't share intelligence with you or we would have risked exposing the whole operation during a highly sensitive political climate. We were risking an all-out war if the Pakistani government had rumbled what we were up to.'

'The simple fact is you cut a deal behind our backs, Simon. You left those boys there to die in exchange for the freedom of some low-level turncoat informant, bartering information on a non-existent weapons dump for his life.'

'We didn't know it was non-existent at the time did we? How were we to know? The local intel had been inaccurate.'

Hand glowered, fists tightening by his side. 'When our team went in deep behind enemy lines to capture Mahood in his brother-in-law's village, you had already bloody cut a deal and spirited him away. It was a death trap and you let us walk right into it.'

'We couldn't have known that they would lay such a heinous ambush. No one meant for those soldiers to get hurt. It was a very difficult time for us all.'

'My boys nearly died. I lost my job, Simon'. Again came that stare.

'Hardly old boy. An honourable discharge. A very healthy Army pension. More medals than you can shake a stick at. It was your time to go anyway. And regardless, my people tell me that you've created a highly lucrative enterprise freeing kidnap victims on the private market whilst leveraging a pretty powerful network to boot. Doing well for yourself it seems, Charles, and probably only thanks to the top brass sweeping the fact that you went rogue under the carpet. An MI6 recommendation, I may add.' Prentice looked pleased with himself.

'I did what needed to be done and I'd do the same again in a heartbeat.' Voice raised. Stark.

'Charles. You commandeered a bloody US Apache helicopter at gunpoint and flew it into a burning enemy village.'

'We all know the story'. Tense. Fractious.

'Yes. The Hand of God. The type of story some men's reputations are built upon.'

Both men now simmering on the edge of fury. Hand continued unapologetic.

'I saved three lives which you had put at unnecessary risk. Three of our finest men.'

'The ends justify the means? You were lucky things worked out, Hand, or the blowback from a buggered up rescue mission on an operation that didn't exist would have been totally catastrophic.'

'You should have told us what you knew.'

'Do I need to remind you that we were at war? Tough decisions have to be taken, Charles.'

Hand breathed in deeply, checked his watch and turned to go.

'What do you know about Boris Golich?' Simon called after him searchingly.

Charles stopped and turned around. The question hung between them for a while.

At length, a measured reply. 'He's a very dangerous man.'

'Walk with me.'

●

The two men walked along Shepperton Lock in silence for half a mile or so. It was a quiet and picturesque piece of river flanked on one side by a number of elegant houses with large glass frontages designed so the owners could derive optimum pleasure from expansive and scenic views. Across the narrow, undulating river lay Pharaoh's Island. An unusual free standing island in the Thames, it was home to a cluster of glorious houses, often of unique architectural design, and accessible only by boat. Moored in front of these properties bobbed a succession of powerful looking motorboats and over-designed gin palaces. On their side of the river, the two men passed a number of gaily painted house boats and barges. They walked in silence along the grass until they reached two barges conjoined to each other. The first, a working functional house boat, charming in springtime but, Simon noted, not particularly practical for an unrepentant British winter. Or indeed for those in need of plenty of standing closet space to hang their best Savile Row suits. The boat tethered to the port side of the river was sheathed in a heavy white tarpaulin. The men paused to read a sign which had been erected on the river bank. It read:

The little boats of Dunkirk project. This boat is being renovated to its former glory. It is estimated that this boat served on over 350 missions and during the Dunkirk rescues saved an estimated 165 lives. Please give generously to help with the cost of this privately funded renovation project so that future generations can enjoy the majesty of our brave and historic boats.

Hand stuffed a crisp twenty pound note into the plastic envelop stapled to the sign.

'There will always be wars, Charles. It's incumbent on us as servants of the nation to pick the right battles.' And then, deliberately catching his eye, 'We're on the same side you know, old boy. Men like us need to work together for the common good.

So I suppose you'd better tell me, Charles, why are you looking into Boris Golich?'

Hand raised his eyebrows quizzically. Feigning a practiced bafflement.

'Come don't deny. Don't do me that disservice. We know you still have contacts. You've been using an encrypted security clearance traced back to your old job to find out everything you can about Golich and his Rublex Corporation. In addition there's a certain inquisitive lady named Ella Philips, who we've tied to your operation, who has been putting herself around to find out what she can.'

A gravid pause. 'Where's all this going, Simon? Why should you care who we look into? We're a private business and this is a private matter.'

'I was rather hoping we may be able to help each other out. I've had a favour pulled from an old colleague in government who needs help fast. He's trying to shine a light on uncovering shady money trails stemming from Rublex and this Golich character before he binds the British government to an embarrassing commitment which could damage relations with some of our overseas trading partners and stain our good name in the international money markets.'

'You're talking about Russian Mafia money. The Vory.'

'So you do know about this then. I was rather hoping you would be able to help. What have your people been able to find out, Charles? We know Golich has become "Pakhan" now, the criminal mastermind who pulls the strings and a man whose reach is so far inside the Kremlin he only needs to sneeze and the Russian president gets bloody haemorrhoids. If we leverage the usual channels to follow the money and Moscow gets so much as a sniff of it, we risk closing down our whole operation. We practically operate over there under licence these days anyway. We can't bet the farm and risk upsetting years of careful contact grooming and intelligence gathering on this one, Hand.'

'And if we choose to assist your colleague, to furnish him with what we've found?'

'Then I shall ensure that Her Majesty's Secret Service "misplaces" certain evidence accrued against one Tom Hunter following the siege at the Nigerian Embassy last October. I believe you two are still professionally acquainted are you not?'

Charles Hand gripped his fist tightly. Fingernails turning white as they dug into his palm. He was backed into a corner, outflanked. Practically invited it upon himself. Hand stepped away and after a few moments of composed consideration he turned and spoke quietly. 'We'll trade. Set up the meet.'

Chapter 26

I moved fast. It wouldn't be long before Bob Wallace's body was discovered and I didn't need heat from the Guardia Civil who would soon be crawling all over the course and examining the scene of the crime. I decided to move cross country in the twilight through this tract of undulating rural land that had been carved out to produce a notoriously testing golf course. I would approach the truck park from behind, thereby avoiding any unnecessary contact.

The few kilometres back to the equipment truck enclave disappeared quickly. In the Regiment, we'd trained relentlessly. Despite incessant cuts from the Ministry of Defence, the British Army still retains some of the latest technologies and an impressive array of multi-purpose vehicles designed to transport soldiers across inhospitable war zone terrain. Sometimes, however, a soldier has no choice but to travel for miles on foot, often in adverse weather conditions and under the constant threat of ambush or engagement from a hostile enemy. It has always been the same throughout the ages and remains the case today even in these advanced times of robot soldiers and drone spy planes. Covering huge distances in double-quick time was referred to as a 'yomp'. My feet had developed a hard leathery skin to them which obscured the sensitive nerve endings and blocked out the pain. Now muscle memory returned to me as I tracked over the course's immaculate lush greenery. Solid legs and brisk rhythm propelling me forward at pace, eating up the ground beneath. Whoever we were up against had shown no compunction in the violent murder of Bob Wallace. The Target was still missing and it stood to reason that the longer it took to get to him, the less chance there was in bringing him back alive. Time was grinding forward relentlessly and I wasn't prepared to wait on ceremony.

Taking up an offensive position, shielded by the unwieldy branches of an aged sprawling olive tree, I checked over the Beretta. Turned it over carefully in my hands. Screwed on the silencer that Mickey had so kindly furnished. The oily looking guard remained on his crate, now whittling on a piece of wood with a fat curved blade used to slowly strip it of its bark. The rest of the man-made clearing between the trucks was empty. The hut beyond dark and lifeless. Ghosting silently from my vantage point, I was able to slip up to the guard unnoticed. It was only when almost upon him that he looked up from his handiwork, startled, eyes bulging wide. He rose fast to draw his weapon, triggering me in turn to spring at him hard. Leading with the butt of my gun, smashing into his nose, shattering cartilage against bone and into his face. He squealed like a stuck pig. Snorted in pain as blood spurted freely before crumpling onto the ground, squirming in agony. A sharp well-placed kick, steel toe-cap against temple, rendered him unconscious. Seconds later, his hands were secured together behind his back, cable ties biting tightly into fleshy wrists. I rolled him under an adjacent truck with the sole of my boot and on checking around me, gun muzzle primed, I pushed forward into the hut. I'd been expecting a golf equipment store or some kind of caddy shack but inside resembled more of a mission operations centre.

A large central table, strewn with maps and papers filled the main part of the central room. The walls were encased in large cork notice boards, pinned with charts and lists. A long shelf ran along the back of the hut upon which a kettle and several chipped tea-stained mugs sat. Beneath it stood a small squat fridge. I leafed quickly through the papers on the table trying to find anything that might point to Daniel's whereabouts. There was nothing seemingly pertinent to the job in hand. However, the extensive documentation revealed significant gambling and extortion activity, listing names with betting and payment activity detailed. This was coupled with neatly presented tables holding the names and addresses of local businesses and their 'taxes' payable week by week. The European Golf Tour travelled to a different country every seven days. This group increasingly looked like a network of sophisticated criminals shaking-down businesses at every stop of the merry-go-round, surreptitiously raking in hundreds of thousands of euros at each event.

But I wasn't a cop. I didn't care what these scumbags did to make their money. All I cared about right now was getting a lock on Daniel Ratchet and hopefully getting him back alive. Like I said, if the Target is still breathing when it is brought to safety, it means a bonus payment on top of my standard engagement fee. And that meant more to me than saving a life or putting the world to rights.

I entered the smaller room. It was done out as a personal office with desk and chair, smart metallic filing cabinets lining the walls. A bone dry pot plant, sporting crinkled leaves framing limp petals, gamely struggled to add colour to the sterile environment. I tugged on the top drawer of the nearest cabinet. It was locked shut. From my boot I fetched out my Bowie knife from the hidden leather sheath. The cabinet drawer was tough, clearly reinforced. The spring lock stubbornly resisted the tension of my blade. I gripped the knife handle tighter and leaned my weight down on it hard, twisted my wrist to pry open a gap between cabinet drawer and sturdy metal frame. No dice.

Heavy, thumping footsteps drummed into the hut, breaking my concentration. I dropped into an instinctive crouching position behind the partition wall of the small office. Hunkering down onto my haunches, balanced on my toes, primed to spring upwards leading with shoulder at first contact. Thinking fast: no windows in the hut and only one entrance meant no natural escape exits. I had company and unless I was going to pump a volley of holes into a wall and kick my way through, in the process alerting the whole world and the entire Guardia Civil to my movements, then the only option was to fight my way out.

I'd experienced enemy engagements going in many different ways. But even with the element of surprise on my side this time, I just knew in the pit of my stomach that this wasn't going to go the good way. I watched the massive hulking form of a lumbering mono-browed thug fill the space of the main room of the hut. He was shadowed closely by a skulking grey-hued figure, redolent of a sickly hyena looking for an easy meal. I recognised him as the caddy labelled as 'Razor' in the briefing notes Ella had compiled.

Given the size of this place, there was no doubt that I'd be discovered in seconds. I double checked the ammo clip in my piece and exhaled deeply. A massive thigh waded across the floor towards the office, floorboards creaking under heavy boots. With my back to the partition, crouched on my haunches, I angled the barrel of the Beretta round the crack in the open door and fired, two soft thuds piercing just above the knee of that meaty leg. It was enough to bring the huge man crashing down, bouncing chairs out of his path as he fell.

'What the hell?' shouted the hyena as his powerful sidekick collapsed while clutching his leg in agony. I moved swiftly. Blazing a volley of shots in front to create some cover, I rolled out of the office and pushed into the main room of the hut. Better a moving target than a sitting duck. I was caught by a slug to my shoulder tearing through the flesh and knocking me into the wall. The wounded giant had pulled a Glock from his belt and, from his sprawled position, was letting rip a succession of rounds in my general direction. Razor was flush, backed up against the wall of the hut, keeping away from the gunfire. Figuring he wasn't packing a weapon or it would already have been deployed in the tear up, I rolled hard to my right and threw myself forward at him. Dived face first over the large table in front of me, sliding, scattering papers like a speedboat's wake through a still pond. The move bought me vital seconds. The mono-browed beast was unable to twist his injured body to meet my new position and get a line of fire on me with the Glock. I landed shoulder first on the other side of the table. Turned in a single motion and emptied my clip, riddling the assailant's back and ribs with a scorching of hot lead. Razor fled from the hut in a blind panic.

I had learned the hard way, through losing the closest of mates, that in the heat of theatre you should never leave a threat alive that may serve to later compromise you. That threat might be live ammo or weaponry which could be used against you later during a contact or it may simply be leaving an enemy alive who might recover from their injuries sufficiently to become the one who finally calls out your number. At least that's how I justified it to myself. I crawled towards the slumped muscled torso of the beast, my shoulder soaked in claret from the bullet wound. Pain thumped through me. Adrenaline surged through my body. The blood was up.

●

The freak lay slumped over moaning in pain and I pushed him onto his back on the floor. He wheezed. His thick muscular neck looked too thick to snap. I picked up a chair lying next to him, positioning one of the legs over his face. He looked up at me pitifully. I stamped down on the seat of the chair driving it into his eye socket and down through to the back of his skull.

What the fuck was it with me and using impromptu pieces of furniture to kill scumbags? First tables and now chairs! I guess if the hostage recovery game ever stopped paying so well I could always take my uncanny product familiarity and make a new career move working at an Ikea store.

I scrambled to my feet and piled down the steps of the hut. The hunt was on for a fleeing hyena.

And it didn't take long to spot him. In fact he hadn't got far at all, making the basic strategic error of heading through the open space of the car park to escape when he could have covered his movements by cutting through the trucks back onto the golf course. Gripping my shoulder to try and stem the flow of blood, I started after him hard. Gaining ground, I shouted for him to stop, gesticulating ominously with the barrel of my empty gun.

Razor wasn't to know that I hadn't been able to reload and I figured that a warning of impending violence may be sufficient to jolt him into compliance given that he couldn't get away quick enough from the recent fire fight. He stood panting next to a gleaming, new red BMW, waiting for me to reach him with hands raised. I greeted him by throwing a hard right cross, catching him square on the jaw and knocking him backwards over the bonnet of the car. Picking him up by the lapels I shook him hard. Yelling into the contorted face before me, 'What do you know about Daniel Ratchet you piece of shit? Where the fuck is he?'

'Nufink man, I swear it. Please. Please don't kill me,' came the rasping reply. His hands feebly gripped my forearms in a vain attempt to free himself from my grasp. The gleam of an old fashioned gold watch on his wrist, incongruous with the trendy casual sports gear he wore, caught my eye. I followed a hunch, recalling Bob Wallace's comments on Daniel's distress at having had his grandfather's watch stolen earlier that week.

Intense. Aggressive. Inches from his face. 'Tell me why you are wearing Ratchet's watch then you pathetic little fuck? You want me to shoot you in the face right now you worthless runt? Don't fucking lie to me unless you want to die.'

I held my gun against his ear. Hot breath on his cheeks.

'Okay, okay. I'm sorry. Please just ease up man. It wasn't my idea, I swear. It was Andy what made me take it. Sergei wanted the pressure turned up to push through some player deal, to get the new agent in our pocket. And Andy likes to play games man. I just do what I'm told innit.'

'Where is he now?'

'I swear I don't know nufink man, for real.' I tightened the grip on his neck and squeezed.

'Look I just hear bits and pieces alright. They don't tell me the plans.'

I figured he was probably telling the truth. I wouldn't share vital information with this specimen either. I doubted he was part of the brains trust of some tight inner circle.

'Tell me what you know and don't hold back or you're dead meat like that giant-carnival-side-show-freak back there. Understand?'

'Daniel Ratchet was pissing off a bunch of people. He's been here five minutes and he's already sticking his nose in where it don't belong. He was asking the wrong questions about tournament fixing and contracts and the like. He's got Andy's back up and was holding out on Sergei. All I know is that's a silly mistake man, thems not to be fucked with them guys'.

'Where the fuck is he now?' I shouted. Patience draining fast.

'He had some information about the player fixing that goes on out here on Tour. He was snooping about with that crazy coach Wallace.

Had some kind of evidence on the scores and stats that prove a pattern apparently. Me and Sorlov had to find some fucking device, give him a slap. We couldn't find it and we couldn't find him neither.' Razor was flustered. Babbling. 'Listen mate. I swear, me and the caddies, we're just into a bit of gambling, making a few shakedowns from town to town that's all. It turns a nice trade and the bosses keep things organised so it doesn't spill over and raise too much bother with the local roz. They all know it goes on but we're just an irritant, a nuisance that can be put up with. They don't want to cause a fuss or Rublex will pressure the Tour into ensuring that they don't stop at that course next time. That's a fortune lost to the local community from tourists and the like. They don't want to miss out so they don't go grumbling when we come knocking on a shakedown. Besides, we've gone an made sure that we got some of the senior local police in these places in real deep on the betting ledger—they like a flutter and then when we hold what they owe over their heads they tend to do what we tell 'em. But honest, I didn't know it was going to get heavy. I didn't know they were gonna take him.'

I leered down at the snivelling rat, giving up his mates as quickly as he could get it out. As much as I needed the intel to get to the Target quickly, I also hated squealers who'd grass given half a chance. If you didn't have the balls to even make a pretence of holding out for your boys, then frankly that made me sick.

I reached back and slapped Razor across the mouth with the back of my hand. It's called a bitch slap for a reason. I'm right handed. The slug had hit my left shoulder so I was able to give it some real purchase. A whimper and then a trail of blood dribbling from the corner of his swollen mouth.

Shouting came from across the car park. I jerked my head backwards to see two uniformed hotel security guards running at speed towards where I held Razor over the Beema. They were obviously concerned at the altercation and intent in breaking up a fight in the grounds of this high-class establishment. That could mean possibly detaining us until the Guardia Civil arrived and that was not a chance I was prepared to take.

I met the first of the two uniforms with a scything right elbow to the side of his neck knocking him out cold. With my left hand still gripped around Razor's collar I pivoted and kicked the second skinnier guard hard under the ribcage. A liver shot. I felt his ribs crack under the heavy tread of my combat boot. The authority drained out of his face and a moment later he was groaning, contorted in pain and fighting for breath, as he squirmed on the tarmac.

I turned back to Razor. 'Who has got him? Where could they have taken him, rat?'

'I'm not sure, really I'm not. The boys have talked about a villa outside Madrid. A fat place where they enjoy whores and piles of coke when we've had a good run. It's like a reward for us to let our hair down now and again.' Nervously he looked up at me. A sideways glance. 'I've not been allowed to go yet.'

'Where is it? Exactly where?' I repeated slowly, bending him further over the bonnet so his back arched steeply, accentuating his vulnerable position.

'There's an address inside the hut.'

I grabbed Razor by his hair and spun him so he was bent over the car bonnet face down. Roughly pinned his arms behind his back and looped his hands and then ankles in turn with cable ties pulled from my pocket, cruelly pulling them tight to pinch off the circulation in his arms and legs. Slammed his face into the car hood with a single crack and let him slump unconscious to the asphalt, heaped between the two parked vehicles. Clutching my shoulder to apply pressure through the blood sodden shirt I jogged back towards the hut.

There was work to do. And now Hunter was on the scent.

Chapter 27

SPAIN. SESENA. OUTSKIRTS OF FRANCISCO HERNANDO VILLAGE.

Daniel Ratchet was broken. A hollow shell. Confidence shattered, now taken beyond any level of pain and suffering he could have imagined. Beaten, tied up, starved and humiliated. No resolution offered itself. He couldn't reason with these men given they barely spoke English. Besides, they treated him no better than an animal. Nothing existed behind the darkness of their eyes. He'd probably be dead now if Black Leather Jacket Man hadn't put Bad Breath Man on a leash when he did. His mind raced over the decisions he had taken in the last few days. Beseeching questions pressed to which there were no good answers. *Why had he been drawn in to looking into corruption on the Tour? What place was it of his? Why had he questioned the Aaron Crower contract and believed Bob Wallace when no one else had batted an eyelid about player fixing despite it probably going on right under their noses for years?* He scratched at the walls in anguish. *Couldn't he just be sodding happy for once? How could he not have taken this life-changing career opportunity without screwing it up?* He wondered if he would ever see his sweet vulnerable Matilda again.

Daniel languished in the dank lonely wallows of despair for an indeterminable period. The once significant and finely calibrated increments of time now blended together into a single, meaningless void. Bitter remorse licked mercilessly at his soul. Hope seeping into the deep pit of abject darkness where only the ashes of his dreams remained. The pitiful remnants of his life. And in macabre tandem to the grip of his misery, a sticky pungent film formed and tightened on his skin; the drying remains of excrement, left unwiped from his face.

Alone with his thoughts. Deafened with silence. He could hear the blood throbbing round his head and pulsating in his ears. Haunting kaleidoscopic images of his worried parents and life back home in Sheffield cascaded through his mind's eye. And then Matilda. His beautiful, brave Matilda who had somehow tried to warn him of the impending danger with that email. So close to happiness. How he yearned to see her again.

He awoke from a period of fitful sleep. Sat up, pulling cold knees close to his chest. The fact was that the choices he had made had got him into this mess. He couldn't change that. He was here and in this situation. He either lived or he died. They wanted his computer and presumably the incriminating evidence about Rublex and the golf Tour on it. They'd now made that clear. Wily old Bob Wallace had been right all along. If that was what they wanted he could just tell them where it was and perhaps they'd let him go?

Wise up son. Men like this do not go to these extremes just to let me skip off into the sunset when they get what they want. Right now that tablet and the video stored on it is probably the only thing keeping me alive.

If they were determined to gain the information, however, he knew in himself it wouldn't take long for them to extract it. He was weak. These guys knew what they were doing. It wouldn't take much pressure for him to spill his guts and that could be game over.

They'd said to wait for somebody to arrive. Some Russian or Eastern European sounding name. They certainly wanted the tablet. If they were Russian, then it had to link to Rublex and the dodgy agreement that he had raised concerns about. Things had started going bad right after that. The video he had recorded had proven that Sergei was involved in the tournament fixing. But surely he couldn't be involved in his kidnapping too? The man who had been so kind to him, so generous in lending him the credit card. Giving him that amazing watch. Could it be so?

He would reason with the man. Perhaps he could promise to keep quiet and this whole situation might disappear. But they'd murdered the driver of the meat truck. He'd heard the gunshots with his own ears and had a body dumped upon him in the car boot. That was probably to eliminate any link to his disappearance from the golf course. These men were ruthless. He didn't know who was coming or if it was even Sergei at all, but Daniel figured he didn't have much time. It was imperative that he now try to take matters into his own hands if he wanted to stay alive. His only option was to try and escape.

●

Daniel braced himself and slapped his own face hard, sharpening his focus. He scanned the room through tear-streaked eyes. It was practically bare. No windows. Flaking paint. The child's foam mattress. The cracked plastic bucket. The doors were locked and bolted from the outside, first a heavy studded wooden door which was secured by an outer gate of iron bars. Not a lot to work with then. Daniel smiled weakly to himself at the ridiculous situation. On closer examination of the plastic bucket he noted the crack had exposed a sharp edge. Daniel listened at the door for signs of movement, for any presence outside.

Nothing.

Appling pressure to the side of the bucket and working the crack further, he now twisted and cajoled the weakness in the plastic using an urgent ripping motion. The cheap bucket splintered at its base and Daniel kept forcing it until he was able to break off a single shard of sharp green plastic. He placed the bucket back in its corner with the broken side facing the wall. The shard slipped into a trouser pocket. Daniel's heart soared.

With no hatch in the door for interaction with prisoners, any bottles of water or what little food that Daniel had been provided with had been thrown at him round the corner of the opened door. This meant that if they wanted to see Daniel then they needed to unlock and open both doors, his only way out of there. Daniel rose to his feet and, for the first time since his ordeal, he started to stretch out his beleaguered body. His head was still sore and he had a fat lump of swelling across his right cheek with open lacerations inside his mouth from where he had been struck. His neck and the top of his shoulders ached from lying cramped on his side. He tried to shake it out a little. The movement made him wince. It felt like he was carrying a full set of cracked ribs. He checked and a smear of yellowish bruising, the colour of a rotting pear, covered the entire right hand side of his body under his shirt. Legs were weak and stiff from the forced inactivity and he lacked in energy from the poor nutrition of the previous few days. Besides this, he was functional and he was alive. And he was now also armed with a weapon, of sorts.

Daniel called out for water. Fairly gently at first and then building to a wailing crescendo which left no possible room for doubt that the prisoner needed attention. The footsteps started down the hall. Daniel braced himself. Keys rattled in lock, the crash of metal grate flying against wall.

'Shut fuck up, little bitch.' Gruff, staccato words like machine parts working against each other. Daniel waited behind the door crouched and coiled. Heart pounding. Bad Breath Man bowled through the door with a black leather belt in his hand, buckle swinging menacingly. Daniel didn't skip a beat. He pounced as soon as his captor was a step inside the door forcing the sharp plastic shard tight to his throat. He unwrapped the belt from the man's wrist, forcing his face against the wall of the dingy cell.

'Where are the keys for the door?' he demanded, and then rapidly, screaming in desperation, 'Keys? Now motherfucker!'

'In lock,' came the stifled, begrudging response. Daniel checked over his shoulder quickly to verify. Kicked him swift and hard in the back of the knee. Pushed the guard face first into the wall and down onto his shins. Darted through the open door, slamming it hard. The euphoric sound of turning key signalled the reversal of fortune was complete. Jailor had become the jailed. Trapped inside the very cell which had served as Daniel's own cage of despair. He couldn't actually believe that his feeble plan had worked. Freedom surged, dizzying him.

●

Pocketing the key, he spun around to face a long dark corridor expanding before him. He was alone, no sign yet of Black Leather Jacket Man. If the two of them had been summoned to his cell by his commotion there would have been no chance of getting through that door and the repercussions didn't bear thinking about. It had been worth the risk.

In one sweaty hand he gripped the plastic shard, the thick belt wound round the palm of the other with a foot or so of slack leather swinging pendulously from the weight of its heavy metal buckle. Edging gingerly forward in the dark, feeling like a primitively armed gladiator about to enter the arena and meet his fate. The hammering on the cell door and angry shouting from behind echoed along the corridor spurring Daniel forward with renewed intensity.

Scuttling through the darkness towards a semicircle of faint white light, growing broader with every step, made him feel that he was entombed within a labyrinth. Fear abounded. Instead, however, of being pursued by the Minotaur as had Theseus, Ratchet's paranoid imagination presented monstrous Russian guards at every turn. On reaching the end of the corridor, he arrived in a kitchen pantry area replete with large white porcelain sink, industrial-size washing machine, dryer, and other heavy utility units. Vast shelves heaving under the weight of food tins, bottles of oil, dense packets of flour and dried meats lined the walls. Industrial-sized bags of rice sat squat on the floor below. Out of one such sack, tell-tale grains spewed forth across the floor from a small hole chewed in its base: rats. Through the end of the pantry could be spied a large Spanish-style kitchen. Edging closer, Daniel peered cautiously through the saloon doors and found himself looking at the rear of a uniformed maid standing over a sink of steaming milky water, industriously scrubbing at a burnished pot. The kitchen was dominated by an old-fashioned and sturdy-looking range cooker. In front of this stood a beautiful, solid rectangular wooden table, the type perhaps sawn in a single piece from the heart of an aged Spanish fig tree. To the side of the kitchen, a patio door painted white with red trim led out towards extensive manicured grounds surrounding the hacienda.

He tiptoed forward. The maid gently sang to herself in Spanish, swaying her ample backside in rhythm to her simple tune. Totally preoccupied with her chores, back facing the pantry. Now, sliding through the swinging wooden gates, fearful that the slightest squeak from their hinges might alert of his presence, he crept soundlessly across the stone floor. Daring to not even breathe for fear that she might summon help and he would be recaptured. Only on reaching for the patio door did a surge of electric panic grip him as the dreadful possibility occurred that it may be kept locked. This exit was the only viable option to escape as there was just no way to make it past the maid without being seen.

She can't know what these men have done to me. She is local household help, can't be part of the gang. Perhaps I could reason with her? She might speak English. I wish I'd bloody bothered to take those community classes in conversational Spanish instead of sitting in the pub. No. Get real son, this woman is not going to help you, she is going to scream blue murder when she finds a strange man she can't understand creeping up on her armed with a plastic knife and a swinging leather belt.

With no choice then for it but to work, Daniel delicately tried the handle of the door, easing it down fully, feeling like forever for the lever to engage and operate the mechanism of the door latch. He pushed on it gently and, to his total relief, it eased open. Daniel finally exhaled. Stepped forward, gleefully puffing out his cheeks, expelling hot breath. A hasty glance behind him found the reassuring sight of fleshy bottom cheeks wobbling gleefully, unmoved from the sink. He stepped out into the dazzling sunshine.

Chapter 28

ENGLAND. LONDON. RIVER THAMES.
THE LONDON EYE. 14.00 HRS.

Derek Hemmings shuffled towards his turn in the queue, fidgeting nervously. He was decidedly ambivalent about the coming meeting. On the one hand, he was certainly excited about the prospect of seeing what MI6 had discovered and learning more about Boris Golich. The long overdue favour he had exacted from Simon Prentice should produce results that his limited resources were just not capable of. On the other hand, he certainly did not possess a head for heights and the prospect of spending the next thirty minutes suspended high above the river Thames in a small glass capsule, buffeted by wind and rain, filled him with dread. Whomever he was meeting apparently had a flare for the dramatic, texting him a series of complex instructions for the meet, finally culminating in his arrival here for 14.00 precisely. The London Eye was a busy tourist attraction on the bank of the river Thames, resembling a fun fair big wheel, providing stunning panoramic views across the city of London. *When it wasn't overcast and tipping with rain, that was*, grumbled Derek petulantly into the promotional pamphlet that had been thrust into his hand. Vertigo, meanwhile, didn't seem to particularly mind, whatever the weather.

The pod swung to a halt before him. Doors slid open grandly. The capsule had been allocated as private. Derek swallowed and clambered inside. A low block bench filled the centre of the space. A man in a smart military-style overcoat stood gripping the rail which traced around the centre of the big transparent egg, transfixed by something on the horizon. The doors swung shut and the pod rattled and shunted forward.

'I gather we have a mutual friend,' said Derek, opting to sit well away from the glass and keeping his eyes fixed squarely into the middle distance.

'I'm afraid not,' flashed the curt reply.

'Pray tell, why I am here then?' sniffed Derek beginning to lose his currently fragile patience. His stomach lurched and the pod began to climb the steep ascent on the wheel.

'Simple. You need information about Boris Golich. I'm here to provide some enlightenment,' answered Charles Hand dryly, spinning to face Derek for the first time and taking a single step towards the seats rooted in the middle of the bubble.

'It's a matter of utmost gravity. Have you been apprised of the context?' The now distinctly unwell looking civil servant was turning somewhat green around the gills.

'I appreciate that you are being inculcated to enter the British government into a business commitment with one Boris Golich and that you are rightly reticent so to do.'

'Yes. That indeed would be an accurate appraisal. Do you have the information I need to put a stop to this madness then?' Derek just wasn't taking to this man.

The Hand of God stared out over the steeple of St. Paul's Cathedral and across the City of London. He paused before answering. 'My organisation is currently engaged on a job that leads to the door of Boris Golich. There's been a crime. Kidnapping or murder of a young British man and in the course of our investigation we've been led to believe that several agents of the Rublex Corporation are involved.'

'I see,' said Hemmings wringing his hands tightly as furrows of concentration battled for pre-eminence across his disturbed and furrowed brow. 'A grave affair... What else have you discovered? I'm of the volition that the whole organisation is a front to launder substantial sums of dirty Russian Mafia money. If we can tie this to Golich and validate the origins of the money trail then the government just couldn't get involved with this cursed gas exploration deal off the Falklands. I need to prove it before it is too late. I fear that if we enter into this agreement now then the repercussions of opening the gates of Europe to Golich's stolen energy and the flood of black Vory money will be catastrophic.'

Hand looked down impassively, the act inducing Derek to continue with pressing urgency to make his point.

'Britain will be complicit, sir, in legitimising a corrupt Russian organisation which will contaminate both our fine reputation in the world order and damage relations beyond repair with our hard won international trading partners.' For some reason he flung his hand out grandly, gesticulating over the city that they were now suspended above. Derek's passion for his cause was even transcending into the theatrical.

'We may create some jobs in the short term but frankly I am of the mind that British-sanctioned gas exploration in the waters surrounding the Falkland Islands, to which Rublex have acquired pre-emptive rights, would place us at risk of inciting a new war with Argentina and their South American partners who contend territorial ownership. Only they would be better funded this time by their wealthy and insatiable Chinese paymasters who are avaricious for new natural energy assets.'

The Hand of God well understood the implications of war and he didn't appreciate being lectured upon the subject. He probed in response. 'Have you considered what will happen if the deal gets derailed? It may be wise to be careful what you wish for.'

'Well, yes, I have actually,' Derek sniffed. He considered himself somewhat of a political intellect and this was an opportunity to demonstrate that he understood both sides of the equation with a fair and balanced rationale.

'The counter argument, and a real danger that I think concerns the PM, is that if the British don't work with Rublex, then they may just approach the Chinese themselves direct, build an offshore platform as base for the workers and cut us out altogether. They wouldn't get a free ride for gas distribution into Europe, but I suppose the Chinese would open those doors themselves by leaning on the governments of the impoverished European nations like Italy, Spain, and Greece, whom they have been propping up financially since the great recession, through the purchase of government bonds as a backdoor policy veto.'

Hand had heard enough and was tiring of the meeting. Perhaps it was not such a good idea to have arranged it in a moving capsule that couldn't be left until it had docked. 'It's a complex situation indeed. But one that can only be handled with true integrity, Mr Hemmings. If you have searched your heart, studied the facts, and made your decision for the right reasons and in the best interests of Great Britain, then you will have done the right thing.' Derek's cheeks flushed pink.

'I will turn the use of our gifted researcher Ella Philips over to you. She has already started to uncover trails of laundered money through a network of accounts feeding into Rublex. Vast totals paid in primarily small denominations appear to be filtered through a series of legitimate subsidiaries and recycled back into the corporation.' As he spoke, Hand splayed his fingers to depict an ever-expanding web.

He continued. 'We believe that the kidnapping was instigated at a professional golf tournament in Spain and we have men on the ground at the scene right now. You may know that Rublex is the main sponsor of the European Tour and supports many of the leading players also, on an individual basis. When we were called in on this job, we looked into potential suspects and the murky past of their wealthy owner came to bear.' He stole a glance out over the Houses of Parliament unfolding beneath them. 'Seems he is keeping some pretty interesting company these days. Then MI6 got in touch and availed us of our support for the Foreign Office. We have joined the dots, so to speak.'

'Can any of this illegal financial activity be documented and proven beyond reasonable doubt?' Hemmings pressed for some proof.

The glass pod slowly continued its inexorable decent to the boarding platform on the bank of the river. Charles Hand turned to his companion and spoke quietly but firmly, his face expressionless.

'Our job at this moment, Mr Hemmings, is to find and to hopefully rescue a missing Briton. To bring him back safely. We are running out of time. Meetings such as these serve only as a distraction from this vital work. We are not tasked with investigating international organised crime, financial or otherwise. Not unless it helps to resolve our work faster and save the lives of those we are paid to rescue.'

'Sir, I implore you. I cannot do this on my own. I need to be able to demonstrate the veracity of these unfounded claims, to prove to the world that Golich is not who he says he is. I need documentation to show the Prime Minister. This is about doing the right thing. This is about serving the best interests of our country.'

Hand considered this for a good full minute before answering. He stood stiffly staring through the rain splattered glass over the city, lost in thought. 'As I have already said, we'll help you how we can, Mr Hemmings. Ella will pass over all that we have found to date. She can alert you to the trail of accounts. I'm confident that you will be able to follow it at your end to find the evidence you require to make your Boris Golich a persona non grata to the British government.'

'I understand. I'm indebted to you, sir. Thank you for your help. I have nowhere else to turn now.' He felt flat.

'Don't thank me. Save your thanks for Simon Prentice of MI6, Mr Hemmings. When it comes to doing the so called right thing, to which you alluded, MI6 never fails to disappoint. But, as you know only too well yourself, leverage only requires a single point of pivot.' The statement was both cryptic and barbed. The cabin rocked to a halt and the doors swung open mechanically, signalling the conclusion of their circular trip.

Chapter 29

I reached the caddy shack again, nestled amongst the eerie shadows of the truck park, door hanging open upon its hinges. Everything was as it had been left following the tear up. My eye followed a succession of discarded papers and upturned furniture leading to a massive, unmoving carcass, spread out like some freakish shop dummy twisted into an action pose. The body occupied a large portion of the free floor space. A chair balanced unevenly on three legs, the fourth impaling the eye socket of the dead man embedded firmly into his skull. A dark crimson puddle of viscous blood had seeped across the wooden floor, filling random cracks in the floorboards like spilt paint. Flies buzzed, circling the body in geometric oscillation. The pitiless scene would no doubt be discovered at some point soon. I needed to work fast. Gathering up pages of scattered documents and files from the floor I quickly leafed through them scanning the words as I went. Records of bets, odds for players finishing in specific positions in certain tournaments, names and numbers mostly. I didn't have time for this, nor to bust open those stubborn filing cabinets in the adjacent office and trawl through their contents. That could take an age and I needed to get going fast or the body count was going to grow. With Daniel Ratchet possibly becoming the next name on that list.

I checked around me in case I'd missed anything obvious. Something not necessarily in my nature but that I'd drilled myself to do in the field. Take a step back if you can before letting rip. So:

empty coffee cups sat unwashed in the sink. Kitchen towels and drying up cloths lay folded, unused. A packet of biscuits spilled their contents across the counter at the back of the hut. The walls were bare except for a fat cork notice board hanging on the side wall. Score cards, a detailed yardage map of the golf course, an extensive list of tournament tee times and a calendar were pinned to it. A topless blonde woman in a golf visor as white as her teeth, perched precariously on the side of a red sports car cupping a pair of obscenely large and inviting breasts. The month of May was well represented. To the left of the calendar a hand-written note pinned to the board caught my eye. I walked over and examined it. It read:

Pussy Palace! Carascalle, Mimbreras 4, 03201 ELCHE

The mongrel in the car park had mentioned this place where some of the crew went to celebrate a good streak on the take with coke and whores.

Pussy Palace circled in red with a residential address sounded like it must be that place. I tore the note from the board using my good arm, the other now hanging limply by my side as it throbbed in agony. A soggy, bloody angry mess. The pain scrambling my thoughts. Stuffed the paper into my pocket. Grabbed a wodge of kitchen towels from the counter. Dampened them under the warm tap and held the paper tight against and into the bullet wound in my shoulder. Stemmed the bleeding as I winced in pain.

Noises now from outside. I piled out of the hut fearing I would be disturbed at the scene of a murder at any moment. Tipping down the steps, I clocked two burly television engineers, matching beer guts spilling out competitively from under sweat patched T-shirts. They were hauling heavy cables out from under one of the trucks. At the level they were stooped, if they happened to glance ninety degrees to their right under the adjacent truck, they would spot the bound, gagged and unconscious body of the oily-looking guard I had neutralised earlier. I turned and moved fast, heading in the other direction. Head down. The fewer people who could provide my description after the carnage in the hut was discovered, the better.

I put some distance between us and redialled the latest encrypted contact number to reach HQ. Ella picked up right away as usual.

'Hey soldier,' she purred in her throaty, posh girls' school, accent, 'you making progress?'

Sex on a stick.

'Think so, Ella. Although I've gone and picked up some lead for my troubles.'

'Are you injured Hunter? A bullet?' she pressed urgently.

'I'll live. Although I need some space to get patched up before it properly slows me down. Don't worry about me. Just get me some intel, will ya? I've got an address and I need you to process it. I think they may be holding Daniel there. Find out what you can. How far is it from here? Whose name is the deed of ownership in? Try and get a visual on it, different routes in, point of access, that kind of thing. I'll check in with Mickey and then get down there as soon as I can.'

'Give me a little time, Tom. I'll check Google Earth but doubt it's got the detail you need. If that's so, then I'll have to hack access to a US spy satellite system. I'll come back to you when I can, but this stuff usually takes a few hours and I know we have to move fast. Use the time to get yourself patched up will you?'

'Sure. Thanks. Find me a way in. There's no point me just tearing off without preparing first. It won't help Daniel if I get taken out before I can even get to him. And Ella, you'd better tell the Hand of God that his mate is dead. They've killed Bob Wallace.'

●

The Range Rover was parked a mile down the road from the golf course behind some rusting oil storage tanks. I slumped into the front seat, breathing hard now and sweating. The throbbing hole in my shoulder clawed at my energy. I grabbed the medical kit, which Mickey had so efficiently provided, from out of the dash box. Tore the sleeve of my shirt off and tended to the wound. First I cleaned it gingerly with a sanitised wipe before taking a pair of small metal tweezers and fishing inside the hole of burnt, blooded flesh for pieces of shrapnel and bullet. The pain was immense. But bittersweet. At once like revisiting an old, unpleasant, yet strangely familiar place and being compelled to explore. I'd been here before and I knew the drill. Knew I needed to get the metal out of me fast, sanitise the wound, get stitched and bandaged up before I lost any more blood, before I'd become no use to anyone. Not to myself and least of all the Target. I worked nimbly and relentlessly. Clamped my teeth together to absorb the pain, pressure so tight on my jaw I felt the enamel itself might shatter. Proper job done and I'd felt every piece of it. I knew that most of the scraps of lead were removed as best I could. Black wiry butterfly stitches knotted in place. Only now could I risk numbing the pain. Before I dressed the shoulder, I fired up a hit of morphine and injected a weeping syringe needle direct into my deltoid. Then padded and bandaged it tight.

The phone lay idle. Nothing yet from Ella. She'd be a while yet getting me the information I needed, so I sparked a Marlboro cigarette, inhaled deeply and smoked it slowly to the butt. Locked the doors of the motor. Eased back further in my seat, inclining it below the window line. I closed my eyes and allowed the deep flickering purple and yellow light to wash over me like coloured dye spreading over blotting paper. I welcomed the colours as they sunk into me, feeling myself falling deeper away piece by piece, letting go of the pain. Slipping away. Letting go. Despite knowing that it always ended in blood. Always so much blood. Maria.

Sundown, yellow moon, I replay the past
I know every scene by heart, they all went by so fast

The slow repetitive click-clack, click-clack of the oversized ceiling fan as it lugubriously cycles above me. The sash window held open by an army boot, balanced on its heel and jammed tight between frame and ledge. The tread of its deep furrowed sole caked in dried flaking mud. Shouts and yelps and laughter from children playing on the road below. An old fashioned wooden cabinet. Drawers yawning open, crumpled clothing spilling out. The heavy framed mirror with its chipped corners, flecks of shaving cream splattered across it leaving an unintended language of indecipherable hieroglyphics. The old fashioned gramophone sits hissing and spitting as it sticks, relentlessly scoring across the slither of vinyl held beneath its predatory needle.

If you see her, say hello, she might be in Tangier
She left here last early Spring, is livin' there, I hear
Say for me that I'm all right though things get kind of slow
She might think that I've forgotten her,
don't tell her it isn't so

We had a falling-out, like lovers often will
And to think of how she left that night,
it still brings me a chill
And though our separation, it pierced me to the heart
She still lives inside of me, we've never been apart

Another drop of sweat scores its way down my forehead as if in slow motion, gliding over the contours of my cheek and jaw. Finally splashes onto my chest. I'm so sorry, Maria.

Fucking wildly, uninhibited, in the hot sticky afternoon. The air thick and heavy. The room smells unmistakably of raw sex. She should have been teaching local kids that day, part of the UN Aid programme. But I'd persuaded her to play hooky. Craved her every moment, every chance I could. This beautiful, intense, passionate woman consumed me. She had helped me to heal, helped me to become human again. Even after all of the horror and damage that I'd seen. That I had caused. After all of the horror and damage that I had become.

If you get close to her, kiss her once for me
I always have respected her for busting out and gettin' free
Oh, whatever makes her happy, I won't stand in the way
Though the bitter taste still lingers on from the night I
tried to make her stay

I see a lot of people as I make the rounds
And I hear her name here and there as I go from town
to town
And I've never gotten used to it,
I've just learned to turn it off
Either I'm too sensitive or else I'm gettin' soft

The fan spins. Relentless. Click-clack, click-clack. The gramophone still stuck on Dylan's' baleful lament. Imploring, reaching for one more touch, one more interaction with love lost.

And I do see her. I see her tied with rope. I see the pain in her eyes, pleading, beseeching me to save her. But I do not. I do nothing. I don't help her because I'm bound helpless myself. Each of my limbs tied and taped with clinical precision. No movement possible. And finally I am hooded. And in the dark recess of Hell that becomes me I strain to amplify every slightest sound, unable and defiantly unwilling to turn it off. I hear everything; the totality of barbaric detail. But I cannot help her. I'm fucking useless. Impotent. Maria.

And they delight in my suffering with each grain of her agony. No perception of depth or space. Just pitch blackness. I hear slow and purposeful movements. Steadied and practiced as they take their time.

Then the sudden violence of a rapid SHINK, SHINK slicing through the heavy air right next to my ear. I recoil from the savagery of the sound. Steel blade honed on whetstone. Guttural laughter sickens my stomach.

Then scrabbling, clawing. Heavy blows as bone meets flesh. The sorrowful whimpers. An animal broken and in pain. My Maria.

Silence, pregnant with meaning. Nothingness, an eternity in the pitted darkness that envelopes me. Until this is shattered with shards of screaming so primal that I may never quieten the sound again.

And I listen to the screaming as I strain with all force against the bonds until finally, defeated, I lie exhausted. Maria's begging has now stopped too, replaced only by a low imperceptible moan. Her suffering, the result of a series of sadistic cuts and intrusive insertions strategically executed, designed to administer the utmost pain possible to bear.

And I cannot escape the reverberations of this endless torture even as the door closes firmly and stillness is sucked back into the room. The click-clack of the oversized fan above us. The hiss and *spit of the old gramophone as it pours out its doleful lyrics. No noise from the street below now. And one sound cutting through it all. The persistent PAT, PAT, PAT that is hardly noticeable at first but that builds in deafening waterfall as comprehension washes over me. Maria bleeding out onto the wooden floor. I listen, haunted, as every splash takes her further away from me.*

Sundown, yellow moon, I replay the past
I know every scene by heart, they all went by so fast
If she's passin' back this way, I'm not that hard to find
Tell her she can look me up if she's got the time

I am with her until the end, sharing in her pain and her suffering. I absorb it until it becomes my own. This is my fault. She is innocent. Punish me for God's sake, please torture me instead. Maria, I'm so sorry.
Our bloodied souls entwined, conjoined in anguish.

And though our separation, it pierced me to the heart
She still lives inside of me, we've never been apart

Chapter 30

A wall of heat hit Daniel hard in the face. The bright sunlight stung his eyes as he eased through the kitchen patio doors. He had to put distance between himself and the house quickly. It wouldn't be long before he was discovered missing and the two thugs, who had been doing such a princely job baby-sitting him, came to take their retribution. He shivered in the sun, as he remembered the beatings. Running his hand tenderly across his throbbing ribs, Daniel prayed he wouldn't have to take any more.

The winding pathway that led away from the back of the house was made of smooth white pebbles, adorned on either side by a lush green lawn well-watered by a pulsating sprinkler system. Suddenly conscious of the loud crunch emanating from his footsteps Daniel stepped onto the damp springy Bermuda grass and broke into a jog. The garden was exquisite. Vibrant flowers of exotic reds, yellows and purples splattered across vast green bushes. Bendy fronds and stooping palms swayed together to some unheard rhythm all of their own making. Lemon trees dazzled with ripe yellow fruit nestled amongst a mess of dark green foliage. Humming birds and nimble bees busied themselves in the natural beauty, dancing and twirling under golden sunlight. It was a wondrous garden but Daniel was in no mood to appreciate it. He was scared. Dripping in sweat. Out of breath and racked in pain from the punishment he had absorbed in the preceding days. The aching in his ribs made it hard to suck oxygen into his lungs.

Head down, Dan. Keep moving forward.

The snap of a gunshot fired from the house cut through the sky, running through Ratchet like an electric shock. He ducked instinctively, although from the distance of the sound he knew the gun couldn't have been aimed directly at him. It was a warning shot. The escape had been discovered and he was now being hunted. Pressing on, not daring to look behind, branches tore at his skin as tangles of undergrowth were hastily brushed aside in the desperate attempt to make distance from the hacienda. That distance wouldn't hold for long though. Dogs barked, shouts and fractious voices abounded. A group had been rounded up to recapture him and he knew he would soon be surrounded from different sides.

Adrenaline was pumping around Daniel's ragged body as he set hard into a small copse of fruit trees, each encircled by a neat border of hay on freshly turned soil. He ducked and weaved through a tangle of dry caustic branches and pulled up clear in the shadow of an imposing dry stone wall at the back of the property. It encircled the grounds of the villa.

Huge in scale it had obviously been there for many years, a hand-built monument to privacy and protection from outsiders. At this moment, however, with the bitter irony not lost on him, Daniel was on the inside and desperate to get out. The baying of dogs beyond the fruit trees grew louder. There was no gate in the wall and nothing immediately visible to help scale it. But the wall was constructed in the old Spanish artesian method of laying heavy stones on top of and surrounded by each other with no cement or binding agent. Held in place only by their collective mass under the relentless force of gravity; serving resolutely immoveable under the heavy yoke of this most irrefutable of masters.

Daniel jammed his foot into a space between the stones and leveraged himself up using fingertips to claw at the vertical mass of rock above. Next step upwards he scraped his cheek on the rough wall and by the time he was able to haul his arms over the top, some fifteen feet from the ground, his fingertips were bloodied and his kneecaps swollen and split from scraping against the jutting chips of rock.

'Freeze or I shoot!' The shout came from below him. Daniel looked back into the garden to see a muscular brown-skinned man with a shaved head standing on the grass below, waving a semi-automatic machine gun in his hands. Two spiteful looking dogs snapped and scrabbled up at the base of the wall snapping at his dangling legs. Daniel hung there motionless. Heart pounded inside throat.

'Capture him you idiot,' came a barked order beyond, as the rest of the search party caught up. The muscled skinhead turned to look and Daniel took advantage of that brief moment with gun barrel lowered. Hauled his knee onto the top of the wall and without pause to look at what lay below, hurled himself straight over the edge and into the unknown.

●

Suspended in time, stomach firmly in mouth, the beleaguered body dropped through the air like a stone. The landing was hard, first hitting with his shoulder and then jolting the side of his hip onto the hard ground below. He rolled into a crumpled heap and moaned. Spat the dirt from inside his mouth. He could hear an argument ensuing behind the wall. Pulling himself to his feet and brushing himself down, Daniel looked cautiously up and down the dirt track. It was deserted except for what looked like farm machinery parked behind several dishevelled out-buildings. A little girl in a long dirty pink T-shirt and flip-flops several sizes too big, was playing with a hoop about a hundred yards away. She was totally absorbed in what she was doing, hadn't looked up. The drop had clattered him hard, knocked the stuffing out sideways. Daniel didn't feel he had it in him to set off running again. But he had to get away now. His captors would scale the wall in no time and, if he was caught again at this point, he was dead meat. Thinking on his feet, he limped across the road and, checking that he was unobserved, pulled open the rotted wooden door of a rickety farm storage building. The dry boarding splintered in Daniel's hands, flaking away from the door and he squeezed through the gap into a dark spacious void.

Inside and safely out of sight, the prey exhaled deeply, feeling the tension fall from his shoulders for the first time in days. He shivered and rubbed the goose pimples off his arms, noticing that the dark cool space was several degrees lower than the outside temperature, far away from the remorseless attentions of a vindictive sun. With his eyes adjusting slowly to the gloom, Daniel groped his way forward. Froze suddenly. Then grunting in disgust, spitting and scrabbling wildly at his face to remove the sticky tangled mess of cobwebs that had enveloped him. A bat flustered and flapped loudly, swooping from one corner of the dusty grain store to the other causing him to drop to the floor instinctively in fright. Straightening up and squinting around to get his bearings, Daniel could make out that the farm building was little more than a utility barn which had seen better days. It was now ostensibly being used for storing discarded old equipment and some rotting harvest produce. The floor was made of dirty, cracked poured concrete coated with discarded kernels of grain and dust. A rusted combine harvester, emasculated by the removal of its two front wheels, lay abandoned to one side of the space. A collection of ancient scythes, hoes, and a burly wooden ladder lay piled against a large wooden water barrel. One corner of the barn was dominated by bales of tightly packed straw stacked up high. Daniel nodded in appreciation. *That's got to be the perfect hiding place.*

Chapter 31

ENGLAND. LONDON. WESTMINSTER.

'Alexander, please could you come through to the office? I'd like to bring you up to speed with certain developments,' Derek Hemmings breathed excitedly into the intercom at his assistant. He leant back in the crimson leather chair, a smile of quiet satisfaction softly building across his crinkled mouth. A pigeon strutted pompously along the window frame through which a soft natural light poured into the room. The brusque meeting with Charles Hand had actually led to new avenues of enquiry and provided compelling information which had previously been inaccessible. For the first time since his meeting with Boris Golich at the club Derek felt like he had the upper hand, his instincts were about to be justified.

He'd stuck his neck out, at significant personal risk to his long and established career, in order to best serve and protect his beloved nation. *Done the right thing indeed, old boy.* And now he could feel, nay practically taste, that he was to be vindicated. But there was probably more to it and, on reflection, he had secretly accepted that this whole escapade was to some extent the daring mission that he had always longed to take for MI6; previously forsaken on account of the manifold sacrifices made for Alice and choices taken to provide a stable future for their nascent family. So yes, of course he had fantasised that the resulting fallout of saving the country from this poisoned chalice would provide the perfect swan song to an industrious and less than glittering career. Recognition. Perhaps some minor honour or other and the chance to finally get one over on that supercilious Scottish shit Andy Bartholomew. Derek Hemmings considered that he had every right to smile and enjoy the moment of impending victory.

'You wanted to see me, sir?' the smart young man purred as he stepped briskly into the office, snapping the door into place.

'Yes, Alex. I wanted to share some good news with you given all the late nights and assistance you have provided me in researching the Boris Golich situation.'

'Really, sir? That does sound exciting. And you should know sir that I'm always at your service. Privileged, in fact, to simply be able to aid you in your important work.' Gushing. Even by Alex Gontelmoon's very own high standards, forged in the machinations of an expensive public school education where prefects whimsically dished out bare-bottom canings to younger boys who hadn't displayed the requisite levels of idolatry, he was plumbing new depths of gratuitous obsequy.

Derek continued unabashed. Beckoned Alex towards him conspiratorially. He was rather fond of his assistant, considered himself something of a mentor. 'I've pulled some favours from the top. I'm being sent classified data imminently which will conclusively prove that Boris Golich is a notable crook and that the gas exploration deal with Great Britain must be halted at all costs.'

'That won't be happening any time soon, Hemmings,' boomed a brash Scottish voice from the doorway. Derek spun in his chair to find a red faced Andy Bartholomew striding confidently into his office, a slim manila file clutched in his hands. He was sweating profusely, a fat blue vein angrily throbbed on the side of his blotchy neck.

'How dare you fucking cross me, you useless old prick,' he seethed. Derek rose slowly from the chair to meet him, only for a fat sweaty palm to slam into his chest forcing him backwards into the seat.

'What the devil,' he blustered.

'You're finished pal. Your career is fucking toast. You're out. As of today, Hemmings. Sans pension too, *Old Boy.*' Andy spat the last two words with pure disgust, mere centimetres from Derek's face, expelling his diction with the vehemence of a motocross rider splattering a muddy trail. He continued: 'Our mutual friend here, Mr Gontelmoon, has been very enlightening regarding your undercover detective work, you sad old goat.' Andy gloated ostentatiously, fanning the loose sheaf folder in his hand whilst nodding towards Alex. 'You certainly are an ambitious young man. Aren't you, Gontlemoon?'

'Alexander?' Derek enquired sternly, his gaze unreturned as the young civil servant fixed a dogged stare at the thick carpet nestling around his fiercely polished shoes.

'Oh yes,' chortled the ebullient Scot savouring his moment of triumph, 'and a fucking good judge of character too it seems. Shown he knows how to back a winner wouldn't you say, Double-O Nothing?' An attempt at an exaggerated Sean Connery impersonation, designed to heap further humiliation on his older colleague.

'Alex here needed to back the winning horse to further his career prospects in Whitehall. Guess what? It turns out that was me, pal.'

'I don't know what on earth you are banging on about, Andy,' Derek retorted, his poker face devoid of emotion. *I'll see your stake and raise you double, to hell if my hand consists of a nothing but a bag of spanners, I'll bluff this out.*

'Have you been drinking at lunch again? I'm afraid I don't have time for your petty shenanigans. I really do need to get on with some proper work, so if you'll excuse me.'

'Everything's right here in this file, you slippery old bastard. The unauthorised activities. Refusing to sign the trade agreement and putting thousands of British jobs at risk. Disrespecting a powerful new ally of the United Kingdom and, to add injury to insult, making clumsy enquiries into Boris Golich's past to try and stymie what's already been agreed at the highest levels of Government.'

Derek sat stony faced, listening purposefully, calculating his next move.

'I have your letter of resignation freshly typed out inside this file, Hemmings. It's already been accepted. It just needs your signature. Sign it by the end of the day or I'll personally make sure you are escorted from the building under a dark cloud of dishonour and a wave of unpleasant negative publicity. How would little Alice like that then, d'you think?' he snorted.

At the cruel mention of his wife's name, Derek winced visibly. But by then Andy had already turned and flounced out of the office shadowed by a smartly dressed traitor. The simple file tossed upon the desk top, nestled innocuously amongst the other papers, understated in its deadly purpose.

Chapter 32

I woke with a rancid taste in my mouth and the familiar pervasive sense of bitter regret. Rubbed my milky eyes, pulled the knife from the inside of my boot. Gritted my teeth and tore the blade against the back of my hand slowly, deliberately. Blood bubbled fiercely to the surface of the skin and snaked its way back towards my cocked wrist. The body's reaction to the cut sent pain receptors instantly to my spinal cord, releasing chemicals which stimulated the hypothalamus in my brain. The signal to the adrenal glands, immediately released adrenaline and noradrenaline hormones to raise my heart rate, increase respiration, and slow down my digestion in readiness for a situation of either fight or flight. I'd learned this. Remembered it all well. It worked. But in this instance, the standard biological response to pain served a more powerful personal purpose. To cleanse my thoughts, to flush away the violent haunting memories that were branded onto my soul.

Besides, I needed to function effectively if I was going to be able to neutralise the savage criminals who had taken the Target. I checked my shoulder wound which seemed to be a little less tender already, not bleeding overtly. I redressed the burnt fissure scarring, padded it extensively with wads of cotton wool, strapped it tight and then rolled an Elastoplast tube over my arm to keep everything in place. Overall movement was slightly restricted but it would have to do. I popped a couple of pain killers into my mouth and swallowed them dry. It was time to get moving.

I gunned the engine of the Range Rover, squealing back out onto the road, heading in the direction of the mountains towards the Pussy Palace. I'd make some ground and check in with Ella for intel en route.

I drove for two straight hours, fast and efficient, mindlessly staring at the empty tarmac ahead of me. My thoughts were a binary tract vacillating between the memorised image of Daniel Ratchet's face and a parade of contorted dead bodies that I'd both encountered and generated in the past few days. The stark images played out to a backdrop of dull throbbing pain that licked away at my energy. Pangs of hunger finally roused me. I urgently wanted to reach the Target but experience had taught me to slow down, prepare, wait for the right intelligence before busting a move. That meant refuelling when I had the chance, so I pulled off the dusty highway round to the back of a single-pump petrol station that fronted a corrugated iron box serving as a restaurant. Parked up next to a beaten and rusted pickup truck, sporting muscular looking winching gear on its flatbed. The structure of the restaurant may have been rudimentary on the outside, but inside it was beautifully appointed. Instead of the cheap, uncomfortable fast food joint I was expecting, the whole restaurant was panelled with wood and framed with hanging baskets. Lovely bright green vines springing from the ceilings and walls. A pretty brunette waitress smiled a greeting at me as I clambered inside. She showed me to a table in the corner and instead of the typical offering of greasy burgers and all-day breakfast fry-ups that were staple nosebag in English roadside diners, I was presented with an extensive menu of delicious sounding tapas dishes. Too many options.

As I flicked through the pages of dishes listed within the fat menu, I reflected on my situation. On the choices I took. War had made me selfish. I often felt as if the normal rules of a civilised world didn't apply to me. I knew I had become desensitised to emotion and empathy, as if the nerve endings of my soul had been burnt away in some hellish explosion. I was torn between a harsh reality of danger, fear, and adrenaline; and a series of increasingly traumatic and inescapable flashbacks that transported me to relive moments of pain and cruelty so powerful that I could even taste the gunpowder in the air, hear the screaming. The scent of Maria's perfume consuming me. Always there in the background, surprising me at the most unexpected moments. Blurred lines. The means of escape I had chosen was to step on the accelerator of living experience. Not so as to hide, but in order to simply feel more. And to grip desperately onto what I could to stop it slipping from my grasp. But like a wet beer bottle, sometimes the harder I gripped, the faster it slid from my hands. I had rebuilt my life only to have it smashed from under me. I remembered when the pain was at its worst, taking more and more drugs until the Hand of God had found me and dragged me free. I still drank heavily and popped pain pills for fun. When alcohol wasn't an option, for operational purposes, I drank coffee like it was going out of fashion. And when one addiction had abated I merely substituted it for the next. Killing had first become normalised to me and later I realised it was thrilling, gratifying. And sex. I craved sex from the moment I awoke until the moment my brain shut down through either exhaustion or intoxication. I didn't care which.

But a man like me, with certain skills and experience, a man prepared to go to the dark places that others wouldn't, who could hold his hand inside the flame longer than the rest, still had his uses. I got the job done. And besides, there was always a chance that as long as I could keep lying to myself and everyone else that I was participating in normal life, that I felt the same as everyone else - that if I smiled at their jokes and cared just a little about their banal concerns, I might make it through to the other side. And that was all I needed.

I ordered a San Miguel. Slugged it down thirstily on arrival, immediately ordering a second. The recent action I'd seen had induced a powerful hunger, carnal appetites, and I knew that where I was headed things were going to get bloody. If I was going on a killing spree then I'd need to replenish myself.

I ordered greedily and leant back in my chair, taking pleasure from watching the little senorita waitress sashaying her arse around in those tight jeans and wiggling her hips between the tables as she tended to the other customers. The food duly arrived. Lots of little circular terracotta dishes filled the table and I helped myself to liberal servings of succulent lamb, plump beans, and crispy calamari heaped together on the same plate. Simple hearty food. I swallowed down the other beer, fully aware that the local police turned a blind eye to driving under the influence, something that was simply deemed to be part of the indigenous culture. The waitress took her time cleaning the table. She paused, deliberately catching my eye. 'You're English, no?' she said coyly, her head tilted to one side as she dabbed her cloth at a thick smear of split sauce.

'Yeah. English,' I responded, noticing cute dimples set into the soft skin of her rounded cheeks.

She continued, 'I like English. I study it well. I want to go there.'

I grinned up at her and she blushed, looking down at the table before returning my gaze, eyelashes fluttering. 'English are polite. Nice. Not like Russians. They are rough in here, you know. Always causing trouble. Problems for us. For my family.'

'You have Russians in here?' I countered.

'Yes. Often they stop here. Get drunk. Break things. Every month.'

'I see,' I muttered, eyes narrowing to slits. 'Well that's just no good, is it? I'm looking for some Russians myself. I've got business to attend to.'

She leant towards me and traced her fingers across my bandaged shoulder. 'I like that. I think you are a good man.'

I held her gaze for a long moment and nodded, pushing back the chair as I stood up. Slowly made my way towards the back of the restaurant and kicked open the men's toilet. I took my time over a long and satisfying piss and when I reopened the door to the washroom I found she was standing there swaying slightly, hands clasped together in front of her. She smiled, stepped towards me and, in a single motion, I grabbed her wrist, pulling her back into the men's toilet, closing the door behind me with the heel of my boot.

I kissed her hard, my tongue swirling inside her mouth whilst she backed up until flat against the wall. Her fingers played in my hair. I responded, running my rough hand over her elegant neck and throat and down over her T-shirt, squeezing her pert breasts hard. She gasped. Raised her knee upward and wrapped her leg around me as I pawed and mauled at that tight arse with a rampant hand. She was panting hard now and I was in no mood to take my time slowly with this horny little Spanish bitch. Finding the back of her head I twisted my fist, entwining it into her hair and pulling her head back. I sucked and bit eagerly at the soft elongated neck presented in front of me, inducing involuntarily whimpers and moans as she writhed again humping hard against me. Forced her forward so she was bent leaning against the wash basin, pretty face, already jewelled with beads of perspiration now just inches away from the stained cracked mirror. Holding one arm twisted loosely behind her back I tore her jeans and black lace panties down from over those smooth hips in one movement. She groaned deeply and arched her back, causing those curvaceous, buttocks to thrust out towards me. I growled and forced myself inside her sex with a single, primitive trust.

'Oh yes. Give it to me, bastardo,' she pleaded as I mercilessly banged into her, grunting as she lifted off her feet with each individual thrust. Retained the savage intensity of the coupling for several delicious minutes before finally exploding into her hard. With one arm wrapped around her waist I pulled her pelvis back onto me and ground my hips against her raggedly abused behind as forcefully as I could muster. Exhausted I collapsed over the back of my little Spanish conquest, crushing her with my weight and forcing her pretty face to squash flat against the cold mirror.

'Fuck. You are delicious,' I panted as she wriggled from underneath and turned to face me, pulling up her jeans from around her knees. She stood up on tiptoes and kissed me, running her finger tips across my face and down the vivid scar on my neck.

'Thank you,' she purred in that glossy Spanish accent. 'I want you come back and visit me when you return this way. You promise me no, English?' She looked earnestly at me before adding, 'Only after you find your Russians. I want you make them pay for me.'

I cupped her face in my hands and kissed her full and hard on the lips before pushing the door to the washroom open. Threw a fist full of euros onto the table, more than amply covering the bill for the meal and, I considered devilishly, a fair consideration for services rendered.

When I stepped out into the car park, the pickup was gone. I jumped into the motor, stretching my cramped muscles out in the car seat. Checked my phone, a red dot blinked reassuringly on the screen, highlighting the location I had requested with links to detailed access plans of the surrounding area. The whole process taking a few hours to set up. The party house where the hostage had been taken was still a good four hours' drive towards Madrid from my current location. The Target would have to sit tight for now. I sent a signal back to the team in England so that Ella could track the progress and keep Mickey informed of my movements in case backup or an escape route out of there was required should things go tits up. In response, a bright sonorous tone announced the delivery of a new text message nagging for attention. It was another of Ella's quasi-poignant military history quotes:

A good battle plan that you act on today can be better than a perfect one tomorrow.
- Gen George S. Patton

I grinned and stuffed the device back into my pocket.

Chapter 33

Boris Golich grunted as he climbed off the bony porcelain-skinned whore beneath him and wiped the sweat from his hairy belly. He rolled onto his side. Reached for the mobile phone set on the cabinet next to the circular bed decorated with a crumple of black satin sheets. He scrolled pensively through a long list of text messages. The humiliated young girl groped wordlessly at a puddle of skimpy clothing not long since discarded on the wooden floor. The oligarch didn't look up, instead he sighed aloud, a solitary line crinkling across the bridge of his nose.

He read the message a second time. Progress had been hindered with the UK gas deal and one man at the Foreign Office in particular didn't appear to subscribe to the very British sense of fair play that Boris regarded with such alien admiration. His men on the inside apparently had things in hand but, irrespective of this, Golich reasoned that not only had his crucial deal schedule been placed at risk but he had also been lied to and disrespected. Not an acceptable situation. After all, he had the very word of the British Prime Minister himself as to the validity of the deal and surely he was not a man with whom to trifle. He punched in a curt reply before tossing the phone idly aside. The casually dispensed-with whore slipped from the bedroom, head bowed, without a backward glance.

He had sent an SMS; Short Message Service. The radio frequency signal instantly transmitted a micro packet of code from the handset over the ether to the nearest base station. This, in turn, forwarded the incoming signal carrying the data onto the network of the receiver's mobile device at a slightly different frequency. The message was received only an instant later. The device in question was held by an Anglo-Russian sleeper cell deep inside the reaches of the British government.

It read simply: 'English bitch must die'.

●

Derek Hemmings knocked reticently upon the shiny black door of the Secretary of State for Foreign and Commonwealth Affairs on the top floor of a grand old building in Whitehall. Inside it sat Brian Weston, Member of Parliament, Cabinet Minister, Head of Department. A man more suited to bringing a cutlass to the negotiation table than a pen. Brian was Derek's ultimate boss, known ubiquitously throughout this building as The Minister. He was also the man who was about to bring Derek's career to a premature end, only months before he was eligible for full pension, gold watch and the litany of accolades and platitudes owing on account of laborious and devoted service to the country. It was a painful situation but one which could simply not be avoided. *Out-played this time, old boy* Derek thought to himself. What hurt the most was that he'd been shafted by the one man he truly detested above all.

'Come.' The solitary bark from inside the sweeping oak panelled office summoned Hemmings into the metaphorical lion's den. He turned the door handle, wiped clammy hands on stiff suit trousers, and entered, his throat dry and coarse.

Shuffling inside, the slim sealed envelope quivered slightly within his tight grasp. It contained the letter of resignation so kindly crafted by Andy Bartholomew on his behalf. He hadn't bothered reading it, knowing it would be as blunt and inelegant as the author himself. *No finesse. No class*, Derek mused to himself with disdain. The same skills and guile were just not required like they used to be in order to forge a career within the great halls. Now it was all self-promotion and crude attempts at powerbase alignment. Still, if that's what was required, perhaps he should have moved with the times and he might not be in the bloody mess he was now, and all over the principal of doing the right thing. What was the use in that if it didn't make one blind jot of difference?

The room was dark, lit only by the glow of a single lamp emanating from under an oversized green shade. He could make out two figures in easy chairs positioned to one side of the spacious, richly appointed room. A tall mahogany cabinet, glass doors yawning open, displayed a copiously stocked bar, generous array of cut glass, and innumerable bottles of spirits.

'Do come in, Derek. I'm told you have something for me.'

'Well, yes sir, I'm afraid I do'.

'Not your day is it.' A flat statement. No response required.

'I can't say that it is,' Derek sniffed bitterly. He stepped forward towards the cluster of Chesterfields extending the envelope, offering it to the Minister.

'I don't believe that any introduction is necessary?' Weston nodded towards the occupant of the chair with the back facing Derek. Charles Hand sat stony-faced, nursing a cut-glass tumbler of neat Scotch in which jagged splinters of ice bobbed, partially submerged. He turned slowly, directed his eyes to the empty chair without breaking his scowl and addressed Derek directly with the words: 'We need to talk.'

●

'It seems you are in grave danger, old boy,' the Minister intoned conspiratorially as he thrust a tumbler of amber liquid and chipped ice towards Derek. He continued, 'This is real James bloody Bond stuff, Hemmings, and I don't know how you of all people have wound up in the middle of it. Hand will fill you in, but it doesn't make a pretty picnic. What we're about to share with you is classified, and some way above your pay grade, I may add. We're only obliged to share it because somehow you've got yourself right in the fucking centre of the whole affair and have apparently just become a target.'

Derek stiffened, he felt the blood draining from his face. 'A target?' he stammered.

Now Hand interjected. 'Our team have intercepted intelligence which indicates that you are to be murdered on the specific and direct orders of Boris Golich at some point in the next few days.'

'Murdered? You can't be serious? But, how?'

'Probably a staged car accident, perhaps a hit and run. Or even the latest favourite, a bungled mugging after work somewhere.' A factual unemotive response.

'Christ,' Hemmings mumbled to himself. 'I suppose I didn't actually mean how... more like how come? Why me?' and his voice trailed off.

'Listen, Derek,' chimed in the Minister, 'you've put yourself in harm's way for the sake of the country. You've risked your career and you've pissed off some very serious individuals in high places in the process. It hasn't gone unnoticed.'

'I was trying to do the right thing,' came the doleful reply.

'And you bloody well have done, sir! That's why I'm refusing to accept that phoney resignation of yours,' Weston fired back, leaning forward and clamping his hand onto Derek's bony knee. 'Tell him what you know, Hand, for fuck's sake.'

'After our most pleasant meeting on the London Eye, my team undertook additional forensic accountancy investigation into the money trail. Ella really went the extra mile on this one. It seems that your gut feeling was correct, Golich's business empire is fuelled by dirty money via Vory criminal networks and all of it is washed clean in plain sight. The money streams are from six separate strands of Russian Mafia families, or 'Bratva', which literally means "brotherhood". Derek noted that Hand used the same splayed finger motion as he had done in the London Eye as he said this.

'In days gone by, Golich used to be the 'Obshchak' for these families, the man responsible for collecting the money from their feared brigadiers in the field and tasked with bribing the government and any other officials that got in the way. He used this position of influence to get, shall we say, a little too close to that arch-ruthless-bastard-in-chief who has occupied the office of the Russian Primacy for too long for anybody's good. He leveraged their relationship to remove the heads of the families, literally in some cases—exile in others—to seize a stranglehold of control for himself. He now holds the position of 'Pakhan', or overall head of the united family. It's the Russian equivalent of the Godfather. Boris Golich is omnipotent. And their crime money is now sanitised across the globe through a network of genuine business deals with established and respected organisations.' He stole a glance at the Minister. *Was that a sneer?* thought Derek.

'And, of course, high profile sponsorship deals in golf and motor racing. All gilded with a halo effect from the endorsement of irreproachable friends in high places and insidious political influence.'

'The PM?' proffered Derek guardedly from beneath a pair of arched silver eyebrows.

'I'm afraid so.'

'I thought playing golf at Queenwood together sounded just a little too cosy. I take it all this can be proved then. Unequivocally, I mean?'

'Before this major gas exploration deal cropped up, Golich had selected the benign environs of the European Golf Tour to funnel his dirty money through. As you know I have men on the ground right now searching for a sports agent who appears to have uncovered corruption in the sport at a high level through overt sponsor influence on players, illegal gambling and tournament fixing. We are working on the premise that this sports agent has since been kidnapped or murdered to prevent the information being exposed.' Derek listened, chewing off an errant hang nail from an already beleaguered thumb.

'As a body hasn't surfaced as yet, we have to work on the assumption that the Target must be withholding access to this information. The alternative that they've disposed of the body is not one that we can bring ourselves to consider right now when there is a chance he is still alive. Epecially given the defiant ethos of the Vory where they have never been shy about leaving their victims on display to perpetuate their terrible reputation.' Hand shook his head solemnly and continued.

'It's apparent that they are ruthless in achieving their own ends and will stop at nothing to meet them. The Pakhan won't deviate course. His immense reserves of money talk loudly and when Boris Golich talks, people listen very carefully indeed. Infiltrating the governing body of a sport to sanitise his company's image and launder some petty cash, however, is small potatoes compared to the Falklands gas deal, as you well know.' Hand nodded towards Derek.

'This deal impacts real people's lives, their jobs and their families. He has literally played world governments off against each other in their bid to woo him. And once you have entered that orbit, it seems apparent that there is no going back, regardless of who you may be.' The men let this hang there for a while as they considered the implications.

'He sounds capable of anything,' croaked Derek, somewhat despairingly and shifting his gait uncomfortably from buttock to buttock.

'Indeed so. The local mayors in regions where Golich's organisation owns assets, Russia, Kurdistan and Ukraine, are replaced at will or simply disappear if they don't play ball. It's the same with dissenting journalists. Anyone who crosses the little bastard. We have evidence surrounding a protest group of eight Uzbekistani wives from blue collar families, angry at the poor treatment of their husbands following an accident at a refinery which left people maimed. They pursued one of his companies through the courts. Each was found beaten and raped in their own homes on the same night. It was no coincidence.'

'Bastard,' snorted the Minister, before draining his glass.

'It gets worse,' continued Hand, voice unwaveringly steady. 'It was hard to find but there is a certain company located in the Cayman Islands, Hamilton Advisory, of which the sole director and employee went to Eton with our very own upstanding Prime Minister. It turns over seventy million a year and serves as principal advisor to a group of luxury developments situated on the Caspian Sea. These are 'black holes', vast chasms for Mafia to pour dirty money into and remove again freshly laundered. The residencies and casino resorts are supposedly constructed with the highest quality materials to the finest specifications, fit for the most demanding Emirate Sheik, but they never see a single visitor. The companies that build them for Golich use local work gangs, forced labour and cheap materials, if they even get built at all, that is. They are protected by local government from tax implications and inspection. A torrent of fee capital is directed from Hamilton Advisory via two numbered bank accounts both which are attributable back to the PM.'

'I'm afraid, Derek,' said the Minister censoriously, 'that it has become clear the PM is up to his neck in this for personal gain and he's endeavouring to commit Great Britain to a shotgun wedding with a notorious gangster. All under the noble subterfuge of creating countless jobs that will forge his legacy.'

'I bloody knew something was amiss,' said Derek stunned at the news. 'And Golich wants to get rid of me, I suppose, because I've been a thorn in his side and delayed the timings of the deal?'

'And challenged his authority, don't forget that,' chimed in the Minister. 'He has an inpatient intolerance for insubordination it seems,' smugly reflecting at the spontaneous alliteration. 'And you've gone and pissed the little thug off, Hemmings. Not the done thing really.'

Hand levelled things out again. 'We've uncovered a few more in Whitehall on the payroll as well, including your friend Andy Bartholomew.'

'I always knew he was a toad,' said the civil servant triumphantly, brightening up for the first time. 'What happens now then?'

'Well, for starters, it is imperative that you lie low,' said Hand taking control. 'We've arranged for you to stay in the building tonight, in the executive suite. Telephone Alice and tell her you'll be pulling an all-nighter. Make it convincing, the less she knows about this the better.'

'She's not in any danger is she?'

'Nothing immediate that we have detected. The sleeper cell has orders to eliminate you alone for now, although we know the Vory have a history of using family members as leverage and to mete out their frightful revenge. The Minister has authorised a plain clothes officer to be placed outside your home as a precaution, Derek. I have requested that he be joined undercover by Phil Manning, one of my Unit's guys who has been working the Golich connection in London. Alice will be safe, I can promise you that.'

'This is all rather unpalatable,' murmured the older man, wringing his hands nervously.

'We need to wait and let this play out a little further, so we won't be disrupting Bartholomew just yet. We need further firm evidence of collusion and corruption before any arrests can be made.'

'Indeed,' added in the Minister, 'the PM is a powerful man. Many have underestimated him at their peril. I'm bloody going to make sure he swings for this. We'll take the whole sordid matter to the press before Britain commits to a deal with that nasty Russian crook.'

'Oh, I'm certain that you will, Minister,' Derek spoke from the corner of his mouth, 'and basking in the plaudits for having prevented such a debacle on the international stage will no doubt reflect nicely on someone with aspirations for the top job.'

'Why of course,' came the dry response. 'Someone's got to show some leadership to get us out of this mess. But your part won't be forgotten either, Hemmings. You'll have your pick of where you want to go next, Commander Hemmings of MI6, is it? If you've still got the fight left in you old man.' He flashed a wolfish smile and settled back into the chesterfield, glowing with overt satisfaction.

The Hand of God stood briskly. He scowled, 'Gentlemen, when you've quite finished congratulating yourselves, there's a lot of work remaining to be done. Do not forget that people's lives still hang in the balance.'

Chapter 34

SPAIN. SESEÑA. OUTSKIRTS OF FRANCISCO HERNANDO VILLAGE.

The tranquillity of the afternoon was shattered as the wooden door to the barn was unceremoniously kicked open. Ratchet's hiding place instantly flooded with sunlight, a myriad of falling dust particles playing within the captivity of the sunbeams.

'Find him,' someone barked over the background score of snarling, salivating dogs. Men took to the barn energetically, kicking over equipment and rifling through grain bins, armfuls of produce heaped onto the floor. Black Leather Jacket Man stood legs apart in front of the mass of tightly wound hay bales, brandishing an Uzi. His weapon of choice lay nestled within hairy muscular arms like a sleeping baby. Blowback-operated, select-fire and closed-bolt, it is manufactured entirely of polymer for a lighter carry, the large lower portion of the gun comprising of grip and hand guard. The grip section was recalibrated from the regular Uzi, using Israeli engineer Uziel Gal's 1948 design, so that it can be operated with both hands to deliver greater control when in full-automatic fire given it is such a small lightweight firearm. The gun has a cyclic rate of fire of twelve hundred rounds per minute with minimum recoil and kick back. It's capable of delivering punishing volleys of bullets at sub-sonic speed, ripping apart any living thing within a deployment of fifty metres. But to its Russian master, it was simply a familiar old friend, sharing raw memories of putting the hammer down on the mean streets of St. Petersburg in the aftermath of Perestroika, operating as one of the Bratva's most feared Boyeviks. The term literally meaning 'warrior' was hard earned amongst the Vory as a family enforcer. The Russian letters 'МИР' tattooed on the back of his hand denoted the pride taken in a violent and murderous past.

He now held that hand aloft to command silence. The group responded by halting their frenzied activity exactly where they stood. Black Leather Jacket Man grinned.

'I know you in there, little bitch,' he called, mimicking a child in song. 'Come out and say hello, Daniel, or you going to eat my gun right now.'

The group waited for a reaction. Nothing stirred. The man wiped the corner of his mouth slowly, spat onto the floor and suddenly jerked the barrel of the Uzi upward spraying a rapid burst scorching into the haystack. He unleashed the entire clip, finger tense and white on the trigger long after the magazine had extinguished itself. He ran forward, a maniacal grin over his face and using the butt of the gun started to smash into the dishevelled hay pile, frantically searching beneath. Two others joined him and, within a minute, the entire stack had been torn apart. Loose hay was strewn everywhere across the concrete floor with errant scraps floating all around them. There was no sign of the escaped prisoner.

Ten feet away, Daniel Ratchet had witnessed the uncontrolled drama through a crack in the wooden barrel within which he crouched, submerged to his nose in stagnant rain water and pungent alginated slime. He'd initially considered the haystack as the perfect hiding spot. Heart pounding inside his chest, he'd been transported back to frenetic childhood games of hide and seek as packs of eager energetic cousins sought him out. Realising an obvious hiding place to him would be also one to his pursuers, he'd changed his mind and chosen to squeeze into the water-butt, soaking himself to the skin in the process. Now, petrified with fear and holding his breath to the limit of consciousness, Daniel didn't dare move a sinew.

From his hiding place he watched transfixed as the little girl in oversized T-shirt and flip flops that he'd seen playing innocently with stick and hoop on the dirt track outside was frog-marched into the barn. She was shoved to the floor in front of Black Leather Jacket Man, who reached down and hoisted the child to her feet by a fistful of hair. Watched her amused, smirking, as she squirmed and screeched like a scolded cat.

'You see man in barn? Did you see man go in barn or no, little pig?' he shouted into the crying girl's face. Unable to form the words out of shock and probably unable to speak English too, the child kept shaking her head vigorously, tears streaming down her grubby face.

He called out into the space of the barn. 'Daniel. Now listen good little bitch. You come out and say hello or I gut this pig right here.' He pulled a long stiletto blade from a sheath on his belt and held it tight against the girl's throat as she struggled for breath through uneven gasps and sobs. 'This is your fault, Daniel. You can save her if you come say hello. Don't cause this problem for little pig. Come out here right now bitch.'

Defeated. Beaten. Exhausted. No move to make and no will to make it. Trapped. This was finally, at last, the very end.

Daniel emerged from the barrel at the side of the farm building, water pouring off him from every angle onto the floor. He was a total mess. The putrid water stung at his eyes. The men rushed towards him as one. His bedraggled frame was hauled up and thrown onto the unforgiving floor. Shaking his head to clear it, he opened his eyes in time to find a meaty fist closing in on his face at prodigious speed. It smashed into the bridge of his nose and Daniel felt cartilage splintering, blood spurting uncontrollably. He reached for his face, attending to the damage. As he did so another blow rained in forcing his palm to bang hard against his mouth, knocking his two front teeth back into his mouth in the process. He grunted with pain. A stiff knee to the groin put him down again. Gasping for breath on the cold stone floor, he watched the legs of the little girl scurrying away as she escaped to freedom through the open barn door.

Chapter 35

SPAIN. CARASCALLE, MIMBRERAS 4,
03201 ELCHE. 21.24 HRS.

I parked the Range Rover alongside a high metal fence lined with conifer trees, dead straight and as far as the eye could see. Lazily scratching my finger down the length of my scar, I popped the soft pack and jammed a Marlboro into my mouth. Scorched it alight. I hadn't been passed by another car for near on twenty minutes since I pulled off the main road. I was scouting the grounds of the address found in the caddies' hut, using insights sent through from HQ for discreet access points to the party house. Pussy Palace! I smiled to myself. *I'm gonna take these Russian pussies and fuck 'em over real good.*

I waited until dusk started to draw in and then grabbed a canvas bag of assorted goodies that Mick had provided earlier: namely stun grenades, ammo clips, and a couple of spare pieces. I was tooled up, itching to get inside and spring the Target.

The location to launch the assault had been specifically identified. A mesh metal fence at the side of the property obscured from view of the main house by fronds. It swayed and folded awkwardly under my weight as I scaled it, making it hard to control. I flipped over the top, landing on my feet in a crouching position. An automatic video camera was rotating through an arching sweep of the perimeter along either side of the grounds. Ella had provided intelligence that each sweep took twelve seconds before it returned to cover the area of assault. I commando-crawled forward quickly into a clump of bushes a couple of metres out of the range of visibility. I mentally regrouped, then cocked the Beretta. If the guys inside were anything as mean as the ugly giant bastard I'd tangled with back at the caddy shack, then this was going to get messy. I scanned the grounds again for signs of guards or dogs but saw none. Darkness was descending hard and remaining stationary was not an option unless I wanted to take a bullet in the back of my skull.

Comrades often told me that they were bewildered by my ability to recall seemingly innocuous details from theatre and the heat of battle that they had long since shed. Otherwise important facts in a real life grown up world passed me by. But when I was in a heighted state of arousal, deep in the thick of the fight, I seemed to notice everything. To drink in the detail, to feel the energy, to notice enhanced colours and smells. Everything slowed down. My music.

Edging closer, I took in more of the property. Built on several tiers, it sprawled out in ungainly design, appearing uncomfortable with its own vulgarity. Rather than retaining the beautiful traditions of classic Spanish architecture, the house and outbuildings were a mix of extravagant modern opulence and overbaked kitsch. Together it simply didn't work, resulting in an overblown statement of tasteless nouveau riche misjudgement. The marbled drive was dominated by a water feature that would have been out of place at a palace three times the size of the main house. Sculptures of five life-sized stone stallions reared up out of foaming jet streams which shot twenty feet into the air. The front of the house boasted pillars fit for a Roman emperor's mausoleum, framing a door of such stature that it looked as if it might hold an army at bay for weeks. The unmistakeable pulse of bad eurotrash dance beats emanated from within. I kept moving fast. Crouched low. Head down. Finger comforted by the torque of trigger pressure. Those old pals, flesh on metal.

The back of the property was a similar grotesque coupling of bad taste aligned to ostentation. A massive swimming pool, which I could just about tell from the ground was designed to resemble a water-filled palm tree, took up the majority of the space. It came complete with hot tub, a deserted bar in the centre of the main pool with stone columns rising to serve as seats. Brightly coloured inflatable lilos, rubber rings, and what looked like an inflatable sex doll floating face down, occupied the gently rippling water. The music was louder from the back, the patio doors were wide open. From my vantage point in the shrubbery, I watched a tableau of figures on the deck and through the glass doors just inside the house. A woman dancing with her hands in the air and sporting an obscenely skimpy hot pink bikini was writhing between two men, one slugging from a large square shouldered bottle of spirits. Three serious looking guys, each competing for the award for heaviest stubble, played cards round a small table, piles of notes and coins stacked proprietarily in front of them. Fat cigars glowed in an ash tray, surrounded by bottles of beer perspiring in the heat. A Magnum revolver had been tossed casually aside on the glass top.

I turned my piece over in a meaty palm, considering the options. If I was going to get the Target out quickly, then I would need surprise on my side, and that simply wasn't going to be achieved by kicking things off with a blazing gun fight. I revisited the access points on the building that Ella had identified and sent to my phone.

At that moment, a fat man in long shorts and socks, stomach proudly protruding and hanging low over his belt, staggered out of the double doors. Wrapped within the grasp of one thick arm was the squirming skinny body of a teenaged girl dressed in heels and a yellow bikini. His other hand clasped a bottle of tequila by the neck. Clearly in a party mood, he was trying to encourage the others to join in the revelry. Swearing loudly in what sounded like a joke Liverpudlian accent, he gesticulated grandly. I recognised the face from Ella's 'cast of characters' and had clocked him outside the caddy shack. It was Billy Boy, the caddy. An unpleasant character and proud recipient of a long arrest record, mainly for bar fights and vandalism. One charge was for indecent assault on a German tourist who had rebuked his incessant flirtations only to be lifted off her chair, laid on top of the bar and held down with one arm whilst he buried his face under her skirt literally eating her out in front of a baying crowd. She'd fled in tears to the police station whilst afterwards Billy would claim to all and sundry that she had loved every second. The vicious bite marks and bleeding across her vagina and inner thighs, coupled with months of counselling thereafter, told of a very different story. His identification at least verified I was in the right place.

Unnoticed, I doubled back in the direction I had just come from. Try as I might, I realised some time ago that I really wasn't cut out for stealth. With my build, I was more of a brute force kinda guy, not made for reconnaissance detail. Some of my pals in the mob had been perfect at it. Small wiry guys who could run all day carrying three times their body weight in backpacks and who could fit into tight spaces to become practically invisible when staking out the enemy. Tough as nails, some of those boys. They'd follow you into Hell and back. But this guy, Tom Hunter, was more the proverbial sledgehammer that you'd use to crack a walnut. It was well documented that I loved a nasty tear up, something even the top brass in the army had recognised by decorating me with more pieces of tin than could fit across my chest. That was before I got myself kicked out for being a naughty boy though. But not before the Hand of God had protected me from the powers that be time after time.

I tracked around the side of house, keeping as low as I could. The darkness was falling hard and, from what I'd seen, these guys weren't making security their number one priority. I was pretty confident that I had remained undetected or I sure as hell would have known about it by now. Moving quickly, I located the ground floor window I was seeking, open on the inside for ventilation but with a metal screen in place for rudimentary protection. Behind the window lay a storage room, a graveyard for some decrepit looking sun loungers, parasols, a washing line contraption and some pretty standard household appliances. I checked around me before extracting the hunting knife from my boot and jacked it firmly between the wooden frame and screen for leverage. To my surprise it pinged out of place instantly and flipped back into the room, rattling angrily on the concrete floor. This was clearly only a token effort at security, one designed more to keep out stray cats than highly trained killers.

I rested my forearms on the window ledge and heaved myself up so that my torso was half-wedged through the open space, legs dangling below against the wall of the house. It was a pretty tight squeeze but I could twist and wriggle my shoulders so that I fitted through the space and, using my hands out in front of me to take my weight on the floor, I was able to flip my legs over to follow me through. I grimaced and ground my teeth together as I sucked up the pain that shot through my shoulder. It was an untidy dismount and wouldn't have won many points from a panel of discerning gymnastic judges. Regardless, I was inside.

The corridor which led to the storage room was empty. They were probably keeping the Target tied up in a bedroom somewhere on the upper floors but I needed to check each room as I went, both to ensure that I didn't miss him and also to secure the area so we wouldn't be met with a nasty surprise that might outflank us on our retreat. Aside from the storage room, which was nothing more than a drab concrete box, the rest of the house, as far as I could make out, was done up with incredible finery in bold reds and golds. The floors were made of a polished black wood, punctuated at intervals with delicate ornamental tables standing in splendid isolation displaying individual artefacts, statues or sculptures. Huge canvases of modern art, splashed with eccentric arrays of colour upon them, adorned the walls at every turn. For a guy like me who had lived out of a bag country to country and from job to job for the last few years, it all seemed a little overcooked to say the least.

I checked the first two rooms and found them empty. The first a spacious gym with hard plastic flooring was filled with exercise bikes, treadmills and littered with freakishly sized free weights and dumbbells. The plasma screens were left blaring out music videos to an invisible audience. The second room was filled with a large mahogany dining table anchored in its centre by four chunky silver candlesticks and surrounded by formal upholstered chairs. An oil painting of Red Square in Moscow dominated from one end of the room. The spectacular bay window looked out across the brown hills to the east and beyond.

The door to the third room along the corridor was left slightly ajar. Without needing to peer through the crack between door and frame a succession of animalistic grunts and moans emanating from inside left no doubt that it was occupied. A voluptuous black woman was kneeling on the couch facing towards the door, sandwiched between two men. She was being hammered from behind at one end by an angry looking man covered in spindly tattoos, inked across his arms and torso like the musings on an errant schoolboy's desk. All stars and crosses and sickles and scythes. His jeans slumped untidily around his ankles, a black

T-shirt rolled half way up a matted hairy stomach. At her front, another equally unpleasant character was fucking her mouth with remorseless aggression. He was pulling at the nipples of her huge chocolate-coloured tits, flopped over the edge of the couch, using them as handles to bring the lips of her plump mouth closer towards him. He had his back to the door. The three of them were totally engrossed in their feverish joint enterprise.

One of the men called across at his buddy. 'Next time we come back, we stop off again at the roadside restaurant and take our sweet time with that hot little piece of shit waitress. I want to tie up her daddy and make him to watch as we tag team it. Remember how we laughed when Sorlov made the slut dance for us?' It was a Russian accent.

'Hell, yes. She'll take some punishment and then serve us beer all night long.' High fives all round. They were very pleased with themselves.

Russians, golf caddies, party in full swing just like Razor had said. This was all I needed to know.

I reached round the door frame and coldly fired a shot over the left shoulder of the blowjob recipient and into the forehead of the man facing towards me as he took the surprised girl from behind. His eyes remained open for the short journey it took the .22 calibre bullet to bore through his skull, demolish the frontal lobes, penetrate the cortex and then exit directly through the cerebellum at the back of his brain. The devastating high impact damage was delivered in just a fraction of a second. He collapsed backwards, the look of ecstasy from pumping the luscious bottom of his juicy black whore, still frozen across his face. Time now hung in glorious suspension with the next events seeming to occur simultaneously. His partner in crime spun around as I stepped fully into the room to engage him, callously slitting his throat in single motion causing blood to glug and spurt from the artery in his neck like a can of beer shaken before opening. The girl looked up shrieking unintelligibly, her face and naked torso now drenched in her 'lover's' claret. I reached down and bitch slapped her with the back of my hand hard onto the floor to shut her up. Kicking the bleeding man out of my way as he scrabbled on the polished wooden tiles creating frantic patterns with his own voluminous bloodletting. I moved around the couch to prevent the whore from crawling away to get help. Heard spluttering and gurgles as the life drained out of him, one hand clamped to his throat.

'Shut the fuck up unless you want to get smoked too,' I growled into her terrified face. Tears seeped uncontrollably through thick false eyelashes. Her glossy lips trembled. The message was clear but, in case she didn't speak English, I held my gun up to her head and put my finger to my lips demonstrating that silence was required or there would be consequences. Grabbing her by the hair, I pulled out the verifiable identification photograph of Daniel that Ella had sent to my phone. Shoved her face into it. 'Where is this man?' I said slowly and clearly. The woman was sobbing. She looked at the picture and shook her head. I asked again relaxing my grip, concerned she was about to lose it altogether.

'Is this man here? Is he in this house?'

Still trembling, she shook her head again. 'No man. Not here,' was all she said.

I heard shouts from the garden. I'd been compromised. I hadn't used a silencer on the gun. Noting the number of occupants to the property, I had figured that we were never really going to be able to simply slip in-and-out unnoticed. May as well make an entrance. And from what I'd seen about the way that these guys operate, if there was a little noise and a little blood as we got to know each other, then so be it. Leaving the room in carnage behind me, I pushed out again into the corridor and then into the main hall. A barrage of sub-machine gun fire poured down on me from the first floor landing atop a broad staircase. I wasn't hit but the marble flooring around my feet was chewed up badly enough for me not to want to ponder the merits of holding my position whilst he readjusted his aim. I rolled forward and took cover behind a smallish palm tree potted inside a huge terracotta jar. The machine gun rattled, sending relentless swathes of bullets into the walls all around me. I steadied myself and pumped three rounds up and into the general direction that the fire was coming from, buying some time. Sprang a stun grenade from my pack and tossed it onto the first floor balcony. The explosion is designed to elicit sensory deprivation to those within the blast vicinity using the combination of huge sudden noise impact and white light flashes. It's quick, unexpected, and very effective. I tossed the bomb and moved from my cover point simultaneously. The distraction had its desired affect and I was able to sprint directly under the balcony to escape the sweeping range of the machine gun. After the shock of the stun grenade had faded I heard movement above my head, a regrouping. I listened carefully, adjusted my position slightly and then, holding the Beretta aloft, emptied the remains of my clip up into the plaster ceiling. A heavy thud and cries of pain told me I had hit the unsuspecting shooter standing directly above me.

If I was going to find Daniel quickly I figured that a hostage could take me to him and provide some bargaining power to get us out alive. I pushed against a closed door and entered inside a games room hosting an empty drinks bar and full-sized pool table with balls scattered over an immaculate blue baize. A cinema-sized plasma screen on one wall was silently showing hardcore porn. On the other hung an enormous eight foot square mirror framed with heavy gold leaf painted on dark wood. I couldn't shake the impression of encountering a ghost ship cast adrift without its crew. Turned to back out the way I had come. Suddenly a tall cupboard built into the wall sprang open and two men burst out at me shouting and waving pool cues. Seems they had been shooting a game together and enjoying the flick when the gun fight in the hallway alerted them to an intruder and they had holed up until now. The pool cues indicated they weren't packing heat. I raised my gun and coolly squeezed the trigger. Nothing. Hadn't changed the fucking clip. The bullets were totally spent and the timing couldn't be worse. Now the first guy was on me and using the end of the pool cue to smash into my wrist, causing me to drop my piece, much use as it was anyway. I pivoted in a single deft turn and stamped down on the inside of his knee causing him to buckle. As he fell I caught him with a powerful uppercut hearing the crunch of teeth as jaw shattered against fist. I caught his shoulders as he slumped and slammed his face into the hard wooden frame of the pool table rendering him out cold. Three moves. Three seconds. Punishing and precise. His mate came at me with renewed vigour. He was a big solid lump, probably six foot four and heavy set with it. My guess was nineteen stones of fat and muscle. Soya meat, as I tended to call it.

Too many weights makes you slow, mate, I observed wryly to myself, remembering the words of a fearsome Maori hand-to-hand combat instructor that the Hand of God had used to drill us. *Size and strength matters less than precision of action and taking the right decisions quickly. Hit first and above all hit hard. Do whatever it takes and get out alive.*

But now he was close in, real close, and speed wasn't a factor as he was able to force me over the pool table, choking me from behind with the cue he was wielding. He pinned me down and squeezed the grip of the wood against my neck. This was tight. I was exerting a massive effort of brute strength just to keep the cue from crushing my wind pipe. It was a fairly even match. If I didn't wriggle free somehow before I blacked out then this was going to end very badly. I kicked out wildly but he used his massive thighs to pin my legs under the table, leaning every ounce of bulk over and on top of me. Snarling face inches from mine, so close I could smell the stench of tobacco on his breath. My right hand was wedged between the cue and my throat. I used my left to blindly grope around on the table for a ball. Checked myself. Given the position my body was trapped in, trying to smash a pool ball against his head wouldn't do much damage and might only serve to really piss this animal off. So I gambled. Recoiling my left arm to generate leverage, I flung the ball as hard as I could up and into the mirror hanging behind us. It shattered instantly with a loud crash sending showers of razor sharp shards flying down onto the back of my assailant. The impact shocked him into loosening his grip for just an instant. The heavy mirror frame itself followed seconds later collapsing from its hook and crashing onto the Russian's neck. Pieces of mirror had flung into my face and I could feel trails of warm blood snaking their way down my cheeks. I heaved the brute up, rolling to one side. He shook the mirror from his back and lumbered towards me. I wasn't going to let myself get into another bear hug with fatty again, so I reached across him diagonally and grabbed the wrist of his right hand as he flung out a fist.

Now spun and bent at the knee to grab at the handle of my knife, left hand to left boot. Rose fast, pivoted in an arch on my toes and hurled a left hook stabbing the blade several inches inside my attacker's right ear. He howled in agony and I thrust forward, relentlessly twisting and driving the knife deeper and deeper, working to bore it into his head. I kicked him in the stomach and watched him sag to the floor like a sack of wet cement. No way these guys were all just golf caddies. They know how to shoot and they know how to fight dirty. Got to be Russian ex-soldiers if you ask me.

Thus far I counted four-and-a-half to five bodies, depending on the fate of Machine Gun Harry upstairs. But still no eyes on the Target. I reloaded a fresh magazine clip into the gun, wiped my blade clean on the shirt of my recently deceased games partner. Slotted it back into the sheath inside my boot.

●

The sound of shouting and pounding feet alerted me to new company. Probably the guys from the card game, I figured. I exited from the games room and decided to break for the stairs. If Daniel was here after all then I knew now he must be on the upper floor. Three guys packing an assortment of revolvers and other small arms appeared in my line of vision, firing wildly. I crouched to one knee, exhaled to steady myself and returned fire managing to catch one of the group flush in the thigh. He flew backwards like a cigarette tossed from the window of a speeding car. I rolled another stun grenade towards them and, using the flash as cover, bounded sideways across to the stairs, shooting intermittently in their general direction. Checked for enemy contact around the stairwell and found none so I turned my attention back to the others. I took the steps three at a time, firing continuously ahead of me to ensure a clear path and pin back any prospective ambush in waiting. Reached the top deck. I dived flat onto my stomach, rolling to the side and away from the line of fire. Landed on the injured shoulder and it fucking hurt like hell, the pain masked until now by the rush of so much adrenaline. I just shrugged it off, growling. There were more urgent matters at hand.

I scoped the surroundings. The centre of the upstairs landing was occupied by a figure slumped against the wall in a pool of blood, head resting upon chest, a redundant AK-47 submachine gun upon his thighs. The shooter from my earlier contact in the hallway had bled out from the bullets fired from underneath. Judging by his clothing and a congealed puddle of blood spooling around his groin area, death would have been as slow and painful as much as it would have been unexpected.

I took to my feet. Pressed on, ignoring the dull aching pain resounding in my shoulder. I fired a volley of bullets into the base of the closed door of the nearest bedroom to drive any inhabitants back. Kicked it open and entered the room. Beyond the bed and handcuffed to a thin metal pipe that ran the length of the skirting board sat two women huddled together on the floor. I say women but these were little more than emaciated teenagers, heavily made up and wearing tawdry see-through night dresses of the sort that might be found in the window of a grubby back-street sex shop. I recalled the name of this place scrawled on the address found in the caddy hut: Pussy Palace. From what I'd seen so far, this fine establishment was doing its best to comply rigorously with the Trade Descriptions Act. It was obvious that these girls were being kept locked up like this until their talents were again required by the guests of the house. It made me sick.

'It's okay. I'm gonna get you out of here. Don't worry. Do you speak English? Engleese?' I soothed.

'Yes. God. Thank you,' one of the girls replied behind pretty tear-stained eyes. 'I'm American. She's Russian. You've got to help us. They tricked us into coming here weeks ago from Puerto Banus. They had a yacht. Told us there was a party, told us there would be modelling scouts there.' She scrambled to her knees reaching out her hands.

Moving fast and keeping one eye out on the door behind me I ushered the girls to scoot to the side before putting a single bullet through the pipe, shredding it. A hard stamp with a size fourteen combat boot broke it apart and I helped the girls to slide their cuffs off between the two broken pieces. They'd have to figure out how to get them off their wrists later for themselves but at least they could run and make a break for freedom now.

'Are you okay?' I asked.

'I don't know,' she replied shaking her head as the tears streamed down her cheeks. She looked pretty broken. The Russian girl kept her eyes to the floor.

I pulled out the picture of Daniel and spoke quickly. 'Have you seen this man in the house? He's been kidnapped. Do you know if they are keeping him here?'

'There's no one else here. This is a party house. We've been raped in every room of this shithole. The guests come and go. So do the whores. The guards aren't sober enough to hold a prisoner here that isn't for their own entertainment.' Her face was contorted with disgust as she spoke and her hands involuntarily moved to cover her body as if to offer some kind of protection from the memory.

'Fuck,' I hissed under my breath. 'This is the wrong place. I've got to move and move now. You girls make sure you get out of here. Run and don't look back. You sure as hell don't want to be here when these animals come looking.'

I'm not paid to be a hero. I'm paid to spring kidnap Targets and bring them back. Dead or alive. *Focus on the job in hand, do whatever it takes. Don't look back.* Didn't give it a second thought leaving those girls behind to fend for themselves. Perhaps I'm wired up the wrong way. Perhaps my sense of right and wrong has been eroded. What I do seems to be morally regarded as on the side of right, in the righteous biblical sense, that is. But not all the Targets we rescue necessarily deserve to be saved, nor are they wanted free for the right reasons. It's not for me to make those calls. I'm nothing more than a wind-up toy moving forward relentlessly in the direction that I'm pointed. And I sure as fuck don't consider myself a good person.

I ducked back onto the landing and made it across to a first floor window to peer out across the grass. A heavily muscled man in a black tank top and jeans was clutching a pump action shotgun to his chest. Standing with his back to a garden wall, illuminated by the light from the house and the brilliant silver crescent moon, he was casting anxious glances around him to all sides. My best guess was he'd heard the commotion, seen the litany of dead bodies and was now well and truly spooked. I didn't know how many more of these guys there were but my priority now was getting out in one piece, getting the Range Rover, and finding a new lock on the Target's whereabouts without wasting any more precious time. All I could do was pray that this wild goose chase hadn't made me too late. Right now Tank Top Boy was in the way of my making a fast exit.

I eased open the window silently and, crouching to one side, nuzzled the barrel of the Beretta through the open gap. I whistled once. Loud and shrill. Tank Top Boy turned automatically to look and as he fractionally presented his torso to me square on. I double-squeezed slugs out in quick succession, tearing two adjacent holes into his stomach. He dropped the shotgun, clasping his hands across the gaping wounds in a desperate attempt to stem the blood which was beginning to seep down the paving cracks slowly in the direction of the swimming pool. The dying man sat down, a twisted look of bewilderment spreading across his face. He'd seen neither the gun nor the author of his fate.

I flipped open the window and assessed the drop. Twelve, maybe fifteen feet at my best guess. I arched my body, levering through the gap onto the window ledge, so that my legs hung dangling below like an oversized child perched precariously on a playground swing. The grounds were deserted. I pushed myself off and landed on the soft grass below, rolling in a textbook parachute landing. Sprinted out across the well-tended gardens, keeping relatively low until I found the section of bent metal fence that had folded under my weight earlier. It was harder doing it in reverse with the metal grill bending towards me. With no toeholds to power off, I had to jump up vertically and grab the very top of the fence, using brute strength to pull my body up and eventually to swing a leg over the top in the most lamentably graceless of efforts. *Something to work on, for sure.* Gravity did the rest. I landed on the other side of the fence and steadied myself on my feet. Checked around me in all directions, all senses alert for enemy pursuit coming after me in the darkness. Clear. Time for Hunter to move out.

Chapter 36

SPAIN. SESEÑA. OUTSKIRTS OF FRANCISCO
HERNANDO VILLAGE.

'Please relax. May I offer you a glass of cold water to refresh
yourself?' Sergei Krostanov stood over Daniel Ratchet, bathing
him in the warmth of his most benevolent of smiles. The
disenfranchised body was upright on a hard back chair bound
with rope across feet, thighs and upper torso. Hands were tied
tightly behind back. The body was exhausted, limp save for the
support of its bonds.

'It's good to see you again, Daniel. My colleagues tell me you
have been on a little, how shall we say, excursion? What is it Daniel?
You want to leave us is that it? Don't you like our hospitality? It's
a little rude to repay such generous hosting in this way don't you
think? To leave, without even so much as a goodbye.'

The face remained impassive. Noise was being received by the
ears but the words washed over them, like waves lapping at the
seashore. The brain didn't know if it could induce the vocal cords
to respond, for the lips to form words. The victim didn't know if he
could or how he was supposed to react.

'Dan-i-el,' Sergei cooed softly, like his name was a nursery
rhyme. A lullaby in his ear. 'Daniel. You have something that I
need and I'm afraid I will have to insist that you tell me where it is.'

The mouth opened. Throat straining to speak. The biological
mechanisms sought to respond to the command sent from the
brain. But the mouth was dry. No sound came out. He tried again.
Finally his throat croaked. And then:

'I don't know what you mean.'

'Daniel. I know that you and the incorrigible Mr Wallace have been spreading dreadful lies about me.' He spoke calmly, measured. Impeccable English with an irrefutable and ever-present thread of hard-boned Russian accent cutting through it. That unblinking cold stare. Piercing blue eyes so pale they could be mistaken for grey. Shark's eyes. No window to the soul. *Perhaps he has no soul.*

'No honestly. I haven't Sergei.'

'Liar.' The retort was sharp and followed by a sudden crisply delivered slap striking Daniel hard across the cheek. His face stung hot with a crimson flush of shame.

'You have been seeking to implicate me in the corruption of players and the manipulation of tournament outcomes. I'm sure you appreciate that this cannot be tolerated.'

'It was Bob's idea. I wasn't sure. I just wanted to check. Things didn't add up.'

'You have some documents and a video I believe, purporting to substantiate this, Daniel. They are stored remotely on your personal tablet device. We cannot find this. I want you to tell me where it is. I do not wish to be forced to hurt you.' The words were even, measured in tone.

The eyes stared blankly back towards the figure pacing before them. 'Daniel, your parents have been calling and calling. They are very worried, Daniel. They are also very annoying. They have been upsetting my friend, Mr Randy Hughes, wanting to know what is going on. Have you been found yet? What are we doing to help? Boo hoo. Do you think we should give them some news Daniel? Good news perhaps? Or maybe some bad news? Maybe send them an appendage from your worthless little body to shut them up? Do you think that might work?'

The torso twisted and strained on the chair.

Sergei's face suddenly softened. His tone now gentle and

calm. 'Come now. I merely wish to clear my name, Daniel. You can understand this, can you not my friend? I need to see what information you have in this respect so that I may simply defend my honour and prove that I am a worthy ambassador for our great game of golf. Do you remember how kind, how generous I was towards you when you needed help?'

'You've kidnapped me and half fucking killed me to get that computer. It's obvious I was right all along. You're a freaking psycho.'

'Where is tablet?' Sergei flashed loudly in a surge of anger, his immaculate diction briefly slipping.

'I can't tell you,' Daniel said, half pleading.

'Stubborn boy,' he murmured, shaking his head. And then, almost as a throwaway afterthought, 'You will pay for your insolence and you will tell us.' He casually lit a cigarette and inhaled deeply, surveying the captive tied to the chair like a hungry predator looming over a newly discovered burrow of helpless newborns. He circled around the back of the chair and bent down so his face was uncomfortably close. He held the angry ember of the lit cigarette tip aloft, moving it to within a centimetre of Ratchet's left eye. Unable to recoil, fixed tightly by his bonds, Daniel blinked wildly as smoke spiralled into his eyeball, tears trickling freely down his cheek.

'Is this so important that it is worth losing an eye for, Daniel?' Sergei enquired, appearing genuinely interested.

I can't betray you Matilda. My dear, beautiful Matilda. I just can't.

'Please. I don't know where it is. I gave it to Michael. He has it. I swear'.

'Michael Hausen? The physiotherapist at the training centre?'

'Yes, yes. I gave it to him to look after.'

'We will check for this. If you are lying to me I shall be most displeased, I can assure you.' Sergei straightened up to leave but checked himself. He leaned back in towards Daniel and casually stubbed the cigarette out on the side of his neck, tossing the butt dismissively onto the floor. He exited smartly, leaving the cell behind him filled with rabid screams.

Chapter 37

I punched the freshly memorised contact number into the new disposable phone. I had been grabbing some kip, pulled up in a lay-by in some dusty Spanish shithole of a town, the kind littered with high-rise blocks that no one wanted to live in during the good times let alone in the long distant aftermath of a financial crisis. Still, on the bright side, some global business sectors were thriving. I could think of at least two that were booming: Kidnap & Ransom on one side and Hostage Recovery on the other. The Unit was prosperous.

'Where the bloody hell have you been, Hunter?' Ella exclaimed with a tone of practiced injured innocence. 'We've been trying to reach you.'

'I've been a little busy. Had to find out that the Target wasn't at that address the hard way.'

'Sorry Tom. We checked out the address you gave us. It's a viable location for us to assume the Target was being held at. Things have changed, we've got fresh intel on the movements of one of the key suspects in this shake up. Mickey's getting a lock on the Target. We need you there right now.'

'I could probably have done with knowing that before I crashed the wrong party. Don't think I was the most popular guest somehow.'

'Well if you answered your bloody phone sometimes, it might just make communication a little easier,' she teased.

'Okay, okay. Mea culpa,' I grinned into the handset. 'Guess I was just eager to crack on.'

'What went down?'

'Helped a couple of damsels out of a jam I guess, but I used a little too much force.'

'Stop it. You know I love Dylan too, Tom,' she cooed. 'Blood on the Tracks?'

You know your music, babe. It did get a little messy in there.'

'Not more bloody body count? You'll have police forces from all over Europe looking for us now as well as the whole of Africa. You're clearly all right though and back to your charming self. And how could I not have guessed that women were involved somewhere?'

'I've only got eyes for you, Ella. You know that.'

'Enough!' she giggled. 'I've been doing some research for Charles. This whole gig runs deeper than just a few rogue caddies, Tom. Read the bloody report this time and I'll get back to you when I receive the latest location co-ordinates from the tracker Mickey placed on Sergei Krostanov's car. We're closing in on Daniel's real whereabouts at last and we're going to need you there sharpish. And please, Hunter, be bloody careful.'

I hung up the phone and scanned through the report.

Originally founded as an entity named Rublucon, Rublex Corporation had its murky origins from foundation in 1986 during the transition of the USSR at the time of perestroika. An aggressive and suspected unauthorised takeover of previously state-owned oil and gas fields in Siberia had turned the prodigiously youthful and ruthlessly ambitious owners into billionaires overnight. Rublucon had rapidly expanded into new markets and territories enriching those officials who enabled its growth whilst building a morass of enemies along the way. Growth was seemingly always at the expense of the common man, with thousands of homeowners and farmers displaced to make way for new infrastructure in specific territories. After the land grab, the business ostensibly cleaned itself up and was renamed Rublex. There wasn't much information on the ownership of the organisation.

By the turn of the millennium, Rublex's operation had sanitised itself further. Reach had spread internationally and there were photographs on the Internet of Boris Golich, one of the original founders, socialising with world leaders. The conglomerate would now withstand all scrutiny and was considered beyond reproach. A massive pipeline had been constructed through Kurdistan and down through Turkey, providing access into Europe. The latest news was of a gas exploration in the international waters off the Falkland Islands with several national governments interested in partnering to develop the resources. The sanitisation of this once dubious organisation seemed complete.

The report also contained details of the fifty million pound sponsorship deal with the European Tour, now in the second year of five. They supported the overall Order of Merit sponsorship and end of season championship, something of a big money bonus shoot-out which replaced the successful and long-standing Race to Dubai. In addition to this, they funded provision of the physiotherapy truck and a fleet of personal trainers available to those players without one already in their team. There were pictures of Krostanov everywhere: with players, at dinners, with the Tour committee. Ella had updated her cast of characters and mugshots too. The 'usual suspects', as she referred to them every time she pulled profiles together regardless of the job. She'd been thorough with the catalogue of caddies and officials who could possibly be linked to the disappearance. Using state of the art image recognition software, she had searched for further images documented around the world to link them to those under suspicion in the kidnapping. She had found some of Sergei in an American investment prospectus for an oil exploration company in Uzbekistan. A strapping man in his thirties. In one grainy image, he was standing in front of a corrugated iron hut, framed by a backdrop of vast rugged mountains wearing a hard hat and smiling. He held a clip board, his arm clamped around a mine worker. Tough beginnings. A world away from the opulent and refined environment of the golf Tour where he now seemed so central. There was a caption accompanying the photograph.

Site manager Sergei Krostanov with engineer Andrei Sharplov at the Uzbek oil refinery pumping station, 10 September 1999.

Ella had highlighted the name in red to make a point. Andrei Sharplov. I zoomed in and centred on the face of the other man in the picture. Scanned through the list of other faces to compare. He was also wearing a hard hat and the photograph wasn't the best, but the bone structure and those eyes, even early traces of that sculpted beard, were all the same. There was little doubt. Soviet mining engineer Andrei Sharplov and former colleague of Sergei Krostanov was now Aaron Crower's caddy on the European Golf Tour, Andy Sharples.

●

Two old men, skin leathered from years of exposure to the sun, played cards over tiny cups of coffee outside the beleaguered café opposite. They looked up in unison, briefly startled by the thrust of the engine. Then resumed their trusted early morning ritual which served as an unspoken distraction from the slippage of time, lives winding down like the setting moon over water. Nothing else in the town stirred as I sped through dirty deserted streets and back out onto the motorway. Reinvigorated by news of Daniel's location.

●

SESEÑA. OUTSKIRTS OF FRANCISCO HERNANDO VILLAGE

'Get lost again did we, Tommy Boy?' Mickey called over to me as I pulled off the road about thirty miles south of Madrid. We were sheltered under a large shady fig tree which cast long shadows over a cluster of disused farm buildings. 'I hope she was worth it mate. I've only been 'ere for four blinking hours.'

'They inside?' I nodded towards the large hacienda style property at the back of which we were parked, judiciously ignoring the well-meaning jibe.

'It's well-protected. I've clocked at least six different heavies coming and going so far but there's bound to be more inside the compound we don't know of.'

'And Krostanov?'

'Yep. All parked up. If our sources are correct, he's probably attending to some business with Daniel in there right now. Assuming the kid's still alive.'

'I'd usually wait for night fall to lead a strike but I think we're running out of time. Is Hand sending in anyone to assist? Where's Phil Manning when you need him?'

'Phil's in London, mate. He's working the Golich angle in town. It's getting serious at that end too with an assassination order made on some government official or other so it's just you and me on this one pal.' He slapped me hard on the back displaying something near to genuine affection.

'What have we got in the way of heavy artillery, Mick?'

'How did I know you'd bloody ask that? You do love your toys,

Tommy', he chuckled. I followed the wiry little character about fifty yards to a clump of dry thorny bushes nestled behind a masonry shed, probably used to house livestock at some time or other. Partly covered in the undergrowth, an old Spanish bakery van lay concealed. Mickey had clearly swapped vehicles at some point. He unlatched the back of the van and I peered inside. An assortment of various weapons were neatly strapped against the metal sides of the van. I selected a snub nose Kalashnikov machine gun. It fired an armour piercing round with greater range, accuracy and penetrating capability than those sub-machine guns which load pistol-calibre cartridges.

Smirked at the irony that this fine *personal defence weapon* as they were known, was in fact a product of the Russian Motherland. The 'PDW' label was used to justify their existence, in my opinion, by the powerful American gun lobbies. They had flooded the black market since the early nineteen nineties, when it became a trusted favourite of the notorious Jamaican Yardie drug gangs. But this was Russian weapon technology through and through and now I'd be using it on some of their own. I strapped it over my shoulders.

'Big guns too, Mick?' I nodded inside the van.

'Quite proud of myself on this score actually, mate.' He straightened, appearing pleased as punch.

'I have only managed to acquire our very own M9A1. Yeah, a bazooka! I didn't like doing it, mind, but the Hand of God set me up with a meet with them ETA Basque fellas and they were happy to trade. Seems they bought a load off the Portuguese Defence Forces after they'd finished fighting them Marxist guerrillas in Africa during their colonial wars in the mid-seventies and just had them lying around. Hand figured that if it's just you going in there on your tod then you'd want me to at least clear you some space.'

'A bloody antique then?'

'I've done some testing and trust me, mate, the rocket launcher has still got some grunt in it. You all good for small arms too?'

'Need some mags for the Beretta, but otherwise I'm good to go. You're on point for this one, Mickey. I'm gonna need you to smash the gaff up a bit with that bad boy.' I nodded to the big metallic tube that Mickey was caressing like a six year old with a new favourite Christmas present. 'Draw their fire whilst I bust in. Keep hidden and be ready to get us the fuck out of Dodge when I come out with the Target. That van's good cover. It's slower than the Range Rover but we won't get picked up as easily.'

'Sounds like a plan, mate. Make it happen, Tom.'

This was going to be an in and out job. Crude but effective. And just my style. Mickey was tasked with blasting the crap out of the east side whilst I penetrated the kitchen door on the patio at the rear from the west. Once I was inside, I would be taking out anyone who didn't look like either a kidnap victim, and I'd met a few in my time, or resemble the picture of Daniel Ratchet that I had committed to memory. Not particularly scientific, I know, but there was no time to get fancy and I wasn't here to be making new pen pals.

The message from Ella buzzing through on the phone didn't improve matters.

The graveyards are full of indispensable men.
- Charles de Gaulle

Funny thing. That girl had an unnerving sense of pertinence and timing with her quirky military quotations. Not particularly helpful given that more often than not they had a knack of turning out to ring true to the situation. My stomach churned. I'm not sure it was what I needed right before going into theatre.

Chapter 38

The stage was dark. A screen curved across its back, displaying a changing montage of uplifting and iconic images. Oil fields. Gushers. Mountains. Sunrises. Teams of smiling workers. Gas tankers in rapid convoy on otherwise empty roads. Bustling offices. Graphs depicting positive growth spikes. The Union Jack fluttering in slow motion. The legend which ran across the top of these pixelated images read:

A NEW UNION FOR GROWTH. DELIVERING ECONOMIC SUSTAINABILITY AND CREATING BRITISH JOBS.

Rows of journalists and especially invited delegates from government and the ranks of the Ministry of Trade and Investment and Department for International Trade sat patiently facing the stage waiting for the activity to begin.

Andy Bartholomew strode purposefully onto the centre of the stage. He cleared his throat and paused briefly to survey the audience who studied his every move.

'Welcome, Ladies and Gentlemen. Thank you all for coming. I know that today has been somewhat shrouded in secrecy but until now the government hasn't been in a position to release details of the historic deal which my department has been working tirelessly on. A deal we've agreed in order to generate and guarantee seven thousand British jobs over the next ten years!'

The audience erupted into spontaneous applause. Bartholomew

looked really rather pleased with himself.

He continued. 'As you well know, ladies and gentlemen, there hasn't been much real cheer for the economy in Britain since we cast off from a toxic Europe over the last wee while. Well this government has bucked that trend at last! We have beaten off fierce international competition for this deal and we have created a union to deliver fiscal growth, to safeguard and create British jobs!'

More applause. Andy savoured every last morsel, not deeming to commence his next sentence until the very last strike of hands coming together had completed.

'Therefore without further ado,' he rolled his R's like a bugler trilling the arrival of the regimental goat, 'I am honoured to introduce the Prime Minister to share the details on this momentous day.'

The Prime Minister swaggered onto the stage, tracked by a spotlight. Announcements of this type usually took place in Westminster, not amidst this poor imitation of American-style political razzmatazz. It had been Bartholomew himself who had choreographed the slick stage-managed announcement, apparently so as to generate maximum media interest and impact around the globe.

'Thank you. Ladies and gentlemen, you've no need for me to remind you of the torrid economic and political climes through which we have lived and served and although, over the last couple of years, there has been something of a modest upturn, due to strict austerity measures and the manifestation of Brexit, we know that many parts of the European Union continue to wallow in the swamps of financial despair. During this sorry chapter of our time trading partners have collapsed, currencies have fallen, banks have gone bust, businesses have failed, jobs have been lost, lives have been ruined.' He paused for the implications to settle and continued on with some gusto to announce the steps taken to consign these bitter memories to history once and for all. The speech detailed how, in the face of stiff foreign competition, the government had secured a trading alliance with the Rublex Global Corporation, one of the most prodigious and fastest growing oil and gas distributors in the world. The historic deal, partially funded by the UK, would create a minimum of seven thousand jobs for British workers over the next ten years and was worth an estimated seven billion pounds to the UK economy. It was, he hoped, a defining moment. He turned, half-facing the vast screen stretched behind him as the lights dimmed again and a video vignette offering detailed factual content on the deal danced into life.

As the audience settled, fixated on the images playing out in front of their eyes, a figure emerged from a throng at the back of the room. Calling out as he approached the stage, a thick sheaf of papers waving in his hand, The Minister, Brian Weston, shattered the silence within the room.

'Prime Minister! Stop this charade. You have left me with no choice.'

A hundred heads swivelled in unison to watch as he sprang onto the stage. 'Stop this nonsense, Prime Minister. I beseech you. Stop this at once.'

'Take a hold of yourself, man,' warned the Prime Minister stepping towards him.

'Prime Minister. I cannot allow this to proceed. You have chosen to consort with Boris Golich, a man whom we have now unequivocal proof of involvement in the most audacious of criminal activities.' He faced the audience urgently. 'You have opted to commit Great Britain to a commercial relationship with a Russian Mafia overlord via the veiled guise of oil and gas exploration which is merely a front for laundering dirty drug and extortion money. You risk tarnishing our standing on the international stage through supporting such nefarious criminal activity and costing us millions in the unwarranted joint venture infrastructure fees needed to facilitate this cursed deal.'

'Have you lost your mind, Minister? You simply have no grounding for these quite absurd and unsubstantiated allegations. I won't tolerate such insubordination.'

'Stand aside,' the Minister admonished. He depressed a button on a clicker which, until now, had been concealed within the pocket of his suit jacket. The visuals on the screen changed. Now a series of enlarged scanned documents were presented there.

Warrants for Boris Golich's arrest under the charges of conspiracy for the acts of the organisation of murder, extortion, embezzlement and various other criminal atrocities committed in several of the old Eastern Bloc countries. Additionally, a number of bank statements highlighting a series of large off-shore payments made to numbered accounts purported to link the Prime Minister to Hamilton Advisory, a consultancy advising Rublex on the marketing of incomplete or non-existent casinos and resorts. The PM held a fixed smile on his face, conjuring mock laughter as his head rocked from side to side in faux disbelief. Hoots and howls of derision from the audience followed. Displayed on the screen next came photographs of abandoned building sites at the locations of these ghost developments. Then followed swiftly by screen grabs of sexy marketing material featuring quoted endorsements in the name of the UK Prime Minister. Apparently they had 'strong investment potential, impressive sustained occupancy rates and unparalleled facilities'.

The audience, slowly comprehending the gravity of the facts presented, grew steadily as one in audible discontent. Camera blubs flashed, smartphones were held aloft to capture the action. Within moments those journalists who were live Tweeting at the launch had alerted the world to the sensational turn of events and the debacle was already trending.

The President of the United States of America had just weighed in himself with a Tweet regarding the importance of commercial transparency, the need for probity in politics and high moral standards across public life. A frenzy of responses had begun. Journalists and MPs jostled for position, crowding the stage in a menacing cluster, intent on exacting answers. It was nothing short of an unedifying scrum which soon overwhelmed the event security.

Sensing the moment was at hand, the Minister signalled over to the side of the stage, summoning a portly middle-aged man accompanied by a ruddy-faced police constable tightly buttoned inside his smartly pressed uniform.

'Prime Minister, you'll need to accompany these fine gentlemen of the establishment to answer a few questions.' He looked towards the Special Branch officers at the side of the stage who were detailed to protect the Prime Minister in public. He shook his head and raised his voice issuing a directive. 'Stand down please. There is a warrant in place.'

'Prime Minister, in the next few days I shall be tabling a vote of No Confidence in the House of Commons surrounding your leadership of both the Party and of the country. We will submit our letters demanding your resignation to the 1922 committee. You are in no position to carry on given your apparent errors of judgement and clear lapses in moral fibre. I'm challenging for the leadership at once.'

Chaos ensued. Chairs were knocked backwards as reporters and staff alike rushed forward jostling for position, shouting questions, reaching over one another for photographs and for answers.

At the back of the room a flustered Andy Bartholomew hurried out through the emergency exit. Head down, coat tails flapping behind all aflutter.

Chapter 39

SPAIN. SESEÑA. OUTSKIRTS OF FRANCISCO HERNANDO VILLAGE.

A deafening explosion shattered the surrounding peace of the rural Spanish countryside. A gaping wound now torn into the side of the hacienda building like a screaming mouth with jagged broken teeth. Rubble lay everywhere. Thick clouds of brick dust swirled in the baking sun. Shattered concrete lay strewn indiscriminately over the grass. Shouting swiftly followed.

Mickey followed up his first strike with the bazooka by firing a well-placed and equally damaging second just above it into the first floor, nearly taking off the entire corner of the building. Within a matter of seconds, the beautifully constructed architecture of this fine old building had been decimated. The noise of warfare perforated the air. Even though we were in a sparsely populated region of the countryside, away from the main conurbations, there was no way that these huge explosions weren't going to draw someone's attention to the hacienda at some point. I don't think Mickey had factored in an engagement with the Spanish military when he sourced our gear for the mission. That was something we could do without if we were to get Daniel free quickly.

Using the cover created by the explosions, I smashed open the glass of the kitchen door using my forearm, in perfect synchronicity. Leaning in and fiddling with the handle on the inside, I discovered to my dismay that the door was already unlocked. 'Congratulations Einstein,' I muttered to myself and kicked open the door frame, scanning left and right behind the pugnacious snout of the Kalashnikov.

The kitchen was clear. Footsteps clattered on a stone floor somewhere outside. Reaching the door I dropped to one knee. In my experience, an enemy running towards you at speed will be expecting to shoot at a height of about two metres, or at the level of the head of an average man standing. Adjusting your gun muzzle at speed to just one meter, or the height of a man kneeling, takes that extra, vital second, leaving ample time for me to get my rounds off and bring them down.

I waited, kneeling inside the door frame of the kitchen. Eye fixed to the target-scope. Shooter cocked and primed. Forefinger resting a light tension on the trigger. Two burly men, revolvers waving in front of them as they ran, cantered around the corner of the staircase. The clatter of my magazine emptying itself echoed round the vast bare hallway as the bullets spat out in a spiteful rage of fire. They didn't even see me crouching as they sped towards the sound of the assault on the building. I dropped the men inside seconds, ripping scorched bloody holes through chests and necks and thighs, sending the pair of useless carcasses tumbling to the cold floor in an unseemly tangle of limbs before casually reloading. I tracked the empty corridor round to an opulent marble atrium. Stepped over the useless, lifeless bodies. Sticky footprints left inside the dark pooling of glossy crimson.

A bullet whizzed past my head and thudded into the thick wooden frame of a large painting hanging on the wall. I ducked hard, bobbing and weaving away from the direction of fire. Spinning furiously, I returned shots in short random bursts, pinning back the shooter so I could hold a new position. Bullets hailed down on me from the top of the sweeping staircase, leaving me trapped in the crosshairs between two deadly angles. To my left, the gunman resumed and intensified his firing. Sharp fragmented chips of wall plaster cut into my skin as I worked my big frame into the tiny space presented under a table displaying a large ornamental vase. I was getting some serious heat and, if it carried on like this, it wouldn't be long before one of these stingers had my number on it. Cold sweat soaked the back of my shirt. Angling my barrel upwards, I took aim at the ceiling over the shooter who was viciously peppering me with shrapnel from his nest at the top of the staircase. Squeezed the trigger and let the beast rip into the plaster above him. It was like a hammer being taken to a wedding cake. Vast chunks of plaster cascaded down onto the top tier of the staircase, crushing the sniper under a deluge of heavy debris, blunt trauma administered with instant and direct effect.

The other shooter stopped as well, distracted temporarily by the recent architectural adjustments. I commando-crawled from under the table, moving steadily towards the direction of attack. The gunman had withdrawn now behind a door and I managed to hold him back with a consistent popping of my piece into the wood and surrounding walls. With no return fire coming back my way, I scampered a retreat into the corridor from whence I had just emerged.

Another crash into the roof of the building. Mickey was doing his bit to cause chaos all right, but if he kept on like this, there wouldn't be much of the property left standing by the time I located the Target. This was a big house and I needed to find Daniel quickly. I wasn't going door to door searching him out this time if I could help it. In and out as fast as possible was the plan.

Then, from out of nowhere, the butt of a revolver smashed into the side of my head, splitting it open and knocking me sideways into the wall through the force of the blow. A bull of a man in a black leather jacket, sporting a face not even a mother could love, grabbed me roughly by the shoulders before throwing me head first back into the wall.

Where were they breeding these gigantic beasts? He should have just fucking shot me in the head when he had the chance. Done us all a favour.

He grabbed my hair, pulling my head back, and thrust a revolver into my face, smirking. I winced up at him through blood-encrusted eyelids. Thinking fast and hedging that the gun could be out of bullets, I feigned collapse. Slumped deliberately and unexpectedly leaving him to take the full weight of my body in his fist supported only by my hair. It stung like hell as thick clumps ripped out of my scalp by the root. But the surprise action, submission as opposed to expected aggression, delayed my would-be execution for just long enough to grab the handle of my Beretta and, with it still securely fastened to my belt, I managed to pull it away from my thigh and squeeze off a couple of rounds direct into the foot of the thug looming above me. He bellowed and let go of my hair, hopping in agony. Falling to the floor in a heap, I scrambled quickly to my feet and kicked off from the corridor wall to slam powerfully into the wounded Russian beast. I hit him in the midriff. Hard. Uncompromising. Cut him in two with my shoulder, forcing him to double over and wretch. A solitary memory skipped through my mind of the days when I would relish spear tackling some chunky high stepping Number Eight peeling off the back of a scrum on a desolate mud-covered rugby pitch. He may be big but he didn't have much fight in him. As he straightened up to face me, I jabbed him with a swift left in the throat. Clean. Clinical. Not hard enough to smash his windpipe but enough of a precise blow to cause instant swelling, making breathing hard. He choked and spluttered, eyes watering uncontrollably. I pulled the Beretta loose and forced it inside his mouth, pulling up the picture of Daniel stored on my phone and holding it in front of his face.

'Where is he?' I demanded. The goon shook his head, still gasping for breath. 'Where is this man?' I shouted and pushed the barrel of my gun deeper into the recesses of his throat, making him gag. He nodded resignedly and I pulled the gun free, keeping it trained on his head.

'Take me to him, motherfucker,' I ordered, shaking him by the collar of his leather jacket like a badly behaved dog. Even if this lump 'didn't-speak-the-English', he'd got the message sure enough. I pushed him down the corridor, gun jammed into the middle of his back. Blood was smearing on the exquisitely-patterned stone floor as he dragged the injured foot after him. Every so often, in order to keep the hustle going and drive him on at a faster pace, I delivered a well-placed kick with my steel toe cap into his calf muscle, bouncing the trailing leg ahead of him. We passed a number of side rooms and intriguing passages that flowed out like the unexplored tributaries of a coursing river until gradually the corridor grew colder, gloomier, undeserving of the need for decorative attention or the warm yellow sodium lighting. Forced my hostage forward until he came to a natural halt in front of an outer gate of iron bars against a heavy studded wooden door.

He grunted, inducing me to shove him forward so that his nose was touching the metal. With the gun still pressed menacingly into his back I pulled each arm up onto his head interlocking a set of inordinately thick fingers. Patted him down causing the reassuring jangle of key chain inside trouser pocket. Handed Daniel's jailor the keys and forced him to unlock and then open the gate and door as I stood harrying him from behind.

It swung open slowly, heavy on its frame before finally unveiling the pathetic scene before me. There was no mistaking the Target. Daniel Ratchet sat slumped, bound with rope to a wooden chair, listless and unmoving. Blood caked his face, his sallow skin, his shirt. His trousers were damp and beneath the chair his feet wallowed in a puddle of dark and odorous urine. On his neck, an obscene inflamed burn, weeping pus, broke the smoothness of pale white skin. I pushed my captive hard, forcing him to limp inside the cell as I called out to Daniel checking he was still alive. The boy stirred and slowly opened his eyes to look up at me in weak desperation.

'It's all right, mate. I'm here to get you out of this place,' I said, stepping towards him as I spoke. As I reached the chair, the leather jacket took a step towards us. I half-turned and, without warning, fired point blank into his face splattering blood and brain matter particles in a disgusting spray over the cell wall behind. He had expended his use and with an exhausted Target to now get out of the building alive we couldn't afford to be slowed down any further. Drew my hunting knife and cut Ratchet loose.

Daniel slipped off his chair and onto the floor. I slapped his face, then shook him and with no given response repeated the action over and over. His eyes flickered and after a short time they opened drowsily.

'Wake up man! Pull yourself together, Daniel. We're getting the fuck out of here. NOW!' Slowly he kicked into gear, visibly starting to function one piece at a time, first waking to salient consciousness, then motor skills starting to fire, now gaining spatial awareness. He looked up at me helplessly. Throat so dry, desperately trying to speak. His mouth formed the words before any noise escaped. Finally he managed to croak at me, annunciating a single audible word.

'Matilda,' was all he said.

I lifted him off the floor and hauled him over my shoulder, head draped over my back, legs dangling at the front of my chest. I hadn't any water to give him and even if I had been carrying a full on emergency first aid kit there was no time to administer treatment. I was in the fucking field. We needed to fall out and now. I pressed forward, supporting Daniel with my left arm wrapped over his lower back, gun firmly gripped in my right. He was a tall, rangy kid which made him difficult to keep hold of, but he didn't weigh as much as some of the army bergens we had carried back in the mob on twenty mile yomps across the moors. Checking left and right, I exited the cell and set off at a steady pace down the corridor, precious cargo in place. I guessed the remainder of those still inside the building were being kept busy by the barrage of explosions assailing the property from Mickey's bazooka frenzy. The dingy corridor remained empty and we covered the distance fast.

Dripping with sweat and panting hard, I heaved the dead weight of Daniel's body onto a hardwood mahogany counter in the kitchen and stretched out my injured shoulder. I was numb from the bullet wound taken back at the golf course and my deltoid was now almost entirely locked into one place. I had grown used to the dull throb of pain threading down my side, strangely savouring the familiarity of the cruel sensation as it wracked my body. The electric impulses between the damaged nerve endings and pain receptors in my brain told me that I was living, not merely some fragment of a disturbed dream sequence. I was able to feel something for real, the receptors signalling to my brain that I still inhabited this body and had not yet thrown off this mortal coil. Was not yet in Hell.

The kitchen was empty. A large copper pot bubbled on the range. A set of ancient cow bells hanging above, a rustic trophy of yesteryear. The table in the centre of the room was typical of the archetypal Spanish country kitchen and I could picture a family spanning three generations gathered round over a hearty breakfast engrossed with one of the patriarch's rambling stories. My ruminations were quickly shattered by a long-haired olive-skinned man in a white T-shirt banging through the kitchen swing doors to our left holding a hunting rifle. He wore jeans with cowboy boots. A hand rolled cigarillo hung from lips that presented themselves in a perpetual sneer. The scene could have been lifted straight out of some dodgy Western.

I grabbed Daniel. Pulled his limp groaning body from off the countertop and down onto me as we fell to the floor behind the kitchen table. I shunted forward and, grabbing the ankles of its front two wooden legs, heaved sharply backwards, flipping the heavy unit onto its side. Presenting the thick wooden front as a shield for the two of us. Cowboy Boots unleashed a couple of cartridges whizzing into the table top. They stuck fast. The table was solid. Fig wood. Old school and built to last. Lucky it was a low calibre rifle, probably best suited for shooting rabbits and birds in the surrounding countryside. Even so, if whoever furnished this place had chosen to go with some modern self-assembly flat-pack crap instead, the boy and I would be cashing in our chips right about now. I pointed the nose of the Kalashnikov over the top lip of our makeshift barricade and returned fire, lashing bullets around the kitchen before us. The rattle of the gun, accompanied by metallic echo of bullets bouncing into tiles, pans, and the cooking range created a raucous musical cacophony around us. Cowboy Boots retreated back behind the flapping swing gates. I waited, head down, forefinger caressing the trigger of my smouldering weapon. Counted fifteen seconds of silence in my head. Nothing. I jammed the barrel of the shooter over the top of the table and blasted another short burst of fire. No response, so I peered around the side of the table. The kitchen was empty. Then I saw it. The pointed toe of that scuffed cowboy boot just visible an inch or so from under the swing gates. I aimed low, at knee height, to where I projected the man was standing and gritted my teeth. Squeezed the trigger and let the gun do its work. Leapt over the table closing forward to ensure I had the best angle to make a hit. Gun fire blasting ahead of me, keeping him pinned back, I kept shooting until I could practically engage the enemy hand to hand, clip emptied in full. Crashed through the swing gates and found Cowboy Boots just beyond, taken down in a bloody pile clutching at his legs. He looked up at me dolefully, grasping feebly for the rifle by his side as I leapt forward onto his chest. Slit his throat from ear to ear. Butcher work with cold steel in the kitchen somehow felt right.

I turned, then strode back to grab the Target to get the hell out. A slobbering thick-shouldered American pit bull bounded in from the corridor and launched itself at Daniel, who lay curled up at the base of the upended table. By the time I reached him, it had clamped its jaws into his leg and was shaking it furiously. Ratchet's resistance was limited to a low moan. I pulled out my Beretta and aimed at the devil dog. The mechanism jammed. Fuck. No shot. I flung the gun at its head missing narrowly, bouncing off its thick neck. The dog didn't even look up. I stepped in and kicked it square in the side as it ripped at the flesh on Daniel's leg like it was toying with a bone in the back yard. I felt ribs shatter and crumple under my boot. The mutt yelped. Attention turned from the Target towards me. First job done. It snorted and set after its new prey. As the dog came into me I dropped my shoulder and smashed my fist down hard into its nose knocking it sideways and sending it rolling. It righted itself unsteadily and, in a slavering frenzy, came straight back at me, snapping and growling with the myopic purpose of pure animalistic fury. I had succeeded in my objective of deflecting the dog's attention but, with no time to reload the mag on my Kalashnikov and the Beretta spent, I wasn't going to stand there and trade blows, so I scooted back quickly onto the counter and flipped my legs onto the tiled kitchen top. As the animal jumped up barking, wildly trying to reach me, I grabbed a round copper saucepan and fended it off, striking it in the mouth and skull, batting at it animatedly. Finally the dog gave up and prowled threateningly, pacing in a tight circle below me, panting hard. I rose to my feet upon the counter, stooping my neck to keep my head from bouncing on the ceiling. There was just no way I could bring myself to finish off man's best friend down there if I could possibly help it. It wasn't the mutt's fault, even if that Hound of Hell was giving me and the Target some serious problems to think about, with no time to waste. I scanned the kitchen. A little further down above the counter was a spice rack hanging off the wall. Next to that hung a long string of onions, garlic and a thick dried Spanish sausage that was curved into a U-bend shape. I bundled across the counter-top and grabbed the cured meat. Whistled down to the slathering frenzied Pitbull to grab its attention and waved the charcuterie above its nose, just out of reach. It followed the swaying of the sausage hypnotised; all malevolent intent on mauling me to death seemingly forgotten in an instant. I hurled the chorizo stick around the kitchen door and out into the corridor, from where we had entered. The dog bolted after it. In a single motion I bounded off the counter and across the tiled floor just in time to reach the door with my boot and slam it shut. The dog flung itself against it in frustration. I breathed out hard. The beast barked and snarled as it scrabbled against the wood, feverishly trying to get inside the kitchen and back at us. I patted the spare pocket of my cargo pants and slotted the final magazine into the machine gun. Reaching over I hauled Daniel up by his shirt and out of the foetal position he had adopted in the shadow of the table; our improvised defence shelter.

There was little doubt. This was bad. The Target was in a right fucking mess. Couldn't stand. Blood was soaking through his trousers. I bent down and using the fireman's lift technique flopped him again over my heavily strapped shoulder. We made it through the same kitchen door which I had unnecessarily smashed in earlier. Over the patio now at a trot. I made a vain attempt at checking for contact as we ran but the truth is I was knackered from carrying a twelve stone deadweight on my back and from some pretty brutal fighting to get us outside. Plus, I was carrying a gunshot wound which was sapping my energy more than I had bargained for. There was no use pretending otherwise, if we were going to survive this we needed to get out of the compound and fast.

Chapter 40

By the time we reached the vast dry stone wall at the back of the garden, I was drenched in sweat. We'd threaded through lush vegetation and beds of vibrantly coloured and exotic smelling flowers. I rested briefly on several occasions to readjust the Target's body, shifting the weight on my back, catching my breath. I kept talking to him as we went. The kid was worth more to me alive.

'Keep it together man. You're gonna be okay. Daniel, are you listening to me, mate?' The occasional grunts returned back at intermittent intervals told me that at least he was still breathing. That's all I needed. *Tom Hunter is seeing this job home.*

I fished the pre-pay mobile phone from my pocket and dialled Mickey from the list of previous calls. He answered on the second ring.

'Take your bloody time why don't cha, Hunter? What you doing, making new friends in there or something?'

'Something like that, Mick. Something like that.'

'I've been keeping 'em busy for ya, Tom. There's three or four of them up there returning fire whenever I punch holes in that gaff.'

'Yeah. So I heard. Good job. We're by the back wall in the compound, Mickey. Target's incapacitated. Living but he's in bad shape. I can't get us both over this wall with him on my back, it's just too much weight with this wounded shoulder and what we've been through busting out of there.'

'I'd make a nice fat hole for you to walk through, mate, but I've spent my wad on our little fireworks show. No rockets left I'm afraid.'

'What do you have Mickey? They'll be down here any second now.'

Moments later, a thick, hairy old rope lashed over the wall about twenty metres down from where we were crouched. I jogged over to it and shouted back 'Got it, Mick. Is it secured, mate?'

'It's on the front of the van. Tie the kid on and I'll winch him over.'

It was a pretty rudimentary plan but it was all we had. I pulled the rope across the top of the wall and secured it around Daniel's waist. The engine revved from somewhere behind us and I helped push the limp body upwards, bent in half under the strain of the rope. It didn't look comfortable but he made it to just before the top and I hollered. Mickey jammed on the handbrake keeping the van fixed. Our precious cargo hung precariously from the taught rope. A full minute later, Mickey's head popped up furtively from the other side of the wall, the very image of a wizened meerkat on the Serengeti surveying its territory. He reached over and grabbed hold of the dangling body. Began hauling him over.

Gun shots whistled into the wall. I hit the deck and rolled automatically, finding cover beneath an orange tree. Daniel was a sitting duck, he couldn't have made an easier hit. A slug caught him flush in the buttock as Mickey pulled him finally over the wall. His cries were reminiscent of a wild animal in distress.

'Tom he's been hit! He's been hit!' came the urgent shout from beyond the wall.

'Get him out of here. Now,' I called back. 'I'll meet you in the town by that old casino. If I'm not there in fifteen, just go.'

'Gottcha. Oh, and Tommy, think you might be needing this, mate.'

A spare ammo clip landed softly on the grass ahead of me.
Golden.

Inside a minute I heard voices. From my vantage point amidst the orange grove, I scoped four guys. One was smartly dressed, immaculately presented in a fine suit. Judging by this and other factors such as body language, including his directive gesticulations to the others in the group, he was clearly in charge. Of the other three, two looked like local lads. Hired muscle. T-shirts, jeans, trainers, sun-darkened skin, hair slicked back. The fourth was cut from a style I'd encountered before. Bigger than the others by a head, skin a milky white, shoulders square as an aspirin bottle encased within a shiny black leather jacket wrapping. Agitated feet pawed at the ground. He wouldn't be best pleased when he found out I'd pasted the face of his stunt double all over the cell wall. Or maybe he already had.

I quickly assessed the options available to me. There was now one full magazine clip in the Kalashnikov, thanks to Mickey's spare. The Beretta was spent, lying back on the kitchen floor. And I had my knife. They had shot Daniel and seen him flip over the wall. Perhaps they thought I had also managed to make it over and would divert all their efforts to outside the perimeter. But the group were fanning out now and that wasn't a chance I could take. They were checking the bushes and trees, clearly hunting for unwelcome guests. I figured that most people pinned back in my situation would try to scale the wall or find a weakness in the fencing surrounding the compound. But I wasn't most people and I'd been in tighter scrapes. This was no time to panic. If that's what was expected, I was going to do the damn opposite. I'd breeze right out of the front gate, just like I owned the place.

I skirted the orange grove and tracked back up towards the villa. Watched as the group split up, tracing the back wall, and spied one of the two hired Spanish goons as he half-heartedly used the barrel of his rifle to prod and poke into the foliage. Felt my blood rising the way I often did before a kill. I locked on him, enjoying the fact that I knew that these precious moments were the last he would experience, whilst he remained oblivious. His life was in my hands now and I would decide to take it in whichever manner I wanted. Concealed by the lush greenery, I stalked him to within only a few meters. I was so close now I could make out the thin slick of sweat which covered his biceps and hairless forearms. Muscles sculpted through hours in the gym, not natural strength, more for show than for hard work. He'd need a few years yet to put a bit of man on him but I wasn't going to allow him that privilege. Abandoning his efforts, he skulked round the side of the building, studying the gaping hole in the brick work left by Mickey's earlier bombardment like a ripped stage curtain left unsewn. I watched as he scuffed his way through the rubble, blazing a cigarette alight.

And I'm breathing hard. Heart thumping. The blood pumping and coursing through me. I can feel my nerve ends tingling. Fuck, I feel so alive. And then I can't contain it. Have to taste it. I pounce and I'm on him before he's exhaled his first drag, punching my blade into his stomach and twisting it as I lift him off his feet. He bends double and as his feet scrabble for the ground I catch him with a left hook smashing into his temple. Leaving go of the knife handle, blade still embedded inside him, I follow up with a right uppercut driving into the underside of his nose with speed and force. He crumples at my feet pathetically, bloodied, motionless. Endorphins surging. Waves of serotonin flooding my brain. For a brief moment all pain is washed away.

I'd seen this happen once before in a street fight, a man killed with a single punch to the nose, death from internal bleeding. I love 'the sweet science', as it is known. I'd trained myself to be a switch hitter in the boxing ring, unusual in being able to deliver equal force from both the orthodox and southpaw stances. I wasn't ambidextrous, so it took practice. Hours on the heavy bag, setting the balance correctly, shifting the weight to administer power from the body core, not just arm punches. I'd trained myself to avoid injury as much as improve my boxing technique. If, like most sluggers, your stance is naturally conventional, it's far easier to break a hand in the heat of a tear up. You've thrown your hardest punch with spiteful intent, usually a straight right. If the feet aren't correctly placed, this moves the body out of alignment and off balance. Should that first punch connect, depending on what is thrown back, then oftentimes you will want to follow up with a rapid second blow to drive home your dominance in the altercation. The new position now lends itself to you throwing an overhand left coming from the side. If you don't focus on putting your fist in the right position, driving through with the first two knuckles, keeping the fifth metacarpal bone out of the way, then breaking a knuckle will occur nearly every time. There's a reason why hand injuries (amongst other fight damage) are attended to so frequently on Accident and Emergency wards on a Saturday night. A common result from booze-fuelled wild swinging pub brawls, often just a lot of bluster and a few mistimed scrappy blows. Typically all over inside a minute, but a broken hand is an unnecessarily painful way to make your point, even if you do come out the victor.

I looked down with disdain at the deflated sack of meat, discarded lifeless amongst the rubble. As far as punches went, that one was a hall of fame peach and one I would no doubt recall with relish from time to time in the dull moments of transit between jobs.

A radio handset, fixed to the belt of the hired Spanish muscle who had just been on the receiving end of my best attentions, crackled into life. A thickly-accented voice speaking in syrupy English was moving through the channels asking the group to report activity. The stock response echoed over the airwaves twice: 'Clear'. Then the name 'Alejandro' was called, a pause and then twice again in irritable succession. I scooped up the handset and issued a muffled response, same as the previous answers. Held my breath. Waited, uncertain if my brief impersonation had done the job. The radio crackled again: 'Keep searching the grounds. Secure the area.'

They wouldn't be looking for anyone at the house for a while. Sticking close to the villa and slinking in the stretched-out pattern of hazy shadows, I soon made it around to the impressive frontage of the building. The yawning driveway stretched out ahead of me. No sign of patrols left or right. I furtively checked about me again and taking a deep breath set out straight ahead into open cover. Sprinting hard out across the drive, jinking as unpredictable a path as I could fathom in the quickest time possible towards the gate. It felt like I had a supersized luminous bullseye burning onto my back, and I was fully expecting to be taken down by a bullet at any moment. Any rudimentary marksman standing at the first floor window in the front of the house would have an easy shot and plenty of time. But it was a calculated strategy. The team was distracted, focused on searching the grounds and beyond the perimeter wall. My move was the least expected and I gambled against stacked odds that no one would think to be guarding the front door.

●

I made it onto a dusty main road a few hundred meters beyond the main gate before I finally stopped moving. Hands on knees.

Panting for breath. Sucking hot heavy air into my lungs. Sweat dripping from every pore in my shaking body, stinging my eyes. Shoulder opened up and starting to bleed again. Not what I needed right now.

I set off, striding down the road, still breathing raggedly. A mile or so down, an unwashed, red Fiat Punto chugged by, travelling at around twenty kilometres an hour. I let it pass before stepping out into the empty road behind it and, crossing my arms above my head, waved and shouted at the driver flagging him down. It came to a gentle stop fifty meters ahead of me and I bounded up to it. In fairness to the rather concerned looking driver, the sight of a battered ugly mug like mine, scarred and stained with sweat and blood looming into the car mirror would make most people uneasy. Smiling in through the mud-splattered window, my best lopsided grin in place, I could barely get a greeting out before the studious looking young man with horn rimmed glasses and perfectly groomed hair looked up anxiously and began very slowly moving to deploy the central locking and secure the car doors.

'Do you speak English?' I asked louder and slower than was really polite, trying not to let an increasingly fraught expression show across my face.

'No Ingleses. Perdóname,' came the response accompanied by a flapping of hands. The nervous man clearly regretting having stopped at all.

'I need a lift please,' I shouted simultaneously trying the door handle. The engine revved. Sensing that I was about to lose my ride I pulled out the Kalashnikov, smashing it through the glass window. The driver froze, sweaty palms held submissively in the air, a contortion of fear carved into the fixed mask of his face. I swiped out the excess jagged glass around the door frame with the gun barrel and flipped up the plastic lock. Motioned to the driver to get out on his side and followed him round the vehicle as he moved, weapon trained perpetually upon him. I motioned for him to lie down on the road and as he did so I sprang into the empty driver seat, revving the high pitched engine before shunting off down the road towards the local town.

I reached the old casino just a few minutes later. I'd miscalculated. On foot it would have taken me at least twenty minutes to cover the ground plus I'd had some action to contend with. Pulling into the deserted car park, I looked around for activity, signs of Mickey and the van. The old casino had fallen from grace since its heyday in the nineteen fifties when it must have been quite a grand affair. A tattered sign, paint peeling and framed by a chain of bare circular light bulbs worn from years under the baking sun, depicted silhouettes of girls in fishnet stockings, high heels and bodices bending provocatively with hands on knees. Faded glory or not, you couldn't mistake what this place had once been. Now it stood empty, boarded up with plain wooden planks and rusting nails. The car park was a dusty vacant lot, typically deserted in daylight but frequented by whores and their clientele after dark, a fitting use perhaps given its somewhat racy past. I checked my watch a second time. It was seventeen minutes since I had seen Mickey disappear with Daniel over the wall and I had instructed them leave without me on fifteen. I was getting twitchy. Could I have been followed? Those guys were known to be connected, probably had eyes everywhere on the payroll. A moving shadow suddenly caught the corner of my eye. Startled, I jerked sharply around to find a quizzical face only inches from my own, staring straight back in at me through the car window.

'You're always fucking late, Hunter,' Mickey scoffed at me. 'Get in the back of the van with the Target sharpish and stay the bloody hell out of sight. We've got to move out right now.'

Chapter 41

SPAIN. COUNTRYSIDE.

In the back of the old bakery van, Daniel was burning up. I poured water into his mouth from a plastic bottle and mopped hot sweat from his brow. He was murmuring something incomprehensible. Something about Matilda. Of course I'd read in the briefing notes that she was his recent girlfriend but didn't reckon that the unhelpful woman I'd interrogated at the golf course car park warranted that much concern. Still, whatever it took to get him through. He was in a bad way. Beaten, tortured, mauled by a savage dog and shot. Doubted that he'd had much in the way of food, water or sleep during his ordeal. If I wanted good money, then I needed him to make it. He had to stay awake.

The van trundled through the rolling Spanish countryside, Mickey driving, a flat cap pulled down low on his head. Concealed in the back, Ratchet and I were keeping out of sight. We knew these guys were connected and that they'd be coming after us at high speed. Hiding in plain sight, we were gambling on the fact that they wouldn't figure on us trying to outrun them by pootling along in a battered bakery van with a top speed of fifty kilometres an hour. We passed golden fields knitted together like a patchwork quilt. Sturdy hedgerows and trees neatly lined the roads providing layers of never-ending symmetry. Mickey flicked on the radio and the whine of sickly bubble gum Europop filled the van. Twenty minutes or more passed without seeing another car.

'Hold on boys. What's all this?' the call filtered back at us. 'Fucking road-block, Tommy. Look lively.'

I peered up through the front seats and out of the windscreen. We were held in a small queue of cars on a narrow country road. Ahead of us two police cars were parked at angles across from each other on either side of the road. Officers of the Guardia Civil, buttoned up in full uniform and hats, were walking up and down the row of cars with clipboards, making enquiries of the drivers through their windows. It was too late to pull a U-turn and take another route without drawing unwarranted attention to ourselves.

'You think this is for us, Mick?' I said.

'Couldn't say. Don't see how it could be, do you? How connected are those Ruskies anyway? Guess we're about to find out. Not sure how I'll explain that I can't speak Spanish driving a van like this without them wanting to look in the back. If it goes tits up, mate, we're going to have to fight our way out.'

I grabbed an M16 semi-automatic assault rifle from the rack and loaded a new clip in preparation. It had been a firm favourite of the US military since the early sixties, first adopted by the US Air Force and then by the Army where it was used heavily in Vietnam. It's a lightweight shooter manufactured from a mix of steel, aluminium alloy, composite plastics and polymers so you can strap it to your back and go for miles without being slowed down. It's gas-operated and air-cooled, with a rotating bolt. The use of direct impingement keeps the weight down further by doing away with an additional gas cylinder, piston and rod; cycling the action instead directly with gas which is fired from a cartridge straight to the bolt carrier. A lighter, simpler gun and fewer operating parts to worry about. Now that really flicks my switches. I checked Daniel over, he was looking comfortable enough for now. Traffic was starting to move up ahead.

The expected knock arrived on the glass window. Mickey dutifully wound it down, smiling. The policeman stooped. 'Hola,' he said dryly. Mickey nodded.

Up ahead another policeman was waving cars through with an impatient ferocity. He called down to his colleague and the message was relayed. A grunt. A tap of the clipboard on the bonnet of the van. Waved us through. Mickey half-turned, winked at me and weaved the old vehicle through the roadblock and out onto the open road. I shook my head, exhaled and placed the M16 to one side. Turned back to Ratchet and reapplied some wadding tightly down against the weeping bullet wound in his buttock, keeping the pressure on hard to stem the bleeding. *Florence fucking Nightingale.*

Less than five minutes down the road, the whoop of a siren and the flicker of blue lights alerted us to a squad car closing on us fast from behind. With no ability to outrun them, we reluctantly pulled over. The same policeman as before came to the window, a stern uncompromising look upon his face. He fired something in rapid Spanish at Mickey. No response. He tried again. Mickey looked back at him this time and simply said, 'Do you speak English gov?'

'English? Si, I speak some English. Please get out,' he sniffed with a supercilious air of tangible distain.

Mickey dutifully did as he was asked and I strained to listen through the sides of the little van as they stood together on the hot tarmac.

'Do you own this vehicle please?'

'Um. No it's a rental'

'You rent this?' The response incredulous.

'Yes from a friend. I work for him running errands'.

'We have reports of a vehicle being stolen with this description coming from Alicante this morning. Do you have papers?'

'Yes. Surely. I'll have to rummage around in the back for them though. That okay?'

Footsteps approached the back of the van and Mickey made a

loud show of opening the back doors. I primed myself with the M16 cocked as the doors slowly swung open. Watched as the expression on the policeman's face changed in sequence from sudden shock to serious concern as he absorbed the tangible threat of a machine gun pointed direct at his heart. It was probably the most action he'd encountered in his pen pushing, traffic counting career to date. It certainly didn't look like he wanted to be there.

'Tie him up, Mickey. Leave him by the side of the road. If we smoke him we'll only draw more heat. We're supposed to be on their side anyway.'

'Haven't worked out who we can trust on this one yet. Intelligence that Ella provided shows that these Russians have bought their way right up the establishment in a load of countries. Some local policeman who's probably on the take from half the neighbourhood already can be easily bought. We can trust no one on this job, Hunter.'

'Agreed. But I'm not killing him for the hell of it when it'll cause problems later getting back to London. We leave him tied up out here in the sun to work on his tan and crack on.'

We left the policeman, gagged with one of his own socks, hands and feet tightly bound with rope, sitting in his underwear in a dried out ditch as we clattered away towards the city. Our destination was the central hospital. Whilst waiting for me to turn up at the old casino, Mickey had been on the phone to Ella back at HQ. Given Daniel's critical state of health and the fact that he remained in a perilous situation, until his kidnappers were either apprehended or neutralised for good, Charles Hand had secured private treatment in the city hospital at Barcelona. We weren't to stop until we got there under any circumstances whatsoever, not even for the Spanish police.

We drove for an hour in near silence. The Target was slipping in and out of consciousness. There was little that could be done to ease his discomfort. Even so my fist gripped his clothing willing him to hold on until we reached Barcelona. The heat was thick and oppressive inside the van, choking already parched throats even drier. Every bump and pot hole on the neglected road surface jolted through us like electricity, serving as a merciless reminder of each painful niggle and injury carried by my exhausted body. The elixir of adrenaline which had previously coursed so flagrantly through my veins was now dissipating. Mickey drove us forward in solemn silence as if steering a hearse at the head of a funeral cavalcade. Guiding us steadily closer towards our destination, eyes fixed upon the road.

The open countryside narrowed and the battered bakery van crawled up a winding road rocking gently from side to side as it made the tight turns. We pulled into a village. Passed squat sandy coloured houses. An old woman bowed with age and dressed head-to-toe in black lace inched slowly up the road, relying on the aid of a homespun crooked stick which looked as if it had been whittled and shaped from a severed branch. The centre of the village was dominated by an austere looking church. Its size and ornate architecture entirely incongruous against the backdrop of such simple dwellings in the surround. Turning a dusty corner the van slowed. Mickey cursed under his breath. Ahead of us, police cars of the Guardia Civil stretched across the road, uniformed policemen flanked their vehicles, guns drawn. A welcoming committee.

Chapter 42

Michael stretched his muscled body out and rolled uncomfortably on the couch inside the physio-truck. He was restless and unable to sleep. A lot had been going on around the Tour since Spain and, whilst gossip had been rife in the last few days, few of the facts had been substantiated. The circus had inevitably left town on schedule following the conclusion of the tournament and the players and their entourages were now starting to reappear in dribs and drabs at the course on the outskirts of Munich for the BMW Championship. It was cooler in Germany than the searing heat of Spain. Time never stood still on the Tour. There was always the next event, always another trophy to play for, always another cheque.

One of the old golf swing coaches was reported in the media as having passed away at the last event, natural causes. Talk amongst the players was that it may have been a robbery gone wrong but the story had been carefully managed by the European Tour Public Relations team. Police reports were obscured and the media had played ball. The last thing these luxury resorts hosting their prestigious events with high paying sponsors wanted was any negativity which may be generated through a perceived association with criminality. Matilda had taken some time off from travelling with the Tour. Michael had always been protective of the beautiful, vulnerable girl whom, in many ways, he regarded as a younger sister figure. It had been an unspoken bond between them and Matilda had often depended on him as a deflector to the multitude of testosterone-fuelled chancers who came sniffing around as she tried to do her job. The only time she had trusted anyone, allowed anyone to really get close to her, was her new boyfriend Daniel Ratchet, a fresh player manager to whom Michael had also taken a shine. But no sooner had he arrived on the scene than he had gone missing. She was clearly very upset and it had all got a bit too much for her to be around the events.

Michael squirmed and twisted uncomfortably, squashing his face deeper into the stiff cushioning of the couch. More worries danced through his mind. In the process of trying to bolster his meagre pay packet and support his family, he had lost a lot of money to a certain unpleasant group of caddies who ran a book gambling on tournaments. He'd had a few early wins using inside knowledge of the players' physical conditions. He'd doubled-up backing some nailed-on favourites only to see the results slip out of his grasp at the very last moment of the final day of action. Unheralded performances and he'd lost large. Failure to pay up had seen him sink deeper on the interest payments. Recently he'd been on the receiving end of some beatings and scare tactics and, frankly, it frightened him. Things were getting out of hand and no one seemed to be in a position to do anything about it. The caddies were acting like a law unto themselves.

Trouble seemed to be escalating too. Apparently some big tough looking guy with a nasty looking scar had stuck a gun in Matilda's face in the car park back in Spain, asking questions and scaring the crap out of her. It had been the last straw and she had taken sick leave for the next couple of weeks. He couldn't help but worry about her. On top of all of this, right before Daniel had gone missing, he had left his personal tablet for Matilda, stashed secretly right here in the truck. Michael had discovered it whilst cleaning up at the end of the Spanish leg of the Tour and with all the recent goings on, he had of course been curious, particularly given that the guy had then vanished into thin air. Michael liked Daniel. He was different to the other player managers they encountered out here who were arrogant and brash, treating them like the hired help or, in Matilda's case, some cheap whore they could paw or gawp at. So he had wanted to help him and, with all the recent goings on, it was apparent that he needed all he could get. Unable to give Matilda the computer for safe keeping as yet, seeing as she had left in such a hurry, Michael had dutifully taken care of things. The way he always did, in his efficient and dependable way.

The dark plays tricks on the mind when you are sleeping alone in a truck within the isolation of an empty green field site during the set-up of Tournament Week. No fancy comfortable hotel for him. Over time one got conditioned to the sounds of the nocturnal wild animals calling to each other at night. The lonely lament of the wind. But now a different noise from somewhere outside the truck held the attention of the big German. A chill ran down his spine. Sitting bolt upright, rubbing his eyes. T-shirt soaked in sweat. Head groggy. There it was again. Almost imperceptible. Persistent. Deliberate. The sound of a light yet aggressive filing at a level that wouldn't have woken him if he had been asleep. Michael threw the blanket to one side and levered his chunky frame down onto his bare feet. The noise continued unabated. There could be no doubt anymore. Someone was trying to get in.

A nine iron leaning at a jaunty angle against the table, casually discarded by one of the players, was snatched up shakily as a ready weapon.

Gripping the club in his meaty left hand, the sleepy giant padded over to the door. He waited in the stillness. Breath held tight, a silent prayer on his lips. Each thump of his heart was simply deafening. And the scraping just kept on and on tormenting him until finally a solid clunk and a satisfying click as metal slotted gently against metal linking the machine manufactured components into place. The handle turned.

Michael stammered, 'Wer ist dort bitter?' and then after a short time, 'Who's there please?'

Silence. He called out again. A split second later, the door was kicked open violently and two masked men charged up the little metal steps in close succession and piled into the truck interior amidst a clatter of noise and fury. Michael didn't even have time to swing the club. He jabbed it into the ribs of the first man, slowing him down but the second was on him instantly, clawing at him, grappling round his broad chest and knocking him backwards. It was enough to keep him occupied whilst the lead assailant rallied and catching him flush with a well-timed shoulder charge slammed against his legs, bringing him down.

Michael was overwhelmed by both the suddenness of the attack and the combination of aggression and sustained force from the two men. Working together, they pinned him to the floor. A black sack was roughly forced over his head and its cord pulled tight. Punches rained down on his face and ribcage to the point where Michael Hausen eventually gave up struggling, instead curling up his knees and using those big hands and solid forearms to shield himself. Within a further couple of minutes, a skipping rope, borrowed hastily from the training kit in the truck, was tied tightly at each end around his wrists and ankles which were forced behind his back. Hausen was bound immobile, left trussed up and writhing helplessly on the floor.

A voice. 'You've got something we want, Michael.' The ensuing swift boot to the ribs generated a muffled grunt by way of response. 'Where's the tablet, you Kraut bastard? Don't waste our time or you will be in for some real trouble,' threatened a cockney sneer.

Michael said nothing. The kicking continued. Legs, torso, head. Finally, tired out from their exertions, the interrogation began again in earnest. 'Where's the fucking computer? We know you've got it, Sausage Meat, we've been told,' screamed an enraged Scottish tirade just inches away from the hooded head. This could only have been Sean.

Michael gritted his teeth, his eyes tightly shut too. He hated that voice with a passion. Sean had tormented him, burnt him. Now he was being beaten on again. He may have been helpless but he had something that they wanted. And he knew how important it was, what it meant. He wouldn't betray Daniel. And he wouldn't betray himself again. Not to these bullies. There was clearly too much at stake. The German swallowed hard. And right there within the darkness of the hood and the restrictions of his bonds, shrouded in fear, Michael fought against the instincts of his natural disposition and silently he took his bravest decision.

●

Streams of sunlight cut through the branches of the canopy of proud overhanging trees. The truck park was contained, sealed off with ribbons of thick blue tape. Swarms of uniformed police clustered together writing notes and taking photographs, bagging evidence and interviewing passers-by. Michael Hausen's lifeless body, bound and trussed like a sucking pig prepared for roasting on the spit at a medieval banquet, had been discovered at mid-morning the next day. Except that when the policemen were finally able to untie and un-hood the victim, they had been unable to make an immediate positive identification of the body. Every bone and tooth in its face was smashed and broken into a messy bloodied pulp. The body lacerated and grotesquely smeared with green greying bruising. The ruptured skin and crushed ribcage, which had apparently been jumped gleefully upon like a child's trampoline, depicted a swollen purple tapestry of pain.

But Michael had chosen not to utter another word. The coveted tablet had not been surrendered. He had neither betrayed Matilda nor broken Daniel's trust. Picked on for his prodigious size and exploited for a sorry lack of bravado since he was a boy, the lifelong victim had chosen this moment to display the true courage which always slumbered within him. In the stoic acceptance of his death the man had at last found the strength that made himself complete.

Chapter 43

'Only seventy kilometres to Barcelona and this has to bloody 'appen. Another pissin' roadblock. We can't afford to sit here idling forever. I might have to even switch the engine off and push it through mate, we are that low on blinkin' petrol now. If we don't find a gas station soon, we are going nowhere fast, Tom.' Mickey slammed his hand against the steering wheel of the bakery truck in frustration. 'Hold up. This looks serious, Hunter. The roz have come mob-handed. How's the patient doing back there?' he enquired twisting his neck birdlike to peer into the back.

'Target's not in good shape. We haven't got long, I reckon. He's still bleeding. We can't bloody stop for this lark, we just haven't got the time, mate. Besides, they've probably found that cop in the ditch by now. We ain't getting through this one without a scrap.'

'Take it easy for now. Let's suss them out. They might be on the lookout for a lost cat for all we know. We're miles away from the Russians by now, it's probably not even related.'

'I'm telling you I don't like it,' I replied, grimacing as I picked up the assault rifle and yet again checked the magazine was fully stocked. Pure habit.

Mickey rolled the van up closer towards the three police cars which were blocking the road in zigzag fashion, beaming a broad and unconvincing smile. A tall, mahogany-skinned policeman, proudly sporting a bushy moustache, waved us forward insistently. We coasted to a proximity of around fifteen feet in front of him when the powerful rattle and snap of machine gun fire tore into the windscreen of the van, shattering it instantly, pouring a shimmering waterfall of glittering broken glass over the front seats. Mickey was pinned back into his seat, body shaking and contorting as it was riddled with bullets. He stood no chance. Torn full of holes. We were compromised, trapped in the jaws of a deadly ambush.

The gunfire turned onto the body of the van and I launched myself at the back doors flinging them wide open. With M16 grasped tight in my left hand, I squeezed out a wide arching volley of indiscriminate fire to pin down our assailants and try to free up our position. Had to clear us a way out. Grabbed the Target by the scruff of his neck, pulling his languid body out of the van after me and down onto the road. Seconds later, bullets screamed through the sides of the van, stabbing raggedly through the metal. Head down, I grabbed Daniel again and, pumping my legs hard, pulled him across the road at pace. I laid him on his back behind a low white stone wall that framed the neatly kept front garden of a small house on the roadside. Sweating. Puffing hard. Bullets spitting spitefully past my head. The Guardia Civil were agitated, firing their pistols at us in random bursts from behind the bonnets of their parked vehicles. I returned shots with interest, keeping them busy, but something didn't add up.

Where did that machine gun come from? Police don't shoot first and ask questions later. They knew we were coming. This was a planned ambush.

They murdered Mickey. And there had been nothing I could do.

The intensity of the gun fight slackened and, seizing the opportunity, I scoped around me for a safer place to decamp. The low wall provided cover for Daniel lying stretched out prone behind it, but even when I crouched low it did little to protect my muscular bulk. *Same as airline seats*, I thought to myself wryly, *big guys always get the raw end of the deal.* It's why Ella booked me business class whenever I flew on a job. She was always thinking of me.

I clocked a tall, narrow, white building some twenty yards back past the roadblock. I fired at intervals, enough to keep the Spanish Police pinned back. Indolence or incompetence, I wasn't sure which, but they certainly appeared to be in desperate need of a firearms refresher course. Two men left the building and walked briskly up the road to join the officers behind their cars. One was considerably taller than the other and walked with a limp. He wore a black leather jacket, his companion smartly dressed in tailored suit. They stepped closer into focus. Sergei Krostanov and the lumbering goon I had met earlier that afternoon. I pumped out a volley of slugs towards them with renewed venom. Everything slotted into place at once. The Guardia Civil were on the payroll of the Russians. They'd been tracking us. This had indeed been a trap all along. They were still after the Target.

I held my fire and waited a long minute. Thinking hard. *Mickey was dead.* We were outnumbered and outgunned. Squatting behind an impossibly tiny wall for cover.

I needed to get the Target, who I had just met and had barely yet managed to speak, a man who was half dead and couldn't walk, into a hospital in Barcelona as quickly as possible.

And our only transport had been shot up into little pieces.

If that wasn't enough, they had now had serious reinforcements in the shape of two crazy Russians, who hated my guts, wielding a shit-packing machine gun - probably a mounted Browning M2 or similar judging by the shudder of its rounds.

The odds against us were stacked heavier than a weighted coconut shy at a travelling fair.

The pause in the action and arrival of their paymasters seemed to change up the energy. Two of the uniformed policemen lost patience and, presumably riding on the confidence of their superior numbers, crept slowly forward towards the van. A rudimentary attempt at battle strategy, a basic plan designed to outflank me. But the machine gun started up, covering their slow progress and giving me no option but to return shots at it as the Browning swept all before it, tearing up plants and thumping slugs into the stone wall, scorching the reddish earth in a rabid snarl of shrapnel.

The policemen reached the van and crept around the other side, keeping tight, hidden from our view and the position from whence Ratchet and I festered in perilous predicament. Head down and as out of sight as I could make myself behind our inadequate defences I considered the options. I might have sussed their weakly executed plan but that didn't mean I was really in any position to do much about it. The hail of bullets kept coming at us. I recalled that Mickey had said that we were almost out of petrol. That might be a blessing in disguise. I stuck the nose of my gun over the top of the wall and trained it on the gas tank of the van. Squeezed hard. Trigger finger white. Straining. A ferocious stream of bullets pumped into the side of the van and up across to the engine.

Explosions require three elements to occur spontaneously: fuel mixed with oxygen in the right proportions, and a source of heat. The boat-tailed, streamlined, and tapered projectile known ubiquitously as a bullet, propelled through the air at a velocity of around one hundred and eighty-six miles per hour out of the barrel of my shooter and into the near empty gas tank. I was gambling that the paucity of flammable liquid within, which had been the cause of my friend's consternation, might mean that the ratio of oxygen to inflammable fuel could be close at least to the desired ratio of one to fifteen. The epic explosions seen in the movies where the hero shoots up a car, creating huge noise and a monstrous ball of flame, are something of a fallacy.

I got lucky. The van was old and inefficient, its fuel tank perhaps not totally vacuum sealed. The bullets sparked a reaction, just as I hoped. The tank blew, not Hollywood production style, but enough to fling the two policemen, pressed against the van, into the road unconscious. What was left of the limited petrol not burnt up in the muted explosion seeped onto the tarmac. Flames engulfed the bodies rapidly. I watched as Krostanov signalled to the men behind the roadblock to stand down from assisting their police colleagues whilst he stood back impassively observing the charred bodies in the fire. His card was well and truly marked.

The flames provided all the distraction we needed. Grabbing the Target by his lapels I backtracked, dragging him up to the front door of the house in whose garden we had taken refuge. I fired a single shot into the lock and hoofed it open with a kick which any overworked mule would have been proud, shuffling us inside. A solid looking wood sideboard stood in the entrance hall. I heaved it forward, tipping it over right up against the front door, jamming it shut. They would be up on us pretty sharpish now there was no gun fire to keep them at bay. I dragged the moaning body into the kitchen and left him stretched out under the kitchen table, a bloody smear from the gunshot wound in his buttock leaving an unseemly trail across the tiled floor. That he was making any noise at all by this stage was only a positive sign. I made it to the front window in time to clock the remaining three officers approaching at speed. Two stopped in stunned rapture over the smouldering bodies of their fallen comrades. I smashed the glass in the window with the muzzle of the M16 and slotted them where they stood, allowing purposeless compassion to become the agent that sealed their fate.

Did that make me the same as Krostanov? I brushed the irritating thought away. I had no duty of care to these men. This was not my troop and I was engaging an enemy in battle.

The third member of their band, witnessing the fate of the others, hesitated on his advance towards the house, uncertain whether to now opt for the sanctuary of retreat. Trapped in a virtual no man's land, out in the open and vulnerable. Too far to turn back, not close enough to attack with any real impact. Surprised by the uninvited visitor of long mislaid memory, my mind's eye jumped to the pleasant greenery of an English village cricket pitch on a competitive Saturday afternoon. His eyes redolent of the batsman caught between wickets, about to have his stumps smashed by an eager keeper as his playing partner pulls late out of a tight run scoring opportunity. Sheer desperation turning to discontented resignation. A bitter taste of injustice as the ineffectual confronts the inevitable. But nostalgia was brushed easily aside when I spared him no quarter for his indecision, coldly slotting a hole between his eyes. Watching as he slumped to his knees and toppled forward face first. Life taken. An inauspicious innings brought to a premature end.

The Browning took out the remainder of the lower ground floor windows as the Russians advanced on us. The policemen had served their purpose in slowing us down and these criminals were ruthlessly pursuing us themselves. By now the clip for the M16 was running low on ammo. Returning fire and wasting indiscriminate bullets was not an option. I needed to regroup and find us a way out. Fragments of broken glass crunching under foot, I backpedalled out of the front room, fast. This unstoppable wave of shit just kept on coming at us.

As I made it into the hallway, the noise of a crying child pierced the silence of the house. I hadn't even considered that the occupants of the place might actually be inside. This was a seriously unwelcome complication. Enemy contact any second now. No time to check on Ratchet in the kitchen. Had to work on the assumption he was still alive. The stairs creaked and groaned under my weight as I took them two at a time, bounding up to the first floor.

And so I found them cowering in a back bedroom. A family of five. Three children under eight years old, two skinny little gap-toothed brothers and their pretty bronze-skinned older sister, with neat fringe and saucer wide brown eyes, huddled around the skirts of their leather-skinned mother. The terrified father stood frozen as I entered the room. He displayed a look of unmitigated panic. I held my free hand aloft in a calming motion and put my index finger to my lips gesturing for silence. The father slunk back deeper into the room to stand protectively in front of his brood. I wouldn't allow these innocent people to fall into the cross fire of my bloody war with these ruthless Russian gangsters.

The sound of the front door being repeatedly kicked hard until its blockade crashed to the floor told me that our guests had arrived downstairs. The rhythm of bullets snapping around the hallway to clear the way and the unmelodic tones of their twin deflection and destruction gracelessly announced their intentions. These visitors were not here for tea and sympathy. I glanced around the bedroom, looking for inspiration. There was a single bed, neatly made up and adorned with white lace. A simple wooden chest of drawers. A solid looking wooden wardrobe. A tasselled blue rag rug partially covered the sanded wooden floor boards. A painting of the sea, and small fishing boat hung on the pristine white plastered walls. The window was slightly ajar so I prowled across to it and peered out onto a small rectangle of thick yellowing Bermuda grass littered carelessly with a small red tricycle, bats, balls and water pistols some fifteen feet below us. Beneath the window, roughly five foot down, was a small tile ledge probably one foot wide and running the length of the house through which the main rain gutter was supported. I pushed the window open and ushered the agitated mother towards it, picking her up under her arms and lowering her until wavering tiptoes found the tiles and she was able to steady herself below the window. The situation was pandemonium and the family didn't have a great choice in deciding what they should do. In the end, they had chosen to co-operate with the big guy with the scar holding an M16 rather than chance their luck with the guys downstairs making all the commotion and shooting up their home. I couldn't explain the situation in Spanish even if I wanted to, but frankly there was no time and I was just glad they moved fast without me having to get heavy in order to make them see sense. I lowered the children one at a time out of the window by a succession of gangly, wriggling arms and legs down to their waiting mother. They edged along the tiled ledge holding hands, flat against the wall. Their crumpled father turned to follow them but I caught his arm, spinning him to look me in the eye. The furrowed brow melted as I handed over the gun and nodded down the stairs, a look of understanding and resignation forming in its place. Next I moved sharply over to the wardrobe and tore out the contents of hanging shirts, trousers, skirts and blouses littering them over the floor. Rocked the empty wooden carcass back and forth until I found its pivot. Rested it on my shoulder. Shooting pain and gritted teeth. Heaved it upward, head inside, a sickly marzipan stench of mothballs filling my nostrils and choking deep into my lungs. I staggered blindly towards the doorway and now, guided by my willing friend, edged out onto the landing. Measured footsteps menacingly trod the staircase below us just as I leveraged it off my back, tipping it downward over the banisters and into the stairwell beneath. Crashing. Skidding. Sliding. Finally crunching to a definitive halt as it wedged itself firmly between wall and stairs blocking the way up. An angry shout below told us that the intervention had been just in time.

I pointed to the gun and gestured with a pretend shooting motion to my petrified accomplice. Gun fire rattled into the wardrobe. He looked up at me through nervous bushy eyebrows and I nodded. He squeezed the trigger in return, knocked backwards somewhat by the unexpected kick of the gun, the bullets stamping a messy uncontrolled pattern into the neatly plastered walls of his staircase. No way near accurate but the noise alone was enough to tell the Russians that the route upstairs was well covered.

Leaving the man of the house to protect the staircase for now, I moved quickly back into the bedroom. Looked out of the open window. Staring straight ahead onto the garden you couldn't make out the petrified family frozen on the ledge below. I hoisted myself onto the window frame and jumped the fifteen feet to the grass below landing on my toes and automatically rolling the way we had been drilled at parachute school. The training always kicked in, muscle memory was still good. It was the slug I had taken that again caught me hard as I made contact with the lawn. Pain searing, eyes watering, I remained lying face down with the thick grass rubbing coarsely against my face waiting for the screaming set off inside my brain to subside. My body throbbed. The energy drained from my limbs. Seconds passed. I can't take it. *Fuck. I am a corpse waiting to happen. Stretched out stationary on the lawn. Easy pickings. Move out soldier. Fucking move out. NOW.* I hauled myself weakly to my knees and, clutching my sticky weeping shoulder, staggered up off the grass and back against the outside wall of the house. Rocking with pain. No gun. A house full of injured and vulnerable people, relying on me to protect them from the enemy inside.

There was only one chance now and that was to come up on these bastards where they didn't expect it. I steeled myself and with jaw clenched, re-entered the house. I half expected my phone to flash through a text from Ella back at base with some quote or other from Henry V about the rounding on the opposition and seizing the upper hand. All very well for him, but this wasn't five thousand men on horseback entrenched together on a muddy field in an unmoveable position. This was one freakishly big Russian homicidal maniac and his psychotic boss. Tooled-up and really pissed off.

●

I made it through the kitchen undisturbed. Daniel was lying very still under the kitchen table. Blinking occasionally, he looked like he was lapsing in and out of a coma. There was no time to check on him. From inside the downstairs hallway the sounds of swift exchanges of bullets told me that the owner of the house was getting into his newly appointed role of sentry and gun emplacement.

Then the shooting from upstairs suddenly halted, indicating to me that the seriously depleted magazine clip may have finally expired. Two minutes lapsed. Still no exchanges were given. I peered round the kitchen door and could just make out the thick legs of the Russian as he reached above him and pounded the butt of his gun into the wardrobe smashing splinters of wood apart as he endeavoured to clear a route up the staircase. He'd be through there in no time. I drew my knife and stealthily crept into the hallway on my hands and knees, tracking the cedar wood banisters and trying to keep out of sight as best I could. The Russian was preoccupied with his violent assault on what was once a sturdily made old fashioned piece of furniture. The element of surprise was in my favour. The blood lust was up, my senses heightened. My mind emptied itself completely as pure instinct took over. With his attention absorbed fully above his head I reached a chunky forearm through the wooden railings behind him. A deft flick of the wrist twisted the blade, slicing across his Achilles tendon to rip it away from his ankle bone. The tendon flipped and rolled up into a tight little ball just below his calf. Howling, he crashed down the remaining stairs in a tangle of legs and arms clutching at his foot, gun sliding and spinning down after him. It was all I needed. A second later I was on him. Knees pinning his arms and chest to the floor held under my entire weight. Blade plunging wildly at his face, neck, heart in an inhuman adrenaline fuelled frenzy. Not halting, even after he had stopped writhing below me, until totally exhausted. I collapsed forward on top of the body, panting hard. Sweating, shaking, unable to move. This had been my last throw of the dice. I wasn't carrying heat and he was heavily armed. In my current physical state with my shoulder the way it was I would be no match for a man like that in a fist fight. I had nothing more to give. Gambled seven lives on one last play.

Rolling away, I could feel my arms and face bathed in a coating of warm gooey blood. The carcass to my side was a mess. It looked like he had been caught in the gears of a combine harvester, chewed up and spat out. Detached from the process, I mechanically patted him down for weapons and removed a revolver, concealed in an inside pocket. Stared numbly at my handiwork, butchered and mangled, on the floor. I felt no remorse. Nothing but pure animal exhilaration from the kill. I licked the salty blood from my dry lips and right there and then vowed I could never speak of this to another human being.

I turned my back on the kill-room and returned to the kitchen, finding the Target unmoved. There was still no time to be wasted. This village would be overrun any minute now.

I pulled Ratchet out unceremoniously by his feet from under

the kitchen table and checked his pulse. I slapped him crisply round the face until his eyes flickered awake.

'Come on man. Keep the fuck with it, Daniel. Stay awake, mate, we're getting the hell out of here,' I urged, dragging him upward first against my knee and then hoisting his limp body onto my back as we part-staggered, part-trotted out into the garden. The woman and children remained stationary on the ledge, clinging to the side of the house in terror, peering down on us as we made our escape. I kept moving forward, head down.

●

We rounded the front of the house. The van was still smoking. Bodies lay dead at every turn. The scene that stretched before us depicted a sorry massacre. An animated group of villagers clustered across the road, chattering with concern and gesticulating at the carnage. Some made urgent phone calls whilst others filmed on their mobiles. Four young men, chests puffed out, were starting across the road together to take a closer look at the chaos. Ignoring them steadfastly, we continued unfazed, doggedly determined to exit the area as quickly as we could and avoid the next wave of law enforcement. I laid the Target on the bonnet of a blue Fiat Uno parked on the road. Not caring about witnesses by this point I smashed my elbow against the glass window of the passenger seat, shattering it into fragments across the inside of the vehicle. Reached inside and flipped up the plastic lock. Pulled open the door. Eased back the front car seat and laid Daniel gingerly onto the back seat before locking two seatbelts across him to hold the body in place. Sweeping broken glass away as much as possible, I clambered through the car and inserted myself into the driver seat. Less than half a minute later, the wires under the dashboard sparked a connection and the motor roared into life. Gunning the engine, we squealed away. Not a moment too soon, I reckoned, given they would probably be calling the army out to back up the decimated local police force any time now. I spun the wheel and floored it back the way we had come through the only route that wasn't blocked out of this little linear village. The way Mickey had driven us in. Only now Mickey wasn't leaving with us. He lay slumped in the burning wreckage of an old Spanish bakery van, riddled with so many treacherous bullets. They'd taken my friend.

There was nothing I could do. And I can never erase that.

As I blinked back hot tears, recalling the many times Mickey had supported me on dangerous missions, and saved my bacon from far too many unsavoury scrapes, I was reminded of Ella's prescient words prior to the losses— painful losses— suffered on the Nigerian Embassy job. Words taken from the Anglo-Saxon poem, Beowulf, which depicts tales of a hero of the Geats in Scandinavia who victoriously battles and overcomes both a terrible monster and its fiercesome mother in defence of the King of the Danes. Words that had since been branded into my memory:

'Then Beowulf spoke, son of Ecgtheow… "Bear your grief Wise One,
It is better for a man to avenge his friend than to refresh his sorrow.
As we must all expect to leave our life on this Earth we must earn some renown, if we can, before death.
Daring is the thing for a fighting man to be remembered for."
The Ancient arose and offered their thanks to God,
To the Lord Almighty, for what this man had spoken.'

I swallowed hard. This grief was going to be hard to bear indeed, but whatever else happened I knew I would walk through the fires of hell to be certain of avenging Mickey.

Chapter 44

ENGLAND. LONDON. WESTMINSTER.

'I'm calling a motion of 'No Confidence' in the Chamber, Alistair. I've written to the 1922 Committee. The process has begun. Other letters will soon be submitted to reach the minimum threshold and force the vote. There is no way that the PM can continue to lead the Party whilst he is being investigated for criminal activity and after this monumental Rublex debacle.'

The Minister circled his friend and trusted Whip impatiently. Alistair Worrell was an impeccable dresser. His suits, cut of the finest cloth, were always immaculately pressed and off-set by the ever-present splash of colour from one of any number of different silken handkerchiefs which would peek rakishly from his top pocket; hinting at a certain repressed creative flair bubbling under the surface. He was an intelligent man and one of some considerable discretion, a powerful attribute for a successful career in politics. He had secured a double first in classics at Cambridge and entered into politics young. He combined his ferocious intelligence with a reputation for tireless hard work and for simply getting the job done, whatever job that may be. He had grown to become the trusted aide and confidante, the right-hand man even, of one of the genuine power brokers still remaining within government. So good had he become at influencing, cajoling, leveraging toxic snippets of information and massaging egos that his boss, Big Beast as he was, had long since declared him indispensable. He would not now further progress through the party ranks. Simply because he had proven himself to be too good, too proficient in the dark arts. Not only couldn't the Minister bear to be without such sought after skills for his own ends, but he would also not allow them to be deployed for any potential rival.

Alistair spoke, 'You were instrumental in uncovering the seedy underbelly of this deal with Golich, Minister. Instrumental in undermining the PM on the day of his big announcement. We orchestrated the public humiliation. It's an act of out and out rebellion and a dangerous path we tread, if I may say so, sir. The PM didn't get where he is today without being a calculating, ruthless bastard. He has many supporters who are capable of some pretty nasty and effective stuff, as you rightly know. You won't have an easy ride of it I can assure you.'

'Alistair, I need to know you can generate the support required to elicit a full-scale change in the leadership of the party and bring the vote to bear.'

'I shall have the appropriate words in the appropriate ears as ever, Minister. I can make no promises and even if we think that we have the commitment of the necessary votes, one can never be certain until the final ballots are cast.'

'Let the chips, then, fall where they may.'

●

Derek Hemmings sat hunched up facing the window in his office from which, if he really strained his neck, he could just about see onto the corner of Whitehall lit up by the street lamps. He fixated on a tiny chip in the corner of the heavy glass pane. Pale and drawn, his legs jigged up and down uncontrollably. Bony fingers worried at a fraying corner of material on his suit jacket, making it decidedly worse. Things had just got very real and rather serious indeed.

Six minutes earlier, he had taken a brief phone call at his desk. And Lord God Almighty, whilst he, Derek Sinjon Hemmings, remained in the sanctity and security of his office, pretending to be working long hours alone on an intense project in adherence to the Minister's advice, there had been a break-in at his home. A back window smashed. His little Alice alone and vulnerable. Soaking in her regular pre-bed lavender bubble bath. Dear Alice, unaware of the danger that her own husband had so selfishly placed her in. The danger that he had been unable to warn her about.

Her blood-curdling screams had apparently alerted Phil Manning to the situation. Charles Hand's man had been provided as an additional security measure to protect the property should the imminent threat on Derek's life come to fruition. What the dickens Her Majesty's 'Finest' constabulary were doing at the time, Heaven only knows. They were supposed to be guarding the family, so thank goodness for that bloody man Hand after all. The Hand of God they called him. Now Derek knew why. And good for Alice too. His wife, always so buttoned-up and fastidious. *She could scream the bloody house down when it served her purpose.*

A smartly dressed young man had been found inside the house apparently. The trained killer sent to remove Derek Hemmings, the thorn in Golich's paw. Manning had ordered him to stop. To surrender his weapon. Request ignored. Gun raised to shoot. Armed. Resisting apprehension. Civilian endangerment. No second warning. Shot down where he stood. Shot down inside the Hemmings's family home. Blood pooling over their new cream carpets at the top of the staircase, carpets that Alice had thus far not permitted the sole of a single outdoor shoe to meet. And a body, there lying prostrate, lifeless where it had fallen. Alice screaming blue murder. *God help us.*

So the order to suppress Derek Hemmings had been given. To maim and to murder. Boris Golich's traitorous sleeper cell inside the British Government had been awakened

And there inside his erstwhile mentor's home, Alexandrov Gontlemoon lay dead.

●

Pacing around the snug at Chequers, his Buckinghamshire country retreat, nursing a cut glass tumbler of finest Napoléon brandy, the Prime Minister was lost deeply within his own thoughts. He was in a veritably atrocious mood. A fact to which one member of the household staff at least could attest. His interview at Scotland Yard had lasted for five straight hours. It centred predominantly on the alleged impropriety of his relationship with one Boris Golich, the Russian oligarch and international businessman. To his mind, the Prime Minister had been paraded like a common criminal, certainly not afforded the courtesies deserved of the leader of the country. His finest hour had been usurped and turned into a mockery in full view of the world's media who were now baying for his blood. He reflected on the precipice walked between success and failure, how he had so narrowly missed out on the chance to become immortalised as a national hero through creating seven thousand well needed jobs for the nation following the hitherto cold, abstemious years of bitter recession, austerity and European-exiting trauma. He also lamented the lost chance to amass great personal wealth which had so tantalisingly been promised. Certainly Mr Golich's exotic incentive scheme which accompanied the, now defunct, gas exploration deal was capable of holding one's attention.

He drained his glass and hurled it in disgust, smashing it inside the wastepaper bin to the side of his desk. The bitter taste of betrayal still lingered in his mouth. They had gone for the jugular all right. No holding back in seeking to finish his long and distinguished political career.

So, the Minister sought to out-manoeuvre the arch political strategist himself and remove him from office once and for all. But this leader of men had clung to the rocks of power for far too long to be finished yet. Not by a long shot.

Composing himself as he lifted the ornate bone handled telephone receiver sitting upon his leather-topped writing bureau, the Prime Minister made a rapid succession of calls. He spoke fluidly and animatedly, relishing the emergence of a newfound energy as he beseeched, bullied, and cajoled. And by the time telephone receiver was settled back in its cradle for good, cages had been rattled, loyalties divided, and a calculated plan had been set in motion.

Chapter 45

SPAIN. NEAR ESTANYOL. VILOBI D'ONYAR.

Slowing as we turned a tight corner at the exit to the village, a figure stepped off the curb in the periphery of my vision. The passenger door flew open and Sergei Krostanov hurled himself into the seat thrusting an old fashioned Colt revolver into my face.

'Keep your hands on the steering wheel and continue driving please. Retain a steady pace. These mountain roads can still be dangerous even at this time of year,' he offered dryly, hovering the gun a few inches from my temple.

We drove in silence for a few miles, passing at one point a fleet of four polished white police cars driving at high speed, lights flashing and sirens blaring as they sped back in the direction of the village. Finally he spoke. Measured tones.

'Your ingenuity has impressed me. I also wished to avoid these new police given how you have spoilt all of our plans. I appreciate the lift.' He smiled to himself, glancing into the back of the car at Daniel. 'I'm still going to need that tablet, you little traitor,' he snapped, momentarily losing the veneer of polished decorum worn as such a practiced mask.

'He's half-dead. He can't help you. He can't even speak. I'm taking him to hospital in Barcelona. If he makes it there you might get your precious tablet. You'll never get it if he doesn't.'

'Do you think you give the orders here? I don't see you holding a gun any more big man, do you?'

I kept my eyes fixed on the road, ignoring him assiduously. Struggling to keep my cool. Hands gripping the wheel. Knuckles white. And then the Russian began to roll the bottoms of his suit trousers up. 'Do you see these, big man?' he asked drawing my eyes towards the large eight pointed stars tattooed onto each of his knees. 'You know these? It means I am a boss. 'Avtorityet'. I kneel to no man. I am a brigadier of the family. It means respect. It means that a pig like you does what I say.'

'Vory,' I growled in response.

'Yes Vor. The Bratva. Mafia. Crime lords. Thief-in-Law. Whatever you want to call us. We are all powerful. We buy the police so they do our bidding. They work for us now. We will never obey their laws. The governments of countries from around the world fear our wrath. We have always operated outside of society by our lifelong vow, but society now bends to our will. I have even made your quaint little game of golf dance like a puppet to our tune so we can run Rublex oil through Europe! This gives me the greatest of pleasures. The whole of Europe has always viewed mighty Russia as some feral mongrel cousin. We even spoke French at court for three hundred years instead of our beautiful mother tongue, so ashamed was our disgusting nobility by our lack of sophistication in eyes of the world. I came from dirt. I saw the privileged take this game of golf in summer. It was not for boys like me. I knew they played it in rich countries. I hated those people and I hated those countries. I wanted very much back then to destroy everything they stood for, to destroy this game of the rich. And now we run the game and it is so. You must listen carefully and understand me 'big man', even you proud Englishmen now bow to the Vory.' He rattled the gun and his free hand against the dashboard in front of him in a theatrical drum roll. An announcement of fact.

Something inside me snapped. The road ahead bled from single carriage way into a main road with multiple lanes. As we approached the turning I stepped down on the accelerator. 'What are you doing? Slow down now,' Krostanov screamed. We came up towards the apex fast and I quickly slotted my seat belt into place. 'Stop now. I order it,' he screamed at me waving the gun furiously.

The threats meant nothing. I was resolute. Committed. Metres from the junction, I pulled down hard onto the steering wheel and swerved off the road. The scene played out as if in fragments of a dream. The bonnet of the Fiat Uno crunched into the metal sign post at sixty kilometres an hour. It crumpled on impact. The inside of the car was filled with unintelligible shouts and cries. Daniel and I were thrown forward and jolted hard against the protective belts. But we remained in our seats. Shaken. Rattled. The force of the crash tore the seat belt into my shoulder with such force it felt as if the wound had been flushed with a red hot poker. When I eventually looked to my side I found the front windscreen had been smashed right through by the flying body of my uninvited passenger.

Seconds felt like years as my brain stretched the elasticity of the linear temporal continuum on which perception exists, scrambling and fighting to compute millions of tiny pieces of information as to the state of my body, the external environment and the exposure to near and current danger following the shock of the crash. This biological response explains why trauma victims often hold and replay vivid recollections of minute and seemingly insignificant fragments of their experiences. Why I was still haunted by the flashbacks.

Slowly I unbuckled the seatbelt. I managed to lever my body and pivot to kick open the twisted metal of the door. I staggered from the car. Took a drawn out moment and steadied myself, savouring the feeling of my feet being on solid ground as I lumbered slowly away from the concertinaed motor. Two cars had pulled over some way behind us and the drivers were getting out to see how they could try and help. They called out to me as they jogged over but there was only one thought in my mind. My first consideration was not for my injuries or even to rescue the Target from the wreckage. Instead I was myopic in my dreadful purpose.

At the front of the crash site, I located the man responsible for Mickey's death. Lying on his back upon the grass verge. His forehead was badly cut, sliced open to the skull. The contours of his face were mapped with a network of tiny lacerations. By the odd angle his body was positioned in, it looked as if he had broken both arms, shoulder blade, and collar bone. A bitter scowl twisted with pain, fixed across his face. The Vor was conscious.

I stood over him, looking down with unblinking eyes, as he writhed in agony beneath me. 'Help me. Help me please,' he rasped. Held his gaze, then viciously stamped my boot heel down onto his knee cap shattering the patella bone and rupturing the conjoined cartilage with cruel and scientific precision. The quiet moan of pain emanated from deep inside him. I shifted my weight and brought the boot down again, this time onto his second knee cap, smashing it beyond all repair. That noise again. He tried to twist away in pathetic desperation.

'Now you couldn't kneel again if you wanted to, you worthless motherfucker.' I hocked up a globule of phlegm from the back of my throat and spat it into Sergei Krostanov's beleaguered face. 'That's for Mickey.'

But his eyes still flashed with indignation, a futile last act of defiance. I knelt beside him on the grass. Our stares collided, an unflinching channel of emotional intensity between us as I placed my hand firmly over his mouth and nose. He wheezed, twisted hard and then spluttered as he fought desperately for oxygen. A protruding blue vein pulsed prominently down the centre of his forehead, his face red and blotchy. Finally the fight left him and, submitting to the inevitable, his eyes once again locked onto mine but now in a sad embrace of human fragility. I watched remorselessly, his life fading as he suffocated within my grip.

One of the passers-by who had stopped his car at the roadside to help with the accident was now gingerly picking at pieces of metal and trying to reach inside. He looked very stressed. The other man had reached me as I finished with the Vor.

'Tú lo mataste' he said quietly at me in disbelief. He was shaking. I ignored it and kept walking. 'You kill him' he said louder in English after me.

I stopped in my tracks and fixed the good Samaritan with a steely glare, eyes narrowed to slits. I pointed directly at him. 'The crash killed him. You saw nothing'. The man dropped his eyes to the ground, nodded and said nothing.

I returned to the vehicle and motioned for the do-gooder, who was now leaning inside the car, to move aside. He looked relieved to be given permission to stand clear of a possible impending explosion from the wreckage. The Target had survived the crash. He was clearly fucked, but somehow managing to cling weakly on to life. Daniel was proving to be quite a fighter. I respected his stubborn refusal to submit to the welcome seduction of death after everything that he had gone through. I unbuckled the seatbelts, his bloodied form perversely resembling an oversized sausage cooking on the grill. Reached in and pulled him out of the car. Cradling the limp body, draped across both of my outstretched arms, we turned away from the contorted metal and walked solemnly towards the motorway intersection.

A blur of vehicles raced past us as we stood, steadfast, on the edge of the road. There's no doubt that we would have made an unusual and alarming sight and one that many of the drivers rubbernecking clearly felt best to avoid. But it wasn't too long before a huge juggernaut pulled to a halt on the hard shoulder just in front of us. The driver wound down the window and in a strong Dutch accent shouted down at us. 'Are you guys all right? Is he injured? Can I help you?'

'He's in a bad way. We need to get to the hospital in Barcelona. Are you headed that way mate?'

'Sure. I can take you. There's a turning off the motorway which heads straight there. It's not far from my route. But don't you think you should get an ambulance to take you there? I have a phone if you need one.'

'There's no time to waste. Thank you though. Can I bring him up to the cab?'

'Sure. Come on up. There's a little day cot back here where he can rest.' The driver swung open the heavy door to his cab and scampered down a couple of short metal steps. He helped me to carry Daniel's limp body up into the cab of the huge eighteen-wheeler, carefully protecting his head as we manoeuvred him through the door and into the back.

'What happened to him? He looks in a pretty bad way no?' he said and then, after running his eye over my blood-stained face and shirt, 'Come to mention it, so do you. You guys been in an accident or something? You look like you've been in the wars.'

'If I told you mate, you wouldn't believe me. Just put it down to a car accident.'

'That car also fire bullets does it?' he said cautiously as he stared at the sorry wound in my shoulder.

'Best you don't ask. Seriously. I'm sorry but we need to get going.' And then glancing down at the Target, 'He's fading fast.'

The driver, whose name I established was Joost, generously handed me a large bottle of water which I tried to get Daniel to drink from in vain. I left him alone to rest.

We drove in silence for the next thirty or so minutes, eating up miles of tarmac. With Ratchet secured in the back cot and as safe as he could be for now I was able to relax for the first time in days. I closed my eyes for a few seconds, briefly seeking some much needed respite, having been running on a high octane mix of anger and pure adrenaline since as far as I could remembe. I fell into a deep sleep, instantly enveloped by a comforting velvety shroud knitted of urgent images and dreamy fragments shooting into and through my unconsciousness. And time leapt forward before I was shaken groggily awake.

'Hey, buddy. We're getting pretty close. It's the turn off at the next junction.'

I shook my head to clear it. 'Thanks. You've really helped us out here mate. Things were looking pretty dicey before you turned up.'

The juggernaut swung off the motorway at the signs for the city of Barcelona. We followed a snug series of recently laid one-way roads connected by a complex pattern of roundabouts until we finally arrived at the highly modern and frighteningly clean building on the outskirts of the city. Why they didn't just make buildings to look like buildings any more was beyond me. I wouldn't have recognised it as a hospital, it was so modern in design. We wheeled into a sparsely occupied car park and pulled to a halt. 'Well. This is it. I hope your friend will be all right.'

'Thank you. He might be now—on account of you.' I offered my hand in a gesture of friendship. We both carried Daniel off the truck and, because our injuries might be in need of some serious explanation, I suggested that I carried him alone into the hospital. The trucker slapped me on the back and I cradled the Target in my arms through the electric doors and into the air conditioned cool of a starkly modern post-apocalyptic reception area.

Somewhere behind us a huge engine roared and then a Klaxon blasted sounding a final farewell.

Chapter 46

The early morning sun reflected brilliantly on the windows of The East India Club, glinting out mercurially through a patchwork of cloud over St. James's Square. Two of London's ubiquitous overfed pigeons squabbled on the pavement over the grubby remains of a hotdog bun ignoring, with practiced nonchalance, the blacked-out Mercedes Benz as it pulled up outside. The Minister stepped calmly out onto the pavement. Leant backward slightly and rocked his shoulders from side to side, audibly cracking several vertebrae into place.

Derek Hemmings piled out of the back seats behind him, nervously smoothing his suit. Decisions needed to be taken on the way forward. Late last evening they had been summoned to a breakfast meeting with the Prime Minister. It was a curious thing given the battle lines had very much been drawn. No clear reasoning had been provided but, with curiosities peaked by a number of cryptic clues, there had been little doubt that attendance was mandatory. Given the unpleasant altercation at the public unveiling of the huge jobs and investment deal, leading to the PM being taken in for police questioning, the two of them were not exactly looking forward to the engagement. Derek's stomach was in fact a bubbling, twisting testimony to this very fact. So much so that he hadn't managed an attempt at breakfast, nor swallowed so much as a mouthful of hot coffee. The truth was that he had not yet recovered from the stark reality of what had occurred inside his own home. The horrific danger that Alice had been placed in on his account. A point that was not lost on her either. She was requiring an inordinate amount of attention and fussing to keep frayed nerves at a settled peak. This was the first time since 'the incident', as it was now labeled, that Derek had been allowed to leave the house, a kindly neighbour sitting with her in his place. Shaken by the specific threat to his own life, naturally, he also remained unsettled by the bitter betrayal of the aide for whom he had fostered near-paternal affection. Despite his enduring malaise however, given that he had already come so far in his quest to do the right thing, Derek had resolved that he owed it to Queen and country to see things through.

The front door to the club was opened with aplomb by a portly man in smart red jacket and bowler hat. They entered a small room, usually reserved for card games, to be greeted by a welcoming aroma of freshly brewed coffee. The Prime Minister sat alone at the felt covered table, hands clasped as if in prayer. After a moment of staged silence he gestured to the empty seats. Cleared his throat.

He began, 'I want you to know I've drawn a line.'

The Minister replied, 'How very generous of you, Prime Minister.'

Derek noted the barbed spar and assiduously avoided any eye contact.

'You miscalculated, Minister. Played your hand too early.'

The bathos of the remark was not lost on the trio given they sat in a room designed for serious gambling.

'Pah! You've been caught with your grubby little paws in the till. End of story, sir!' the Minister snapped, smashing back his riposte.

Anyone for tennis? Thought Derek to himself miserably.

'I'm afraid that just won't wash. Better men than you have looked into this matter in forensic detail. The only thing linking me to

Golich apparently is a job taken by my old school pal in a foreign country. He's taken full culpability. And I will of course publicly distance myself from the little turd. Nothing else is provable. This won't drag me down, not in the long term.'

'There is a vote of No Confidence to be scheduled in the House. Call it a long overdue coup if you will. I'm running for the leadership.'

The Prime Minister smiled enigmatically and leaned backwards in his chair. Derek shifted uncomfortably and started to wonder if he could ask for a cup of the rich fragrant coffee that wafted around the room and smelt so good. Or, he fretted, had that moment passed in terms of polite etiquette, eclipsed entirely by the overt sniping? He swallowed drily and kept his council.

'I take it you've canvassed for support on this one, Minister? Counted those votes home already have you? Convinced that this stink is going to stick aren't you?' A dismissive, derisory tone.

'Shouldn't I?' enquired the Minister, for the first time sounding a little less than sure.

'Well I'm certain you've got your best men on it. How is Alistair anyway? I'm sure you can be confident that he will be able to marshal at least fifteen percent of the party to submit letters of support for the motion and then gain a majority to vote against me, especially after all I've done for them. Bringing them back to power after so long. Giving them jobs, reward, responsibility, purpose. Oh, by the way, is he still shagging that sixteen year old Filipino houseboy that he's got stashed away in his Fulham pied-à-terre? One wouldn't want a big scene made about that now would we? The fallout of these things can be so unpleasant. It's the families in these situations that I, for one, always worry for.'

Derek snorted, uncontrollably. Covered his face with both hands, humiliated. Stared down at the table. The Prime Minister looked directly at him for the first time and raised a hawkish eyebrow.

'You were the cause of this in the first place by all accounts, Hemmings. What's a no-mark civil servant on the verge of fading away into the obscurity of retirement doing prying into affairs that don't actually concern him anyway?'

Derek blushed. 'I was doing the right thing, sir.'

The PM sniggered audibly.

Hemmings rallied to his theme. 'I was looking out for the interests of this noble country at a time when, I'm sorry to say, our leader was displaying a spectacular dereliction of duty.' His face was flushed with anger now.

The Minister looked at him proudly. 'You've underestimated the depth of feeling surrounding this, Prime Minister.'

'And you've underestimated the power of national support for generating seven thousand jobs following the years of pain after Brexit. The country wants this. They don't give a monkey's red arse about Golich's past. They want a proactive leader, someone who will stick their neck out for growth.' His diction was at once immaculate, crystal clear and the epitome of self-assurance.

Their eyes locked. Hard. Unflinching. Neither prepared to look away first. Finally the Prime Minister spoke again.

'Humphrey has done the rounds. He's spoken to the troops. Some were a little nervous about yesterday and the Golich relationship but on balance they are still with me. You'll squeeze fifteen to twenty percent of the vote. I've still got the whip, Minister. We'll smash you in a leadership contest and you should know it.'

The Minister gripped the table with both sweaty palms. Derek exhaled and made eyes at the bubbling coffee jug.

'Why are we here?' he said finally. His tone flat, deflated.

'I don't want a battle, Brian,' the PM oozed. 'I need you on my team. I'm not going to suffer for this and I don't see the point in losing one of the biggest stars of the front bench in the process.' He smiled insincerely across the green felt at them both, riding his momentum. 'Is this really worth your career, Brian? Of course I understand very well that after the rigmarole of yesterday and the public denouncement of the Rublex deal that some explaining needs to be done, some managing and massaging of the situation. And yes, of course, someone will indeed need to take the fall.' With that the Prime Minister raised his eyebrows and chuckled, arms open in a gesture of generosity. 'Who do you think that should be, Derek? How would you feel if I suggested that a certain Andrew Bartholomew could be lanced on the harpoon for this?'

Derek glanced sideways at the Minister and then back at the PM. 'I'm listening,' was all he said.

'Here's the trade gentlemen. We'll continue the gas exploration but won't deal with Golich. He's off the menu for good. But we'll try to find a partner we can progress with to build infrastructure for those jobs. Minister, you'll call off the vote of No Confidence. Come out in support of me and I'll give you any tenure you desire. Your pick of the top jobs. Heck I'll even endorse you to take over from me when my term is up. I'll recommend you as successor and won't stand for another re-election. So much cleaner than all this messy in-fighting which just serves to weaken the party, don't you say?' He waited whilst the rhetorical question settled between them. 'Hemmings, you'll get a bump up to MI6. A final hurrah. A kicker to the pension fund, something to impress upon the little lady. And best of all old boy, you get to stick the knife right between Bartholomew's shoulder blades yourself. Whatdayasay chaps?'

Derek looked at the Minister, who was looking right back at him.

The Minister cleared his throat. He spoke with a quiet intensity. 'Well played, Prime Minister. It seems you have yourself a deal'.

Chapter 47

'Do you speak English?' I pressed forcefully. The fat nurse at the hospital reception was squeezed tightly into a baby pink uniform. Her saucer brown eyes sat atop a pair of pudgy cheeks all framed with a frizz of thick black curls. Studiously completing a complicated looking form, she resembled some sort of serious over-stuffed cuddly toy. The look I received back at me couldn't hide the alarm on her face as I stood before her desk dangling a bloodied body in my arms. She began calling for help in Spanish, unbridled urgency in her voice. All eyes in the waiting room were fixed upon us.

Two porters appeared from nowhere, dressed head to foot in powder blue, fussing around me and trying to ease the Target from my arms. I stood steadfast.

'I need to speak with Doctor Cavestendros. This is urgent.'

The request elicited a series of blank looks. I repeated the name loudly whilst shrugging off the unwanted attentions of the hospital orderlies. A brief phone call later and we were finally directed down a well-lit corridor.

I kicked my steel toe-caps twice against the base of the clinic door to announce our arrival. Entered sideways, careful not to bang Daniel's head on the frame. Smiled to myself. It would be just my style to get this far and finish the lad off with a concussion whilst carrying him inside the hospital. A small man in a white coat, thick-framed glasses and a carefully crafted goatee beard rose from his chair and guided me towards a medical table. I laid the Target flat as the concerned doctor busied himself checking for vital signs.

'Charles Hand sent me. He said you'd be expecting us'.

'Yes. Everything is arranged. There will be no police record of the gunshot wounds. You guys weren't here. And of course the treatment is taken care of. Do you know what has happened to him?' he asked as he inserted a cannula into the vein and then attached a saline drip to the bung to feed the arm of the ailing patient. 'I need the truth.'

'What I know is this. He's in a bad way. Has been for the last ten hours or so since I've been with him. He's lost quite a bit of blood. He was shot in the arse. Mauled by a dog. Think he took quite a beating before I sprang him.'

'Bad day at the office then,' the doctor replied without cracking a smile.

'He's gonna make it, right? You'll have to attest that I got him here alive.'

'He's very weak. Surprisingly stable given the bullet wound. But you got him to me in the time frame in which surgery can be performed and can make a difference. So the good news is once we stabilise your friend, we can operate. Then we will sanitise his wounds, replace the blood he has lost, and medicate him correctly. He needs fluids. I don't think he's eaten or drunk for some time. In my view he has a better than fifty percent chance of making it through this but that will drop by nearly ten percent each hour from here on in unless he gets the treatment he needs.'

Fucking close call.

It had been a rough ride but I could handle those odds after what we had been through together. I nodded. Backed up. Slumped into a plastic chair to the side of the room. Closed my eyes. Head spinning.

'We can't work with him until he has taken on the fluid. Your shoulder needs care too. It's seeping'

'Yeah. I took a lump of lead a day or so back. Got the bullet pieces out. Tried to clean it up. It feels all wrong now though I gotta say.'

'Let me see. It's not good that you haven't had treatment for so long. It hasn't been sanitised properly. You may have an infection by now.'

He moved across the room and cut away the sleeve of my shirt to give the unfettered access he needed. Carefully cleaned the wound. Injected local anaesthetic into the shoulder. I watched as he took a set of metal tongs resembling some form of medieval torture implement and fished around inside the scorched angry wound for what seemed like an age. Gritted my teeth. A second later, a tiny metallic clatter into the bowl told me he had removed the remaining shrapnel that my own primitive attempt must have left inside my arm. He dressed the shoulder tightly, packed with clean gauze and wadding, and secured my arm in a sling.

He smiled at me. 'No arm wrestling for you for a while, okay?'

'Sure thing, Doc,' I said, grinning back at him. I flicked my head over at Ratchet as a nurse tended efficiently to his medical requirements. 'Will he need to stay in overnight?' I asked, catching myself staring at her arse as she reached over the examination table causing the hem of her uniform to ride up a little.

'He'll be here for quite some time I should think. We'll determine the best course of treatment for his injuries. He will need surgery, but we need to check him for signs of internal bleeding. He seems to have been beaten pretty badly. I have my instructions to look after him. You've done your bit. He's in safe hands now.'

'Thank you,' I said holding his gaze before getting to my feet and stepping to where the Target lay stretched out, motionless. I placed my free hand on the back of Daniel Ratchet's head and held it there tenderly for a moment. Nodded once at the doctor. About turned. Never looked back.

Chapter 48

ENGLAND. HAMPSHIRE. FARNBOROUGH AIRPORT.

The Lear Jet sat idling on the runway strip at Farnborough Airport as the pilot completed his final checks. Inside the opulent cabin was a short martini bar, a very large flat screen and two white leather swivel chairs that faced each other across a faux marble table. Boris Golich sat impassively in one of the seats, speaking on the phone. The blonde head of a young stewardess bobbed up and down under the table, busying herself in his lap.

'Boris Golich for Trade Minister Zhou,' he barked into the handset. He waited a beat for the familiar voice of the Chinese politician to answer. 'Zhou, it's Boris. I'm willing to resume our discussions. The British have got cold feet on the gas deal. There is a considerable opportunity for The People's Republic to secure this vast natural resource for yourselves and leverage the desperation of our naïve Argentinean friends. You know my terms. You have until close of business tonight.'

He hung up the phone with a single jab of his stubby forefinger and slightly adjusted the angle of his seat. As the hum of the jet engines increased in pitch, Boris Golich lazily produced an oversized Cuban cigar from his jacket pocket and scorched it alight. The wheels left the runway and folded neatly into the undercarriage of the plane.

A contented look settled across his perfectly lineless face.

Chapter 49

ENGLAND. SUSSEX. GATWICK AIRPORT.

The airport bar was quiet and dimly lit. An elderly couple sat together wordlessly, content in the silence of each other's company. An impossibly young-looking bartender stood, shuffling from foot to foot, looking bored. A man occupied the corner table with his back to the bar, a bottle of Scotch and two glasses set before him. I moved across the room and joined him silently. He filled the glasses.

'To Mickey,' he said as he raised his glass.

'To Mickey,' I repeated solemnly. Took a deep swallow of the golden liquid.

Charles Hand refilled the glasses. 'To fallen comrades,' he said draining his whiskey.

'Fallen comrades.'

'It's good to see you, Thomas. You did well out there, in a difficult situation. You recovered the Target. Alive. Daniel Ratchet is safe thanks to us. He'll recover from his injuries given time. We can get the lad back to his parents.'

'It was touch and go for a while, boss.'

'I know. They don't mess about, the Russian mob. They're a nasty, uncompromising group of individuals.' He paused. 'I trust that you made them pay for killing Mickey, Thomas. I know it must have hurt you. Badly. Watching as it all happened so fast and being powerless to help him. I hope it didn't stir up bad memories. Mickey was one of the best.'

I nodded. A lump in my throat.

The Hand of God pushed back his chair. Rose. Pushed a brown padded envelope across the table towards me. 'Ten thousand pounds as usual. Plus ten for bringing him back alive. Take some time off, Thomas. I'll be in touch when we need you again. And for crying out loud, take Ella out for dinner or something, will you? That poor girl keeps asking after you.'

I was still grinning as he walked away.

I sat in silence, alone, lost in thought for a while. The fine Scotch whiskey was slowly diminishing in the bottle before me as I greedily savoured the mellow, peaty flavour. I gathered myself and checked my phone for any messages. An unopened text from Ella sat neglected:

So sorry about Mickey. We all loved him Tom. xoxo

I blinked back a tear. Figured I might just take the Hand of God up on his suggestion after all.

But no sooner had it entered my mind than that thought melted like rooftop snow on a hot chimney stack. Standing at the entrance to the bar was a curvaceous red-haired woman with white porcelain skin, hugging a man and pulling two tiny children close into her legs. They said their goodbyes and she stood as they walked away, still waving after them for some time. Finally, she turned and, pulling a smart red case behind her, she wiggled into the bar. I watched as she stood deliberating, just a couple of metres from me, and eventually ordered a drink. The skin-tight, three-quarter length creme trousers and red high heels she wore perfectly accentuated the plumpness of her rounded bottom. I felt the warm glow of the whiskey in my stomach. She turned, clutching a bottle of beer, her French Tip nails wrapped tightly around the neck. She was looking for a place to sit. I kicked the chair opposite me out from under the table and gestured to it. She smiled and looked awkwardly around.

'It's okay. I don't bite you know,' I said. And then, 'Please. Join me. I could use the company.'

She thought about it for a moment and then, seeming to shrug almost imperceptibly, she stepped across towards me smiling and eased herself into the chair. 'That's quite the line' she threw back at me, manicured eyebrows raised challengingly. 'What happened to your arm?' She eased a perfectly painted fingernail down the sling.

I leaned forward eagerly. 'I could tell you, but I don't think you would believe me.'

'Try me. I might like it.'

'Really?'

'Sure stud. Somehow I'm starting to think I might enjoy hearing about you getting badly injured.'

'Ah well. You know, it was just the usual shit. Saving kittens from trees. Rescuing damsels in distress, that kind of thing.'

She snorted. 'You must be some kind of regular hero then,' she teased.

I flashed my best lopsided grin. 'I do my best.' Held her gaze for a second too long. 'So, listen. I'm only going to say it once. So, you can pretend you didn't hear me, finish your drink, and carry on with your life. But you look like the kind of girl who might be just crazy enough to be able to step outside of the predictable boring bubble of this existence every now and then. Might realise that we're really only on this rock for a tiny amount of time. Might grab an adventure in life when one happens to come along. I like that. And I like you.'

She looked down at her drink and smiled. A few seconds later she flashed back up at me, big eyes open wide. 'Say it then,' she whispered.

'Your flight better not leave anytime soon. My hotel is close by.'

She groaned quietly. Then the hint of a cruel smile flickered on the corners of her mouth. 'I hope you have two rooms reserved stud. One for you and one for your ego! Go to hell big boy and if I were you, I would retire those useless chat up lines for good.'

My jaw slackened.

She pushed back her chair, took a swig of beer and walked casually away. I watched after her in disbelief, her hips rolling as she crossed the bar. She knew for damn sure I was looking. Finally, reaching the exit to the bar, she half-turned her head back towards me and delivered a deep sultry wink. Then she was gone.

Golden.

Chapter 50

ENGLAND. SURREY. WENTWORTH.
EUROPEAN TOUR HEADQUARTERS.

Five weeks had passed by since Tom Hunter had rescued him from his Vory kidnappers. Daniel Ratchet had felt strong enough to fly back to the UK. He had healed well under the discreet supervision of Doctor Cavestendros in Barcelona. Charles Hand had facilitated Mr and Mrs Ratchet in visiting the Spanish hospital to see their son. The whole saga had been a blur. Draining. Daniel felt as if he had been caught up and spat out by a spiteful tornado. He wasn't quite sure what was actual memory and what had twisted into cruel imagination.

He walked slowly up the steps of the smart European Tour Headquarters in Wentworth, tucked away in an affluent and leafy part of the Surrey countryside. His stomach churned with apprehension. This was the chance to tell his side of the story. To seek some redress with the Tour and finally expose the tournament fixing in which the Rublex Corporation, principal sponsor of the European game, was so instrumental. He had managed to speak briefly to Silvio by phone and had agreed to meet him here as a representative of Crown Sports.

He entered the building and was shown into an empty room, flooded with natural sunlight. It was airy and oval shaped. The walls were adorned with paintings of various sizes, mostly depicting early Scottish golfing scenes, consisting predominantly, it seemed, of men in cloth caps swinging primitive looking wooden clubs at leather balls. Ratchet waited nervously for both Francis Broome, Chief Executive of the European Tour, and Silvio to arrive.

Fifteen minutes passed. Then thirty. Daniel paced around the room fretfully. Perhaps he had he got the wrong time. Or had they forgotten about him? Surely the matters he had come to discuss would be considered significant enough to warrant granting him an audience. He bristled.

Finally the double doors to the room opened and Francis Broome entered carrying a large leather-bound portfolio wallet. They shook hands and each chose seats around the fine antique walnut table.

'I'm sorry to hear of your recent trials and tribulations, Daniel,' began Broome. 'We all are, I speak on behalf of the entire Tour. I know you had just joined us as an agent representing some of our players not so long ago, but we're a close-knit family in golf, and we were all so shocked. Especially coming at a time when we have had to contend with the terribly sad deaths of Rublex Corporation sponsorship director Sergei Krostanov, long-standing coach Bob Wallace and physiotherapist Michael Hausen. It's been a torrid time.'

'It's all connected. I was kidnapped by Sergei Krostanov.'

'I've seen the police report,' Broome interrupted, cutting him short. Curt, direct.

'They kidnapped me because I found out about corruption on the Tour. Tournament fixing and unfair undue influence upon many of your key players is rife. The caddies are running an illegal gambling and enforcement ring. It's all bloody fixed. It's a sorry disgrace.' Daniel was enraged. He rose from his seat clenched fists on the table, glaring.

'Daniel, please calm down. We appreciate that you've been through a lot but I really can't sanction such overblown accusations. I won't permit you to besmirch the good name and reputation of the European Golf Tour and our major sponsor. You must be careful that you don't stray into the realms of slander with what you are saying. It's highly contentious.' Broome reprimanded him like he was a child. 'The truth of the matter is that you have been through quite an ordeal. It is known that this can affect someone emotionally. Distort their perceptions so to speak. Sergei kidnapped and tortured you, yes. That has been corroborated. And a dreadful situation that was.' He stepped towards the window and looked away from Daniel unable to hold his eye. 'But whatever criminal actions he took he did so in his own name. They are saying that he snapped. He's been overworked and under immense pressure to deliver the sponsorship programme for Rublex and it got too much for him. This "breakdown" he suffered manifested itself in the terrible criminal behaviour he inflicted upon you. It proves that he was in a disturbed state of mind in that he went on to take his own life shortly after in a motor accident. He must have been feeling enormous guilt for his actions and the suffering caused. It was appalling what you've endured, Daniel, but I maintain that this can only be viewed as the individual and isolated criminal behaviour of a man with personal psychological issues. It is simply not relevant to call into question the probity of the European Golf Tour as an organisation. All this talk of cheating is complete and utter nonsense, I'm afraid. We have conducted an internal root and branch review for our own reassurance and it has turned up nothing. We did find a little evidence of some high jinks from some of the nefarious caddies to which you refer and since then a portion of these disaffected freelancers have moved themselves along and off the Tour, in the wake of so much sorrow.'

Daniel was exasperated now. 'I have evidence. It's all documented. I can prove it. Rublex is ruining the Tour. Why won't you listen to me?'

'Daniel, Daniel, come now, this is pure fantasy. Rublex is the European game's greatest benefactor in our history. They've committed to invest over a hundred million pounds into our Tour through sponsorship and activation to drive the development of the sport in countries all over Europe. I believe that it is one of their principal business engagement activities. They just simply wouldn't do anything to endanger that. Where is this evidence you speak of?'

'It's all saved on a stats programme on my tablet. I've even got a video recording of Sergei and Andy Sharples discussing the corruption at the highest level.'

'Show me.'

'I don't have it. I left it for Matilda Axgren to hold for safe keeping in the physio-truck before I was taken.'

'I see. Well perhaps we had better ask her ourselves then?'

Daniel felt the blood drain from his face at the mention of her name. Matilda. Here. Right now. He hadn't been able to contact her from the hospital. She hadn't been traceable. How he wanted to hold her in his arms again.

'Is Matilda here?' he stammered.

'Yes. And Silvio Flavini of Crown Sports, whom you also know.'

'I was wondering what had happened to Silvio, we agreed to meet here. He's fully aware of everything I've been saying. You must ask him yourself, he'll verify it.'

The older man stood up, ensuring the integrity of the crease in his trousers as he rose. He ambled across the room, opened the double doors, and disappeared for a brief moment. When he returned, he was accompanied by Matilda and Silvio. Daniel stood. She looked beautiful. Yet different to how he had remembered. More grown up, perhaps. Distant somehow. She wore a black business suit, tailored to show off her striking figure, skirt cut just above the knee. No jewellery. Daniel had never seen her looking so professional. But there was something he couldn't place. Her long platinum blonde hair was worn in a tight bun tied behind her head. She carried a smart new Louis Vuitton satchel. She didn't make eye contact with him as she entered the room. Silvio, in corduroy trousers and a casual open neck shirt, was heavily tanned, as always. But Daniel sensed that he was more uneasy than his typical gait, not projecting the usual smooth and relaxed demeanour. He greeted Daniel with a little wave and the hint of an awkward smile, choosing to keep the table between them.

'Daniel,' began Broome, 'I would like to introduce you to the new team at the head of Rublex European Tour golf sponsorship.'

Daniel felt his knees buckle. He gripped the table for support. 'What do you mean?' he asked.

'Matilda has replaced Sergei following his breakdown and absence from the job due to overwork and stress. And of course the tragic road accident. Despite your personal situation, I'm sure you'll concur that it's also a difficult time for her having lost her fiancé. She is still grieving. Silvio will be supporting her in implementing the sponsorship across the Tour on secondment from Crown Sports.'

Daniel had heard nothing after fiancé. Head spinning. Then it landed. Hard. No jewellery. It was the first time that he had seen her without her "mother's" engagement ring, the ring that she claimed she wore to protect herself. That she claimed she wore to feel close to her lost family. All lies. The black suit seemed to show she was in-mourning for Krostanov.

Daniel looked at Matilda with disgust. 'Sergei? Your fiancé all along? How could you?'

Matilda said nothing.

He flipped. 'Breakdown? Road accident? Is that what you are insisting on calling it?' Daniel Ratchet was shouting down at Francis Broome, an unfathomable situation that would have been absurd to consider not more than three months ago. 'That bastard kidnapped me, beat me, nearly bloody killed me, and you call it a breakdown? At least I know his death was no accident. He got what he deserved, executed by the man who saved me. Someone with honour in his blood.' He looked across at Matilda, daring to meet her gaze for the first time. Pale watery blue eyes stared back defiantly. 'How the hell could you work for Rublex, Matilda? You know what's been going on. Didn't you find the tablet I hid for you? All the evidence is on it. The video recording of Sergei discussing the fixing of events so they could manipulate the odds in their illegal gambling ring and cheat the big money Asian gamblers. My programme outputs detailing the tournament fixing patterns, the statistics analysis coupled with electronic versions of sponsorship contracts for individual players incentivising them to throw places and drop shots.'

'You mean this tablet, Daniel?' Matilda said coldly, fishing in her satchel and producing the computer.

'Yes! Thank you. All the evidence is on there. Finally you'll see I was right all along.'

'There's nothing on here, Daniel. I don't know what you mean. I found the computer you left for me on the desk in the truck. I've been through everything and there is no data that you speak of. I discussed matters at great length with Mr Golich, owner of Rublex, about the way forward and he was most obliging. And, of course, regarding my future on the Tour with the advice of the kind Mr. Broome,' she smiled beatifically towards him. 'There is no evidence of this corruption. Somehow you are confused.'

She found the tablet I left for her on the desk in the truck? I didn't leave my tablet on the desk. It can't be so. Is she lying to me again?

'Matilda. I trusted you. I loved you. How could you betray me like this?'

'Don't be silly. What we had wasn't special. I was merely playing my part in helping Sergei to secure the players for his sponsorship contracts. I need this job. I have to pay for the treatment and care for my brother. Sergei was firstly a mentor of mine. We met when I was studying in Russia and later he got me the physiotherapy job on the Tour. He knew my desperate family situation and we came to an understanding. Over time our relationship blossomed. There was always every aspiration for me to progress within Rublex given my background of studying business. My degrees. You won't stop that from happening.'

'I think that settles it then, Daniel,' Francis Broome chimed in condescendingly. 'You are angry now, but in time you will come to realise what really happened and you will accept that Rublex will have a big part to play in golf for many years to come. The reputation of the Tour and our primary sponsor remains intact. Without this evidence you speak of, any claims you make to the contrary will of course be vigorously denied and contested in a court of law.'

Daniel looked around the room at each in turn. He shook his head and then, without uttering another word, he hurriedly left the room. Broken. Dejected. Confused.

He trailed down the steps, eyes brimming with the bitter tears of shame. His parents, who had barely let him out of their sight since their unhappy reunion by his hospital bed in Barcelona, were waiting where he had left them. Sitting in the front of their Vauxhall Vectra. They had driven him to the meeting in a show of familial support. Daniel climbed dolefully into the back seat.

'What happened son?'

'Nothing. They wouldn't listen. I can't believe it after everything that I've gone through. I can't. It was all just a lie. I don't want to speak about it.'

'You need to accept it, Daniel. These aren't our sort of people, boy. You've aimed above your station and this is the result. You've tried your best to help people and you've been hurt. I've arranged a job for you with me back in Sheffield at the insurance firm. You can move back in with us at home.'

Daniel placed his head in his hands. Silent. Head spinning. The desolation was absolute.

The car pulled away slowly, cruising smoothly down the neat road that bisected the fairways of the beautiful Wentworth Club's golf course. They tracked the winding tarmac through lush forest and out into the countryside. No one spoke. No one had anything to say. Daniel remained inconsolable.

Time passed. The motorway spread out before them. Inside the vehicle the stress remained thick and heavy. What few innocent comments passed between them to lighten the mood were ignored or merely grunted at in response. Daniel sat in an unhappy trance, hypnotised by a blur of passing pylons, road signs and speeding cars. He felt as if he was now being transported towards his final terminus – a limited life without the possibility and potential that he had so cruelly been permitted to taste.

And then the sound of a ringing mobile phone cut through the emptiness inside the vehicle. Daniel fumbled around in his pocket and, after what seemed an eternity, finally engaged the call. Mumbling in answer.

'Good afternoon. Is that Daniel Ratchet?'

'Yeah,' sniffed Daniel, half-expecting a salesman to tell him he could claim back some non-existent Payment Protection Insurance on a no-win-no-fee deal.

'Daniel. It's Brooke Anderson from the Laureus World Sports Academy.'

'Oh. Hi,' Daniel said, brightening up moderately.

'I'll cut to the chase. I'm notifying you that we are publishing your article in our 'Sport for Good' magazine.'

'Article?'

'Yeah. The one you submitted on corruption in golf and the undue influence of sponsors on top players in order to further their own objectives. Particularly the Rublex Corporation. We're very impressed with the evidence you have compiled. The statistical patterns, the undercover video recording of the principal wrong doers admitting their crimes, the background narrative. It's a compelling case you make regarding a very serious issue. Action needs to be taken.'

'Um. What article? I didn't write an article or submit one to Laureus.'

'Your representative spoke to us and sent it on a memory stick on your behalf. A German guy. One Michael Hausen?'

Michael. So it was Michael who had found the tablet. He must have seen the evidence on there and in conjunction with his own personal experiences at their hands made the connection between the caddy gambling ring and the Russian Vory. He took matters into his own hands—must have written the article to make sure that those who stood up for truth, for justice and for opportunity in sport would get the evidence to expose Rublex for what they really are. That bitch Matilda must have been in on it all from the start. Smoothing the way with her beautiful and tantalising sexuality to encourage susceptible golf agents to sign dodgy sponsorship deals with Krostanov.

Once the man she had used to get her leg up, and obviously over with, on the Tour, the man to whom she became engaged, had proven himself to be losing control of the situation she needed another means to achieve her ruthless ambitions. Krostanov went to extreme lengths to find and eradicate all traces of evidence linking Rublex to corruption. It seems Matilda must have used it as a bargaining chip to replace him and secure his job with Boris Golich, even before he was dead. No honour amongst thieves as they say.

But before he had been murdered, Michael must have figured out that Matilda wasn't to be trusted and wasn't going to act. He'd read the information contained on my tablet and understood the implications. He'd pieced together the connection to the gambling ring and the danger they posed. He realised that I had been kidnapped and Bob Wallace butchered probably as a direct result of discovering the truth. Given such a serious situation, it had taken genuine, unprecedented bravery for Michael to act and to ultimately sacrifice his life. To do the right thing.

'Yes. Thank you. That's fantastic.'

'Not only that Daniel. We're so impressed by your efforts that we'd like to make you a job offer. On the strength of the Rublex exposé we are accelerating the launch of a new division at Laureus centred on corruption across sport worldwide, supported with a new endowment of five million dollars. It will be run from a new Miami base. We think a young hungry guy like you with significant experience in exposing major corporate sports corruption would be perfect to head it up. We'll need you to come to London right away to discuss things. Can you make Monday morning at nine o'clock? What do you say?'

Daniel's heart soared. 'Thank you,' he stumbled. 'I'll be there!' He bounced on his seat, his dad watching intently in the rear view mirror as he rapped his knuckles in sheer delight on the car window.

He ended the phone call. Sat back in disbelief. Stunned into silence again. 'Who was that love?' his mother enquired curiously from the front seat. Daniel shook his head incredulously.

'Who was that? That was the voice of justice and the final deed of a man who against the odds found it within himself to do the right thing. A hero who I had betrayed for the love of a woman and sent to his death. And in return I think he might very well have just saved my life.'

ACKNOWLEDGEMENTS

To:

Matthew my Publisher – for holding no fear from the glare of writing in Technicolor.

Tom my Agent – for strapping in, holding tight and bringing it home.

David my Editor – for every ';?!:' and your effervescent erudition.

Bob Dylan – for unprecedented generosity, as greatest lyricist and winner of the Nobel Prize in Literature, for allowing me to use your words in mine.

Lee Child – for driving the genre, leaving the rest in its wake as 'barnacles on the boat'.

MJ – for never no doubt and for helping wild ideas soar.

DJ Judge Jules – for reading and re-reading from the start. For being one of the 'Renaissance men'.

For all manner of kind help and support in the process of making it happen:

Ross

Colin

Matt

John

Bob

Andy

Xav

Michelle – for giving shelter from the storm. This book was born in the eye of a hurricane.

ABOUT THE AUTHOR

Ted Denton was offered a bursary at an early age to serve as a commissioned officer in the British armed forces.

Fascinated with geo-political relations and bipartisan negotiation Ted has engaged with government departments and NGOs, undertaking extensive global travel.

He went on build an exciting career through founding a private international consultancy.

Ted is passionate about boxing, writing and adventuring.